TAN
TH

HEATHER GRAHAM

FULL FORCE

ELLE JAMES

MILLS & BOON

First Published in Great Britain 2019
by Mills & Boon, an imprint of HarperCollins*Publishers*
1 London Bridge Street, London, SE1 9GF

ISBN: 978-0-263-27435-6

0919

MIX
Paper from responsible sources
FSC® C007454
FSC
www.fsc.org

This book is produced from independently certified FSC™ paper to ensure responsible forest management.

For more information visit: www.harpercollins.co.uk/green

Printed and bound in Spain
by CPI, Barcelona

TANGLED THREAT

HEATHER GRAHAM

For Roberta Young Peacock,
a true Florida girl, with lots of love
and best wishes.

Prologue

The History Tree

"They see her…the beautiful Gyselle, when the moon is high in the sky. She walks these oak-lined trails and sometimes pauses to touch the soft moss that drips from the great branches, as if she reaches out for them to touch what is real. In life she was kind and generous. She was beloved by so many. And yet, when brought so cruelly to her brutal and unjust death at the infamous History Tree, she cast a curse on those around her. Those involved would die bitter deaths as well, choking on their own blood, breath stolen from them as it had been from her," Maura Antrim said dramatically.

The campfire in the pit burned bright yellow and gold, snapping and crackling softly. All around them, great oaks and pines rose, moss swaying in the light breeze. The moon overhead was full and bright that night, but cloud cover drifted past now and then, creating eerie shadows everywhere.

It was a perfect summer night, and perfect for storytelling. She was glad to be there, glad to be the storyteller and glad of the response from her audience.

Maura's group from the resort—teenagers and adults alike—looked at her, wide-eyed.

She refused to smile—she wanted to remain grave—though she was delighted by the fascination of the guests assembled around her. She had been grateful and pleased to be upgraded to her position of storyteller for the Frampton Ranch and Resort, an enterprise in North Central Florida that was becoming more renowned daily as a destination. The property had been bought about five years back by billionaire hotelier Donald Glass, and he had wisely left the firepit and the old riding trails as they were, the History Tree right where it grew, the ruins of the old plantation just as they lay—and amped up the history first, and then the legends that went along with the area.

Maura wasn't supposed to be on tonight—she shared the position with Francine Renault, a longtime employee of Donald Glass's hotel corporation, probably second in command only to the main resort manager, Fred Bentley. The two of them were known to argue—but Francine stayed right where she was, doing what she wanted. Despite any arguments, Donald Glass refused to fire either Francine or Fred, who, despite his stocky bulk, moved around the resort like a bat out of hell, always getting things done.

Fred Bentley had watched Maura at the start of the evening; she thought that he was smiling benignly—that he approved of her abilities as a social hostess and storyteller.

It was hard to blame him for fighting with Francine. She was…a difficult personality type at best.

And sharing any job with Francine wasn't easy; the woman had an air of superiority about her and a way of treating those she considered to be "lesser" employees very badly. Francine was in her midthirties—and was a beauty, really, a platinum blonde, dark-eyed piece of perfection—and while Maura had turned eighteen, Francine considered all of Donald Glass's summer help annoying, ignorant children.

The young adults—or "camper" summer help—were fond of gossiping. It was rumored that Francine once had an affair with Donald Glass, and that was how she held on to her position—and her superiority.

Glass was married. Maybe Francine was blackmailing him, telling him that if she wasn't given a certain power, she'd tell his wife, Marie, and Marie—or so rumor had it—could be jealous and very threatening when she chose to be. Hard to believe—in public Marie was always the model of decorum, slim and regal, slightly younger than Donald but certainly older than Francine.

Teens and young adults loved to speculate. At Maura's age, the thought of any of the older staff together—all seeming so much older than she was at the time—was simply gross.

Tonight, by not being there, Francine had put herself in a bad position.

She hadn't shown up for work. A no-show without a call was grounds for dismissal, though Maura seriously doubted that Francine would be fired.

Maura looked around, gravely and silently surveying her group before beginning again.

She didn't get a chance—someone spoke up. A young teenager.

"They should call it the Torture Tree or the Hangman's Tree…or something besides the History Tree," he said.

The boy's name was Mark Hartford, Maura thought. She'd supervised a game at the pool one day when he had been playing. He was a nice kid, curious and, maybe because he was an adolescent boy, boisterous. He also had an older brother, Nils—in college already. Mark's brother wasn't quite as nice; he knew that many of the workers were his own age or younger, and he liked to lord his status as a guest over them. He was bearable, however.

"The Torture Tree! Oh, lord, you little…heathen!"

Nils had a girlfriend. Rachel Lawrence. She was nicer than Nils, unless Nils was around. Then she behaved with a great deal of superiority, as well. But, Maura realized, Nils and Rachel *were* at the campfire that night—they had just joined quietly.

Quietly—which was amazing in itself. Nils liked to make an entrance most of the time, making sure that everyone saw him.

Rachel had her hands set upon Mark's shoulders—even as she called him a heathen. She looked scared, or nervous maybe, Maura thought. Maybe it was for effect; Nils set his arm around her shoulders, as a good, protective boyfriend should. They made a cute family picture, a young adult male with his chosen mate and a young one under their wings.

Maura was surprised they were on the tour. Nils had said something the other day about the fact that they were too mature for campfire ghost stories.

"Torture Tree—yes, that would be better!" Mark said. He wasn't arguing with Rachel, he was determined that he was right. "Poor Gyselle—she was really tortured there, right?"

Mark and the other young teens were wide-eyed. Teenagers that age liked the sensational—and they liked it grisly.

"She was dragged there and hanged, so yes, I'm sure it was torture," Maura said. "But it was the History Tree long before a plantation was built here, years and years ago," Maura said. "That was the Native American name for it—the Timucua were here years before the Spanish came. They called it the History Tree, because even back then, the old oak had grown together with a palm, and it's been that way since. Anyway, we'll be seeing the History Tree soon enough," she said softly. "The tree that first welcomed terror when the beautiful Gyselle was tormented and hanged from the tree until dead. And where, so they say, the hauntings and horrors of the History Tree began."

Maura saw more than one of her audience members glance back over the area of sweeping, manicured lawn and toward the ranch, as if assuring themselves that more than the night and the spooky, draped trees existed, that there was light and safety not far away.

The new buildings Donald Glass had erected were

elegant and beautiful. With St. Augustine just an hour and a half in one direction and Disney and Universal and other theme parks just an hour and half to the south—not to mention a nice proximity to the beaches and racetrack at Daytona and the wonder of Cape Kennedy being an hour or so away, as well—Frampton Ranch and Resort was becoming a must-see location.

Still, the ranch had become renowned for offering Campfire Ghost Histories. Not stories, but histories—everything said was history and fact…to a point.

The listeners could hear what people claimed to have happened, and they could believe—or not. And then they'd walk the trails where history had occurred.

"You see, Gyselle had been a lovely lost waif, raised by the Seminole tribe after they found her wandering near the battlefield at the end of the Second Seminole War. She was 'rescued' by Spanish missionaries at the beginning of the Third Seminole War, though, at that point, she probably didn't want or need rescuing, having been with a Seminole family for years. But 'saved' and then set adrift, she found work at the old Frampton plantation, and there she caught the eye of the heir, and despite his arranged marriage to socialite Julie LeBlanc, the young Richard Frampton fell head over heels in love with Gyselle. They were known to escape into the woods where they both professed their love, despite all the odds against them—and Richard's wife, Julie. Knowing of her husband's infidelity, Julie LeBlanc arranged to poison her father-in-law—and let the blame fall on Gyselle. Gyselle was hunted down as a murderous witch, supposedly practicing a shaman's magic or a form of voodoo—it was easy to blame it on traditions the plantation workers didn't really understand—and she was hanged there, from what was once a lover's tree where she had met with Richard, her love, who had promised to protect her..."

She let her voice trail. Then she finished.

"Here, in these woods, Gyselle loved, not wisely, but deeply. And here she died. And so they say, when the moon has risen high and full in the night sky—as it is now—those who walk the trails by night can hear her singing softly 'The Last Rose of Summer' with a lovely Irish lilt to her voice."

"What about the curse?" a boy cried out.

"Yeah, the curse! That she spoke before she died—swearing that her tormenters would choke on their own blood! You just said that she cursed everyone, and there are more stories, right?" Mark—never one to be silent long—asked eagerly.

Maura felt—rather than saw—Brock McGovern at her side. He was amused. Barely eighteen, he'd nevertheless been given the position of stage manager for events such as the campfire history tour. He'd been standing to one side just behind her as she told her tale with just the right dramatic emphasis—or so she believed.

He stepped forward, just a shade closer, nearly touching her.

"Choking on their own blood? Kind of a standard curse, huh?" he teased softly and for her ears alone.

Maura ignored him, trying not to smile, and still,

even here, now, felt the rush she always did when Brock was around.

Brock was always ready to tease—but also to encourage and support whatever she was doing. He had that ability and the amazing tendency to exude an easy confidence that stretched far beyond his years. But he was that sure of himself. He was about to leave for the service, and when he returned, he planned to go to college to study criminology. Barely an adult, he knew what he wanted in life. She was sure he was going to work hard during basic training; he'd work hard through the college or university of his choice. And then he'd make up his mind just where he wanted to serve—FBI, US Marshals, perhaps even Homeland Security or the Secret Service.

He shook his head, smiling at her with his unusual eyes—a shade so dark that they didn't appear brown at times, but rather black. His shaggy hair—soon to become a buzz cut—was as dark as his eyes, and it framed a face that was, in Maura's mind, pure enchantment. He had already had a fine, steady chin—the kind most often seen on more mature men. His cheekbones were broad, and his skin was continually bronzed. He was, in her mind, beautiful.

He'd often told the tales himself, and he did so very well. He had a deep, rich voice that could rise and fall at just the right moments—a voice that, on its own, could awaken every sense in Maura's body. They had known each other for three years now, laughed and joked together, ridden old trails, worked together… always flirting, nearly touching at first, but always aware that, when summer ended, he would head back down to Key West and she would return to West Palm Beach—about 233 miles apart, just a little too far for a high school romance.

But this summer…

Things had changed.

She had liked him from the time she had met him; she had compared any other young man she met to him, and in her mind, all others fell short. He'd been given a management job that summer, probably because he was always willing to pitch in himself, whether it came to working in the restaurant when tables needed bussing or hauling in boxes when deliveries arrived. He'd gained a lean and muscular physique from hard work as much as from time in the gym, and he had a quick mind and a quicker wit, cared for people, was generous with his time, and was just…

Perfect. She'd never find anyone so perfect in life again, Maura was certain, even though she knew that her mother and father smiled indulgently when she talked about him in glowing terms—she was, after all, just eighteen, with college days and so much more ahead of her.

This summer they'd become a true couple. In every way.

A very passionate couple.

They'd had sex, in her mind, the most amazing sex ever, more meaningful than any sex had ever been before.

Just the thought brought a rush of blood to her face.

But…she believed that they would go on even

through their separation, no matter the distance, no matter what. People would think, of course, that she was just a teenager, that she couldn't be as madly in love as she believed she was. So she was determined that no one would really realize just how insanely fully she did love him.

She turned to Brock. He was smiling at her. Something of a secret smile, charming, sexy…a smile that seemed to hint that they always shared something unique, something special.

She grinned in return.

Yep. He had become her world.

"Take it away," she told him.

"The curse!" he said, stepping in with a tremor in his voice. "It's true that while being dragged to the tree—which you'll see soon on our walk—the poor woman cried out that she was innocent of any cruel deed, innocent of murder. And she said that those who so viciously killed her would die in agony and despair. The very woods here would be haunted for eternity, and the evil they perpetrated on her would live forever. They had brought the devil into the woods, and there he would abide."

He smiled, innately charming when he spoke to a group, and continued, "I think that storytellers have added in the choking-on-blood part. Very dramatic and compelling, but…there are records of the occasion of the poor woman's demise available at the resort library." He set his flashlight beneath his chin, creating an eerie look.

"And," Maura said, "what is also documented is that

bad things continued to happen on the ranch—under the same tree, the condemned killer, Marston Riggs, tortured and killed his victims in the early 1900s, and as late as 1970, the man known as the Red Tie Killer made use of the tree as well, killing five men and women at the History Tree and leaving their bones to fall to the ground. But, of course, we don't believe in curses. The History Tree and the ranch are perfectly safe nowadays…" She looked at Brock. "Shall we?" she asked.

"Indeed, we shall," he said, and the sound of his voice and the look that he gave her made her long for it to be later, when they had completed the nighttime forest tour—and were alone together.

They walked by the grove, where there was a charming little pond rumored to invigorate life—a handsomely written plaque commemorating the Spaniard Reynaldo Montenegro and his exploration of Florida.

Brock said to the tour group, "Here we are at the famous grove where Reynaldo Montenegro claimed to have found the Pond of Eternal Youth."

It was as great tour; even the adolescents continued to ask questions as they walked.

"I'm happy to have been the tour guide tonight," Maura murmured to Brock. "But I can't believe that Francine just didn't show up."

"If I know Francine, she'll make a grand entrance somewhere along the line, with a perfect reason for not being on time. She'll have some mammoth surprise for everyone—something way more important than speaking to the guests. Hey, what do you want to bet that we see her somewhere before this tour is over? Here, folks," Brock announced, "you'll see the plaque—an inquisition did come to the New World!"

The copse, illuminated only by the sparkling lights that lit the trail, offered a sadder message—that of tortures carried out by an invading society on the native population it encountered.

They passed the ruins of an old Spanish farm and then they neared the tree.

The infamous History Tree.

The tree—or trees—older than anyone could remember, stood dead center in the small clearing, as if nothing else would dare to grow near. Gnarled and twisted together, palm and oak suggested a mess of human limbs, coiled together in agony.

Maura stopped dead, hearing a long, terrified scream, then realizing that she'd made the sound herself.

From one large oaken branch, a body was hanging, swaying just slightly in the night breeze.

She didn't need to wonder why Francine Renault had been derelict in her duty.

She was there…part of the tour, just not as she should have been.

Head askew, neck broken. She was hanging there, in the place where others had been hanged through the years, again and again, where they had decayed, where their bones had dotted the earth beneath them.

Brock had been right.

Francine Renault had indeed shown up before the tour was over.

THE POLICE FLOODED the ranch with personnel, the medical examiner and crime scene technicians.

The rich forest of pines and oaks and ferns and earth became alive with artificial light, and still, where the moss sagged low, the bright beams just made the night and the macabre situation eerier.

Detective Michael Flannery had been put in charge of the case. Employees and guests had been separated and then separated again, and eventually, Maura sat at the edge of the parking lot, shivering although it wasn't cold, waiting for the officer who would speak with her.

When he got there, he wanted to know the last time she had seen Francine. She told him it had been the night before.

Where she had been all day? In the office, in the yard with the older teen boys and at the campfire.

Had she heard anyone threaten Francine?

At least half of the resort's employees. In aggravation or jest.

The night seemed to wear on forever.

When she was released at last, she was sent back to her own room and ordered to stay there until morning.

When morning came, her parents were there, ready to take her home.

She desperately wanted to see Brock.

Her parents were quiet and then they looked at each other. Her father shook his head slightly, and her mother said softly, "Maura, you can't see Brock."

"What?" she demanded. "Why not? Mom, Dad—I'm about to leave home. Go to college, really be on my own. I love you. I'm going to come home. But… I'm almost eighteen. I won't go without seeing Brock."

Her father, a gentle giant with broad shoulders and a mane of white hair, spoke to her softly. "Sweetheart, we didn't say that we wouldn't let you see Brock. We're saying that you *can't* see Brock." He hesitated, looking over at her mother, and then he continued with, "I'm so sorry. Brock was arrested last night. He was charged with the murder of Francine Renault."

And with those words, it seemed that her world fell apart, that what she had known, that what she had believed in, all just exploded into a sea of red and then disappeared into smoke and fog.

Chapter One

"I'm assigned to go back to Florida. To stay at the Frampton Ranch and Resort—and investigate what we believe to be three kidnappings and a murder. And the kidnappings may have nothing to do with the resort, nor may the murder?" Brock McGovern asked, a small note of incredulity slipping into his voice, which was surprising to him—he was always careful to keep an even tone.

FBI Assistant Director Richard Egan had brought him into his office, and Brock had known he was going on assignment—he just hadn't expected this.

"Yes, not what you'd want, but, hey, maybe it'll be good for you—and perhaps necessary now, when time is of the essence and there is no one out there who could know the place or the circumstances with the same scope and experience you have," Egan told him. "Three young women have disappeared from the area. Two of them were guests of the Frampton Ranch and Resort shortly before their disappearances—the third had left St. Augustine and was on her way there. The Florida Department of Law Enforcement has naturally been there already. They asked for federal help on this. Shades of the past haunt them—they don't want any more unsolved murders—and everyone is hoping against hope that Lily Sylvester, Amy Bonham and Lydia Merkel might be found."

"These are Florida missing persons cases," Brock said. "And it's sad but true that young people go to Florida and get caught up in the beach life and the club scene. And regrettable but true once again—there's a drug and alcohol culture that does exist and people get caught up in it. Not just in Florida, of course, but... everywhere." He smiled grimly. "I go where I'm told, but I'm curious—how is this an FBI affair? And forgive me, but FBI out of New York?"

"Not out of New York. FDLE asked for you. Specifically."

"I see."

Egan didn't often dwell on the emotional or psychological, but the assistant director hesitated and then said, "You could put your past to rest."

Brock shrugged. "You know, one of the cooks committed suicide not long after the murder. Peter Moore. He stabbed himself with a butcher knife. He'd had a lot of fights with Francine Renault—the victim found at the tree. They suspected he might have killed himself out of remorse."

Egan offered him a dry grimace. "I know about the cook, of course. You know me—I knew everything about you on paper before I took you into this unit. I'm not sure anyone would have made a case against him in court. That's all beside the point—the past may well be the past. But there's the now, as well. They're afraid of a serial killer, Brock," Egan said. And he continued with, "The badly decomposed remains—mostly bones—of another young woman who went missing several months ago were recently found in a bizarre way—they were dumped in with sheets from several hotels and resorts at an industrial laundry that accepted linens from dozens of places—Frampton Ranch and Resort being one of them."

"I see," Brock said.

He didn't really see.

That didn't matter; Egan would be thorough.

"Yes, this may be a bit hard on you, but you're the one in the know. To come close to a knowledge of the area and people that you already have might take someone else hours or days that may cost a life… You're the best man for this. Especially because you were once falsely accused. And, I believe, you may just solve something of the mystery of the past. And quit hating your own home."

"I don't hate my own home. Ah, come on, sir, I don't want to play any cure-me psychological games with this," Brock said.

Egan shook his head and leaned forward, his eyes narrowed—indicating a rise in his temper, something always kept in check. "If I thought you needed to be cured, you wouldn't be in my unit. Women are missing. They might be dead already," he said curtly. "And then again, they might have a chance. You're the agent with a real sense for the place, the people and the surrounding landscape. And you're a good agent, period. I trust in your ability to get this sorted."

Brock greatly admired Egan. He had a nose for sending the right agent or agents in for a job. Usually.

But Brock was sitting across from Egan in Egan's office—in New York City. He, Brock, was an NYC agent.

And while Brock really didn't dislike where he came from—he still loved Florida, especially his family home in the Keys—he had opted to apply to the New York office of the Bureau specifically because it was far, far away from the state of his birth.

The New York City office didn't usually handle events in Florida, unless a criminal had traveled from New York down to the southern state. Florida had several field offices—including a multimillion-dollar state-of-the-art facility in Broward County. That was south—but Orlando had an exceptional office, close enough to the Frampton place. And there were more offices, as well.

Even if the Frampton Ranch and Resort was in a relatively isolated part of the state, a problem there would generally be handled by a more local office.

"Frampton Ranch and Resort," he heard himself say. And this time, years of training and experience kicked in—his voice was perfectly level and emotionless.

It was true: he sure as hell knew it and the area. The resort was just a bit off from—or maybe part of—what people considered to be the northern Ocala region, where prime acreage was still available at reasonable prices, where horse ranches were common upon the ever-so-slightly rolling hills and life tended to be slow and easy.

There were vast tracts of grazing ground and great live-oak forests and trails laden with pines where the sun seemed to drip down through great strands of weeping moss that hung from many a branch. It could be considered horse country, farm country and ranch county. There were marshes and forests, sinkholes and all manner of places where a body might just disappear.

The Frampton ranch was north of Ocala, east of Gainesville and about forty-five minutes south of Olustee, Florida, where every year, a battle reenactment took place, drawing tourists and historians from near and far. The Battle of Olustee, won by forces in the state; the war had been heading toward its final inevitable conclusion, and then time proved that victory had been necessary for human rights and the strength and growth of the fledgling nation, however purposeless the sad loss of lives always seemed.

Reenactors and historians arrived in good numbers, and those who loved bringing history to life also loved bringing in crowds and many came for the campgrounds. The reenactment took place in February, when temperatures in the state tended to be beautiful and mosquito repellent wasn't as much a requirement as usual. During the winter season—often spring break for other regions—the area was exceptionally popular.

The area was beautiful.

And the large areas of isolation, which included the Frampton property, could conceal any number of dark deeds.

He'd just never thought he'd go back to it.

Certainly, time—and the path he had chosen to take in life—had helped erase the horror of the night they had come upon the body of Francine Renault hanging from the History Tree and his own subsequent arrest. He'd been so young then, so assured that truth spoke for itself. In the end, his parents—bless them—had leaped to the fore, flying into action, and their attorney had made quick work of getting him out of jail after only one night and seeing that his record was returned to spotless. It was ludicrous that they had arrested him; he'd been able to prove that it would have been impossible for him to have carried out the deed. Dozens of witnesses had attested to the fact that he couldn't have been the killer, he'd been seen by so many people during the hours in which the murder must have taken place. He could remember, though, sitting in the cell—cold, stark, barren—and wondering why in God's name they had arrested *him*.

He discovered that there had been an anonymous call to the station—someone stating that they had seen him dragging Francine Renault into the woods. The tipster had sworn that he would appear at a trial as a witness for the prosecution, but the witness had not come to the station. Others had signed formal protests, and the McGoverns' attorney had taken over.

So many people had come forward, indignant, furious over his arrest.

But not Maura. She had been gone. Just gone. He couldn't think of the Frampton Ranch and Resort without a twinge of pain. He had never been sure which had broken him more at the time—the arrest or the fact that Maura had disappeared as cleanly from his life as any hint of daylight once night had fallen.

They had been so young. It had been natural that her parents whisked her away, and maybe even natural that neither had since tried to reach the other.

But there were times when he could still close his eyes and see her smile and be certain that he breathed in the subtle scent of her. Twelve years had gone by; he wasn't even the same person.

Egan was unaware of his reflections.

"Detective Michael Flannery is lead investigator now. He was on the case when you were arrested for the crime, but he wasn't lead."

"I know Flannery. We've communicated through the years, believe it or not. I almost feel bad—he suffered a lot of guilt about jumping the gun with me."

"He's with the Florida Department of Law Enforcement now, with some seniority and juice, so it seems," Egan informed him. "Years ago, when the murder took place, the federal government wasn't involved. Flannery doesn't want this crime going unsolved. He knows you're in this office now. His commander told me that he keeps in touch with you." Egan paused. "It doesn't sound as if you have a problem with him—you don't, right?"

"No, sir, I do not."

Even as a stunned kid—what he had been back then—Brock had never hated Detective Flannery for being one of the men who had come and arrested him.

Flannery had been just as quick to listen to the arguments that eventually cleared Brock completely of any wrongdoing. While Brock knew that Flannery was furious that he had been taken and certain that there had been an underlying and devious conspiracy to lead him and his superiors so thoroughly in the wrong direction, he had to agree that, at the time, Brock had appeared to be a ready suspect.

He'd had a fight with Francine that day, and it had been witnessed by many people. He hadn't gotten physical in any way, but his poor opinion of her, and his anger with her, had probably been more than evident—enough for him to be brought in for questioning and to be held for twenty-four hours at any rate.

"I'm curious how something that happened so long ago can relate to the cases happening now," Brock said.

"It may not. The remains of the dead girl found in the laundry might have been the work of one crazed individual or an acquaintance seeking vengeance, acting out of jealousy—a solitary motive. It might be coincidence the way she was found—or maybe a killer was trying to throw suspicion upon a particular place or person. But…a lot of the same individuals are still there now who were there when Francine Renault was killed."

"Donald Glass—he's around a lot, though he does spend time at his other properties. Fred Bentley—I imagine he's still running the works. Who else is still there?" Brock asked.

Egan handed him a pile of folders. "All this is coming to your email, as well. There you have those who are in residence—and dossiers on the victims. Yes,

Glass and Bentley are still on the property. There are other staff members who never left—Millie Cranston, head of Housekeeping. Vinnie Marshall, upgraded to chef—after Peter Moore's death, I might add. And then…" He paused, tapping the folders. "You have some old guests who are now employees."

"Who?"

"Mark and Nils Hartford," Egan told him. "Both of them report directly to Fred Bentley. Mark has taken over as the social director. Nils is managing the restaurants—the sit-down Ranch Roost and the Java Bar."

Brock hadn't known that the Hartford brothers—who'd seemed so above the working class when they'd been guests—were now employed at the very place where they had once loved to make hell for others.

"Flannery said this is something he hadn't mentioned to you. One of your old friends—or acquaintances—Rachel Lawrence is now with FDLE. She's been working the murder and the disappearances with him."

"Rachel? Became…a cop?" Brock shook his head, not sure if he was angry or amused. Rachel had never wanted to break a nail. She'd been pretty and delicate and… She'd also been a constant accessory of Nils Hartford.

"I guess your old friend Flannery was afraid to tell you."

"I don't know why he would be. I'm just a little surprised—she seemed more likely to be on one of those shows about rich housewives in a big city, but I never had a problem with her. That the Hartford brothers both became employees—that's also a surprise. They made me think of *Dirty Dancing*. They were the rich kids—we were the menial labor. But the world changes. People change."

"Flannery's point, so it appears, is that a number of the same players are in the area—may mean something and may not. There have been, give or take, approximately a thousand murders in the state per year in the last years. But that's only about four percent per the population. Still, anything could have happened. Violent crime may have to do with many factors—often family related, gang related, drug related, well…you know all the drills. But if we do have a serial situation down there—relating to or not relating to the past—everyone needs to move quickly. Not only do you know the area and the terrain, you know people and you know the ropes of getting around many of the people and places who might be integral to the situation."

"Yes. And any agent would want to put a halt to this—put an end to a serial killer. Or find the girls—alive, one can pray—or stop future abductions and killings."

Egan nodded grimly and tossed a small pile of photos down before him. Brock could see three young, hopeful faces looking back at him. All three were attractive, and more grippingly, all three seemed to smile with life and all that lay before someone at that tender age.

"The missing," Egan said. He had big hands and long fingers. He used them to slide the first three photographs over.

The last was a divided sheet. On one side was the likeness of a beautiful young woman, probably in her early twenties. Her hair had been thick and dark and curly; her eyes had been sky blue. Her smile had been engaging.

"Maureen Rodriguez," Egan said. He added softly, "Then and now."

On the other side of the divided sheet was a crime scene photo—an image of bones, scattered in dirt in a pile of sheets. In the center of the broken and fragmented bones was a skull.

The skull retained bits of flesh.

"According to the investigation, she was on her way to Frampton Ranch and Resort," Egan said.

Brock nodded slowly and rose. "As am I," he said. "When do I leave?"

"Your plane is in two hours—down to Jacksonville. You've a rental car in your name when you arrive. I'm sure you know the way to the property. Detective Flannery will be waiting to hear from you. He'll go over all the particulars."

Brock was surprised to see that Egan was still studying him. "You are good, right?" he asked Brock.

"Hey, everyone wants to head to Florida for the winter, don't they?" he asked. "I'm good," he said seriously. "Maybe you're right. Maybe we can put the past to rest after all."

"I LOVE IT—just love it, love it, love it! Love it all!" Angie Parsons said enthusiastically. She offered Maura one of her biggest, happiest smiles.

She was staring at the History Tree, her smile brilliant and her enthusiasm for her project showing in the brightness of her eyes and her every movement. "I mean, people say Florida has no history—just because it's not New England and there were no pilgrims. But, hey, St. Augustine is—what?—the oldest settlement continually…settled…by Europeans in the country, right? I mean, way back, the Spaniards were here. No, no, the state wasn't one of the original thirteen colonies. No, no Puritans here. But! There's so much! And this tree… No one knows how old the frigging oak is or when the palm tree grew in it or through it or with it or whatever."

Angie Parsons was cute, friendly, bright and sometimes, but just sometimes, too much. At five feet two inches, she exuded enough energy for a giant. She had just turned thirty—and done brilliantly for her years. She had written one of the one most successful nonfiction book series on the market. And all because she got as excited as she did about objects and places and things—such as the History Tree.

The main tree was a black oak; no one knew quite how old it was, but several hundred years at least. That type of oak was known to live over five hundred years.

A palm tree had—at some time—managed to grow at the same place, through the outstretched roots of the oak and twirling up around the trunk and through the branches. It was bizarre, beautiful, and so unusual that it naturally inspired all manner of legends, some of those legends based on truth.

And, of course, the History Tree held just the kind of legend that made Angie as successful as she was.

Angie's being incredibly successful didn't hurt Maura any.

But being here... Yes, it hurt. At least...it was incredibly uncomfortable. On the one hand it was wonderful seeing people she had worked with once upon a time in another life.

On the other hand it was bizarre. Like visiting a mirror dimension made up of things she remembered. The Hartford brothers were working there now. Nils was managing the restaurants—he'd arrived at the table she and Angie had shared last night to welcome them and pick up their dinner check. Of course, Nils had become management. No lowly posts for him. He seemed to have an excellent working relationship with Fred Bentley, who was still the manager of the resort. Bentley had come down when they'd checked in—he'd greeted Maura with a serious hug. She was tall, granted, and in heels, and he was on the short side for a man—about five-ten—but it still seemed that his hug allowed for him to rest his head against her breasts a moment too long.

But still, he'd apparently been delighted to see her.

And Mark Hartford had come to see her, too, grown-up, cute and charming now—and just as happy as his brother to see her. It was thanks to her, he had told her, and her ability to tell the campfire histories, that had made him long to someday do the same.

The past didn't seem like any kind of a boulder

around his neck. Certainly he remembered the night that Francine had been murdered.

The night that had turned *her* life upside down had been over twelve years ago.

Like all else in the past, it was now history.

Time had marched on, apparently, for them—and her.

She'd just turned eighteen the last time she had been here. When that autumn had come around, she'd done what she'd been meant to do, headed to the University of Central Florida, an amazing place to study performance of any kind and directing and film—with so many aspects thrown into the complete education.

She'd spent every waking minute in classes—taking elective upon elective to stay busy. She was now CEO of her own company, providing short videos to promote writers, artists, musicians and anyone wanting video content, including attorneys and accountants.

Not quite thirty, she could be proud of her professional accomplishments—she had garnered a great reputation.

She enjoyed working with Angie. The writer was fun, and there was good reason for her success. She loved the bizarre and spooky that drew human curiosity. Even those who claimed they didn't believe in anything even remotely paranormal seemed to love Angie's books.

Most of the time, yes, Maura *did* truly enjoy working with Angie, and since Angie had tried doing her own videos without much success, she was equally happy to be working with Maura. They'd done great bits down in Key West at the cemetery there—where Maura's favorite tomb was engraved with the words *I told you I was sick!*—and at the East Martello Museum with Robert the Doll. They had filmed on the west coast at the old summer estates that had belonged to Henry Ford and Thomas Edison. And they'd worked together in St. Augustine, where they'd created twenty little video bits for social media that had pleased Angie to no end—and garnered hundreds of thousands of hits.

Last night, even Marie Glass—Donald's reserved and elegant wife—had come by their dinner table to welcome them and tell them just how much she enjoyed all the videos that Maura had done for and with Angie, telling great legends and wild tales that were bizarrely wonderful—and true.

Maybe naturally, since they were working in Florida, Angie had determined that they had to stay at Frampton Ranch and Resort and film at the History Tree.

Maura had suggested other places that would make great content for a book on the bizarre: sinkholes, a road where cars slid uphill instead of downhill—hell, she would have done her best to make a giant ball of twine sound fascinating. There were lots of other places in the state with strange stories—lord! They could go back to Key West and film a piece on Carl Tanzler, who had slept with the corpse of his beloved, Elena de Hoyos, for seven years.

But Angie was dead set on seeing the History Tree, and when they'd gotten to the clearing she had started spinning around like a delighted child.

She stopped suddenly, staring at Maura.

"You really are uncomfortable here, aren't you? Scared? You know, I've told you—you can hire an assistant. Maybe a strapping fellow, tall, dark and handsome—or blond and handsome—and muscle-bound. Someone to protect us if the bogeyman is around at any of our strange sites." Angie paused, grinning. She liked men and didn't apologize for it. In her own words, if you didn't kiss a bunch of frogs, you were never going to find a prince.

"Angie, I like doing my own work—and editing it and assuring that I like what I've done. I promise you, if we turn something into any kind of a feature film, we'll hire dozens of people."

Angie sighed. "Well, so much for tall, dark—or blond—and handsome. Your loss, my dear friend. Anyway. You do amazing work for me. You're a one-woman godsend."

"Thanks," Maura told her. She inhaled a deep breath.

"Could you try not to look quite so miserable?"

"Oh, Angie. I'm sorry. It's just..."

"The legend. The legend about the tree—oh, yes. And the murder victims found here. I'm sorry, Maura, but... I mean, I film these places because they have legends attached to them." Angie seemed to be perplexed. She sighed. "Of course, the one murder was just twelve years ago. Does that bother you?" Staring at Maura, she gasped suddenly. "You're close to this somehow, right? Oh, my God! Were you one of the kids working here *that* summer? I mean, I'd have had no idea...

You're from West Palm Beach. There's so much stuff down there. Ah!" It seemed that Angie didn't really need answers. "You wound up going to the University of Central Florida. You were near here..."

"Yes, I was here working that summer," Maura said flatly.

"Your name was never in the paper?"

"That's right. The police were careful to keep the employees away from the media. And since we are so isolated on the ranch, news reporters didn't get wind of anything until the next day. My parents had me out of here by then, and Donald Glass was emphatic about the press leaving his young staff alone."

"But a kid was *arrested*—"

"And released. And honestly, Angie, I am a little worried. Even if it has nothing to do with the past, there's something not good going on now. Haven't you watched the news? They found the remains of a young woman not far from here."

"Not far from here, but not *here*," Angie said. "Hey," she said again, frowning with concern. "That can't have anything to do with anything—the Frampton ranch killer committed suicide, I thought."

"One of the cooks killed himself," Maura said. "Yes, but... I mean, he never had his day in court. Most people believed he killed Francine—he hated her. But a lot of people disliked her."

"But he killed himself."

"Yes. I wasn't here then. I did hear about it, of course."

Angie was pensive for a moment, and then she

asked, "Maura, you don't think that the tree is…evil, do you?"

"*Trees*—a palm laced in with an oak. And no. I'm quite accustomed to the spooky and creepy, and we both know that places don't become evil, nor do things. But people can be wicked as hell—and they can feed off legends. I don't like being out here—not alone. There will be a campfire tonight with the history and ghost stories and the walk—we'll join that. I have waivers for whoever attends tonight."

"What if someone doesn't want to be filmed?" Angie asked anxiously. "You tell the story just as well as anyone else, right? And the camera loves you—a perfect, slinky blonde beauty with those enormous gray eyes of yours. Come on, you've told a few of the stories before. You can—"

"I cannot do a good video for you as a selfie," Maura said patiently.

"Right. I can film you telling the story," Angie said. "Just that part. And I can do it now—I think you said that the stories were told by the campfire, and then the historic walk began. I'll get you—right here and now—doing the story part of it. Oh, and you can include… Oh, God!" Angie said, her eyes widening. "You weren't just here—you saw the dead woman! The murdered woman… I mean, from this century. Francine Renault. And they arrested a kid, Brock McGovern, but he was innocent, and it was proved almost immediately, but then… Well, then, if the cook didn't do it, they never caught the killer!"

Maura kept her face impassive. Angie always wrote

about old crimes that were unsolved—and why a place was naturally haunted after ghastly deeds had occurred there.

She did her homework, however. Angie probably knew more than Maura remembered.

She had loved the sad legend of the beautiful Gyselle, who had died so tragically for love. But, of course, she would have delved as deeply as possible into every event that had occurred at the ranch.

"Do they—do they tell that story at the campfire?" Angie asked.

Maura sighed. "Angie, I haven't been here since the night it happened. I was still young. My parents dragged me home immediately."

She was here now—and she could remember that night all too clearly. Coming to the tree, then realizing while denying it that a real body was hanging from it. That it was Francine Renault. That she had been hanged from a heavy branch, hanged by the neck, and that she dangled far above the ground, tongue bulging, face grotesque.

She remembered screaming…

And she remembered the police and how they had taken Brock away, frowning and massively confused, still tall and straight and almost regally dignified.

And she could remember that there were still those who speculated on his guilt or innocence—until dozens of people had spoken out, having seen him through the time when Francine might have been taken and killed. His arrest had really been ludicrous—a detective's desperate bid to silence the horror and outrage that was beginning to spread.

Brock's life had changed, and thus her life had changed.

Everything had changed.

Except for this spot.

She could even imagine that she was a kid again, that she could see Francine Renault, so macabre in death, barely believable, yet so real and tragic and terrifying as she dangled from the thick limb.

"Oh," Angie groaned, the one word drawn out long enough to be a sentence. "Now I know why you were against doing a video here!"

Angie had wanted the History Tree. And when she had started to grow curious regarding Maura's reluctance to head to the Frampton Ranch and Resort—especially since the resort was supposedly great and the expense of rooms went on Angie's bill—Maura had decided it was time to cave.

She hadn't wanted to give any explanations.

"Angie, it's in your book, and you sell great and your video channel is doing great, as well. It's fine. Really. But because they did recently find what seems to be the remains of a murder victim near here, I do think we need to be careful. As in, stay out of these woods after dark."

"There is a big bad wolf. Was a big bad wolf… But seriously, I'm not a criminologist of any kind, but I'd say the killer back then was making a point. Maybe the bones they found belonged to someone who died of natural causes."

Angie wasn't stupid, but Maura was sure that the look she gave her tiny friend at that moment implied that she thought she was.

"Maybe," Angie said defensively.

"Angie, you don't rot in the dirt on purpose and then wind up with your bones in a cache of hotel laundry," Maura said.

"No, but, hey—there could be another explanation. Like a car accident. And whoever hit her was terrified and ran—and then, sadly, she just rotted."

"And wound up in hotel sheets?"

Maura asked incredulously. Angie couldn't be serious.

"Okay, so that's a bit far-fetched."

"Angie, it's been reported that the remains were found of a murder victim. Last I saw, they were still seeking her identity, but they said that she was killed."

"Well, they found bones, from what I understand. Anyway," Angie said, dusting her hands on her skirt and speaking softly and with dignity and compassion, "I wish you would have just said that you were here when it happened. Let's get out of here. I'm sorry I made you do this."

"You didn't make me do it. If I had been determined not to come back here, I wouldn't have done so. But it's going to get dark soon. Let me shoot a bit of you doing your speech by the tree while I still have good light."

Maura lifted her camera, looked at the tree and then up at the sky.

They wouldn't have the light much longer.

"Angie, come on—let's film you."

"Please—you know the stories so well. Let me film you this time."

"They're your books."

"But you'll give me a great authenticity. I'll interview you—and you were here when the last crime occurred. I'm surprised they haven't hacked this sucker to the ground, really," Angie said, looking at the tree. "Or at the very least, they should have video surveillance out here."

"Now, that would be the right idea. They have video surveillance in the lobby, the elevators—and other areas. But for now, please?"

They were never going to be able to leave.

"All right, all right!" Maura said. She adjusted the camera on its lightweight tripod and looked at the image on the camera's viewing screen. "I've got it lined up already. I'll go right there. You need to get it rolling. The mic is on already, and you can see what you're filming."

"Hey, I've used it before—not a lot, but I kind of know what I'm doing," Angie reminded her.

Maura stepped away from the camera and headed over to the tree. Angie had paid attention to her. She lifted her fingers and said, "In three…" and then went silent, counting down the rest by hand.

Maura was amazed at how quickly it all came back to her. She told the tale of the beautiful Gyselle and then went into the later crimes.

Ending, of course, with the murder of Francine Renault.

"A false lead caused the arrest of an innocent young

man. But this is America, and we all know that any man is innocent until proved guilty, and this young man was quickly proved innocent. He was only under arrest for a night, because eyewitness reports confirmed he was with several other people—busy at work—when the crime took place. Still, it was a travesty, shattering a great deal of the promise of the young man's life. He was, however, as I said, quickly released—and until this day, the crime goes unsolved."

She finished speaking and saw that Angie was still running the camera, looking past her, appearing perplexed—and pleased—by something that she saw.

"Hello there! Are you with Frampton Ranch and Resort? You aren't, by any chance, the host for the campfire stories tonight, are you?"

Angie was smiling sweetly—having shifted into her flirtatious mode.

Curious, Maura turned around and started toward the path.

If a jaw could actually drop, hers did.

She quickly closed her mouth, but perhaps her eyes were bulging, as well. It seemed almost as if someone had physically knocked the breath from her.

Brock McGovern was standing there.

Different.

The same.

A bit taller than he'd been at eighteen; his shoulders had filled out and he appeared to have acquired a great deal more solid muscle. He filled out a dark blue suit and tailored shirt exceptionally well.

His face was the same…

Different.

There was something hard about him now that hadn't been there before. His features were leaner, his eyes…

Still deep brown. But they were harder now, too, or appeared to be harder, as if there was a shield of glass on them. He'd always walked and moved with purpose, confident in what he wanted and where he was going.

Now, just standing still, he was an imposing presence.

And though Angie had spoken, he was looking at Maura.

"Wow," Angie said softly. "Did I dream up the perfect assistant for you—tall, dark and to die for? Who the hell… The storyteller guy is wickedly cute, but this guy…"

He couldn't have heard her words; he wasn't close enough.

And he wasn't looking at her. He was staring at Maura.

"That was great," he said smoothly. "However, I don't consider my life to have been *shattered*. I mean—I hope I have fulfilled a few of the promises I made to myself."

Maura wanted to speak. Her mouth wouldn't work.

Angie, however, had no problem.

"Oh, my God!" Angie cried.

Every once in a while, her Valley girl came out.

"You—you're Brock McGovern?" she asked.

"I am," he said, but he still wasn't looking at Angie.

He was locked on Maura. Then he smiled. A rueful smile, dry and maybe even a little bitter.

"Here—in Florida," Angie said. "I mean—at the History Tree."

He turned at last to face Angie. "I'm here for an investigation now. I'm going to suggest that you two head back to the resort and don't wander off alone. A woman's remains were found at a laundry facility not far from here, and there are three young women who have gone missing recently. Best to stay in the main areas—with plenty of people around."

"Oh!" Angie went into damsel-in-distress mode then. "Is it really dangerous, do you think? I'm so glad that you're here, if there is danger. I mean, we've seen the news…heard things, but seriously, bad things aren't necessarily happening here, right? It's just a tree. Florida is far from crime-free, but… Anyway, thank God that you're here. We didn't really think we needed to be afraid, but now you're here…and thank God! Right, Maura?"

Maura didn't reply. She'd heard Angie speaking as if she'd been far, far away. Then she found her voice. Or, at least, a whisper of it.

"Brock," she murmured.

"Maura," he returned casually. "Good to see you. Well, surprised to see you—but good to see you."

"Investigation," she said, grasping for something to say. She seemed to be able to manage one word at a time.

"I just told you—they found a woman's remains, and three young women who have been reported missing had a connection to the Frampton Ranch and Resort. The FDLE has asked for Bureau help," he explained politely.

"Yes, we were just talking about the young woman's remains—and the missing girls. I, uh, I think I'd heard that you did go into the FBI," she said. "And they sent you…here." There. She had spoken in complete sentences. More or less. She'd been almost comprehensible.

"Yes, pretty much followed my original plans. Navy, college, the academy—FBI. And yes, I'm back here. Nothing like sending in an agent who knows the terrain," he said. "Shall we head back? I am serious. You shouldn't be in the woods alone when…well, when no one has any idea of what is really going on. We're not trying to incite fear. We're just trying to get a grip on what is happening, but I do suggest caution. Shall we head back?"

He was the same.

He was different.

And she was afraid to come too close to him. Afraid that the emotions of a teenager would erupt within her again, as if the years meant nothing…

If she got too close, she would either want to beat upon him, slamming her fists against his chest, demanding to know why he had never called, never tried to reach her and how it had been so easy to forget her.

Either that, or she would throw herself into his arms and sob and do anything just to touch him again.

Chapter Two

"The soil—clay based, some sand—like that covers most of the north of the state," Rachel Lawrence said.

She was seated across from Brock with Michael Flannery in the Java Bar on the Frampton property.

Rachel had changed. Her nails were cut short, clean of any color. Her hair was shorter, too. She still wore bangs, but her dark tresses were attractively trimmed to slide in angles along her face.

Everything about her appearance was serviceable. The girl who had once cried over a broken nail or scuffed sneakers had made an about-face.

She had greeted Brock politely and gravely, and seemed—like Flannery—to be anxious to have him working on the case with them.

"There's the beginning of a task force rumbling around," she'd told him when they'd first met in the coffee bar. "I'm lucky to be working with Michael Flannery—very lucky. But at this moment, while our superiors are listening, and they were willing to accept FBI involvement, they don't necessarily all believe that we are looking at a serial killer and this situation is about to blow up and get out of hand. It's great to have another officer who knows the lay of the land, so to speak."

"Yes, I do know it. And I've got to say, Rachel, I'm happy to see that you are working for the FDLE—and that you're so pleased to be where you are."

She made a face. "Oh, well, there was a time when I thought I wanted to be rich and elite, own a teacup Yorkie in a designer handbag and be supported in fine fashion. But I do love what I do. Oh—I actually do have a teacup Yorkie. Love the little guy!"

It had been far easier to meet back up with Rachel—and even Nils and Mark Hartford—than Brock had expected.

Time.

It healed all wounds, right?

Wrong. Why not? He believed he was, as far as any normal psychology went, long over what had happened regarding his arrest for murder at such a young age—he'd barely been in jail before his parents arrived with their attorney, his dad so indignant that the icy chill in his eyes might have gotten Brock released before the attorney even opened his mouth.

Truly, he had seen and heard far worse in the navy. And, God knew, some of the cases he'd handled as an agent in a criminal investigation unit had certainly been enough to chill the blood.

Still...the haunting memories regarding the forest and the History Tree clung to him like the moss that dripped from the old oaks.

"A Yorkie, huh?" he asked Rachel, remembering that she was there.

They both grinned, and he assured her that he liked dogs, all dogs, and didn't have one himself only because it wouldn't be fair to the animal—he was always working.

Rachel went on with the information—or lack of it—that she had worked to obtain.

"Some of our elegant hotels have special bedding, but...lots don't. The sheets around the remains might have come from five different chain hotels that cover North Florida, Central Florida and the Panhandle, all of which have twenty to forty local franchises. That means that Maureen Rodriguez might have been murdered anywhere in all that area—buried first nearby or somewhere different within the boundaries—and then dug up and wrapped in sheets."

"You checked with the truck drivers making deliveries that day, naturally?" Brock asked her.

She gave him a look that was both amused and withering. "I did go to college—and I majored in criminology. I'm not just a piece of fluff, you know."

Detective Michael Flannery grunted. "She's tailing me—I'm teaching her everything I know. And," he added, "how not to make the same mistakes."

Brock nodded his appreciation for the comment and asked, "Were you able to narrow it down by the drivers and their deliveries?"

"The way it works is that they pick up when they drop off," Rachel said. "So it's not as if they're kept separately. It's almost like recycling receptacles—the hotels have these massive canvas bags. The sheets are all the same, so they drop off dirty and pick up clean replacements. The laundry is also responsible for getting rid of sheets that are too worn, too stained, too whatever. But the driver drop-offs do narrow it down to hotels from St. Augustine to Gainesville and down to northern Ocala. I have a list of them, which I've emailed and…" She paused, reaching into her bag for a small folder that she presented to Brock. "Here—hard copy."

He looked at the list. There were at least thirty hotels with their addresses listed.

"All right, thank you," he told her. "I'd like to start by talking to Katie Simmons—the woman who reported Lydia Merkel missing. And then the last person to see each of the missing young women."

"Cops have interviewed all of them. I saw Katie Simmons myself," Flannery told him. "I'm not sure what else you can get from her."

"Humor me. And this list—I'd like you to get state officers out with images of all the women. Let's see what they get—they'll tell us if they find anyone who has seen any of them or thinks they might have seen someone like them. We need the images plastered everywhere—a Good Samaritan could call in and let us know if they saw one of the women walking on the street, buying gas…at a bar or a restaurant."

"The images have been broadcast," Flannery said. "I asked for you, but come on. We're not a bunch of dumb hicks down here, you know."

Brock grinned. "I'm a Fed, remember?"

Flannery shrugged. "You're a conch," he reminded Brock, referring to the moniker given to Key West natives.

"I get you, but I'm not referring to local news. I mean, we need likenesses of the young women—all four of them—out everywhere. We need to draw on media across the state and beyond. And we need to get them up in all the colleges—there are several of them in the area. All four of the women were college age—they might have friends just about anywhere. They might have met up with someone at a party."

"I'll get officers on the hotels and take the colleges with Rachel. She and I can head in opposite directions and cover more ground." Flannery hesitated. "I've arranged for us to see the ME first thing, so we'll start all else after that—I assumed you wanted to see the remains of Maureen Rodriguez."

"Yes, and thank you," Brock told him. "Do I meet you at the morgue?"

"No, we'll head out together—if that's all right with you. I have a room here and so does Rachel. I'm setting mine up as a headquarters," Flannery said. "I'll start a whiteboard—that way, we can keep up with any information any of us acquires and have it in plain sight, as we'd be doing if we were running the investigation out of one of our offices."

"A good plan," Brock said. "But tomorrow I would like to get started over in St. Augustine as quickly as possible."

"All right, then. We will take two cars tomorrow morning. Compare notes back here, say, late afternoon.

Get in touch sooner if we have something that seems of real significance. It's good that you decided to be based here. Easier than trying to come and go."

Flannery hesitated, looking at Brock. Then he shrugged. "Mr. Glass actually came to me." He lowered his voice, even though there was no one near them. "On the hush-hush. Said his wife didn't even know. Seems he's afraid himself that someone is using this place or the legends that go with it."

Brock drained his cup of coffee. "Can you set me up with Katie Simmons for some time tomorrow?" he asked Rachel.

"Yes, sir, I can and will," she assured him. "She's in St. Augustine."

Brock stood.

They looked up at him.

"And now?" Flannery asked.

"You wanted me here because I know the place," Brock said. "I'm going to watch a couple of the people that I knew when I worked here. See what's changed—and who has changed and how. I'm not leaving the property tonight. If there's anything, call me. And I'll check in later."

"You're going to the campfire tales and ghost walk?" Flannery asked.

"Not exactly—but kind of," Brock said. He nodded to the two of them and headed out, glancing at his watch.

He did know the place, that was certain. Almost nothing on the grounds had changed.

His father had heard about the place—that it was a

great venue for young people to work for the summer during high school. There was basic housing for them, a section of rooms for girls and one for boys. They weren't allowed off the grounds unless they had turned eighteen or they were supervised; any dereliction of the rules called for immediate dismissal. The positions were highly prized—if anyone broke the rules, they were damned careful not to be caught.

Of course, fraternizing—as in sex—had not been in the rules.

Kids were kids.

But with him and Maura…

It had felt like something more than kids being kids.

He still believed it. He wondered if, just somewhere in her mind, she believed it, too.

MARK HARTFORD PROVED to be excellent at telling the stories—despite the fact that he'd told Maura that he was afraid that night. Well, not afraid but nervous.

"You were so good!" he had said to Maura when he saw that she and Angie were going to be in his audience. "So good!"

He'd been just about fourteen when she knew him years before; he had to be about twenty-five or twenty-six now. He'd grown up, of course, and he still charmed with a boyish energy and enthusiasm that was contagious. His eyes were bright blue and his hair—just slightly shaggy—was a tawny blond. He'd grown several inches since Maura had seen him, and he evidently made use of the resort's gym.

Angie was entranced by Mark. But she'd always

been unabashed about her appreciation of men in general—especially when they were attractive. Maura didn't consider herself to be particularly suspicious of the world in general, but she did find that she often felt much older and wiser when she was with Angie—warning her that it wasn't always good to be quite so friendly with every good-looking man that she met.

"I'm sure you're just as good a storyteller," Angie had told Mark.

"I try—I have a lot to live up to," he'd said in return, answering Angie, smiling from one of them to the other.

Maura was somewhat pleased by the distraction. Angie had been talking incessantly about Brock and she'd finally stopped—long enough to do a new assessment of Mark Hartford.

She had decided that she liked young Mark Hartford very much, as well.

They'd already seen Nils in the restaurant. Mark and Nils were easily identifiable as brothers, but Mark's evident curiosity and sincere interest in everyone and everything around him made him the more naturally charming of the two.

"Ooh, I do like both brothers. But the other guy…the FBI guy… Hey, he was the one they arrested—and he turned out to be FBI! Cool. I appreciate them all, but that Brock guy…sexier—way sexier," Angie had said.

Actually, Maura found Angie's honesty one of the nicest things about her. She said what she was thinking or feeling pretty much all the time.

Now the tales were underway. Mark was telling them well. Maura allowed herself to survey his audience.

There were—as there had always been, so it seemed—a group of young teens, some together, some with their parents. There were couples, wives or girlfriends hanging on to their men, and sometimes a great guy admittedly frightened by the dark and tales and hanging on to his girlfriend or wife or boyfriend or husband, as well. There were young men and women, older men and women—a group of about twenty-five or thirty in all.

She couldn't help but remember how her group had been about the same size that night twelve years ago—and how they had all reacted when they reached the History Tree.

She had screamed—so had several people.

Some had laughed—certain that the swinging body was a prop and perhaps part of a gag set up by the establishment to throw a bit of real scare into the evening.

And then had come the frantic 911 calls, the horror as everyone realized that the dead woman was real and Brock trying to herd people away and, even then, trying to see that the scene wasn't trampled, that as a crime scene it wasn't disturbed…

Only to be arrested himself.

Tonight, Maura had her camera; she also had waivers signed by everyone in the group. She'd been lucky that night—everyone had been happy to meet her and Angie—and they all wanted their fifteen minutes of fame. They were fine with being on camera with Angie Parsons.

They were still by the campfire.

She was thinking about Brock.

Determining how much she was going to video after Mark's speech, she looked across the campfire to the place where the trees edged around the fire and the storyteller and his audience.

Brock was leaning against a tree, arms crossed over his chest, listening.

He was no longer wearing a suit; he was in jeans and a plaid flannel shirt—he could pass himself off as a logger or such. Her heart seemed to do a little leap and she was angry at herself, angry that she could still find him so compellingly attractive.

Twelve years between them. Not a word. They weren't even friends on social media.

He must have sensed her looking at him. She realized that his gaze had changed direction; he was looking at her across the distance.

He nodded slightly and then frowned, shaking his head.

He didn't want to be on camera; she nodded.

She turned away, dismissing him.

She tried to focus on the words that Mark Hartford was saying.

The stories were the same. Until they came to the History Tree.

There, a new story had been added in. Mark talked about the tour that had come upon Francine Renault.

He wasn't overly dramatic; he told the facts, and admitted that, yes, he had been among those who had found her.

The story ended with the death of the cook, Peter Moore, who had stabbed himself and been found in the freezer, his favorite knife protruding from his chest.

A fight had gone too far, or so the authorities believed, and Moore had killed Francine. And then later, in remorse or fear that prison would be worse than death, he had committed suicide.

On that tragic note, the story of the History Tree ended. As did the nightly tour.

Mark then told his group that they needed to head back—there had been some trouble in the area lately and the management would appreciate it if guests refrained from being in the forest at night and suggested that no one wander the woods alone.

As they began to filter back, Maura saw that Brock didn't go with the others.

She might have been the only one to note his presence; he had apparently followed silently at a bit of a distance, always staying back within the trees.

She turned when the group left. As they headed back along the trail, Brock stepped from his silent watching spot in the darkness of the surrounding foliage. He walked to the History Tree.

He stood silently, staring up at it, as if seeking some answer there.

Mark was asking if the tourists wanted coffee or tea or a drink before they called it a night.

Angie had already said yes.

Maura turned away from Brock purposefully and followed Angie and Mark. Once they reached the lodge, she would beg off.

All she wanted to do that night was crawl into a hole somewhere and black out.

Her room and her bed would have to do—even if she didn't black out and lay awake for hours, ever more furious with herself that she was allowing herself to feel…

Anything about him. Anything at all.

"I've seen some strange things in my day," Rita Morgan, the medical examiner, said. She was a tall, lean woman, looked to be about forty-five and certainly the no-nonsense type.

"Many a strange thing, and some not so strange. Too many bodies out of the ocean and the rivers, a few in barrels, some sunk with cement." She pursed her lips, shaking her head. "This one? Strange and sad. As long as I've done this, been an ME, it still never ceases to amaze me—man's inhumanity to fellow man." She looked up at Brock and Flannery and shook her head again. "Thing that saves me is when I see a young person get up and help the disabled or the elderly—then I get to know that there's as much good out there as bad—more, hopefully. Yeah, yeah, that doesn't help you any. I just… Well, I can show you the remains. I can't tell you too much about them. No stomach content—no stomach. I had disarticulated bones with small amounts of flesh still attached—and a skull."

She stepped back to display the gurney that held the remains of a young woman's life, tragically—and brutally—cut short.

"It looks as if she was killed a long time ago—

but from my brief, she was only missing about three months," Brock said, looking from Flannery to the medical examiner.

And then to the table.

Bits of hair and scalp still adhered to the skull.

"Decomposition is one of those things that can vary incredibly. I believe she was killed approximately two months ago. Particular to situations like this, the internal organs began to deteriorate twenty-four to seventy-two hours after death. The number of bacteria and insects in the area have an effect on the outer body and soft tissue. Three to five days—you have bloating. Within ten days, insects, the elements and bacteria have been busy and you have massive accumulations of gas. Within a few weeks, nails and teeth begin to go. After a month, the body becomes fluid."

"The skull retains a mouthful of teeth," Brock noted.

"Yes, which is why I believe decomp had the best possible circumstances. Lots of earth—and water. Rain, maybe. Even flooding in the area where the body was first left. As I said, there's no way to pinpoint an exact time of death. It's approximately two months' time. I also believe, per decomp, that she was left out in the elements—maybe a bit of dirt and some leaves were shoveled over her. It's been a warm winter, and the soil here can be rich—and as we all know, this is Florida. We have plenty of insects.

"The question is, after all that decomp in the wild, how in the world did she come to be in sheets at an industrial laundry? But that's your problem. Mine is cause of death. Not much to go on, as you can see, but enough." She pointed with a gloved hand. "That rib bone. You can see. The scraping there wasn't any insect—that was caused by a sharp blade. There's a second such mark on that rib—would have been the other side of the rear rib cage. In my educated estimation, she was stabbed to death. Without more tissue or organs I can't tell you how many wounds she sustained—exactly how many times she was stabbed—but I do imagine the attack would have been brutal, and that she probably suffered mortal damage to many of her organs. There's no damage to the skull."

"Were there any defensive wounds you were able to find on the arm bones?" Brock asked.

Flannery was standing back, letting Brock ask his own questions, since the detective had already seen the remains and spoken with the ME earlier.

"No, there were no defensive wounds, Special Agent McGovern," Dr. Morgan said. "She was stabbed from behind. She might never have seen her killer. Or she might have trusted him—or her. It was violent assault, I can tell you that. But—I am assuming that she didn't want to be stabbed to death—she had to have been taken by surprise. She never had a chance to fight back at all. Some of what I've been saying I'm assuming, but I am making assumptions based on education and experience. I'm the ME—you guys are the detectives. Can't help having an opinion."

"Of course, that's fine, and thank you," Brock said. "The sheets are at the lab? Still being tested?"

"Yes. They can't pinpoint the sheets to a certain hotel because too many of them buy from the same supplier."

She covered the remains.

She looked at Brock curiously, studying him. Then she smiled broadly. "You came out all right, it seems." She glanced over at Flannery. "Despite what you did to him."

"Hey, I acted on the best info I had at the time," Flannery said.

"Rash—hey, he was a newbie at the time. Didn't know his—oh, never mind. But good to see you—as a law enforcement officer, Agent McGovern."

"Well, thank you. I'm sorry, did we meet before?" he asked her.

She shook her head. "I was new in this office. But I assisted at the autopsies for both Francine Renault and the cook, Peter Moore…" She left off, shrugging. "I knew that they'd brought you in—one of the summer kids. Because you were seen in some kind of major verbal altercation with her. And arrested, from what I understand, on a *tip*."

She didn't exactly sniff, but she did look at Detective Flannery with a bit of disdain.

"I say again, I acted on the best info I had at the time. And yeah—I guess he came out all right," Flannery said with something that sounded a bit like a growl in his voice. He eyed Brock, as if not entirely sure about him yet.

"I spent only one night in jail. Trust me, I spent many a worse night in the service," he assured Dr. Morgan and Flannery.

Flannery looked away, uncomfortable. Dr. Morgan smiled.

"Thank you," he told her. "If there's anything else that comes to mind that might be of any assistance whatsoever..."

"I'll be quicker than a rabbit in heat," she vowed solemnly.

He arched his brows slightly but managed a smile and another thank-you.

Brock and Flannery left the county morgue together. They'd come in Flannery's official vehicle; it would allow them to bypass heavy traffic if needed, Flannery had said.

Brock preferred to drive himself, but that day, while Flannery drove, it gave him a chance to look through his notes on the victim.

"She stayed at the Frampton Ranch and Resort three months ago," he murmured out loud. "Her home was St. Pete. She wasn't reported missing right away because she was over eighteen and had been living alone in St. Augustine, working as a cocktail waitress—but hadn't shown up for work in over a week. Says here none of her coworkers really knew her—she had just started."

"The perfect victim," Flannery said. He glanced sideways at Brock. "The other missing girls... You have the information on them, too, right?"

"Yeah, I have it online and on paper. I have to hand it to Egan. He believes in hard copy and there are times it proves to be especially beneficial."

"And saves on eyestrain," Flannery muttered. He glanced Brock's way again. "You know, I asked for you specifically. Hope you don't mind too much. Can't help it. Still think there's something with that damned resort, even if I can't pin it. Well, I mean, back then, of course, it had to do with the ranch. Francine Renault worked there—and died there. But...that tree has seen a lot of death."

He said it oddly, almost as if he was in awe of the tree. Brock frowned, looking over at him. Flannery didn't glance his way, but apparently knew he was being studied.

"Well, bad stuff happens there," Flannery said.

"Right—because bad people like the aspect that bad things happened there."

"You think it should be chopped down."

"It might dissuade future killers."

"Or just cause them to leave their victims somewhere else," Flannery said. "Or create a new History Tree or haunted bog or...just a damnable stretch of roadway."

"True," Brock agreed.

"What drives me crazy is the why—I mean, we all study this stuff. Some killers are simply goal driven—they want or need someone out of the way. Some killings have to do with passion and anger and jealousy. Some have to do with money. Some people are psychotic and kill for the thrill or the sexual release it gives them. Years ago, it was just Francine. Now, that Francine—I didn't find a single soul who actually said they liked her, but it never seemed she'd done anything bad enough to make someone want to kill her. She seemed to be more of an annoyance—like a fly buzzing around your ear."

"Maybe she was a really, really annoying fly—buzzing at the wrong person," Brock said. Then he reminded the detective, "Peter Moore committed suicide. There was no note—but maybe he did do it, because he was afraid of being apprehended, or felt overwhelming remorse or was dealing with an untreated mental illness that led him down a very dark path. Seems to me that everyone accepted the fact that he must have done it—though he sure as hell didn't get his day in court."

Flannery glanced his way at last. "But you don't think that Peter Moore killed Francine any more than I do."

Brock hesitated and then said flatly, "No. And I knew Peter Moore. He hated Francine, but he held his own with her—he didn't really have to answer to her. He was directly under Fred Bentley. I don't think he killed Francine. I don't even think that Peter Moore killed himself."

Flannery nodded. "There you go—see? There was a reason I needed you down here. Damn, though, if it doesn't seem like homecoming somehow."

"What do you mean?"

"I mean, I can't just buy the theory that Peter Moore did it, either. In my mind, the killer might have helped him into that so-called suicide. No prints but Peter's on the knife in his gut, but hell, the kitchen is filled with gloves."

"So it is."

"That beauty is back, as well," Flannery said, glancing his way once again.

Brock didn't ask who Flannery meant. That was dead obvious. Maura.

"Did you ask her up here?" Brock asked him.

"Me?" Flannery was truly surprised. "I barely met her back in the day, and she was fairly rattled when I did… Well, you were there. You didn't ask for her to be here? I'd have thought, at least, that the two of you would still be friends. You were hot and heavy back then, so I heard—the beautiful young ones!"

"I hadn't seen her since that night until I saw her again late yesterday afternoon—out by the tree."

"Ah, yes, she's with that web queen or writer—or whatever that little woman calls herself," Flannery said. He looked over at Brock. "Is that what they call serendipity?"

Brock didn't reply. He was looking at his portfolios on the missing women. He'd already read through them on the plane, but talking things out could reveal new angles.

"All right," Brock said. "Maureen Rodriguez was out of the house and just starting a new life. So she wasn't noted as missing right away. But Lily Sylvester was supposed to check in with her boyfriend. She'd come to the Frampton ranch because she wanted to see it. She stayed at a little hotel on the outskirts of St. Augustine one night after her visit, and then she was supposed to meet with a girlfriend at a posh bed-and-breakfast in the old section of the city. She never showed that day and her friend called the cops right away."

He flipped through his folders.

"Friends and family were insistent about Lily," Flannery told him. "She was as dependable as they come. Is," he added. "We shouldn't assume the worst."

But it was natural that they did.

"All right, moving on to Amy Bonham. She stayed at the Frampton ranch. She told one of the waitresses that she was excited about a surprise job opportunity the next day. She was supposed to be heading in the other direction—toward Orlando and the theme parks. She also stayed at a chain motel the night right after she was at the Frampton ranch and disappeared the next day. I know you certainly looked into her 'job opportunity.'"

Flannery nodded. "We've had officers interviewing people across more than half the state."

"But no one knew anything about it."

"No. But the waitress at the Frampton ranch—Dorothy Masterson—swears that Amy was super excited. Dorothy believed that she was looking for work at one of the theme parks."

"And you checked with all the parks."

"Of course. Big and small."

Brock went on to his third folder. "Lydia Merkel."

Flannery nodded; he'd already committed to memory most of what Brock was still studying.

"Lydia. Cute as a button."

"You met her? You knew her?" Brock asked, frowning.

"I met her briefly—I was in St. Augustine. The wife had her nephews down and I was taking them on one of the ghost tours. Lydia was on our tour. All wide eyes and happiness. Can't tell you how stunned I was when the powers that be called me in and told me that we had another missing woman—and that I recognized her." He glanced quickly at Brock. "You know how it goes with missing persons reports. Half of the time someone is just off on a lark. There's been a fight—a person has taken off because they want to disappear. But I just don't think that's the case." He was silent. "Especially since we found the remains of Maureen Rodriguez."

"And you can't help but think that Frampton Ranch and Resort is somehow involved."

Flannery nodded grimly.

"Lydia had told a young woman she was working with—Katie Simmons—that she wanted to take her first days off to drive over and see the History Tree. We're not just working this alone. I have all kinds of help on this. We do have officers from the Florida Department of Law Enforcement out all over—not to mention the help we've gotten from our local police departments. I keep feeling like I'm looking at some kind of puzzle with pieces missing—except that the frame is there. Because there was only one thing the girls—or young women—had in common."

"They had left or were coming to the Frampton Ranch and Resort," Brock said.

He felt a sudden pang deep in his heart or maybe his soul—someplace that really hurt at any rate.

He glanced over at Flannery. "The four of them are between the ages of twenty-two and twenty-nine," he said.

"Lydia Merkel was—is—twenty-nine. She was at

the ranch with friends for her birthday. On the tour, she talked about loving ghost stories—and how excited she was going to be to see the infamous History Tree."

Seriously—the tree should have been bulldozed.

Not fair—the tree wasn't guilty. Men and women could be guilty; the tree was just a tree—two trees.

"Funny, isn't it?" Flannery asked. "I mean, not ha ha funny, just…strange. Maybe ironic. The History Tree is two trees. Entwined. And you're here—because I asked for you particularly because I knew you were FBI, criminal section—and I'm here. And Miss Maura Antrim is here. We're all kinds of entwined. And I can't help but think that we still know the killer—even if twelve years have gone by."

"Yep. We're all tangled together somehow, like that damned tree. And so help me God, this time I really want to have the answers…and to stop the killing," Brock said quietly.

"You don't disagree with me?" Flannery asked him.

Brock shrugged grimly.

"But you don't disagree—you don't think I'm being far-fetched or anything?" Flannery pressed.

"No, I just wonder what this person—if it is the same killer—has been doing for twelve years," Brock said. And then added, "Although…maybe he hasn't been lying dormant. It's a big state filled with just about everything in one area or another. Forests, marshes, caverns, sinkholes, the Everglades—a river of grass—and, of course…"

"That great big old Atlantic Ocean," Flannery said. "So, there you go. My puzzle. Are there pieces missing? Did the three young ladies who disappeared just run off? Or…"

"Has someone been killing young women and disposing of corpses over the last twelve years?" Brock finished. He took a deep breath. "All right, I guess I'm going to do a lot of traveling. There will be dozens of people to question again. But I think I'll start at the library at Frampton ranch."

ANGIE WAS A late sleeper, something Maura deeply appreciated the next morning. She wanted some on-her-own time.

She had gotten a lot of great footage for Angie's internet channel on the tour the night before.

Martin had ended up loving being on camera—and it had loved him. They were going to do the campfire again that night, get more video and put together all the best parts.

She'd behaved perfectly normally, even though she was ready to crawl out of her own skin. While on the tour, she'd expected to see Brock materialize again.

It hadn't been until the very end that she'd realized he'd been there all along—watching from the shadows, from the background.

But he'd never approached her. She'd seen him later in the lounge, briefly, when she and Angie walked in after the trek through the woods. He'd been deep in conversation with a slightly older man in a suit—she'd seen him earlier and remembered him vaguely. He was a cop of some kind; he'd been there the night that Francine Renault was killed. She had seen him earlier in the day as well, walking around the ranch with a woman. Maura hadn't seen the woman's face, just the cut of her suit, and for some bizarre reason she had noticed the woman's shoes. Flat, serviceable.

And she'd thought that perhaps the woman was a cop or in some form of law enforcement, too.

Angie hadn't seemed interested in talking to any of them—Maura had been glad. She'd left Angie in the lounge, waiting for her appointed drink with Mark, and Maura had slipped quickly upstairs, wanting nothing more than to be in her room, alone.

Once there, she'd lain awake for hours, wondering why something that had happened ages ago still had such an effect on her life—on her.

Why… Brock McGovern could suddenly walk back into her life and become all that she thought about once again. So easily. Or why she could close her eyes and see the man he had become and know that he was still somehow flawed and perfect, the man to whom she had subconsciously—or even consciously—compared to everyone else she ever met.

He hadn't so much as touched her.

And he hadn't looked at her as if he particularly liked her. He'd simply wanted her—and Angie—to be safe. Nothing more. Stay with people. He was a law enforcement officer, a Fed. He worked to find those who had turned living, breathing bodies into murdered, decaying bodies—and he tried to keep all men and women from being victims. His job. What he did.

A job he always knew he wanted.

She had to stop thinking about him, and that meant

she needed to immerse herself in some other activity—research. Books, knowledge, seeking…

She had always loved the library and archives at the Frampton ranch. One thing Donald Glass did with every property he bought was build and maintain a library with any books and info he had on that property. It was fascinating—much of it had been put on computer through the years, but every little event that had to do with the property was available.

The hotel manager—solid, ruddy little Fred Bentley—had never shown any interest in the contents of the library.

Nor, when she'd been alive, had Francine Renault. But the libraries were sacred. No matter what else the very, very rich Donald Glass might be, he loved his history and his libraries, and anyone working for him learned not to mess with them.

For this, she greatly admired Glass. Not that she knew the man well—he'd left the hands-on management to Francine and Fred when Maura had been working there. And back then, she and Brock had both spent hours in the library—often together—each trying to one-up the other by finding some obscure and curious fact or happening. It was fun to work the weird trivia into their presentations.

That had been twelve years ago.

But Brock was suddenly back in her life.

No, he wasn't in her life. He just happened to be here at the same time.

Because a woman had been murdered—and others had disappeared.

Concentrate... There was a wealth of information before her. Bits and pieces that might offer up something especially unusual for Angie Parsons.

The library room was comfortable and inviting, filled with leather sofas and chairs, desks, computers—and shelves upon shelves of files and books.

Donald Glass had acquired an extensive collection; he had books on the indigenous population of the area, starting back somewhere between twelve and twenty thousand years ago. Settlers had arrived before the end of the Pleistocene megafauna era. The Wacissa River—not far away in Jefferson County near the little town of Wacissa—had offered up several animal fossils of the time, and other areas of the state—including Silver Springs, Vero, Melbourne and Devil's Den—had also offered up proof of man's earliest time in the area.

Way back that many thousands of years, there had been a greater landmass and less water, causing animals—and thus hunters—to congregate at pools. Artifacts proving the existence of these hunter-gatherers could be found in countless rivers—and even out into the Gulf of Mexico.

Mammoths had even roamed the state.

By 700 AD, farming had come to the north of Florida. There were many Native American tribes, and many of those were called Creek by the Europeans and spoke the Muskogee language. But by the time the first Frampton put down roots to create this great ranching and farming estate, Florida Indians of many varieties—though mostly Creek—were being lumped together as Seminoles, largely divided into two groups: the Muskogee-speaking and the Hitchiti-speaking.

There were wonderful illustrated books describing fossils and tools found, creating images of the people and the way they lived.

According to the one she pulled from the shelf there had been a colony of Seminole living in the area when Frampton first chose his site.

They had held rites out at what was already a giant clearing in the forest. It was the Native Americans who had first called it the History Tree. The Timucua had first named it so; the Seminoles in the area had respected the holiness of the tree.

Maura—like the writer of the book—didn't believe that the Native American tribes had practiced human sacrifice at the tree. But as war loomed with the Seminole tribe, the European populace had liked to portray the native people as barbarians—it made it easier to justify killing them.

So the tree had gotten its reputation very early on.

Gyselle—who became known as Gyselle Frampton, since no one knew her real surname—had arrived at the plantation soon after it was built in the late 1830s. Spanish missionaries had "rescued" her from the Seminole, but she was fifteen at the time and had been kidnapped at the age of ten—or that was the best that could be figured. Oliver Frampton—creator of the first great mansion to rest on the property—had been a kind man. He'd taken her in, clothed her, educated her and had still, of course, given her chores to do.

She was a servant and not of the elite. She was not, in any way, wife material for his son.

That hadn't stopped Richard Frampton from falling in love with his father's beautiful servant/ward.

But Richard had underestimated his wife. Back then, a wife was supposed to be a lovely figurehead, wealthy to match her husband and eye candy on the arm of her man. Unless she was very, very, very rich—and then it wouldn't matter if she was eye candy or not.

But Julie LeBlanc Frampton had been no fool and not someone to be taken lightly.

She discovered the affair—and knew that her husband loved Gyselle deeply. Perhaps she was angry with her father-in-law for not only condoning the affair but perhaps finding it to be fine and natural. Wives weren't supposed to get in the way of these things after all.

Or maybe the situation was just convenient for her plan.

She hid the taste of the deadly fruit of the manchineel tree in a drink—one that Gyselle usually made up for the senior Mr. Frampton right before he went to bed made up of whiskey, tea and sugar.

The old man died in horrible pain. Julie immediately pointed the finger at Gyselle.

She created such an outcry and hysteria that the other servants immediately went for poor Gyselle. The master had been well loved. And without trial or even much questioning, they had dragged Gyselle out to the History Tree—thought to surely be haunted at that time and also a place where the devil might well be found.

Gyselle died swearing that she was innocent—and cursing Julie, those around her and even the tree.

After she was hanged, she was allowed to remain there until she rotted, until her bones fell to the ground.

Three years later, Julie Frampton died. At the time no one knew what her ailment was—tuberculosis, it sounded like to Maura.

But in the end, the true poisoner did die choking on her own blood—and confessing to the entire room that she had murdered her father-in-law.

"Maura!"

She had become so involved in what she was reading that the sound of her name made her jump.

She'd been very comfortable in one of the plush leather chairs, feet curled beneath her, the book—*Truth and Legends of Central Florida*—in her arms.

Luckily, she didn't drop it or throw it as she was startled. It was an original book, printed and bound in 1880.

"Mr. Glass!" she exclaimed, truly started to see the resort's owner. He usually kept to himself; Fred Bentley was his mouthpiece.

She quickly closed the book and stood, accepting the hand he offered to her.

Donald Glass, in his early sixties now, Maura thought, was still an attractive man. He kept himself lean and fit—and had maintained a full head of salt-and-pepper hair. His posture was straight; his manners tended to be impeccable. He'd never personally fired anyone that she knew of, in any of his enterprises. He left managers—like Fred Bentley—to do such deeds.

He was customarily well liked and treated kindly by magazines when he was included in an article.

Donald Glass used his money to make more money, granted. That was the American way. But he did it all in one of the best possible manners—preserving history and donating to worthy causes all the while.

Whether he was into the causes or simply into tax breaks, no one really looked too closely.

But he tended to do good things and do them well.

"Miss Antrim, how lovely to have you here again," he said, smiling. "And I'm delighted that you've brought Angie Parsons with her incredible ability to show the world interesting places—and provide wonderful publicity for those places!"

"I'd love to take the credit, Mr. Glass," Maura told him. "Angie heard the story about the History Tree. She couldn't wait to come."

"Well, however you came to be here, I'm most delighted. Still sorry—and I will be sorry all my life—about Francine. She was..."

He paused. Maura wondered what he'd been about to say. That Francine Renault had been a good woman? But she really hadn't been kind or generous in any way.

"No one deserved to die that way," he said. "Anyway... I did consider having the tree torn out of the ground. But I thought on it a long time and decided that it was the *History Tree*. They didn't burn down the building when a famous woman died in a room at the Hard Rock in Hollywood, Florida, and..." Again, he paused. "I decided that the tree—or trees—should stay. Not to mention the fact that the environmentalists and preservationists would create a real uproar if we were to cut it down. It's hundreds of years old, you know. And yes—as you learned last night, we do tell the story at the campfire and continue the walk by the tree."

"Trees aren't evil," Maura said.

She wondered if she was trying to reassure him—or if it was something she said but doubted somewhere in a primal section of her heart or mind.

"No, of course not. A tree is a tree. Or trees are trees," he said and smiled weakly. "Anyway, I'm delighted to see you. And thankful for the work you're doing here with Miss Parsons."

"I'm not sure you need us. You've always had a full house here."

He didn't argue.

"I'm sure Marie will be delighted to see you, too."

"A pleasure to see her," Maura murmured.

Marie was perhaps ten years younger than her husband; they had been together for thirty years or so. Like her husband she kept herself fit, and she was an attractive and cordial woman. Her public manner was pristine—every once in a while, Maura had wondered what she was *really* thinking.

Glass lifted a hand in farewell and said, "Enjoy your stay." He started to walk away and then turned back. "I don't mean to be an alarmist, but…be careful. I'm sure you heard. Remains were found nearby. And several young women have disappeared, as well. Whether they ran away or…met with bad things… I know you're smart, but…be wary."

"Yes, I've heard. And I'll be careful," Maura said.

She watched him for a moment as he headed out of the room and then she opened the book again. Words swam before her as she tried to remember where she'd left off.

She heard Glass speaking again and she looked toward the door, thinking that he had something else to say.

But he wasn't speaking to her.

Brock was at the doorway, his tone deep and quiet as he replied to whatever Glass had said.

The length of Maura's body gripped with tension, which angered her to no end.

She hadn't seen or heard from him in twelve years.

He and Glass parted politely.

Brock headed straight for her. He smiled, but it seemed that his smile was grave.

His face seemed harder than the image of him she'd held in her mind. Naturally. Years did that to anyone.

And he'd always wanted to be law enforcement. But that job had to take a toll.

"I thought I'd find you here," he said softly.

"Yes, well, I… I'm here," she said.

She didn't invite him to sit. He did anyway. She wondered if he was going to talk about the years between them, ask what she'd been doing, maybe even explain why he'd just disappeared after the charges against him had been dismissed.

Elbows on his knees, hands folded idly, he was close—too close, she thought. Or not really close at all. Just close because she could feel a strange rush inside, as if she knew everything about him, or everything that mattered. She knew his scent—his scent, not soap or aftershave or cologne, but that which lurked beneath it, particular to him, something that drew her to him, that called up a natural reaction within her. She knew that there was a small scar on the lower side of his abdomen—stitches from a deep cut received when he'd fallen on a haphazardly discarded tin can during a track event when he'd been in high school. She knew there was a spattering of freckles on his shoulders, knew…

"You really shouldn't be here—you need to pack up and go," he said. His tone was harsh, as if she were committing a grave sin by being there.

She couldn't have been more surprised if he'd slapped her.

"I beg your pardon?" she demanded, a sudden fury taking over.

"You need to get the hell out—out of this part of the state and sure as hell off the Frampton Ranch and Resort."

Why did it hurt so badly, the way he spoke to her, the way he wanted to be rid of her?

"I'm sorry. I have every right to be here. It's a public facility and a free country, last I heard."

"No, you don't—"

She stood, aware she badly needed to leave the room.

"Excuse me, Special Agent—or whatever your title may be. You don't control me. I have a life—and things to do. Things that need to be done—here. Right here. Have a nice day."

She stood—with quiet dignity, she hoped—and headed quickly for the door.

How the hell could he still have such an effect upon her?

And why the hell did he have to be here now?

Another body. Another life cut tragically short. His job.

Brock was right; she was the one who shouldn't be here.

Chapter Three

To say that he'd handled his conversation with Maura badly would be a gross understatement.

But he couldn't start over. She was angry and not about to listen to him—certainly not now. Maybe later.

The library seemed oddly cold without her, empty of human life.

Brock needed to get going, but he found himself standing up, studying some of the posters and framed newspaper pages on the walls.

There was a rendering of the beautiful Gyselle, running through the woods, hair flowing, gown caught in a cascade.

Donald Glass didn't shirk off the truth or try to hide it; there were multiple newspaper articles and reports on the murders that had taken place in the 1970s.

And there was information on Francine Renault to be found, including a picture of her that was something of a memorial, commemorating her birth, acknowledging the tragedy of her death—and revealing that, while it was assumed she had been murdered by a disgruntled employee, the case remained unsolved.

Going through the library, Brock couldn't help but remember how shocked he had been to find himself under arrest. He'd been young—and nothing in his life had prepared him for the concept that he could be unjustly accused of a crime. He'd known where he wanted to go in life—but his very idealism had made it impossible for him to believe that such a thing as his being wrongly arrested could happen.

The world just wasn't as clean and cut-and-dried as he had once believed.

Of course, he had been quickly released—and that had been another lesson.

Truth was sometimes a fight.

And now, years later, he could understand Flannery's actions. There had been an urgency about the night; people had been tense. The police had been under terrible pressure.

Brock had usually controlled his temper—despite the fact that Francine had been very difficult to work with. But the day she had been killed, his anger had gotten the best of him. He hadn't gotten physical in the least—unless walking toward her and standing about five feet away with his fists clenched counted as physical. Perhaps that had appeared to be the suggestion of underlying malice. Many of his coworkers had known that he was always frustrated with Francine—she demanded so much and never accepted solid explanations as to why her way wouldn't work, or why something had to be as it was.

Like almost everyone else, he had considered Francine Renault to be a fire-breathing dragon. Quite simply, a total bitch.

She had been a thorn in all their sides. He had just happened to pick that day to explode.

After his blowup, he'd feared being fired—not arrested for murder.

He didn't tend to have problems with those he worked with or for—but he had disliked Francine. In retrospect, he felt bad about it. But she had enjoyed flaunting her authority and used it unfairly. Brock had complained about her to Fred Bentley many times, disgusted with the way she treated the summer help. Her own lack of punctuality—or when she simply didn't show up—was always forgiven, of course, because she was above them all. That night, Brock had been quick to put Maura Antrim on the schedule—as if he had known that Francine wouldn't be there.

Until she was—dangling from the tree.

As the police might see it, after they'd been pointed straight at Brock by the mysterious anonymous tipster, he'd been certain to be on the tour when Francine's body had been discovered, a ready way to explain any type of physical evidence that might have been found at the History Tree or around it.

At the time, Brock had wanted nothing to do with Detective Flannery. He'd been hurt and bitter. He was sure that only his size had kept him from being beaten to a pulp during his night in the county jail, and once he'd been freed, he found that his friends had gone.

Including, he now thought dryly, the woman he had assumed to be the love of his life.

Maura had vanished. Gone back home, into the arms of her loving parents, the same people who had once claimed to care about Brock, to be impressed with his maturity, admiring of his determination to do a stint in the service first and then spend his time in college.

Calls, emails, texts, snail mail—all had gone unanswered. It hurt too much that Maura never replied, never reached out, and so he stopped trying. He had joined the navy, done his stint and gone on to college in New York.

And yet, oddly, through the years, he'd kept up with Michael Flannery. Now and then, Flannery would write him with a new theory on the case and apologize again for arresting Brock so quickly. Flannery wasn't satisfied; he needed an explanation he believed in. He explored all kinds of possibilities—from the familiar to the absurd.

Francine had been killed by an interstate killer, a trucker—a man caught crossing the Georgia state line with a teenage victim in his cab.

She had been killed by Donald Glass himself.

By college students out of Gainesville or Tallahassee, a group that had taken hazing to a new level.

She had even been killed, a beyond-frustrated Flannery had once written, by the devils or the evil that lived in the forest by the History Tree.

Frustration. Something that continued to plague them. But then, Brock had been told that every cop, marshal and agent out there had a case that haunted them, that they couldn't solve—or had been considered closed, but the closure just didn't seem right, and it stuck in his or her gut.

Standing in the library wasn't helping any; Francine Renault had been a dead a long time, and regardless of her personality, she hadn't deserved her fate.

The truth still needed to be discovered.

More than ever now, as it was possible that her murderer had returned to kill again.

Brock left the library.

Before he left for his interviews in St. Augustine that day, he had to try one more time with Maura. He had to find her. He hadn't explained himself very well.

In fact, he had made matters worse.

He had known Maura so well at one time. And if anything, his faltering way of trying to get her far, far from this place, where someone was killing people had probably made her stubbornly more determined to stay.

He'd admit he was afraid.

Beautiful young women were disappearing, and with or without his feelings, Maura was certainly an incredibly beautiful woman.

And there was more working against her.

She was familiar with the Frampton ranch and many of the players in this very strange game of life and death.

"MAYBE WE SHOULD move on," Maura said. She and Angie were sitting in the restaurant—Angie had actually wakened early enough for them to catch the tail end of the breakfast buffet, a spread that contained just about every imaginable morning delight.

The place was renowned for cheese grits; savoring a bite, Maura decided that they did remain among the best tasting she'd ever had. There were eggs cooked in many ways as well, plus pancakes, fruit, yogurt, nuts and grains and everything to cater to tastes from around the country.

Angie, too, it seemed, especially enjoyed the grits. Her eyes were closed as she took a forkful and then smiled.

"Delicious."

"Did you hear me?"

"What?"

"I was thinking we should move on."

Angie appeared to be completely shocked. "I… Yes, I mean, I know now about you—I mean, when you were a kid—but I thought we were fine. This is the perfect place to be home base for this trip. We can reach St. Augustine easily, areas on the coast—some of those amazing cemeteries up in Gainesville. I…"

She quit speaking. Nils Hartford, handsome in a pin-striped suit, was coming their way, smiling.

They were at a table for four and he glanced at them, brows arched and a hesitant smile on his face, silently asking if he could join them.

Angie leaped right to it.

"Nils! Hey, you're joining us?"

"Just for a minute. My people here are great—we have the best and nicest waitstaff, but I still like to oversee the change from breakfast to lunch," he said, sliding into the chair next to Maura. "You're enjoying yourself?" he asked Angie.

"I love it!" she said enthusiastically. "And last night—your brother was amazing. I mean, of course, I know that Maura had his job at one time, and I know Maura, and I know she was fantastic, but I just adored your brother. Keep him on!"

Nils laughed. "Oddly enough, that would have nothing to do with me. My brother reports directly to Fred Bentley, as do I. Couldn't get him hired or fired. But he's loved that kind of thing since we were kids. I was more into the cranking of the gears, the way things run and so forth." He turned toward Maura and asked anxiously, "And you—you okay being back here?"

"I'm fine," Maura said.

"Well, thank you both for what you're doing." He lowered his voice, even though there was no one near. "Even Donald is shaken up by the way we keep hearing that young women have been heading here or leaving here—and disappearing. Seriously, I mean, a tree can't make people do things, but… I guess people do see things as symbols, but—we're keeping a good eye on it these days. We never had arranged for any video surveillance because it's so far out in the woods—and nothing recent has had anything to do with the tree, but…anyway, we're going to get some security out there.

"Donald has a company coming out to make suggestions tomorrow. We have cameras now in the lobby, elevators, public areas…that kind of thing. But dealing with security and privacy laws—it's complicated. I mean, the tree is on Donald's property and it's perfectly legal to have cameras at the tree. And with today's tech—improving all the time, but way above what we had twelve years ago—the tree can easily be watched. Anyway, it's great that you're helping to keep us famous."

"A true pleasure," Angie told him.

He smiled at Angie and then turned back to Maura, appearing a little anxious again. "I just—well, I know you thought I was a jerk—and I was, back then. I did feel superior to the kids who had to work." He laughed softly and only a little bitterly. "Then the stock market crashed and I received a really good comeuppance. Odd, though. It's like 'hail, hail, the gang's all here.' Me, Mark, Donald, of course, Fred Bentley, other staff…and now you and Brock and Rachel."

"Rachel?" Maura echoed, surprised.

"Oh, you didn't know? Rachel is with the Florida Department of Law Enforcement now—she's working with Detective Mike Flannery. They've stationed themselves here—good central spot—for investigating this rash of disappearances. I think it's a rash. Well, everyone is worried because of the remains of the poor girl that were found at the laundry."

"Oh! Are you and Rachel still…a twosome?" she asked.

"No, no, no—friends, though. I have a lot of love for Rach, though I was a jerk to her when we were teens. I'm grateful to have her as a friend. And can you imagine—she's like a down and dirty cop. Not that cops can't be feminine. But she made a bit of a change. Well, I mean, she has nice nails still—she just keeps them clipped and short. Short hair, too. Good cut. She's still cute. But I hear she's hell on wheels, having taken all kinds of martial arts—and a crack shot. Great kid, still. Well, adult. We're all adults—I forget that sometimes. And hey, what about you and Brock? I was jealous as hell of you guys back then, you know."

She certainly hadn't known.

"Of the two of us?" she asked. "And no—I hadn't seen him since that summer. I'm afraid that we aren't even social media friends."

"I'm sorry to hear that. But I guess that... Well, it was bad time, what happened back then." He brightened. "But you're here now. And that's great! I believe you recorded a tour? And more, so far? I'd like to think that you could spend days here—"

"We *are* spending days here," Angie assured him. "I guess we're like the cops—or agents or officers or whatever. We're in a central location. We'll head to St. Augustine and come back here, maybe over Gainesville's way. It's just such a great location."

"Well, I'm glad. That's wonderful. If I can do anything for either of you..."

His voice trailed oddly. He was looking toward the restaurant entrance. Maura saw that Marie Glass had arrived and seemed to be looking for someone.

"Excuse me," he said, making a slight grimace. "Our queen has arrived. Oh, I don't mean that in a bad way," he added quickly. "Marie never meddles with the staff and she's always charming. I mean *queen* in the best way possible, always so engaging and cordial with the guests and all of us." He made a face. "She's even nice when she knows an employee is in trouble, never falters. Just as sweet as she can be—while still aloof and elegant. Regal, you know?"

"Yes, very regal," Maura agreed.

Marie was looking for Nils, Maura thought, and as she noted their table and graced them with one of her smiles, Nils stood politely, awaiting whatever word she might have for him.

But she wasn't coming to speak with Nils. As she approached them, she headed for the one chair that wasn't occupied and asked politely, "May I join you? I'll just take a few seconds of your time, I promise."

"Of course, Mrs. Glass, please." Maura said.

Marie Glass sat delicately. "My dear Maura, you are hardly a child anymore, and though I do appreciate the respect, please, call me Marie."

Maura inclined her head. It was true. She was hardly a child. Marie simply had an interesting way of putting her thoughts.

"I know my husband and the staff here have tried to let you know how we appreciate the publicity your work here will bring us—and free publicity these days is certainly wonderful," Marie Glass began. "But we'd also be willing to compensate you if you want to show more of the resort—if you had time and if you didn't mind." She paused, flashing a smile Maura's way. "We love your reputations—and would love to make use of you in all possible ways. I am, of course, at your disposal, should you need help."

"Oh, that's a lovely idea," Angie said. "I'd have to switch up the format a little—as you know, I bring to light the unusual and frankly, the *creepy*, so—"

"Oh, bring on the creepy," Marie Glass said. She grinned again, broadly. "We do embrace the creepy, and honestly, so many people visit because of the History Tree. But we thought that allowing people to see how lovely the rest of the resort is… Well, it would make them think they should stay here and perhaps not just sign up for the campfire histories and the ghost walk into the forest. If it's a bit more comprehensive, we could use your videos on our website and in other promotional materials."

"I'm happy to get on it right away. Well, almost right away," Angie said cheerfully. "We did have plans to wander out a bit today, but we'll start on a script tonight. Maura's a genius at these things."

Maura glanced over at Angie, not about to show her surprise. So far, she hadn't known they were wandering out that day, and she wasn't sure that she was going to come up with anything "genius" after they got back.

From wherever it was that they were apparently going.

"Thank you ever so much," Marie said, standing. Her fingers rested lightly on the table as she turned to Maura. "We always knew our Maura was clever—we'd hoped to have her on through college and beyond, but, well…very sad circumstances do happen in life. Ladies, I will leave you to your day." She inclined her head to Nils. "Mr. Hartford, would you come to the office with me?"

As soon as they were out of earshot, Maura leaned forward. "Where is it that we're wandering off to today?"

"Well, it was your idea—originally, I'm certain," Angie said.

"Where?"

"St. Augustine, of course. You said it wasn't much of a drive and that we could easily get there and back in a day. I want to head to the Castillo de San Marcos—did you know that it's the oldest masonry fort in the continental United States? And I'm not sure how to say this, but St. Augustine is the oldest city in the country *continually* inhabited by European settlers. Think that's right. I mean, the Spanish started with missions and then stayed and… I have it all in my notes. Though I know you—you may know more than my notes!"

Maura glanced at her watch. It wasn't late—just about ten. If they left soon, they could certainly spend the afternoon in the old city, have dinner at one of the many great restaurants to be found—perhaps even hear a bit of music somewhere—and be back for the night.

"Okay," she said. "I had thought you wanted to finish up around here today—maybe even leave here and stay in St. Augustine or perhaps head out to the old Rivero-Marin Cemetery just north of Orlando. I just had no idea—"

"I thought you loved St. Augustine."

"I do."

"So it's fine."

"Sure. But we don't have permits, and while people film with their phones all the time now, what you're doing is for commercial purposes and—"

"We'll film out in front of places where I might need a permit to film inside. And if you don't mind, when we get to the square, I'll have you tell that tale about the condemned Spaniard who kept having the garrote break on him so that they finally let him go. Now, that's a great real story."

"The square is called the Plaza de la Constitución."

"Right. Yeah, but it's still a square," Angie said, grinning. "It is a square, right?"

"The shape is actually oblong."

"Okay, technicalities are important. But the story is great. About the man."

"His name was Andrew Ranson and he wasn't a Spaniard. He was a Brit and he had been working on an English ship and was accused of piracy. He absolutely declared that he was innocent but met his executioner with a rosary clutched in his hands. While he was being garroted, the rope broke, and the Catholic Church declared that his survival was a miracle. He recuperated, but when the governor asked that he be returned to be executed, the Church refused to give him back. He was eventually pardoned."

"And it's real—proving my desire to show all these stories. We're back to truth being far stranger than any fiction. And there's so much more. It is okay to go today, right?"

"Yes, it is, sure—let's sign this tab and get going right away."

Maura asked for the bill, but as she did so, her old boss came striding over to their table, a massive smile on his face.

Fred Bentley was powerfully built, stocky, not fat,

but to Maura, it had always seemed that a barge was coming toward her when he strode in her direction.

He still had a head full of dark hair—dyed? She didn't know, but he had to be over fifty now, and it was certainly possible. He kept a good tan going on his skin, adding to his appearance of being fit, an outdoor man who loved the sun and activity.

He hadn't been a bad man to work for—he had certainly been better than Francine, who had changed her mind on a dime and blamed anyone else for any mistake.

Maura lowered her eyes for a moment, feeling guilty. Francine had not been nice. That didn't make what had happened to her any less horrible. Maura had to shake the image of Francine's lifeless body hanging from the tree. It haunted her almost daily.

"Maura, Angie," Fred said cheerfully. "Please, not a bill to be signed," he assured them. "What you're doing—in the midst of all this—is just wonderful. We're so grateful, honestly. Anything, anything at all that we can do, please just say so."

Maura smiled, uncomfortable. Angie answered him enthusiastically, telling him how she loved the grounds, the beauty of the pool and the elegance of the rooms, and, of course, most of all, the extra and unusual aspect of the campfire tales and the history walk. She was delighted to tout such a wonderful place.

To her surprise, Maura stood and listened and smiled, and yet, inside, she found that she was suddenly wondering about Fred.

Where was he when Francine Renault had been hanged from the great branches of the History Tree?

ST. AUGUSTINE WAS, in Brock's opinion, one of the state's true gems. Founded in 1565 by Pedro Menéndez de Avilés, the city offered wonders such as the fort, the old square, dozens of charming bed-and-breakfast inns, historic hotels, museums, the original Ripley's Believe It or Not! Museum, ghost tours, pub tours and all manner of musical entertainment.

The city also offered beautiful beaches.

But that day, he hadn't come to enjoy any of the many wonderful venues offered here.

As asked, Detective Rachel Lawrence had set up a meeting with Katie Simmons, the coworker who had reported the disappearance of one of the missing women, Lydia Merkel. She was possibly the last one to see Lydia alive.

They were meeting at La Pointe, a new restaurant near the Castillo—Katie hadn't wanted to talk where she worked, though Brock intended to go by after their meeting, just to see if anyone else remembered anything that they might have missed when speaking with officers before.

The restaurant was casual, as were many that faced the old fort and the water beyond, with wooden tables, a spiral of paper towels right on the table and a menu geared to good but reasonable food for tourists.

Katie Simmons was there when he arrived; if he hadn't seen a picture of her in his files, he would have recognized her anyway. She was so nervous. She saw him as he entered through the rustic doorway, and her straw slipped from her mouth. She quickly brought her fingers to her lips as iced tea dribbled from them. She was a pretty young woman with soft brown hair and an athletic build, evident when she leaped to her feet, sat and stood once again.

She must have realized who he was by the way he had scanned the restaurant when he had entered. Maybe it was his suit—not all that common in Florida, even for many a business meeting.

She waited for him to come to the table.

He smiled, offering her his hand, hoping to put her at ease quickly.

"Katie, right?" he said.

"Special Agent McGovern?"

"Call me Brock, please," he said as he joined her at the table. "And please sit, and I hope you can relax. I can't tell you how grateful I am that you've agreed to speak with me. I know you've already told the police about Lydia, but as you know, we're hoping that we can find her."

Katie sat and plucked at the straw in her tea, still nervous. It looked as if tears were starting to form in her eyes.

"Time keeps going by… It's been weeks now. I don't know how she could still be alive."

A waiter in a flowered shirt was quickly at their table. Brock ordered coffee and he and Katie both requested the daily special, a seafood dish.

"I don't want to lie to you, but I also don't think you

should give up," Brock told her when the waiter had gone. "People do just disappear—"

Katie broke in immediately. "Not Lydia! Oh, you had to know her. She was so excited to have moved here. She loved the city, loved working here—and there was more, of course. Lydia is a wonderful musician. She's magic with her guitar. She has the coolest voice—not like an angel, more like… I don't know, unique. She can be soft, she can belt it out… I love listening to her! She was going around getting gigs—and our boss is a great guy. He does schedules every week and talks to us before he sets them up. That allowed Lydia to set up her first few gigs."

"She was performing before she left here?" he asked.

"Oh, she only had two performances. One was for a private party out on a boat—but good money. They just wanted a solo acoustic player. And then another was at a place called Saint, which is a historic house that just became a restaurant—or kind of a nightclub. Can you be both? Or maybe you could say the same of a lot of places here—restaurant by day, club, kind of, by night with some kind of musical entertainment."

"Thanks. Do you know who hired her for the boat?"

"Sure. An association of local tourist businesses—it's called SAMM," she said and paused to grin. "St. Augustine Makes Money. That's really the name. Only you don't have to be in the city to belong—people belong from all kinds of nearby locations. In fact, half of the members, from what I understand, are really up in Jacksonville. We're the cute historic place, you know—Jacksonville is the big city. And where most people come in, as far as an airport goes." She grew somber again. "But she wasn't working the night before she disappeared. We were out together that night. She was leaving in the morning. She was so excited. Her career—her musical career—wasn't skyrocketing, but it was taking off."

"And according to what I've learned, she did leave in her own car."

"Yes, and she loved her car. It was old, but she kept it up—she kept great care of it. Oh, and that's why she chose her apartment. She could park there for free. Right in this area—well, out a bit—but still in what we consider the old section. I mean, you could walk to her place if you had to."

"Her car was never found," Brock noted. He'd read everything he could about Lydia before coming here today. And, of course, one of the reasons it was easy for law enforcement to consider the fact that she might have disappeared on purpose had to do with the fact that her car had never been found.

Katie was instantly indignant. "I know that—and I'm so sorry, but it made me wonder if the cops are stupid. The state is surrounded by water—oh, yeah, not to mention swamps and bogs and sinkholes and the damned frigging Everglades! Someone got rid of her car. I'm telling you—there is no way in hell that Lydia left here willingly—that she just drove away. Okay, I mean, she did drive away that morning, but… I didn't worry until I didn't hear from her. I know she would have called and texted me pics of the History Tree. When she didn't… I swear, I didn't panic right away, but when I didn't hear from her by that night, I knew something was wrong. I called the ranch, and they told me that she'd never checked in. That's when I called the police. And they all told me she might have just taken a detour. I told them that her phone was going straight to voice mail, and they still tried to placate me. I had to wait the appropriate time to even report her as a missing person with people really working on the case. Then I found out that two other young women had disappeared, and then..."

She broke off.

Brock continued for her, "And then they found the remains of Maureen Rodriguez. Katie, as I said, I don't want to give you false hope. But don't give up completely. People are working very hard on this now, I promise you." He hesitated—an agent should never make a promise he couldn't guarantee he could keep, but...

"Katie, I promise you, I won't stop until we know what happened to her."

She smiled with tears welling in her eyes.

"I believe you," she said.

Their lunches arrived. As they ate, Brock allowed her to go on about her friend. They hadn't known each other that long; they had just hit it off. She loved old music and Lydia loved old music. They had loved going to plays together, too, and were willing to travel a few hours for a show, and they both loved improv and ghost tours and so on...

He thanked her sincerely when the meal was over; she had taken his business card, but also put his direct line into her phone. He promised to call her when he knew something—good or bad—and they parted ways.

He decided to stop by the offices of SAMM next, wanting a list of those involved in the boat event during which Lydia Merkel had played, and then he'd be on to the restaurant where she'd entertained at her one gig on the mainland.

Someone, somewhere, had to know something.

Her car hadn't been found.

She'd only had one credit card; it hadn't been used outside the city. No one disappeared without a trace. There was always a trace.

He just had to find it.

Chapter Four

"I am standing here on Avenida Menendez in historic St. Augustine in front of a home that was originally built in 1763. While it was in 1512 that Juan Ponce de Léon first came ashore just north of here, and 1564 when French vessels were well received by the Native population, it was in 1565 that Pedro Menéndez came and settlement began.

"It was while the Spanish ruled in 1760—nearly two centuries later—that Yolanda Ferrer's father first built the house that stands behind me. In 1762, Spain ceded Florida to the British in exchange for Cuba, and Yolanda and her young husband, Antonio, left for Havana. But in 1783, Florida was ceded back to the Spanish in exchange for the Bahama Islands. Yolanda came back to claim the home her father had built, and the governor granted the home and property to her. At that time, she was a young and beautiful bride, and she thought that she and her husband would live happily ever after—but it wasn't to be.

"Yolanda, deceived by her husband, argued and pleaded with him not to leave her—and then either fell to her death or was, perhaps, pushed to her death, in the courtyard behind the house, where, today, diners arrive from all over the world to enjoy the fusion cooking of one of St. Augustine's premier chefs, Armand Morena.

"Through the years, the house has changed. It stood for a while as an icehouse and as a mortuary. For the last fifty years, however, it has changed hands only once, being a restaurant for those fifty years. But it wasn't just as a restaurant that the building was haunted by images of the beautiful, young Yolanda, sometimes weeping as she hurries along the halls, sometimes appearing in the courtyard and sometimes in what was once her bedroom and is now the manager's office. Yolanda is known to neither hurt nor frighten those who see her. Rather, witnesses to her apparition claim that they long to reach out and touch her and let her know that her story is known and that, even today, we are touched by her tragedy."

Maura finished her speech and waited for Angie to cut the take on the camera. Angie did so but awkwardly, and Maura thought briefly about the editing she was going to have to do. She much preferred it when Angie did the talking, but Angie had already spoken in front of the Castillo and Ripley's, and at the Huguenot Cemetery, the Old Jail, the Spanish Military Hospital Museum and several other places. She had begged Maura to let her do the filming on this one and Maura had acquiesced.

The sun was just about gone. And Maura was tired. As much as she loved St. Augustine, she was wearying of seeing it as if she was reliving that old vacation movie with Chevy Chase.

"Ready for dinner?" she asked Angie.

"Oh, you bet. We're going to have to come back. I loved what I called the square—the Plaza de la Constitución. I mean, that's the whole thing, isn't it? Executions took place there once, and now it's all beautiful, and there is a farmer's market, and people come for musical events and more. I love the streets surrounding it, the beautiful churches and all. I'm so glad we came."

"I've always loved this city," Maura agreed. "But I'm tired and starving. Have you picked out a place you'd like to go?"

There were plenty of choices.

Angie hesitated. She winced. "If I picked a particular restaurant, would you think that I was being ghoulish?"

Maura arched a brow warily. "Ghoulish? I don't know of any new horrific restaurant murders in St. Augustine."

"The restaurant is quite safe—no blood and guts in the kitchen or elsewhere, as far as I know," Angie assured her. "But..." she said and hesitated again. "It is the last place one of the missing girls had a music gig—I think I saw some video—because Lydia Merkel was playing her guitar and singing there not long before she disappeared. It's called Saint."

"Oh," Maura murmured. "Really, I'm not—"

"You wouldn't have even known, I don't think, if I hadn't told you."

Maura had read news reports; she had seen videos

of the young women, including Lydia Merkel, who had worked here in St. Augustine, before her mysterious disappearance.

She hadn't remembered the name of the restaurant where the girl had played, nor even the name of the restaurant where she had worked.

"Please? I can't help but want to see it," Angie said.

Of course, Angie wanted to see it. If the poor woman's body was found and her murder was never solved, she would become another Florida legend.

She didn't have the energy to fight Angie, and besides, she doubted that the restaurant itself had been any cause of what had happened.

"Okay. Is it close? I'm sure you know. Are we walking? I don't think it existed the last time I was up here. I'll google it," she told Angie.

"Two blocks to the east and then one to the south," Angie said.

"We'll leave the car and walk."

Saint was like many restaurants in the historic district—once upon a time, it had been someone's grand home. Maura thought that it might have been built in the 1800s during the Victorian era; a plaque on the front assured her she was right: 1855. Originally the home of Delores and Captain Evan Siegfried.

Abandoned after the Civil War, it had become an institution for the mentally ill in the 1880s, a girls' school in 1910, a flower shop in the 1920s, a home again briefly in the 1950s before it was eventually abandoned—then recently restored by the owners of Saint.

The restaurant's original incarnation as a home was

evident as they entered; there was a stairway to the second floor on the right, and on the left was what had once been a parlor—it now held a long bar and a few tables.

They were led around to what had probably been a family room; there, to the far rear, was a small stage, cordoned off now, but offering a sign that told them that Timmy Margulies, Mr. One-Man Band, would be arriving at 8:00 p.m.

As the hostess led them to their table, Maura stopped dead—causing a server behind her to crash into her with his tray and send a plate of gourmet french fries and something brown and wet and covered with gravy to go flying to the floor.

Maura was instantly apologetic, beyond humiliated, and—what was worse—she had stopped in surprise.

Brock McGovern was seated at a table near the door, deep in conversation with a woman who was wearing a polo shirt with the restaurant's logo but not the tunic worn by the waitstaff.

Of course, now he—like the rest of those in the place—was staring at her.

She truly wanted to crawl beneath the floor.

Apparently he admitted to the woman that he knew Maura; he was standing, about to head her way.

She winced and ignored him, trying to help the waiter whose tray she had upturned, stooping down to help.

"It's fine, it's fine—really!" the young waiter told her, smiling as he met her eyes, collecting fallen plates.

"Oh, dear," Angie murmured.

Then Brock was at her side with the woman who had been at his table.

"Miss, seriously, please, it's all right—this is a restaurant. We do have spills," the woman said.

"I know, but this one was my fault," Maura said.

She was startled when Brock took her arm. She looked up into his eyes and saw that she was overdoing her apology.

She was still looking at him, but she couldn't help herself.

"I am so, so sorry!" she said again.

"Maura, it's all right," he said quietly. And, looking back at him, she realized she was as attracted to the man he had become as she had been to the boy he had once been. And maybe, just maybe, she had been apologizing to him, and he had been telling her that it was all right.

But…

"You never tried to reach me," she blurted as the waiter and busboys—and whoever the woman with Brock was—all scrambled around, cleaning up.

His frown instantly assured her that something was wrong with that statement.

"I did try," he said. "Repeatedly. I called, and I wrote and… I guess it doesn't matter now. There's no way to change the past."

Angie cleared her throat, "Um, excuse me. I think that they want us to sit. Maybe get out of the way? Brock! Wow, weird coincidence. Nice to see you—want to join us? Maura, we really need to sit."

"Yes, of course," Maura said, wincing again—wishing more than ever that she could sink into the floor and disappear. Her mind was racing; she was stunned and felt as if she had been blindsided.

She had great parents. Loving parents. But had they decided that there was no proof that Brock had really been cleared—and that he shouldn't contact their precious daughter? What else would explain that he said he'd reached out but had never actually reached her?

She was still standing. And everyone was still looking at her.

She smiled weakly and took her chair, continuing to be somewhat stunned by Brock's words, wishing that they might not have been said under these circumstances. She supposed that was her fault. But she hadn't been able to stop herself.

"This is charming, absolutely charming," Angie said when they were seated, her eyes on Brock. "We had no idea that you'd be here—and even if we had, how convenient that we came to be in the same place! Have you had dinner? Will you join us for the meal?"

"I have not had dinner, though I did have a great lunch," he said.

"You were here investigating?" Angie asked.

"Yes."

"I know some of what's going on, of course," Angie said. "There's news everywhere these days—even on our phones. Hard to miss. I understand that the last girl who disappeared near the ranch had been living here in the city."

"Yes," Brock agreed. Angie frowned slightly; she'd obviously been expecting more info.

"Do you think there's any possibility of finding any of the missing women alive?" Maura asked him.

"There's always the possibility," Brock said.

"Ah," Angie said, studying him. "A politically correct answer."

"No," Brock said. "They haven't been found dead. That means there is a possibility that they will be found alive."

"Even after the woman's bones were found in sheets?" Angie asked.

"Even after that. It's still unknown if the cases are connected. That three young women have disappeared in a relatively short period of time does suggest serial kidnapping, but whether they were connected to the murder of Maureen Rodriguez is something that we still don't know. But," he added, "as I tried to say, I think it's a dangerous time right now for any woman from the ages of seventeen to thirty-five or perhaps on upward. Frankly, I'd be much happier if all those I knew were in Alaska right now—or Australia or New Zealand, perhaps."

He glanced over at Maura and she felt bizarrely as if her heart stopped beating for a minute.

She had been so angry for so long.

And now she realized that he hadn't been trying to get rid of her, per se—he was worried about everyone.

And maybe, because of the past, *especially* about her.

"But I do say it's a good thing that you stick together," he said, offering them a smile. "So, did you enjoy your day?" he asked politely.

Maura didn't have to worry about answering—Angie had no problem excitedly telling him about all that they had seen and done.

Their waiter—the same man who had collided with Maura—came and suggested that they have the snapper; the preparation of it, a combo of lemon and oil and garlic, was simple but exceptional. The three of them ordered. Maura and Brock were both driving, but Angie was at her leisure, so she indulged in the restaurant's signature drink—the Saint. It came out blue and bubbly, and she assured the waiter she didn't care much about what was in it. It was delicious.

"Have you all finished up here for the day?" Brock asked.

"Oh, yes, Maura is amazing. She knew where to go, what to get—we don't do full-length documentaries, you know. Just little bits. There have been all kinds of surveys about the modern attention span. You'll have tons of people look at something if it only takes them briefly out of their scanning. Unless it's something they really want to see, they pass right by when things become long. Two to three minutes tend to work really well for me. I was doing terribly, then I started working with Maura. She edits, although half the time we get just about perfect in one take."

He glanced over at Maura. "Are you in business together?" he asked.

"No," Maura said.

"Are you kidding? She's in megapopular demand!" Angie answered. "Artists, authors, performers—Maura knows how to make everyone really show off in that two to three minutes," Angie said.

"And I should definitely put in," Maura said quickly, "that Angie is truly a shooting star—her books on truth being stranger than fiction, weird places and so on do amazingly well."

"I have some pretty generous sponsors for my video channel. Whoever knew that being a nerdy and somewhat gruesome kid would pay so well, huh?" Angie asked.

"We never do know where life will take us, I guess," Brock said, turning his attention to Maura once again. "But sometimes you pop before the camera?"

"When Angie wears out," Maura said.

"No, she's great," Angie said. "The video-cam thing loves her—and she's so smooth. A grand storyteller. She'd have been perfect in the old Viking days or in Ireland when history was kept orally and people listened around the fire. Of course, I keep telling her that it can't be her life. We've worked together about three years now and I'm always amazed that she never says no. Work, work, work, I tell her. I put things off when I'm in the middle of a relationship. Maura won't take the time for a relationship."

Maura glared at Angie, amazed that her friend would say such a thing—especially when she'd been flirting with Brock in front of Maura and was unabashedly interested in men. If not forever, for a night—as she had often said.

Maura wanted to kick her. Hard. Beneath the table.

And she might have, except that Angie was a little bit too far away to accomplish the task.

But Brock looked at Maura, something strange in his eyes. “Some of us do make work into everything,” he said.

Angie pounced on that. “So—you’re not married. Or engaged. Or steadily sleeping with anyone?”

Once again, Maura wanted to kick Angie. She damned the size of the table.

Brock laughed. “No, not married, engaged or sleeping with someone steadily. I think you only want to wake up every morning looking at someone’s face on the other pillow when that person is so special that they know the good and the bad of you and everything in between. When you know… Well, anyway…my work takes up a lot of time. And it takes a special person to endure life with someone who works—the way I do.” He sat back. “I’d like to follow you back to the Frampton ranch. Being perpetually, ever so slightly paranoid is a job hazard. I know you’re fine, but…humor me?”

He was looking at Maura.

She still loved his face. His eyes, the contours of his cheeks, the set of his mouth. He’d been so determined and steady when they’d been young, and she had been so swept into…loving him. For good reason, she thought. He’d grown into the man she’d imagined somewhere in the back of her mind.

The man whose face she had wanted to see on the pillow next to hers when she woke up every morning.

“Maura?” Angie asked.

“Um, yes, sure,” Maura said.

Brock stood, heading to find the waiter and pay the check.

"He is so hot!" Angie said. "He's got a thing for you. But if you're going to waste it—"

"Angie, he's working down here."

"You must have been the cutest kids."

"Oh, yeah, we were just frigging adorable, Angie. It was twelve years ago. Come on, let's get the car and head back. I have a lot of editing to do."

"No, you don't. Almost every take was perfect. I should have gotten that check—I'm really making money. Unless, of course, he has a budget for dinners out. I'd hate to ruin his budget."

"Angie, it's all right—look, he's motioning to us. We're all set to go."

Brock wasn't parked far away; he walked them to their car and then asked that they wait for him to come around on Avenida Menendez so that he could follow them.

As Maura waited behind the wheel, she thought about the years that had gone by.

She'd been stunned at first that things had ended so completely with Brock, but slowly, she'd felt that she was more normal—that heartbreak was a part of life. There had been other men in her life. But anytime it had gotten to *we're either going somewhere with this, or...*

She had chosen the "or."

She hadn't planned on making that choice forever, she'd just never met anyone else she wanted on the pillow next to hers every morning.

She wondered what it meant that he'd never found that person, either.

Brock drove up slightly behind her, allowing her to move into traffic. She headed out of the historic district of the city with him behind her, easily following.

"I wonder if I should have ridden with him," Angie said. She glanced over at Maura. "I mean, if you're going to waste a perfectly good man…"

Maura was surprised that she could laugh. "Angie, I rather got the impression that you liked Nils Hartford or Mark Hartford. Maybe even Fred Bentley…"

"Bentley? No, no, no!" Angie said. "I like them tall and dark—or a little shorter but with that ability to smile and charm, something in their eyes, love of life, of who they are…not sure what. But Bentley? Nah. He's like a little tram coming at you—no, no. Although…" She turned in the passenger's seat to extend her seat belt, allowing her to look straight at Maura. "Now, I'd love to find out more about Donald Glass. Power and money! We all know that those are aphrodisiacs. Even when a man is sexually just about downright creepy. Somehow, enough money and power can change the tide, you know?"

"Uh, you know he's married," Maura reminded her.

"Ah, well, I heard that didn't always matter to him so much." Angie said. She laughed. "He even has a younger wife—younger than him. But that's the problem—there will always be younger, and younger will always be replaced with younger still."

"See, a warning philosophy," Maura said.

"But I know plenty of couples where there's an

age difference—both ways!—who are happily going strong. I mean, there are older men who stay in love, and even older women who stay in love with younger men who stay in love."

"Of course," Maura murmured. She wasn't really paying attention to Angie anymore—she was only aware of the car following her.

It seemed forever before they reached the Frampton Ranch and Resort.

Angie talked the whole way.

It was all right. All Maura had to do was murmur an agreement now and then.

At long last, she pulled into the great drive and out to the guest parking. Brock was still right behind her, turning into a parking space just a few down.

He headed over to them while Maura went into the back seat of her car to grab her camera bag.

"An escort all the way," Angie said, greeting Brock as he joined them.

"All the way to the lobby," he agreed.

As they walked, Maura realized that despite the fact that he had joined them for dinner, she had never asked him about the woman in the Saint shirt who had been his companion at his table before she and Angie arrived.

But oddly, she didn't want to ask him in front of Angie. She glanced his way as they neared the entrance to the lobby, once the great entry to the antebellum house. He glanced back at her and, for a moment, it was strangely as if no time had passed at all. She'd always been able to tell him with just a look if they needed to talk alone.

He seemed to read her expression. Or, at least, she thought that he gave her a slight nod.

They walked up the porch steps and then through the great double doors to the "ranch house."

That was rather a misnomer. When the house had been built, it had been based on the Southern plantation style.

The integrity of the plan had been maintained with the registration desk to the far side and the doors leading to the coffee shop and the restaurant on opposite sides—one having once been the formal parlor and one the family parlor. The floors were hardwood, polished to a breathtaking shine without being too slippery—a great accomplishment by maintenance and the cleaning crew. There were great suites in the main house on the second floor while the attic had been heightened and rooms added there. Two wings—once bunkhouses—had become smaller one-room rentals.

Angie had, naturally, taken one of the big suites on the second floor.

Maura just hadn't needed that much space; she'd been perfectly happy up in the attic, and though she enjoyed working with Angie, she liked her own room, her own downtime and her own quiet at times.

"Safely in," Brock murmured.

"Welcome back…did you all decide to hit the entertainments somewhere nearby together?" a voice asked.

Maura was surprised to see that Fred Bentley was behind the registration desk. There was someone on duty twenty-four hours, but it wasn't usually Bentley. He lived on the property, having something of an apartment at the far end of the left wing, and she'd never really figured out what he considered his hours to be, but he was usually moving about in different areas, overseeing tours, restaurants, housekeeping and everything else.

"Our night clerk didn't show," he said, apparently aware that they were all looking at him curiously. "Not appreciated," he added.

Maura didn't think that the night clerk would be on the payroll much longer.

"I ran into Maura and Angie in St. Augustine," Brock told him, answering Fred's earlier question. "It can be a surprisingly small world."

"That is a strange coincidence," Bentley said. "Well, as I said, welcome back. Oh, Angie, Mrs. Glass was hoping that you'd tour the place a bit with her tomorrow, get an idea of what you could do…more videos on the resort as a whole. The swimming pool and patio out back are really beautiful." He nodded toward Brock and Maura. "Those two used to love it—our summer employees have always been allowed use of the pool and gym during their off-hours."

"It was a great place to work," Brock said. "Well, it's been long day. I'm going to head up."

"I think we all are," Maura said. "Good night, Fred."

An elevator had been installed; Maura usually took the stairs, but Angie headed for them and she thought that maybe Brock was on the attic floor, as well. "Night, Angie," he said, heading for the elevator.

"Good night. But long day—I'll take the elevator, too!" she said, joining him and Maura, who pressed the call button.

"I'm in the Jackson Suite," Angie said. "Have you seen the suites?" she asked Brock cheerfully in the elevator. "You're welcome to come see my room."

"I've seen all the suites, and thank you, but tonight… I'm ready for bed," he told her.

Angie laughed softly and said, "Me, too."

Angie was always flirtatious—and she'd honestly stated what she wanted to Maura. Usually her easy way with come-ons didn't bother Maura in the least.

Tonight…

It wasn't the night. It was that she was coming on to Brock.

The elevator stopped on the second floor. Angie stepped out. "Well, lovely day, lovely dinner. Thank you both!"

"Thank you," Angie told her.

The elevator door closed.

"She's subtle, huh?" Brock murmured.

To her surprise, Maura smiled. "Very."

"So, what did you want to ask me?"

He could still read her glances. And in the small elevator, they were close. She wondered if it was possible for so much time to have gone by and there still be that something…

The elevator door opened. They stepped out into the hallway. Brock stood still, waiting for her to talk.

"None of my business really, but that was rather bizarre running into you. And you were with that woman at a table, and then just came on over with us so easily… I…"

"I went in search of Lydia Merkel," he said. "She had a coworker, Katie Simmons, who insists that Lydia didn't disappear on purpose. She'd gotten two gigs playing her guitar and singing, as well as working as a waitress. One of those gigs was at Saint."

"Oh! Well, yes, of course, you were working. And the woman you met… She hired Lydia Merkel?"

"Exactly. Lydia played there the Wednesday night of the week she disappeared. I was hoping to learn something more. But I pretty much gained the same information. The manager did have a few minutes to speak with Lydia. Katie said that she was the perfect entertainment for their night clientele—charming, speaking between songs, performing at just the right volume for diners. She asked her back for a few nights each week and Lydia was delighted. But she had a bit of a vacation planned. She was heading to the Frampton Ranch and Resort, and it was a long-held dream. The manager told her that was fine. Lydia could come in the next week and they'd discuss the future. Of course, as we all know, Lydia never went back."

He paused for a minute and said very softly, "I'm sorry. I never meant to come off the way that I did earlier. But a woman was murdered. Three young women are missing."

"I'm sorry, as well. I thought… Never mind. I don't know what I thought. But you seriously think that…there will be more kidnappings? And that the same person who murdered the poor woman whose remains were found at the laundry has taken these other women?"

He nodded grimly. "From what I've learned, there is no way Lydia Merkel just walked away from her life. I haven't had time for other interviews yet, but I imagine I will find that neither Lily Sylvester nor Amy Bonham just walked away, either. And—while other businesses had sheets and used the laundry and fall in place with other leads as well, the Frampton Ranch and Resort still comes out on top of every list. Maybe I am touchy as far as this place goes, but in truth, I was sent here because of my familiarity with not just my home state but with the Frampton Ranch and Resort. You… you need to be so careful, Maura."

"I will be—I always am. But I'll be very careful. And…thank you."

He nodded. He knew that she was thanking him for the warning—and for telling her just how hard he had tried to reach her years ago.

He still hadn't moved; neither had she.

There were five rooms in the attic. The space was small. The walls were old and solid, and they were speaking softly, but it had grown late.

There was nothing more to say.

And there were years and years of words that they might say.

And, still, neither of them moved.

"I, uh… I'm so sorry for the families and friends of those poor women. And it's truly horrible about that young woman who was murdered, but do you think that they're all related?"

"We don't know. But they did have this place in common. And there's the past."

Maura shook her head. "You mean Francine?"

"Yes."

"But…that was twelve years ago."

"Yes."

"Peter committed suicide," Maura said. "I remember reading about it, and I remember him fighting with Francine. But then again, I remember everyone fighting with Francine. Still, with what Peter did…killing himself. Peter was a bit of a strange man with intense religious beliefs. He also had a temper, which usually came out as a lot of screaming and boiled down to angry muttering. It wasn't hard to believe that he had gone into a rage and dragged her out to the History Tree—and then been horrified by what he had done and regretted his action. Committed suicide."

"That's what was assumed. Never proved," Brock told her. "He was stabbed in the gut, something someone else could have done. Wipe the knife…put it in his hand. Leave him in the freezer. Easy to believe he might have done it himself. Especially when there were no other solid suspects. Just as easy to believe he was stabbed—and that the scene was staged."

He took a slight step back—almost as if he needed a little space. "Well, I'm in room three. I guess we should call it a night. I…uh… Well, you look great. And congratulations. I understand that you're doing brilliantly with your career. But I guess we all knew that you would. You're a natural storyteller—easy to see how that extends to directing people, to making them look great on video."

"Thanks. And you're exactly what you wanted to be—an FBI agent." She paused and took a deep breath. "And… Brock, I never received any of your messages. I don't know if my parents thought they were protecting me… They're good people, but… I am so sorry. I really had it in for you for years—I thought you just walked away."

He shook his head. Shrugged.

"Well, where are you?"

"I'm the last down the hallway, in five," she said.

"I'll watch you through your door," he said with a half smile. "I mean, I'm here—might as well see it through to perfect safety."

"Okay, okay, I'm going. I… I assume I'll see you," she murmured.

"You will," he assured her.

She turned and headed down the short hallway to the end. There, she dug out her key, opened her door, waved and went in.

Finally alone and in the sanctuary of her room, she leaned against the door, shaking.

How could time be erased so easily? How could the truth hurt so badly…and mean so very much at the same time? What would have happened if she had received his messages? Would they have been together all these years with, perhaps, a little one now, or two little ones…

She could have turned to him, laughed, slipped her arms around him. She knew what it would feel like, knew how he held her, cupped her nape when he kissed her, knew the feel of his lips…

Time had gone by. She hadn't received his messages.

She hadn't known he'd tried to reach her; she should have. As soon as she was home, her parents had gotten her a new phone with a new, unlisted number. They'd insisted that she change her email and delete all her social media accounts—not referencing Brock specifically, so much as the situation and the danger that could possibly still come from it.

Maybe she should have tried harder to get in touch with him. But when she'd never heard from him, she'd given up. Tried to move on.

Now they were living different lives.

She pushed away from the door. It had been a long day. She was hot and tired and suddenly living in a land of confusion. A shower was in order.

Maybe a cold shower.

She doffed her clothing, letting it lie where it fell, and headed into the bathroom. And it was while the water was pouring over her that she felt a strange prickle of unease.

It was like a perfect storm.

She was here. Brock was here…

Nils and Mark Hartford were here. Donald and Marie Glass… Fred Bentley…

And then, today her and Angie in St. Augustine, Brock in St. Augustine.

In the same restaurant. At the same time.

She turned off the water, dried quickly and stepped back out to the bedroom. She knew that Brock was working—that they all needed to be concerned. One poor woman was beyond help. Three were still missing, and maybe, just maybe…

There was nothing that she could do except, of course, be smart, as Brock had warned. And suddenly she couldn't help herself. She was thinking like Angie.

A night, just a night.

As Angie had made sure they all knew at dinner, Brock wasn't sleeping with anyone now in his life. There was no reason that the two of them shouldn't relive the past, if only for a night, for a few hours, for…

Memory's sake. If Maura just revisited the past, she might realize that it hadn't been so perfect, so very wonderful, that Brock wasn't the only man in the world who was so perfect…for her.

She knew his room number. It was wild, but…

Yes. It was too wild. She forced herself to don a long cotton nightgown and slip into bed.

And lay there, wide-awake, staring at the ceiling, remembering the contours of his body.

Chapter Five

Brock closed and locked his door, set his gun on the nightstand, and his phone and wallet on the desk by his computer. He shrugged out of his jacket and sat at the desk, opened his computer, keyed in his password and went to his notes.

He quickly filled in what he had learned that afternoon.

The most interesting had not been his conversation with the manager at Saint.

It had been earlier, when he had visited the offices of SAMM.

The event Lydia Merkel had played had been a social for members of the society. It hadn't been a mere boat, but the yacht *Majestic*, and fifty-seven members of SAMM had been invited.

Donald Glass and his wife had been among them.

The contact at SAMM had known that Maureen Rodriguez—or her sad remains at any rate—had been discovered. Every hotel, motel, inn and bed-and-breakfast that used the laundry facility had been questioned upon that finding. But no evidence had led to any one property.

Donald Glass knew about the women who had disappeared. He had never mentioned that he had met any of them.

To be fair, he might not have known that he had met Lydia Merkel. She had been working under her performance moniker—Lyrical Lee.

And, of course, the proprietors of many of the properties that used the laundry service were among those who had been on the yacht.

It was still a sea of confusion.

Except that Frampton Ranch and Resort was the location where the missing girls had been—or been headed to.

Brock filled in his notes, then stood, cast aside the remainder of his clothing and got into his shower. He needed to shake some of the day off. His puzzle pieces were still there, but he was missing something that was incredibly important.

Hard evidence.

And back to the old question—what the hell could something that had happened twelve years ago have to do with the now?

And why, in the middle of trying to work all the angles of the crimes, concentrating on detail and logic, did he keep seeing Maura's face as she stood before him in the hallway?

He knew her so well. He smiled, thinking that she hadn't really changed at all.

She'd been polite, always caring, never wanting to hurt another person.

She'd been so stunned to see him in the restaurant and stopped short and then…

He smiled again, remembering her face. So mortified.

And then trying to clean up the mess herself because she'd caused it. When they had spoken…

She'd obviously been stricken, hearing that he had tried to reach her. He'd seen the pull of her emotions—she had to be angry with her parents, but they were good people and she did love them, and now, with the passage of time, she surely knew that they had thought they were doing what was best, as well.

He showered, thinking that washing away the day would help; sleep would be good, too, of course. He felt that learning about Lydia Merkel and her aspirations to be a full-time musician were another piece of the puzzle—not because she entertained, but because of who she had done entertaining for: the hospitality industry—including the Frampton Ranch and Resort.

Brock and Maura had once been part of that. And they had intended to work part-time through college. His future had been planned out—he'd known what he was going to do with his life. And he had done it.

But Maura had always been part of his vision for his life, and maybe the most important part, the part where human emotion created beauty in good times and sustained a man through the bad.

He wasn't sure he ever made the conscious decision to go to her. He threw on a pair of jeans and left his room, years of training causing him to take his weapon and lock the door as he departed.

Which made him look rather ridiculous as he knocked softly on her door. When she opened it—he hoped and assumed she'd looked through the peephole before doing so—she stared at him wide-eyed for a minute, a slight smile teasing her lips—and a look of abject confusion covering her features.

"Um—you came to shoot me?"

She backed into the room. He entered, shaking his head, also smiling.

"Can't leave a gun behind," he told her.

"I see," she said.

For a moment, they stood awkwardly, just looking at each other, maybe searching for the right words. But words weren't necessary.

He set his holster and Glock down, fumbling blindly to find the dresser beside the door. He wasn't sure if she stepped into his arms or if he drew her in. But she was there. And time and distance did nothing except heighten each sensation, make the taste of her lips sweeter than ever. Their kiss deepened into something incredible. He felt her hand on his face, her fingers a gentle touch, a feathery brush, something unique and arousing, incredible and just a beginning.

His hands slid beneath the soft cotton of her gown and their lips broke long enough for him to rid her of it. He felt her fingers, teasing now along the waistband of his jeans. A thunderous beat of longing seemed to pound between them; it was his own heart, his pulse, instinctive human need and so much more.

Her fingers found the buttons on his jeans.

He couldn't remember ever before stepping from denim so quickly or easily.

Nor did he remember needing the feel of flesh against flesh ever quite so urgently.

They kissed again, his hands sliding down her spine, hers curving from his shoulders and down to his buttocks. They kissed and fell to the bed, and as his lips found her throat and collarbone, she whispered, "I was on my way to you."

He found her mouth again. Tenderness mixed with urgency, a longing to hold the moment, desire to press ever further.

It had been so long. And it was incredibly beautiful just to touch her again, hear her voice, bask in the scent of her…

Love her.

Familiar but new.

Their hands and lips traveled each other. He loved the feel of her skin, the curves of her body, loved touching her, feeling her arch and writhe to his touch.

Feeling what her touch did to him, hands traveling over his shoulders and his back; hot, wet kisses falling here and there upon him; that touch, ever more intimate.

As his was upon her. The taste and feel of her breasts and the sleekness of her abdomen, the length and sweet grace of her limbs.

And finally moving into her, moving together, feeling the rush of sweet intimacy and the raw eroticism of spiraling ever upward together, instinct and emotion bursting upon them with something akin to violence in their power, and yet so sweetly beautiful even then.

They lay together in silence, and once again he heard the beat, the pulse, his heart and hers, as they lay entwined, savoring the aftermath.

At last, he kissed her forehead, smoothing hair from her face.

She smiled up at him. “Twelve years,” she said. And her eyes had both a soft and a teasing cast. “Worth waiting for, I’d judge.”

“How kind. May I say the same?”

“Indeed, you may,” she said, curling tighter against him. “You may say all kinds of things. Good things, of course. My hair is glorious—okay, so it’s a sodden, tangled mass right now. My eyes are magnificent… Well, they are open. And, of course, you’ve waited all your life for me.”

“I have,” he said gravely.

She grinned at that. “You joined the FBI monastery?”

“I didn’t say that. And I’m doubting you joined the Directors Guild nunnery.”

She smiled, but she was serious, looking up at him. “I—I knew some good people.”

“I would expect no less,” he said softly.

“None as good as you,” she whispered.

“Now, that can be taken many ways.”

“But you know what I mean.”

“I do. And don’t go putting me on a pedestal. I wasn’t so good—I was…a bit lost. The best way I had to battle it was to plunge head-on into all the plans I had made. Most of the plans I had made," he added softly.

"I am so sorry."

"Neither of us can be sorry," he assured her.

She kissed him again. For a while, their touching was soft and tender and slow.

But it had been so many years.

Somewhere in the wee hours, they slept. And when morning came, he awoke, and he saw her face on the pillow next to his. Saw her eyes open and saw her smile, and he pulled her to him, just grateful to wake with her by his side.

"Perfect storm," she murmured. "And I'm so sorry for the cause of it. So grateful for…you."

"We can't change what happened then. Now it's all right to be glad that we've…connected."

She nodded thoughtfully. "I keep thinking…there's something in history, something in the books, something that has to give us a clue as to what is going on."

"You need to stay out of it all," he told her firmly.

She rolled on an elbow and stared at him. "How? How would I ever really stay out of it? I was here when Francine was killed. That in itself…it's most horrible that a woman was so cruelly murdered, but, Brock…it changed everything. Changed us. And you do believe that what is happening now is related."

"There is really no solid evidence to suggest that," he said. "In fact, as far as profiling and evidence go, there is little reason to suppose that a killer might have hanged Francine—and then stuck around for over a decade to murder one young woman and kidnap three more. Really, the best thing would be for you to head to Alaska—as quickly as possible."

She smiled. "I would love to see Alaska one day. I haven't been. I'd love to see it—with you."

He was certain that, physically possible or not, his heart and soul trembled. They had just come together—tonight. And, well, thanks to Angie, they were both aware that nothing else had ever really worked for either of them in the years that had been lost between them.

He had never found *her* again. And she had never found him.

He grinned, afraid to let the extent of his emotion show.

"I don't think I have vacation coming anytime soon. But how about Iceland? What an incredible place for you to do legends and stories."

She was next to him, the length of her body close, and she touched his forehead, moving back a lock of his hair. "I don't work for myself—well, I do, but I'm a vendor hiring out my services. We need to be realistic. This is your work and more than your work. And now I'm working here, too. And I can help. I'm not stupid, Brock, you know that. I lock doors. I stay where there are other people. Whoever is doing this—be it a new thing or a crime associated with the past—they're smart enough to work in the shadows. No one is going to be hurt in the resort. You're in room three, and I'm in room five, and I'm not worried at all about the nights. Brock, I'm all grown-up. Quite a bit older than the last time, remember."

"And around the same age—"

"The missing women weren't wary or suspicious. They were just leading normal lives, trying to work and survive and simply enjoy their lives. Brock, most people are wonderful. They will lend others a helping hand. They just want the same things. Maureen Rodriguez was probably a lovely person—simply expecting others to be like that, too. From the little I know, the three missing women were probably similar—expecting human beings to act as human beings, having no idea that a very sick person was out there. I know that there's a predator. I won't be led astray, into any darkness—or off alone anywhere with anyone."

"Okay," he said quietly. "But if we're apart, I'll be calling you on the hour. Oh, screw the hour. Every five minutes, maybe."

"That will be fine. But unlikely. I think most of your interviews and investigations will take more than five minutes. And you really don't need to worry about me today—we'll be videoing out at the pool, in the restaurants—and I'm sure Angie would like to show herself speaking with Marie Glass—maybe Donald, too."

He heard a buzzing from the floor and leaped up. Luckily—he hadn't thought about it when he had left his room with just pants and his Glock—his cell phone was in the pocket of his jeans.

He dug for his phone.

"Yeah, Mike," he answered, having seen the detective's name on his caller ID.

"I'd like you to come with me to the Gainesville County morgue," Flannery said.

Brock gritted his teeth; the morgue meant a body. A body meant that his actions thus far had failed to save anyone.

"One of the missing girls?"

"I don't think so—I believe—or the ME there has suggested—that the remains are much older. But… Well, I'll fill you in. How soon can you be ready?"

"Ten minutes," Brock said.

"Better than me. Meet you downstairs in fifteen. We can grab coffee and head out."

"I'll be there."

"First man to arrive orders the coffee. Never mind—Rachel will beat us both. She'll order it."

"I'll be down."

He hung up and slipped into his jeans, looking back at the bed. Maura was up, staring at him, her face knit into a worried frown.

"I have to go… Not sure when I'll be back. Keep in touch, please. And stick with Angie and Marie Glass—and don't go walking into any old spooky woods, huh, okay?" he asked.

She smiled. "I promise," she told him. "But—"

"Old bones—we have to see what they are. And no—not one of our three missing girls. You'll be here all day?"

She smiled back at him.

"I'll be here all day," she assured him.

He hurried out of her room, heading to his own, hoping he wouldn't run into anyone while he was clad in his jeans only—but not really caring.

He would shower, dress and be ready in ten minutes. He wasn't worried about that.

He did hate that he was leaving.

And hoped it was something he was going to have to get used to doing.

MAURA WAS HAPPY—and determined. No, she wasn't an agent. Or a cop of any kind. No—she wasn't even particularly equipped to defend herself should she need to do so.

But she was smart and wary and everything else that she had told Brock.

Like it or not, she had been at the ranch when Francine was killed. And she was here now, and she was a Floridian and these horrible things were happening in her state. Today she would be filming around the estate with Angie and Marie, and she'd be speaking with all those here as much as possible—especially Fred, Marie, maybe Donald and Nils and Mark.

Her reasoning might be way off. Just because they had all been here twelve years ago and were here now didn't mean a thing. The solution to Francine's murder and answers about the girls who were dead and missing now might be elusive. It was sad but true that an alarming percentage of murders went unsolved. She'd read the statistics one time—nearly 40 percent of all homicides in the US went unsolved each year.

Except on this, while it was in his power, she knew that Brock wouldn't let go.

So, in her small way, she would do her best. And maybe that meant going through the library again—

finding out everything she could about the Frampton Ranch and Resort—and the people who were here.

Maura showered, dressed and set out to edit some of her video from the day before. At nine she decided to go down to breakfast; Angie, she knew, would wake up when she was ready and come down seeking coffee.

Maura took her computer with her, curious to see what various search engines brought up on the ranch. As with most commercial properties, the results showed every travel site on the planet first. And the history of North Central Florida didn't provide any better results. She didn't find much that was particularly helpful—nothing she didn't know already.

Frustrated, she was about to click over into her email when she noticed a site with the less-than-austere title of Extremely Weird Shit That Might Have Happened.

Once there, she read about a strange organization that had sprung up in the area in the 1930s. Various local boarding schools and colleges had provided the members—usually rich young men with a proclivity for hedonistic lifestyles. They had created a secret society known as the Sons of Supreme Being, and considered themselves above others, apparently siding with the Nazi cause during World War II, dissolving after the war, but supposedly surfacing now and then in the decades that followed.

They had been suspected of the disappearance of a young woman in the 1950s, but it had been as difficult for police to prove their complicity as it had been to prove their existence. Members were sworn to secrecy unto death, and in the one case when a young man had admitted to the existence of the society and the possible guilt of the society in the disappearance of the girl, that young man had been found floating in the Saint Johns River.

"My dear Maura, but you are involved in your work!"

Startled, Maura looked up. Marie Glass had come to her table. She was standing slightly behind her.

Maura quickly closed her computer, wondering if Marie had seen what she'd been reading.

"I'm so sorry," she said. "Have you been waiting on me long?"

"No, dear, I just saw the fascination with which you were reading!" Marie said, sliding into the seat across from her. "Today is still a go, right? You and Angie will shoot some of the finer aspects of the resort?"

"Oh, yes, we're all set," Maura said. "Or we will be, once Angie is down."

"That's lovely. I thought we'd start with the pool and patio area, maybe scan the gym so that people can see just how much the resort offers? I know that Angie's forte lies in a different sort of content—as does yours—but she does have such an appeal online. She reaches a big audience. I can't help but think it'd be good exposure."

"Of course. Whatever you'd like."

"It's lovely that Angie Parsons will use her video channel for us."

"She couldn't wait to come here. She's fascinated with the resort."

"Well, her fascination was with the History Tree—"

She paused a bit abruptly, then smiled. “I’ve seen some of Angie’s videos and heard her podcasts and I even saw her speak at a bookstore once. The tree does seem right up her alley. And, of course, since it does seem to draw much of our clientele, I do appreciate the tree. Or trees. But… Well, those of us who knew Francine can’t help but take that all with a grain of salt. Anyway…when do you think we’ll be able to get started?”

“I imagine Angie will be down anytime,” Maura told her. “I don’t want to see you held up, though. Do you want me to call you when she’s had her coffee?”

“Well, dear, this is my plan for the day, but if you could… Oh, there she is now,” Marie said with pleasure.

Maura turned toward the entry to the coffee shop. Angie was walking in with Nils Hartford. She was her smiling, bubbling, charming self, talking excitedly.

She saw Maura sitting with Marie and waved, excused herself to Nils and came over. “Good morning. Mrs. Glass, you are bright and early.”

Marie slowly arched a silver brow. “If one can call ten in the morning early, Angie, yes, I am bright and early.” Apparently in case her words had been too sharp, she added, “But I’m certainly grateful for your work and ready whenever you are.”

“Right after one coffee,” Angie said. “One giant coffee!”

“Wonderful. I’ll just check on the patio area and make sure someone’s darling little rug rat hasn’t made a mess of the place.”

Marie rose and smiled again, perhaps trying to take

the sting from her comment. "At your leisure," she said and sailed out of the coffee shop.

Angie made a face and sat. "If America had royalty, she'd be among it. If she hadn't been born into it, she would have married into it. Oy!"

"She is a bit..."

"Snooty?" Angie said.

Maura shrugged.

"Kind of strange, don't you think?"

"What's that?"

"Donald doesn't seem to be as...well, snooty. Best word I can come up with."

"To be honest, I don't know either of them that well. I mean, I worked for them before, but I was among the young staff—they hardly bothered with us. Fred was our main supervisor at the time."

"Along with Francine Renault?" Angie asked.

"Yep."

"And wasn't your beau kind of like the ranking student employee here?"

"Yes."

Angie smiled and leaned toward her. "And?"

"And what?"

"What about last night?"

"What about it?"

"Oh, you are no fun. Details. Ouch! You can feel the air when you two are close together. I'll admit—well, I don't need to admit anything, I frankly told you that I was deeply into him."

"Angie, you're deeply into a lot of people."

"True. So I've turned my attention to Nils. He is a

cutie, too. Maybe even more classically handsome. Not as ruggedly cool—not like fierce, grim law enforcement. But damned cute. And, hmm, we are here a few more days. I do intend to have some fun."

"Angie—"

"Yes, I mean get laid!" Angie laughed at Maura's reaction. "Too graphic and frank for you? Oh, come on, Maura, you know me."

"And I wish you luck in your pursuits. I'm sure you'll do fine."

"Ah, you see, I shall do as I choose, which is much better than fine." Angie frowned suddenly. "Where is your law-and-order man?"

"He's here working, Angie. He went off—to work."

"Well, I suppose we should work, too. Let me grab my coffee."

"Great. I'll run my computer up and grab the camera."

Angie didn't need to get up for her coffee; Nils arrived at their table with a large paper cup.

"Two sugars, a dash of cream, American coffee with a shot of espresso," he said, delivering the cup to Angie. Her fingers lingered over his as she accepted the drink.

"Thank you so much," Angie said, smiling at him brilliantly. "When we talk about the restaurants, you will be in the video with me, won't you?"

"My absolute pleasure," Nils assured her. He smiled over at Maura. "Morning. I saw you earlier, but you were so involved, I didn't want to interrupt."

"You can interrupt anytime," Maura told him. "I was really just web browsing."

"Anything in the news—or have Brock or that Detective Flannery made any progress on the missing girls? Or, wow, I keep forgetting—Rachel?"

"Not that I know about."

"Something is going on this morning. There was a discovery just south of the Devil's Millhopper," Nils said. "I saw it on the news. Human remains were found. A Scout troop discovered them during a campout."

"I—I probably should have started with the news," Maura said. "I didn't." She didn't tell him that she knew something had been found because Brock had taken off early with Detectives Flannery and Lawrence to investigate. "More human remains. How sad."

Angie didn't seem concerned. "The Devil's Millhopper?" she asked. "That's…a cool name. What the hell is it?"

"A sinkhole," Maura told her. "Devil's Millhopper Geological State Park—it's in Gainesville. It's a really beautiful place, a limestone sinkhole about 120 feet deep. The park has steps all the way down, a boardwalk—sometimes torn up by storms—and beautiful nature plants and trees and all that."

"We need to go there," Angie said. "How did I miss a sinkhole?"

"I don't think it's haunted. But, hey, who knows? Anything can be haunted, right?" Nils asked. "It's not all that far from here—a cool place. Hey, I'd love to take you. I have a day off coming up, if you want to go."

"I'd love it if you could go with me… We'll need Maura, of course, for the video," Angie said.

"I'd love to go with both of you," Nils said.

While Angie smiled back at him, Maura found herself remembering the Nils she had known before—the young man who had thrived on being so superior. She tried to remember if she had noted any of his interactions with Francine. Francine most probably wouldn't have reacted to any of his behavior.

Could Francine have angered Nils…and could he, at eighteen, have been capable of murder?

Ridiculous. He'd been the same age as Brock; they'd all just been kids.

"Seriously, I love the park, too," Nils said, looking at Angie and then flashing a quick smile at Maura. "It's really a pretty place."

"Isn't Florida at sea level? Doesn't it flood?" Angie asked.

Nils looked at Maura again and shrugged. For a moment, he just looked like a nice—and attractive—man. One with a sense of humility—something he had once been lacking.

"Hey, we even have hill country in this area. But honestly, I don't know. It's a sinkhole. It has something to do with the earth's limestone crust or whatever. Geology was never my forte. Hey, we really do have hills in the state—not just giant Mount Trashmores, as we call them. And we have incredible caverns and all kinds of things. Most tourists just want warm water and the beaches, but it's a peninsula with all kinds of cool stuff. I'll find a ghost there for you if you want!"

Angie laughed and even Maura smiled.

"Great—we'll set it up," Angie said.

Maura quickly stood. "Meet you by the pool," she told Angie.

She clutched her computer and ran up both flights of stairs to her room. Housekeeping had already been into her room, she saw.

It seemed so pristine now. Cold.

Maybe just because Brock was no longer there.

She shook her head, impatient with herself. And for a moment, she paused. Being with him again had been so easy, so wonderful, so…perfect.

And she was, perhaps, wrong to dwell so much on one night. Things had torn them apart before.

She was suddenly afraid that events might just tear them apart again.

"WHEN REMAINS ARE down to what we have here," Dr. Rita Morgan told them, "it's almost impossible to pinpoint death to months, much less days and weeks. The bones were found just south of the Devil's Millhopper, as you know, deep in a pine forest. The area was just outside a clearing where the Scouts set up often, but not in the clearing, and it was only because a boy went out in the middle of the night to avail himself of a tree—no facilities out there, camping is rugged—that he came across them. Of course, the kid screamed and went running back for his leader or one of the dads along on the trip, and the dad called the police and… Well, here we are. The bones were scattered and we're still missing a few. I believe that all kinds of creatures have been gnawing upon them, but…there are marks—here, there—" she pointed to her findings "—that were not made by teeth. This young woman—we did find the pelvis, so we can say she was female—was stabbed to death. Oh, these are rib bones I'm showing you with the knife marks. I guess you figured that."

Brock nodded, as did Michael Flannery and Rachel Lawrence.

They were all familiar with the human skeletal system.

"But you think that she was killed sometime in the last year?" Brock asked.

"The integrity of the bone suggests a year—and a few teeth were left in the skull," Dr. Morgan explained. "I'm going to say that she was killed sometime between six and twelve months ago. She was most probably buried in a very shallow grave in an area where the constant moisture and soil composition would have caused very quick decay of the soft tissue, and insects and the wildlife would have finished off the rest. We're still missing a femur and a few small bones. And I'm afraid so many teeth are missing I doubt we'll ever be able to make an identification. We can pull DNA from the bones and compare to missing persons, but as you know, that will take some time."

"She's not one of the three recently missing women, though, right? We are talking at least six months?" Brock asked.

"At least six months," Dr. Morgan agreed. She indicated the pile of bones that were all that was left of a young life, shaking her head sadly. "I wish I could tell you more. She was somewhere between the ages of eighteen and thirty, I'd say. Again—the pelvis is intact enough to know that. We'll keep trying—we'll do everything that we can forensically."

They thanked the doctor and left the morgue.

Outside, Michael Flannery spoke up. "I think that whoever killed Francine Renault twelve years ago got a taste for murder—and liked it. I think that whoever it is has been killing all these years. Maybe slowly at first, fewer victims. I'm not a profiler, but I've taken plenty of classes with the FBI—and I'm sure that you have, too. He's speeding up—for years, he was fine killing once a year. Now—or in the last year—he's felt the need becoming greater and greater."

"It is a possibility," Brock said. "Michael, it is possible, too, that whoever killed Francine did so because she was really unlikable and made someone crack—and that these two dead women we've found have nothing to do with Francine's death. And that the kidnappings aren't associated, either."

Rachel shook her head. "You're playing devil's advocate, Brock."

He was. Brock didn't know why—maybe just too much pointed to the Frampton Ranch and Resort, and he didn't really want it to be involved. Despite what had happened, he had a lot of good memories from his time there.

They now had the bones of two women killed within the past year. Three women were still missing. He'd barely had a chance to scratch the surface of what was going on.

"Come on, Brock. I've been chasing this for twelve years," Flannery said. "I did something I came to learn the hard way simply wasn't right—and now I'm chasing the results of my mistake."

"It wasn't your mistake. You weren't high enough on the food chain back then to insist that the case not just remain open, but that it continue to be investigated with intensity," Brock said. "But say your theory is right. If the killer is at large, then the killer hanged Francine and stabbed Peter Moore to death to make it appear like a suicide and provide a fall guy. That may have been where the killer decided stabbing afforded a greater satisfaction than watching someone strangle to death."

"Where they got a taste for blood," Flannery agreed.

"And you think it's someone who was or is still involved with the Frampton ranch," Brock said.

Rachel watched them both. "Honestly, Nils Hartford was a bona fide jerk—but I don't believe he was a killer," she said, though neither of them had accused Nils. "He… I mean, he and I were never going to make it, but we did become friends. When his family lost all their money, he admitted to me that he loved restaurants and he loved the ranch and that he believed Fred might give him a chance. And as to Mark… Mark was just a kid."

"Kids have been known to be lethal," Flannery reminded her.

"Fred Bentley?" Brock asked, looking at Rachel.

"He wasn't a bad guy to work for—and I think he was well liked by the guests. He's still holding on to his position."

"And he'd oversee any laundry sent out by the hotel," Rachel said.

"If not Bentley…and you're right about the Hartford boys…"

"That leaves Donald Glass himself," Brock said.

Donald Glass—who was married. Who, it had been rumored, had been indulging in an affair with Francine Renault.

A man who had acquired quite a reputation for womanizing through the years.

But would a man brilliant enough to have doubled a significant family fortune have been foolish enough to commit murder on his own property—and leave clues that could lead back to him?

"Time to head back," Brock said. "I say we casually interview all of our suspects. Let them in a little on our fear that the three missing women are dead—and that there is, indeed, a serial killer on the loose."

"Can you get someone at your headquarters tracing the movements of our key possible suspects at the ranch?" Flannery asked Brock. "FDLE is good—but your people have the nation covered."

"Of course," Brock said. He hesitated. "I haven't spoken with Glass that much, but he expressed pleasure that we chose his place as a base. Of course, it's possible that such a man thinks of himself as invincible. Above the rest. But still, I'd say there's another major question that needs to be answered."

"What's that?" Flannery asked.

"Where are the missing women? There are no bodies. Of course, it's difficult for police when adults disappear—they have the right to do so, and often they have just gone off. But the woods were searched.

Bodies weren't found. If it's Glass committing these crimes—or someone else at the Frampton property or someone not involved there at all—he might be taking the women somewhere. Keeping them—until he kills them. If we can find that place…maybe we can still save a few lives."

"And maybe we're all barking up the wrong tree," Rachel said. "And if we concentrate too hard in the wrong direction…well, there go our careers."

"We have to put that thought on hold—big thing now is to find the truth and hope that we can find the missing women. Alive," Brock said. "Agreed?"

Rachel winced. "Right, right. Agreed."

"Agreed. Oh, hell, yeah, agreed," Flannery said.

Brock didn't like what he was coming to believe more and more as a certainty.

A killer was thriving at the Frampton Ranch and Resort.

And Maura was there.

A beautiful young woman who had a history with the ranch.

A perfect possible victim.

Ripe for the taking.

Except that he wouldn't allow it. God help him, he'd never allow it.

He had found her again; he would die before he lost her this time.

Chapter Six

Maura and Angie wrapped up at the pool. Out in the back of the main house and nestled by the two wing additions, the pool was surrounded by a redbrick patio. While the many umbrellas and lounge chairs placed about the pool were modern and offered comfort and convenience, the brick that had been set artfully around managed somehow to add a historic touch that made it an exceptional area.

Maura didn't have to appear on camera; she took several videos of the pool itself and then several with Angie and Marie Glass seated together, sipping cold cocktails, with Marie talking about the installation of the pool twenty years earlier and how carefully they had thought about the comfort of their guests.

A young couple had come out while Maura was filming the water with the palms and other foliage in the background. They'd been happy to sign waivers and be part of the video—laughing as they splashed each other in the water.

When Maura's cell rang, she was so absorbed in detail that she almost ignored it—then she remembered that she and Brock had made a pact and quickly excused herself to answer the phone, leaving Angie and Marie to sit together chatting—just enjoying the loveliness of the pool and one another's company. It was evident that Marie did admire Angie very much. The two women almost looked like a pair of sisters or cousins sitting there, chatting away about the adults around them.

Maura turned her back and gave her attention to the call.

Brock sounded tense—he reminded her to stay with Angie and in a group at all times.

"I won't be leaving here," she assured him. "I'm with Angie and Marie. We're going to go film the restaurants and then the library. We'll probably record in Angie's suite. Are you heading back?"

He was, he told her.

She smiled and set her phone down and looked at Angie and Marie, who were watching her, waiting politely for her to finish her call.

"Onward—to the restaurant," she said.

"Perfect. They won't open for lunch for another twenty minutes," Marie said. "We can show all the tables and will let Nils describe some of our special culinary achievements."

"Yes. Perfect," Maura said.

"Oh, yes, that will be wonderful—we'll have the daily specials, and Nils can serve them. First, Maura can take the restaurant empty, and then some of the food—it's going to be great!" Angie said, always enthusiastic.

Angie and Marie went ahead of Maura; she collected her bag and the camera and expressed her appreciation to the young couple again.

They thanked her—they couldn't wait to send their friends to Angie's web channel when the video was posted.

Maura hurried after Marie and Angie.

The restaurant was pristine when they went in—set for lunch with shimmering water glasses and wineglasses and snowy white tablecloths. The old mantel and fireplace and the large paned windows created a charming atmosphere along with all that glitter. Angie did a voice-over while she scanned the restaurant.

Nils stood just behind Maura; that made her uneasy, but she wasn't alone in the restaurant, she was with Marie and Angie, and a dozen cooks and waitstaff lingered just in the kitchen. She knew that she was fine.

She wondered if Nils made her nervous because she did suspect him of something, or…

If she was just nervous because she didn't like anyone at her back.

When Nils touched her on the shoulder, she almost jumped. "Sorry, sorry!" he said quickly. "I don't want to mess this up—if I do something wrong, you'll tell me, right? You'll give me a chance to do it over?"

"Nils, this is digital. We can do things as many times as you want, but I believe what we're trying for is very spontaneous, natural—just an easy appreciation for what the resort offers."

"Okay, okay—thank you, Maura," he said.

She smiled. "Sure."

Marie was going to sit with Angie. Before she could,

there was a tap on the still-locked door. "Let me just tell them we'll open in a few minutes, right at twelve," Nils said.

Angie and Marie took a seat at a circular table for two right by a side window.

But Nils didn't come back alone.

Donald Glass, elegantly dressed in one of his typical suits and tall and dignified—as always—arrived with him.

"I'd thought it would be good if I popped into one of these videos Marie thinks will be such a thing. If you don't mind. Darling," he told Marie, "would you mind? I think I speak about our wine list with the most enthusiasm."

"No, darling, of course, you must sit in," Marie said.

She rose, giving up her seat. "I'd have thought you might want to do the library," she said. "You do love the library so."

He grinned. "Yes, I'm proud of my libraries. But even then…good wine is a passion."

"Okay, dear."

Maura thought that Marie seemed hurt, but she really didn't show anything at all. She smiled graciously, telling Nils, "They'll need the menus and wine lists."

"Already there, Mrs. Glass, already there," Nils said.

"Okay, then," Maura said. "In five, four…" She finished the count silently with her fingers.

"Angie Parsons here, and I'm still at the Frampton Ranch and Resort. After a day at the oh-so-beautiful pool—and before a night at the incredible historic walk—there's nothing like a truly world-class dinner.

And I'm thrilled to be here with Donald Glass, owner of this property and many more, and—perhaps naturally—a magnificent wine connoisseur, as well."

"Thank you so much, Angie. Marie and I are delighted to have you here. I do love wine, and while we have Mr. Fred Bentley, one of finest hotel managers in the state, and Nils Hartford, an extraordinary restaurateur, manning the helm, no wine is purchased or served without my approval." He went on to produce the list, explaining his choices—and certainly saying more in a few words than Maura would ever know, or even understand, about wine.

But the video was perfect on the first take.

Nils came in as they discussed the menu. He spoke about the excellence of their broad range of menu choices. He suggested that Angie enjoy one of their fresh mahi-mahi preparations, and that Donald order the beef Wellington. That way they could indulge in bites of each other's food.

He might have been nervous, but he did perfectly.

"And now we really have to open the restaurant," he said.

Donald Glass smiled and nodded. "No special stops—we run a tight ship. But, of course, that will be fine, right, Maura?"

"That will be fine. I can avoid other tables, not to worry," she said.

But people were excited when they noted that something was going on.

Many had been at the campfire when she had filmed. They wanted to be involved.

As she spoke to other diners pouring in, Maura knew that Marie Glass was watching her. She turned to her.

"Is that okay?" she asked.

"Yes, yes, lovely," Marie said. She glanced back at Donald, chatting away still with Angie at the table.

They were laughing together. Angie was her ever-charming self—flirtatious. She basically couldn't help it. Glass was enamored of her.

Marie looked back at Maura, her eyes impassive. "Indeed, please, if others wish to sign your waivers, it will certainly add on. Hopefully the food will come out quickly for my husband and Miss Parsons, and we'll be moving on. I can lock down the library, though, of course, Donald will want to be on the video then, too, as I suggested earlier."

"Thank you," Maura told her.

Marie was at her side as she chose a table close by to chat with the guests and diners who arrived—wanting to be on video.

She was startled when she accepted the last waiver and Marie spoke.

But not to her…

Not per se.

She spoke out loud, but it was as if she believed that her words were in her mind.

"And I have always vouched for him. Always," she murmured.

"Pardon?" Maura said.

"What? Oh, I'm so sorry, dear. I must be thinking out loud."

She walked away; Maura went to work.

The head chef himself, a new man, but well respected and winner of a cable cook-off show, came out to explain his fusions of herbs and spices with fresh ingredients.

The videos were coming out exceptionally well, Maura thought.

But she couldn't help remembering the way Donald Glass had sat with Angie—and the way Marie reacted to her husband.

BROCK WAS PARKING the car when he received a message from his headquarters. He hadn't contacted Egan. He had gotten in touch with their technical assistance unit and had reported on the remains that had been found, but it was Egan who called.

Egan wanted to know about the body that they had seen that morning; Brock told him their working theory, thinking that Egan might warn them against it.

He didn't.

Then he put Marty Kim, the support analyst who had been doing extra research for Brock's case, on the phone.

"I did some deep dives this morning," Marty told him. "Before coming to the Frampton Ranch and Resort, Nils Hartford was working at a restaurant in Jacksonville, Hatter and Rabbit. Trendy place. He left there for the Frampton resort, but there was a gap between jobs. I found one of the managers willing to talk. Nils resigned—but if he hadn't, he would have been fired. There was a coworker who complained about sexual harassment. Hartford was managing. The young woman was a waitress. She told the owner that she was afraid of Nils Hartford."

"Interesting. And do we know if the waitress is still alive and well?"

"Checking that out now," Marty told him. "I can't find anything much on Mark Hartford. He went to a state university, majored in history and social sciences, came out and went straight to work for Donald Glass."

"Fred Bentley?"

"He's been with Glass for nearly twenty years—at the Frampton Ranch and Resort for fifteen of them. Before that, he was working at a big spread that Glass has in Colorado."

"Anything on Donald Glass himself?"

"Nothing—and volumes. If you believe all the gossip rags, some more reliable than others, Glass has had many affairs through the years. Some of the women kept silent, some of them did not. He has been married to Marie for twenty-five years, and if I were that woman—I'd divorce his ass." Marty was silent for a minute. Then he added quickly, "Sorry, that wasn't terribly professional."

"You're fine. So…he's still playing the dog, eh?"

"One suspected affair he enjoyed was reportedly with Francine Renault. That hit a few of the outlets that speculate on celebrities without using their names—avoiding legal consequences. Over the years, he did pay off several women. One accused him of sexual assault—except, when it came to it, she withdrew all charges. There was a settlement. But most of these are confidential legal matters, and without due process and warrants, I can only go so far."

"Thanks. He's been spending most of his time and effort down at his property in Florida, right?"

"Oh, he travels. London, New York, Colorado and LA. But yes, most of the time he is in Florida. His trips to other properties tend to be weekends, just twice a year or so."

"Does Marie go with him?"

"It seems he does those trips alone. But, of course, paper trails can only lead you so far," Marty reminded him. "I'll keep searching. I'll naturally get back to you if I find anything else that might be pertinent to your investigation."

He'd parked the car. Detectives Flannery and Lawrence had waited for him.

He reported what he'd just learned to them.

Flannery shook his head. "A man with all that Glass has… Could it be possible?"

"We have nothing as yet, so let's not go getting ourselves thrown out of the resort before we have something tangible, okay?" Brock said.

"Of course not," Flannery said, and he looked at Rachel, frowning. "You should try to get some talk time in with Donald Glass," he said.

"Are you pimping me out?" she asked him.

"Never," Flannery said. "But maybe he'll respond more easily to you on many levels."

"You mean that you doubt that he takes me seriously," Rachel said.

"Rachel, Rachel, you have a chip on your shoulder," he told her.

Brock groaned slightly.

Rachel looked at Brock and he shrugged. "You never know."

"Yes, Rachel, I'm pimping you out—whatever works," Flannery told her. "He might still think of you as the teenager who spent summers at the resort, instead of the whip-smart detective you are now. You might catch him off guard."

She grinned. "Okay, just so I know what I'm doing."

"Let's get lunch," Flannery said. "Oh, and feel free to flirt with your old beau, if need be. I'm sure you've got enough wiles to go around."

Rachel paused before they reached the house, looking at Brock. "Maybe Brock could get Maura on that one," she said.

"Maura is a civilian," he said, hoping he hadn't snapped out the words.

"Yes, but..." Rachel hesitated, glancing at Flannery, who nodded. "Everyone around here always had kind of a thing for Maura. I know that I'd be with Nils—and see him look after her longingly, even though she was a summer hire. And I'd see Glass looking at her, too, and I even think that Francine Renault was hard on her because the others seemed so crazy about her. If she could just draw Nils into conversation—with us around, of course, and see where that leads."

"We do remember that we are professionals, that we play by the book," Flannery said. "But come on, Brock, what led you to law enforcement was the knowledge that you had instincts along with drive. What made me follow your career as you moved on was…well, hell, like I said. You obviously have the instincts for it. Sometimes lines get a little blurred. I am not suggesting that we really use Maura—I'm just suggesting that she could help us chat some of these people up—with one of us right there."

Brock stared at the two of them. He didn't agree, and he didn't disagree. He was surprised by Rachel's words, but he'd been mostly oblivious to others back then. He shouldn't have been surprised by Michael Flannery's passion; he'd always known that Flannery was like a dog with a bone on this case.

Brock would never use Maura. Never.

But on the other hand she was in there interacting with all the persons of interest right now.

Twelve years ago, Maura had been with him; he had been with her. No room for doubt, and certainly, they had never thought to mistrust each other.

Now she had grown into an admirable professional—and a courteous and caring human being. And she was with him once again, although he reminded himself that they had been together just a night. There had been no promises. In the end, whether there was or wasn't a future for them didn't matter in the least. She was a civilian, and that was that.

He raised a finger in an unintentional scold. "She's never alone—never, ever, alone with any of them. With Fred Bentley, either of the Hartford brothers or Donald Glass."

"Right," Flannery said.

At his side, Rachel nodded grimly. He turned and they followed him.

"I'm starving," Rachel murmured as they entered the lobby and tempting aromas subtly made their way out and around them from the restaurant.

"Yeah, it's lunchtime," Flannery said.

"I'll join you soon," Brock told them. He headed to the desk; there was a clerk there he hadn't seen before.

"Good afternoon, sir. How can I help you?" he asked.

"You're new," Brock said.

"I am, sir."

"What happened to the young lady who was working?"

"I don't know, sir, and I don't know which young lady you might mean. Mr. Bentley gives us our schedules, sir. I'm doing split shifts, morning and night now, if I can be of assistance."

"Yes, I understand Angie Parsons is doing some filming here at the resort today. Can you direct me to where they're working now?"

"They're in the library, but they don't wish to be disturbed, sir. Sir!"

Brock turned and headed for the library.

"Sir! I shouldn't have told you. They don't want to be disturbed. Please, I have just been hired on—sir!"

Brock paused to turn back. "It's all right. I'm FBI," he said.

His being FBI didn't really mean a damned thing in this scenario. But he felt he had to say something reassuring to the clerk.

He went through the lobby and down the hallway that led to the library, in back of the café.

The door was closed.

There was a sign on it that clearly said Do Not Disturb.

Well, he was disturbed himself, so he was going to do some disturbing. He knocked on the door.

To his surprise, it opened immediately.

Marie Glass stood before him, bringing a finger to her lips. He nodded. She closed the door behind him.

Angie was holding the camera. He had arrived just before they were to begin a segment. While she loved being the director and videographer, Maura was also a natural before the camera. She smiled right into the lens and said that she was in her favorite area of the resort—the library. She was with Donald Glass, who kept the library stocked, not just here, but at all of his properties, and that he bought and developed places specifically because of unique or colorful histories.

"A true taste of life, the good, the bad and the evil," Maura said, smiling.

"Exactly, for such is life, indeed, and history can be nothing less," Glass said.

Maura knew what she was doing; Glass had been interviewed so many times in his rich life that he was apparently well aware of a good ending.

"Cut! Perfect!" Angie said. "Marie, what do you think?"

Marie smiled—her usual smile. One that maintained her dignity—and gave away nothing of her real thoughts. "Excellent. If we can just do an opening at the entry…perhaps have Fred giving the guests a welcome along with Angie." She turned and looked at Brock. "Oh, would you like to appear in a video, Brock? This was once a home away from home for you."

"No, thank you—though I would enjoy watching," he said. He looked at Maura, who was looking at him then, too. He couldn't read what she was thinking, but she had that look in her eyes that indicated there were things she had to say—but to him alone.

He glanced at Marie. "Not sure my bosses now would like it," he explained.

"Well, we can finish up then," Marie said. "Donald, dear, would you like to find Fred? He has been our general manager now for over fifteen years. He should be shown greeting Angie."

"Good thinking, my dear," Glass told his wife. "Meet you out front."

Donald left. Brock smiled, excused himself and hurried after Glass.

"Sir!"

Glass stopped and turned around with surprise. "Oh, Brock, yes, what can I do for you?" He frowned. "Have you learned anything? I caught a 'breaking news flash' about thirty minutes ago. More remains have been discovered, but those over south of Gainesville. It wasn't… Did they find one of the missing girls?"

He seemed truly concerned.

"No, sir. Whoever they found has been missing much longer. They don't have an ID yet."

"You never know if that's true, or if it's what the media was told to say."

"It's true. They have no identity on the remains yet. Indulge my concern for a moment—there was a young woman working at the front desk here. She might have been just on nights, and I may be a bit overly cautious, but I noticed you have a new hire on the desk."

"We do?"

He appeared genuinely surprised. "You'd have to ask Fred about that. I must admit, I don't concern myself much with the clerks. I worry more about the restaurants and our entertainment staff. But Fred will be able to tell you."

"Thank you."

"Have you seen Fred?"

"No, I haven't, but—"

"He's probably at lunch. I'll take a look in the restaurant. Excuse me."

Brock watched him as he went on by. The man was polite to him—always had been. But he couldn't imagine that dozens of reports were all false—the man evidently had an eye for women and an appetite for affairs.

Did he leave for tours of his other properties because he just needed to work alone, or because he needed space for casual affairs?

Or maybe he didn't really leave every time he said that he was doing so, or go exactly when and where he said that he was going.

Power and money.

Maybe Glass lured young women with those assets.

Brock hurried out front.

Maura wasn't alone. She was with Marie Glass and Angie, and they were standing in broad daylight.

He was still anxious to be with her.

More anxious to hear what it was she might have to say to him alone.

IT WASN'T THAT her work was hard, but Maura was weary—ready to be done.

Most of the videos had gone very smoothly.

Angie spoke spontaneously, and they had needed no more than three takes on any one scene that day. Maura had known what she'd wanted to say—she truly loved any library, especially one as focused and unique as the library at the Frampton Ranch and Resort.

And still, she was tired.

The idea made her smile. She was happy to be tired—because she was happy that she hadn't spent much of the previous night sleeping.

She didn't want to be overly tired that night, though!

Brock appeared on the steps of the porch before Donald Glass got there. He had an easy smile as he joined them and waited for Donald to appear with Fred Bentley.

"The Devil's Millhopper! Sounds like a place I have to see!" Angie said, smiling and looking at Brock.

He shrugged. "It's geographically fascinating—and has great displays on how our earth is always changing, how the elements and organic matter often combine to make things like sinkholes and other phenomena work. Sure—I love it out there." He laughed. "I love our mermaids, too. Weeki Wachee Springs and

Weeki Wachee State Park. Absolutely beautiful—crystal clear water."

"Mermaids, eh?"

"Mermaids," he agreed politely and turned away; Glass was coming down the steps with Bentley. The stocky manager was beaming.

"I get to be in a video!" he announced.

"You do," Angie said.

"With the famous Angie Parsons," Fred said. He paused, frowning. "Or with our beautiful Maura—which is fine, too. Love our beautiful Maura."

Maura smiled. "No, sir—thank you for the compliment. You get to be with our famous and beautiful Angie."

"What do I say?" Fred asked.

Maura already knew exactly where she wanted them to stand for the afternoon light—and how she wanted them walking up the steps to the porch and the entry for the finale of the little segment.

"If you could give a welcome to the Frampton Ranch and Resort—and tell us how you've been here for fifteen years," Maura said. "Naturally, in your own words, and you can add in any bit of history you like."

She probably should have expected that something would go badly.

First, Fred froze and mumbled.

Maura smiled and coaxed him.

Then he went blank.

Then he forgot to follow Angie up the stairs at the end.

He apologized and said that he should be fired—from the video, not the property. He tried to laugh.

Maura encouraged him one more time, and they were able to get a decent video.

Brock stood nearby through the whole painful process, as did Donald and Marie. The owners—the married pair—did not stand next to each other.

Nor did they speak with each other.

And when they were done, Marie thanked Angie and Maura, bade the others good-afternoon and said that she was heading out for some shopping.

Donald thanked everyone and said that he'd be in his office.

Fred thanked Angie—then Maura.

"I was horrible. You fixed me. I guess that's what a good director does. Anyway, back to work for me. See you."

He lifted a hand and started up the steps.

"Fred," Brock said, calling him back.

"Yeah?"

"I noticed you have a new hire on the front desk."

"I do," Fred Bentley told him. "Remember when I was night clerk—well, I don't like being night clerk. Heidi didn't show up at all—and didn't call with an excuse. That's grounds for dismissal, and everyone knows it, so I left a message telling her not to come back."

"You never spoke with her?" Brock asked.

Bentley frowned. "No, I got her voice mail. She must have heard it. She never came back in."

"What's Heidi's last name and where does she live?"

"Heidi Juniper. She lives between here and Gainesville," Bentley told him. His frown deepened. "You don't think that—"

"I'll need her address and contact information," Brock said. "We'll just make sure that Heidi is irresponsible—and not among the missing."

"Of course, of course, I'll get it for you right away," Bentley told him.

When Fred was gone, Angie turned to Brock, repeating Bentley's concern. "You don't really think—"

"I don't know. I think we'll just check on her, that's all," Brock said. He looked at the two of them. "Lunch?"

"Are they still serving lunch?" Maura asked. "They do close for an hour, I think, between lunch and dinner."

"I bet they'll serve us," Angie said. She smiled broadly. "Oh, I do love it when people feel that they owe you."

She started up the steps. Maura was glad; she wanted a few minutes with Brock alone.

She believed that she'd have all night, but she needed a moment now.

But Angie stopped, looked back and sighed impatiently. "Come on! Let's not push our luck too hard, okay? I want them to keep owing me."

She was waiting.

No chance to talk.

Maura started up the stairs to the porch, grateful, at least, that Brock was with her.

Grateful, in fact, that he was simply in the world—and in her part of the world once again.

Chapter Seven

Brock saw that Michael Flannery and Rachel Lawrence were still in the restaurant when he arrived—they had taken a four top, expecting him to join them.

They hadn't expected Maura and Angie, but Michael quickly grabbed another chair and beckoned them all on over.

Angie was happy to greet them both, offering to film some of the campfire fun again with them in it. She hadn't quite figured out that law enforcement officers didn't often want their faces on video that went around to the masses—especially when they worked in plain clothes.

Both politely turned her down.

"I feel like a terrible person," Angie said. "I mean, I'd seen the news. I knew that women had been kidnapped and one had been found dead…or her remains had been found. I just didn't associate it with worrying about the central and northern areas of Florida. And the state has a huge population… Not that having a huge population makes terrible things any better, but statistically, they are bound to happen. I had no idea that the FBI and the FDLE would be staked out at the resort. But I can't tell you how glad I am. Though we did finish here today. And we went to St. Augustine yesterday. I want to see this Devil's Millhopper—the big sinkhole. But I'm not sure if Nils can go right away, and he did say that he wanted to."

Nils must have been close; as if summoned, he was suddenly behind Angie's chair. "While you're waiting to go to the Devil's Millhopper, there's some other cool stuff for Maura's cameras not far from here. Cassadaga—it's a spiritualist community, and the hotel there and a few other areas are said to be haunted. There's a tavern in Rockledge that's haunted, a theater in Tampa… It goes on and on. We can find you all manner of places."

"You need permits for some of them, advance arrangements and all," Maura reminded him.

Nils grinned. "Well, there's more here, too. Hey, I know what we have—and near here! Caves. Yes, believe it or not, bunches of caves in Florida. Up in Marianna, but closer to us—not really far at all—Dames Cave. It's in Withlacoochee State Park, but…outside the state park, on the city edge, there's an area that's not part of any park system. Not sure who owns the land but you can trek through that area and find all kinds of caves."

Maura glanced at Brock; he knew from that look that she definitely didn't want to go off exploring caves alone with Angie.

"Caves! Cool—haunted caves? Weird caves?" Angie asked.

"Oh, yes, there's an area called Satan's Playground. Not in a state park, and not official in any way. I know that Maura and Brock know it—they used to love to go off exploring when they were working here and they had a day off," Nils said. He smiled at Angie. "I'd truly love to explore the Devil's Millhopper with you, if you don't mind waiting."

Angie leaned toward him, smiling. "I don't mind at all. We'd intended to spend several days here."

Nils nodded, apparently smitten; they might have been a match made in heaven.

"Well, hey, Nils, can we still get lunch?" Maura asked.

"No," he said. "But yes, for you. Order quickly, if you don't mind. Chef saw you come in and he said that you're going to help make him more famous, so he'll wait. But he did have a few hours off before dinner, so..."

"I ate," Angie said, smiling. "Two of Chef's lunches would be great, but I just don't think I could manage to eat a second. I suggest the mahi-mahi."

Brock looked at Nils and then Maura. "Two hamburgers?" he asked.

Rachel cast Nils a weary gaze. "Mike and I had the hamburger plate. Chef makes a great hamburger."

"Yes, hamburgers sound good," Maura said.

"Done deal," Nils told them.

When he had walked away, Flannery leaned toward Angie. "I know how important your books and your videos are to you, but for the time being, please don't go off to lonely places on your own."

"I would never go on my own," Angie said.

"Good," Rachel murmured.

"I wouldn't be alone. Maura would be with me," Angie said. She turned to watch Nils. The chef had come out of the kitchen and they were speaking.

"Good-looking man," she murmured.

"So he is. Many women think so," Rachel said, studying something on her hand. "Anyway, the point is..."

"Don't go off anywhere alone as just two young women," Flannery said.

Angie smiled at him. "Detective Flannery, did you want to come along with us? Brock? It could be fun."

"Actually, if you want to see the caves, sure," Brock said.

Maura stared at him, surprised. She quickly looked away.

She knew that if he wanted to head out to the caves, there had to be a reason. And yes, he did have a reason.

Remains had been found not far from the caves.

And there were areas where more remains might be found, or where, with any piece of luck, the living just might be found, as well.

"Nice!" Angie said. "Great—it will be a date. Well, a weird threesome date," she added, giggling. "Unless, of course, Detective Flannery, Detective Lawrence, you two could make it?"

"We're working," Rachel reminded her sharply.

"Yes, of course," Angie said.

"And," Rachel added, "we don't want to be picking up your remains, you know."

Angie stared back at her, smiling sweetly. "Not to worry on my account. Brock will be with us, and when we go to the Devil's Millhopper, we'll be with Nils. Anyway! If you all will excuse me, I just popped in for a few minutes of the great company. We did such a good job with the video this morning that I'm dying to get into the pool."

She stood, motioning that Brock and Flannery didn't need to stand to see her go. "If you take work breaks other than food, join me when you're done."

Angie left them. When she was gone, Rachel stared at Maura.

"You *like* working with her?" Rachel asked.

"She's usually just optimistic about everything," Maura said. "And I guess she has that same feeling that most of us do, most of the time—it can't happen to me."

"Until it does," Brock murmured.

Maura glanced at Brock uncertainly. She had things to say that she hadn't been about to say in front of Angie.

"What is it?" Brock asked her. "We're working a joint investigation here—Rachel and Mike and I are on the same team."

"You want to go to the caves—really?" she asked.

She hoped he would just tell her the truth. "I want to go out to the area south of the Devil's Millhopper we talked about before. The remains today were found between the Millhopper and the caves. I think it might be a good thing to explore around there some more, though it could so easily be a futile effort," Brock told her. "People tend to think of Florida with the lights and fantasy of the beaches—people everywhere. There are really vast wildernesses up here. Remains could be… anywhere."

"It's so frustrating. Nothing makes sense, and maybe we're just creating a theory that we want to be true because we don't want more dead women, and we're all a little broken by Francine's murder. Maybe these cases are all different," Rachel said, looking over at Flannery. "One set of remains in a laundry, another in a forest where a Scout had to trip over them trying to pee. The one suggests a killer who wants to hide his victims. The other suggests a killer who likes attention and wanted to create a display. I mean, it's the saddest thing in the world, the way these last remains were discovered, by a kid…out on his night toilet rounds. Oh, sorry—you guys didn't get your food yet."

Brock waved a hand in the air and Maura smiled, looking down. She hadn't been offended.

But their hamburgers had arrived. And it wasn't how the remains had been discovered that was so disturbing—it was simply that now a second set had been found.

Rachel was looking at Brock with curiosity. "Do you think that the killer could be hiding kidnap victims in a cave or a cavern? Wouldn't that be too dangerous?"

"The better-known tourist caverns?" Brock asked. "Yes. The lesser-known caverns that are just kind of randomly outside the scope of the parks? Maybe. I don't know. He'd keeping them somewhere for days, maybe even weeks. Then there are also hundreds of thousands of warehouses, abandoned factories, paper mills..." He broke off. "I just know that there are three missing women somewhere, and I'd sure as hell like to find them while they're still just missing."

"And not dead," Flannery said grimly. He turned slightly, looking at Maura. "Do you remember anything, anything at all, from back then that might suggest anyone as being...guilty? Of killing Francine Renault."

Maura shook her head, then hesitated, glancing at Brock. He nodded slightly, and she said, "I was stunned—completely shocked—when we came upon Francine's body. When the news came out that Peter Moore had killed himself, I was already far away, and we were young and... I didn't know what else to believe. I—I was exploring on the internet today, though, and came across something that might—or might not—have bearing on this. It's a bit strange, so stick with me. There was a society in this area, decades ago, called the Sons of Supreme Being. They were suspected of the disappearance and possible death of a woman in the 1950s. That's why it struck me as maybe relevant. One of their members was supposed to testify in court—he died before he could. Now, I got this information from a random site—I haven't verified it in any way, but..."

Brock looked over at Flannery. "Have you ever heard anything about this group—this Sons of Supreme Being society or club or whatever?"

Flannery shook his head and then frowned. "Maybe, yes, years ago. I'm not sure I remember the name... When I joined the force, some of the old-timers were wondering during a murder investigation if the group might have raised its head again—a girl had been found in a creek off the Saint Johns River. She was in sad shape, as if she'd been used and tossed about like trash. But her murderer was caught—and eventually executed. Talk of rich kids picking up the throwaways died down. But as far as I know, nothing like that has been going on."

Maura was still looking at Brock.

"You have something else," he said.

She nodded and lowered her voice. "I don't think that Marie Glass realized that she was standing by me or that she was speaking aloud, but…she was watching her husband with Angie. And she said something to the effect that she shouldn't…cover for him. And she acted as if she hadn't said anything at all when she caught me looking at her. But in all fairness… Glass has always been decent to the people who worked for him, even if…"

"He's paid off a number of women through the years," Rachel said. "He was always decent to me. But there were rumors about him and Francine."

Glancing over at Maura, Brock said, "I want to find out if a young lady named Heidi Juniper is all right."

"Heidi Juniper?" Flannery asked him.

"She was working here. She didn't show up and Bentley left her a message that she was fired. He's supposed to be getting me contact information for her. Under the circumstances, I think it's important to know why Heidi didn't show up for work."

They had all finished eating. Flannery stood first. "Rachel and I will get to work finding out about Heidi

Juniper. I was thinking you might want to talk to your old friends Donald and Marie Glass."

"Hardly my old friends," Brock said.

"I'm going to go to the library," Maura said. She paused, looking at them all. "It really wouldn't make sense. Donald Glass may be a philandering jerk, since he is a married man. But he is so complete with his libraries, with his campfire stories…he included Francine's murder in the collection. Would he be so open if he was hiding something?"

"Being so open may be the best way of hiding things," Flannery said. He hesitated, glancing from Brock to Maura.

"Young lady, you are a civilian. You be careful."

"Not many people think that reading in a library is living on the edge," she said, smiling. "Brock will be near, and reading is what a civilian might do to help."

"We thank you," Flannery said. "Rachel…"

She rose and the two of them headed out.

"I'm going to the library with you," Brock told Maura.

"But I thought you wanted to speak with Marie and Donald," she said.

"What do you want to bet that they both show up while we're there—separately, but…"

"You're on," she said softly, standing.

MAURA KNEW WHAT she was looking for—anything that mentioned the Sons of Supreme Being. She delved into the scrapbooks that held newspaper clippings through the decades, aiming for the 1950s. Brock was across the room, seated in one of the big easy chairs, reading a book on the different Native American tribes who had inhabited the area. It was oddly comfortable to be there with him, even though she did find her mind wandering now and then, wishing that they could forget it all—and go far from here, someplace with warm ocean breezes and hours upon hours to lie together, doing nothing but breathing in salt air and each other.

Gritting her teeth, she concentrated on her research.

After going through two of the scrapbooks that went through the 1950s, she came upon what she was seeking.

The first article was on the disappearance.

In 1953, Chrissie Barnhart, a college freshman, had disappeared. She had last been seen leaving the school library. Friends had expected her to meet up with them at the college coffee shop to attend a musical event.

She had not returned to her room.

There was a picture of Chrissie; she had been light haired and bright eyed with soft bangs and feathery tresses that surrounded her face.

The next article picked up ten days later.

In a college dorm, a young man had awakened to hear his roommate tossing and turning and mumbling aloud, apparently in the grips of a nightmare. Before he had wakened his friend, he had heard him saying, "I didn't know we were going to kill her. I didn't know we were going to kill her."

The event was reported to the police and an officer brought the student who had the nightmare in for questioning; his name had been Alfred Mansfield. At first,

Mansfield had denied doing anything wrong. He'd had a nightmare, nothing more. But the police had put the fear of God into him, and in exchange for immunity, he had told them about a society called the Sons of Supreme Being. Their fathers had been supportive of Hitler's rise to power in Germany. After the war, they had made their existence a very dark secret. Only the truly elite were asked to join—elite, apparently, being the very rich.

Alfred Mansfield hadn't known who he had been with, but he was certain he could help bring those who had killed Chrissie to justice. He had simply accepted a flattering invitation, donned the garments sent to him late one night and joined with a small group, also clad in Klan-like masks, in the clearing.

All were anonymous—but he thought that their leader might have been Martin Smith, the son of a wealthy industrialist.

They hadn't killed Chrissie on the day she had been taken; Alfred didn't know where she had been kept. He only knew that he was in the clearing with the double tree when she had been dragged out, naked and screaming, and that the leader had spoken to the group about their need to make America great with the honor of those who rose above the others; to that end, they sacrificed.

Alfred had tried not to weep as he watched what was done to her and how she died. He didn't want to be supreme in any way. He wanted to forget what had happened.

He wanted the nightmares to stop.

He would serve as an informant for the police.

He was released, both he and the police believing that they had taken him in for questioning quietly and that he was safe out in the world. He'd done the right thing by letting the police know, and they would take it from there.

Alfred's body had been dragged out of the Saint Johns River twenty-four hours after his release. He had been repeatedly stabbed before being thrown into the water to drown.

The body of Chrissie Barnhart had never been found.

Maura turned a page to see an artist's rendering of Alfred's description of the murder of the young woman.

She gasped aloud.

It was a sketch created by a police artist. But it might have been the clearing by the History Tree, looking almost exactly as it did today.

Minus the masked men.

And the naked, screaming woman, appropriately hidden behind the sweeping cloaks of the men.

"Brock… Brock…"

Maura said his name, beckoning to him, only to hear him clear his throat.

She spun around. As they had both expected to happen, a Glass had come into the room.

Marie. Brock had risen and was blocking the path between Maura and Marie.

"Mrs. Glass," Maura said, rising. She felt guilty for some reason—and she must have looked guilty. Of something. She quickly smiled and made her voice anxious as she asked, "Did we miss something? I know that Angie will be more than happy to start up again with anything else you'd like."

"Oh, no, dear, I think we did a great job today. I just heard that someone was in the library—I should have known that it was you two! My bookworms. Still, in my memory, the best young people we ever hired for our summer program," Marie said.

"Thank you," Maura said.

Marie was looking at Brock. "Such a shame," she said. "And I'm so sorry. What happened… Well, the mistake cost all of us, I'm afraid."

She did appear as if the memory caused her a great deal of pain.

"Marie, it's long over, in the past—and as far as things went, my life hardly had a ripple," Brock told her. Maura looked at him; he was so much taller than Marie that she could clearly see his face. His look might as well have been words.

She'd been much more than a ripple; losing her had been everything.

She lowered her head quickly, not wanting Marie to see her smile.

"It wasn't your fault," Maura assured her.

Marie was silent for a minute, and then said, "Maybe, maybe I could have… Um, I'm sorry. I didn't mean to disturb you. Get back to it—I have to…have to…do something. Excuse me."

She fled from the library.

"See?" Maura whispered to Brock. "See? There's something bothering her. She has, I think, been telling law enforcement that Donald was with her—*when he wasn't*. Brock, you have to come read this. Donald Glass didn't go to school here, but…if there was ever a candidate for the Sons of Supreme Being, he is one! Do you think that he could be resurrecting some old ideal? And look—look at the police sketch. Well, you have to read!"

Brock sat down where she had been. She set a hand on his shoulder, waiting while he went quickly through the clippings.

He was silent as he studied the pictures.

He turned back to her, rising, and as he did so, his phone began to ring. He pulled it from his pocket, glanced at the ID and answered. "Flannery. What did you find?"

His face seemed to grow dark as he listened. Then he hung up and looked at her.

"What is it?" she asked.

"I think we have another missing woman. Which frightens me. I just don't know how many this killer of ours keeps alive at one time."

"I'll be fine. I'll stay right next to Angie—and the group. We saw Mark Hartford in the hallway—he said that he had twenty people signed up for tonight. Oh, yeah—and Detectives Flannery and Lawrence are staying behind," Maura told Brock.

"I wish you'd just lock yourself in this room until I got back," he said, smoothing his fingers through her hair.

They hadn't slept; they weren't waking up. But they

were in bed, and he was still in love with her face on the pillow next to his.

They'd left the library, making plans. But while talking, they'd headed across the lobby, to the elevator, up to her room.

And then talking had stopped, and they were kissing madly, tearing at each other's clothing, falling onto the bed, kissing each other's bodies frantically—very much like a pair of teenagers again, exploring their searing infatuation.

"Reminds me of staff bunk, Wing Room 11," she had told him breathlessly, her eyes on his as they came together at last, as he thrust into her, feeling again as he had then, as if he had found the greatest high in the world, as if nothing would ever again be as it was being with her, in her, feeling her touch and looking into her eyes.

And it never had been.

"I wonder if Mr. and Mrs. Glass ever knew how much the staff appreciated the staff room?" he'd asked later when, damp, cooling and breathing normally again, they had lain together, just touching.

Their current conversation had started with, "We have to get up. You have to go and see Heidi's family, and I'm taking my camera out for the campfire and ghost walk again."

"No. You're locking yourself in this room."

"No, that would be ridiculous. I'll be with about two dozen witnesses. No one would try anything."

The argument had been done; she did have logic in

her favor. And so they dressed, reluctant to part, knowing that they must.

The evening had been decided.

Brock hesitated. "Do you think that Angie knows we're together again?"

"Probably, but..."

"But?"

"I'm not so sure she'd care. Angie is—Angie. Unabashed. Men are dogs—adorable dogs, and she loves them. But one of her great sayings is that if men are dogs, women definitely get to be bitches."

He frowned, thinking about Angie's behavior at lunch. "Does she know anything about Rachel and Nils having once been hot and heavy?"

"I don't think so. Why would she? She wasn't around way back then. Angie does like Nils. She likes you better, but..."

"I'm spoken for?"

"She might actually think that you're more interested in me—and that wouldn't sit well with her ego. She did tell me that if I wasn't interested, she'd move in."

He laughed. "Well, honesty is a beautiful thing."

"It can be—it can be awkward, too," Maura assured him. "So, are you leaving?"

"Not until I see you gathered with a large group of guests and Angie to head out to the campfire."

"Okay, then, we should go down."

He opened the door for her. They headed for the lobby. It was busy—people were gathering. One was a family, including a mom and a dad and three children:

older boys and a girl of about five. The couple from the pool was going to be at the campfire that night; they greeted Maura warmly. A few people seemed to be alone. There were two more families, one with a little girl, one with twin boys who appeared to be about fourteen.

Angie was there already, chatting with Mark.

"Hey—are you coming out tonight?" Mark asked Brock. He seemed pleased with the prospect.

"No, duty calls," Brock said. "But hopefully I'll catch up by the end."

"You have to go?" Angie asked.

"I do."

"You can't send that other cop?"

"No—because Mike Flannery and Rachel Lawrence are coming here tonight. Rachel knows all about the campfire and the walk and the stories, but Mike has never had a chance to go. And there are things I like to do myself," Brock said.

"Ah, yeah, every guy thinks he's got to do everything himself," Angie said.

"Just on this. Mike and Rachel have really been taking on the brunt of the load. My turn for an initial investigation," he said pleasantly.

He saw that Mike and Rachel had arrived.

"I'll just have a word with Mike—maybe I'll see you later."

He walked over to join Flannery and Rachel, aware that they'd be heading to the campfire any minute.

"Thanks for doing the interview tonight," Flannery

said. "Really. I know you don't want to leave. I swear, we'll watch her like a pair of parental lions."

"I think male lions just lie around," Rachel said.

"I'll be a good male lion," Flannery said. "I feel that I do need to do this. Everyone really knows the stories and the tree—or trees—but me."

Brock didn't want to admit that he really wanted to interview Heidi's parents himself; there were often little things that could be said but lost in retelling. It was always better to have several interviews with family, witnesses and more. And he did owe this one to Mike.

"I'll be back as soon as possible," Brock told them.

"And really, we don't know that you need to be worried."

"I don't know. Glass is looking like a more viable suspect all the time," Brock said.

"Glass won't be out here. No need to fear," Rachel said. "And I may be small, but trust me—I am one fierce lioness."

Brock smiled. "I know," he told her.

He turned. Mark Hartford was deep in conversation with Maura. She wasn't looking Brock's way—she was listening.

He turned and headed out to the parking lot and his car. He knew he couldn't be ridiculous—he'd never keep his job that way.

It was a twenty-minute drive east to Heidi's home in a quiet neighborhood just south of St. Augustine. He noted that the girl lived in a gated estate.

The houses were about twenty years old and reflected an upper-working-class and family atmosphere.

Heidi's parents were eagerly waiting for him. Her mother, Eileen, a slim woman with curly gray hair and dark, tearstained eyes—was frantic. Heidi's father, Carl, bald and equally slim, kept trying to calm her.

"The police didn't even want to start a report until today—they said that she hadn't really been missing. I know my daughter—when she says she's coming home, she's coming home!" Eileen said and started to cry.

"When was the last time you spoke with her?" Brock asked gently.

"She was at work. She said she was leaving soon. It was right at the end of her shift—for that day. Shifts could change, and she didn't care at all. She sometimes worked double shifts, but she said that she wasn't going to work double that day. She was tired. She was coming home. But she never arrived. I waited up. I woke Carl. We drove all up and down the highway. I mean, nothing happened to her here—our community is very secure."

"Did you call her work—talk to anyone there?"

"Some man answered the phone—he just sounded irate. He said that they weren't a babysitting service and she wasn't even with the summer program. That she probably ran off with some friends!"

"You don't know the man's name?"

"He just answered the phone, 'Front desk, how can I help you?'" Eileen said.

"Rude. If I'd known how rude… You'll investigate, right? The detective who called us—Flannery—he was the first one who seemed concerned," Carl said.

Brock nodded. "We'll take this very seriously, I swear," he assured them, taking Eileen's folded hands.

"This is important. Did she say anything else? Had she been having any trouble with anyone there? Had any of the other employees or guests been ugly to her—or come on to her inappropriately?"

"She loved her job," Carl said. "Loved it." He looked at his wife. "She said that Mr. Glass was nice, but she hardly saw him. Or Mrs. Glass. Fred Bentley was her supervisor, and he seemed to be fine. She said he was a stickler for time and the rules, but she was always on time, and she never broke the rules, so they got on fine. Oh, she loved the guy who was like a social director—and she was welcome to use the pool and the gym and go on the walks—as long as she wasn't disturbing or taking anything away from the guests. There wasn't anything she told you that she wouldn't have told me, right?" Carl asked his wife. "As far as I know, she simply loved her job."

"Yes, she did," Eileen agreed. "But…"

She frowned and broke off.

"Please, tell me what you're thinking," Brock said. "Even if it seems unimportant."

Eileen's frown deepened as she exhaled a long sigh before speaking. "Something odd… She was muttering beneath her breath. She said…"

"Yes?"

"Well, I think… I'm not even sure I heard her right. The last time I talked to her on the phone—before she left work and disappeared—she said something like… 'Supreme Being, my ass!' Yes, that was what she was muttering. I didn't pay that much attention—I thought she was talking about a guest—someone acting all superior. I didn't think much of it—people can act that way, when they think they're superior to those who are working. And my daughter would deal with it—and mutter beneath her breath. Yes. I'm almost positive, and honestly, I'm not sure what it can mean, if anything, but… Yes. She murmured, 'Supreme Being, my ass.'"

Chapter Eight

"The beautiful Gyselle," Mark Hartford said, "is sometimes seen in the woods near the History Tree. Running from it. A ghost forced to live where she saw the end of her life. Or, as a spirit, does she remember better times? Is she running to the tree—where she would meet her lover and dream of the things that might have been in life?"

He told the tales well, Maura thought. And even after they had finished at the campfire, he spoke as they moved along the trails into the woods, and finally, to the History Tree.

Mark had asked her to speak twice and she'd obliged; she'd had the camera rolling again, too—she might as well since they were out there. Angie could decide later which night's footage she liked best.

Maura noted with a bit of humor that Mike and Rachel were being true to whatever promises they had certainly given Brock—they hadn't been ten full feet away from her all night.

But at the tree, she found that she wanted it on video

from every angle. She kept picturing the police artist's rendering she had seen that day.

Creepy figures surrounding the tree, unidentifiable. The victim from the 1950s, Chrissie, caught in the arms of one of her attackers.

Were the current victims being held—as she had been held? And if so, how in the hell were they being hidden so well…until their remains were left to rot in the elements?

"You are getting carried away," Angie whispered to her.

"Just a little," Maura agreed.

"Questions—anything else?" Mark asked his group pleasantly.

Maura wondered if she should or shouldn't speak, but her mouth opened before her mind really worked through the thought.

"Yes, hey, Mark, have you ever heard of a group called the Sons of Supreme Being?" she asked.

He looked at her, a brow arching slowly.

His entire tour group had gone silent, all curious at her question.

"Yeah," he said. "I—yeah. I thought it was kind of a rumored thing." He lifted a hand. "No facts here, folks, just stuff I heard at college. They say they existed once. They were a pack of snobs—thought they were better than anyone else. They were never sanctioned by any of the state schools—in fact, I heard you got your butt kicked out if you were suspected of being one of them. They were like an early Nazi-supporter group—seemed they watched what Hitler was doing in the 1930s. But, hey, nothing like that exists now, trust me!" He grinned at his crowd. "I'm a people person. Someone would have told me. Where did you hear about them?"

"Oh, I read something," Maura said. "I was just curious if it had been real or not."

"I can't guarantee it, but I heard that they did exist. No one I know has anything on who the members might have been or anything like that," Mark told her. "Although I did hear that while the rumors of the group started in the 1930s, it really went further back—like way, way back. It was the rich elite even in the 1850s—dudes who came to Florida from the north and all, and built plantations and homes and ranches after Florida became a territory and then a state. They considered themselves to be above everyone else—everyone! If you ask me—a theory I've never spoken aloud before—I have a feeling that Gyselle's death might have been helped along by members—even way back then. Those dudes would have thought that this tree was a sacred spot. And Julie Frampton could have easily whispered into someone's ear. Gotten them to do the deed."

"There is an idea for you," Maura murmured. "Thanks, Mark."

She felt Detective Flannery take a step closer to her.

"Okay, time to head on back, folks. No stragglers—no stragglers. We don't know what's up, but we're asking people to stay close." Mark pointed to the way out.

His group obediently headed back along the trail.

As they came out of the woods, she saw that Brock

was walking from the parking lot toward them. "Brock!" Angie called. "You missed new stuff—the beautiful Gyselle might have been killed by a secret society. Wild, huh?"

Brock frowned and glanced past her at Maura, Mike and Rachel.

"I asked Mark if he'd ever heard of the group," Maura said.

"Oh," he said. "Well, you got something new and fresh on a tour. Great."

He wasn't going to talk, not there, not then—not with others around them. She thought, too, that he seemed tense.

Maybe even with her.

Because, perhaps, she shouldn't have spoken.

But the day was done at last; she wanted nothing more than to get back and close out the world—except for Brock.

She knew that he'd meet first with Mike and Rachel. And, she knew, he'd probably had a rough last few hours—talking to the parents of another girl who had disappeared.

She yawned. "Long, long day—I'm going up to bed," she said. "Angie, we can head out to those caverns tomorrow—at least, I think we can. Brock, can you take the time?"

"Yes. In fact, I think that maybe Detectives Flannery and Lawrence can join us."

Flannery might have been taken by surprise; if so, he didn't show it.

"Yes, we'll all go. Search those woods—close to where the last remains were discovered. You okay with that, Angie?"

"You bet—that will be perfect. Oh, I do hope we find something!" she said enthusiastically. "Oh, lord, that sounded terrible. Terrible. I mean, I didn't mean it that way. Except, of course, it would be cool to find a lair, a hideout—save someone!"

"That would be something exceptional," Maura said, looking at Brock. He still seemed disturbed. "So," she added, "Angie, an excursion tomorrow means you have to wake up fairly early."

"Oh, I will, I will. Meet in the coffee shop at 8:30 a.m.?" she asked.

"Sounds good," Brock said.

"Adventure day—nice break," Rachel murmured.

"You're really going to be there at eight thirty?" Maura asked skeptically.

"Ah, and I even have plans tonight! But yes, I'll be there," Angie said.

"You have plans tonight?" Brock asked her.

"Not to worry—I'm not leaving the property. I'm just meeting up with a new friend in the coffee shop—or not the actual coffee shop, you know, the little kiosk part that stays open 24/7. We'll be fine."

Maura wanted to get away from everyone.

"Okay," Maura said. "I am for bed." She didn't wait for more; she hurried past them and straight for the resort, anxious to get to her room.

And more anxious for Brock to join her.

Brock remained outside, just at the base of the porch steps, with Mike and Rachel—waving as Angie at last left them, smiling and hurrying on up the steps to meet her date.

He quickly filled them in on what Heidi's parents had told him.

Flannery shook his head. "It just gets more mired in some kind of muck all the time. I can see a serial kidnapper and killer, but… You think that there's some idiot Nazi society that has been going on for years—oh, wait, even before there were Nazis?"

"I know, I never heard of it before today—and then that's all that I've heard about. So there is a cult—or someone wants us all to believe that there is," Brock said.

"That could mean all kinds of people are involved," Rachel mused. She frowned. "I never heard what Mark was saying tonight before—that a really narcissistic group being 'supreme' might have existed as far back as the end of the Seminole Wars. Seriously, come on, think about it—and let's all be honest about humanity. At that time, males were superior, no hint of color was acceptable and no one had to say they were or weren't supreme. Society and laws dictated who was what."

"Okay, historically, we know that Gyselle was dragged out of the house to the hanging tree and basically executed there. History never told us just who did the dragging," Brock said. "I do believe that Heidi was taken by the same people who took the other girls—and I don't believe that she's dead yet, and we can only really pray—and get our asses moving—to find them."

"Brock, we have had officers going into any abandoned shack or shed, getting warrants for anything that was suspicious in the least. The state has been moving, but yeah, we need to get going on the whole instinct thing. You think that the caverns might yield something?"

"I think that remains were found very close to them," Brock said. "Anyway, I'm going up for the night. I'll see you in the morning."

"Yep. We'll say good-night and see you in the morning," Flannery said.

By then, the group from the campfire tales and walk had apparently retired for the night. The lobby was quiet as Brock walked across it.

The young man he'd met the night before was on the desk. Brock waved and headed for the elevator, but then noted that he didn't see Angie or the date she was meeting.

He headed to the desk.

"Yes, sir, how may I help you?" the young clerk asked.

"Miss Parsons was down here, I believe. I think she was meeting up with someone in that little twenty-four-hour nook by the entrance to the coffee shop. I don't see her."

"She was down here… I guess she went up."

"Was she alone?"

"I… I said hello, and then I was going through the reservations for tomorrow and okaying a few late departures. I didn't really notice."

Angie's room was on his way to the attic floor. Brock could knock on her door and check on her.

According to what he had seen and learned from Maura, Angie might well have cut to the chase with whomever she had met.

She might be in her room—occupied.

Well, hell, too bad. He was going to have to check on her—whether he interrupted something intimate or not.

MAURA WASN'T SURE what was taking Brock so long, except that he'd be filling Mike and Rachel in on whatever had gone on with Heidi's parents.

She paced her room for a few minutes, then paused as her phone rang.

She answered quickly, thinking it was Brock.

It was not.

It was Angie.

"Maura," Angie said. "You've got to come out—find Tall, Dark and Very Studly, and come on out here."

"Come on out here? Angie, where are you?"

Angie giggled. "Almost getting lucky!" she said in a whisper. "You need to come out here—first. I've found something. Or rather, my own Studly found something for me. Come on, quickly, just grab Brock and get out here."

"Out here where?"

"The History Tree. I have something for you!"

Maura heard a strange little yelping sound—excitement or a scream? She dropped the phone and hurried out into the hallway, just in time to see Brock coming up the stairs at the end.

"Brock, come on. We have to go." Maura said.

"I tried to check on Angie because I didn't see her in the lobby, but she's not answering her door," he told her.

"She isn't there. She's out at the History Tree. Brock—she said that she's found something. She was excited, but then, it was strange—come on!"

She didn't wait for the elevator—she headed straight for the stairs. He followed behind her, calling her name.

"You shouldn't go. I should go alone. Maura!"

He didn't catch up with her until they were out on the lawn, halfway out to the campfire and the trail. He caught her by the arm. "Let me go—you get back in the resort, up in your room—locked in."

"I don't think there's anything wrong," Maura said. "She wanted me to see something. Brock, you're armed and she said to bring you. She just wanted us both to come."

He shook his head, staring at her, determined.

"It could be a trap."

"Angie sounded like Angie. What kind of a trap would that be? Come on."

"No! You don't know—go back into the resort, into your room and lock the door."

She stared back at him.

"Please, Maura, if we're to go on…"

"But, Brock, I just talked to her. This is silly. I'm with you, and… Please, let's just hurry!"

She broke away from him, but he overtook her quickly. "Maura!"

"What?"

"You can't put yourself in danger," he told her. "Let me do my job."

"Oh, all right!"

"Go!"

She did. And since she knew that he'd wait until he saw her heading back into the resort, she turned and headed for the steps.

Something was bugging her about Angie's call. There had been that strange little noise. And then Angie hadn't spoken again. The line had gone dead.

Irritated but resolved, she hurried back into the resort. She waved to the night clerk and headed to the elevator—too tired and antsy for the stairs.

She walked down the hallway, feeling for her phone to try calling Angie again. She remembered that she'd dropped her phone on her bed.

That was all right; she was almost there.

She walked down the hallway to her room and pushed open the door.

The room was dark.

She hadn't left the lights out.

And neither had she thought to lock the door.

She had no idea what hit her; something came over her head, smothering any cry for help she might have made, and then she hit the floor.

And darkness was complete.

BROCK WALKED CAREFULLY through the woods, swiftly following the trail to the History Tree but hugging the foliage and staying in the shadows.

Long before he reached the tree, he heard the cries

for help and the sobs. He quickened his pace, but continued to move stealthily.

When he reached the clearing, he saw that Angie was tied to the tree.

She hadn't been hanged as the long-ago Gyselle had been; she was bound to the massive trunk of the conjoined trees, sobbing, crying out.

Brock didn't rush straight to her; he surveilled the clearing and the surrounding areas the best he could in the darkness. The moon was only half-full, offering little help.

There seemed to be no one near Angie. Still, he didn't trust the scene. It made no sense. Girls disappeared. Months later, remains were found.

None had been tied to the History Tree.

He pulled his phone out and called Flannery. "History Tree—backup," he said quietly.

And then, with his Glock at the ready, he made his way forward, still waiting for a surprise ambush from the bushes.

"Brock, Brock! Be careful, he knows you're coming… He knows… He could be here, here somewhere…"

"I'm watching, Angie," he said, reaching her. He found his pocketknife to start sawing on the ropes that bound her to the tree.

When she was free, she threw herself into his arms. "You saved me. Thank God I called Maura. He might have come back. He might have… He would have killed me. Oh, Brock, thank you, thank you."

Mike and Rachel came bursting into the clearing.

Angie jerked back, frightened by their arrival.

"It's all right, Angie. It's all right—who brought you here? Who the hell brought you here?" Brock demanded.

She began to shake. "I don't believe it! I still don't believe it!" she said, and she began to sob.

MAURA AWOKE TO DARKNESS. For a moment, the darkness confused her.

At first she had no recollection of what had happened. When she did start to remember—it wasn't much. Someone had attacked her when she'd walked into her room.

She touched her head. No blood, but she had one hell of a headache.

Brock had been right. The call had been a trap.

Angie had called…and there had been that little yelp, and then the phone had gone dead. But Brock hadn't allowed her to go with him.

Whoever had done this knew how Brock would react. Knew that he would never allow Maura to chance her own life.

She didn't know who it was. Mark or Nils Hartford? Bentley?

Donald Glass himself?

She tried to move and was surprised that she could. She struggled her way out of the covering that all but encased her. It was a comforter—the comforter from her bed at the resort.

She struggled to sit up and realized the earth around her was cold—as if she were in the ground. Struggling, she sat up—but she couldn't stand. The space was too tight. She could see nothing at all.

On her hands and knees, she began to crawl, blinking, trying to adjust to the absolute darkness. Where was Angie—had they taken her, too? Had Brock raced out to the clearing—to find nothing?

If so…

He'd wake the very dead to get every cop in the state out to start looking.

Maura began to shake, terrified. Then, wincing at the pain in her head, she moved forward again.

Brock would search for her, she knew.

She also needed to do her damned best to save herself.

She paused for a minute, listening. Nothing—but it was night. Late at night. She breathed in.

Earth. Earth and...

She paused, and suddenly she knew where she was—well, not where she was, but what she was in. There was earth, but she'd also touched something hard, a bit porous.

And native to a nearby area. Coquina. A sedimentary rock made of fossilized coquina shells that had been used in the building of the great fort in St. Augustine, that still graced walkways and garden paths and all manner of other projects. But to the best of her knowledge, there hadn't been any at the Frampton Ranch and Resort, unless it had been long, long ago.

Maybe she was no longer near the resort. She didn't know how long she had been unconscious.

She kept crawling, not even afraid of what night

creatures might be sharing this strange underground space with her.

And then, suddenly, she touched flesh.

"WHO, ANGIE? WHO did this to you?" Brock demanded, his arm around her still-shaking body as they headed back toward the resort. Flannery and Rachel had searched the area, a call had been put out for a forensic team and cops would soon be flooding the place.

"It was—it was Donald Glass!" she said, still sounding incredulous. "He was so polite, so gracious, and he said that he wanted me to see something very special. It was him!"

Flannery, right behind them, pushed forward. "Let's see if the old bastard is at the house. Supreme Being. I'll bet he sure as hell thinks that he's one. What the hell was he going to do? Did he think that Angie would die by herself by morning? Or was he coming back to finish the deed—right where he probably murdered Francine years ago?"

As they neared the house, Brock called to Rachel. "Stay with Angie, will you? I've got to go and bring Maura down."

"Don't leave me!" Angie begged, grabbing his arm.

He freed himself. "I have to get Maura."

Rachel had gotten strong; she managed to help Brock disengage a terrified Angie.

Brock raced up the stairs to Maura's room. He could tell the door to her room was open from halfway down the hall. He sprinted into it.

Empty.

The comforter was gone from the bed; her phone lay on the floor.

The breath seemed to be sucked out of him. His heart missed a beat, and for a split second, he froze.

It had been a trap. And he'd been such an ass, he hadn't seen it.

By the time he raced downstairs, the terrified desk clerk was hovering against the wall and Flannery had Donald Glass—in a smoking jacket—in handcuffs.

"No, no, this is wrong—I've been in my room. Ask my wife! Angie! Why the hell would you say these things, accuse me? I did nothing to you. I opened my resort to you. I… Why?"

Angie was shaking and crying, but Donald Glass was agitated, too. He appeared wild-eyed and confused.

"You meant to kill me!" Angie cried.

"I've been in my room all night!" Glass bellowed. "Ask my wife!"

Marie Glass was coming down the stairs, her appearance that of a woman who was stunned and stricken. Her hands shook on the newel post of the grand stairway as she reached the landing.

"Marie, tell them!" Glass bellowed.

Marie began to stutter. Tears stung her eyes. "I—I can't lie for you anymore, Donald."

"What?" he roared.

Brock strode up to him, face-to-face, his voice harsh, his tension more than apparent. "Where's Maura?" he demanded.

"Maura?" Glass asked, puzzled. Then he cried out, "Sleeping with you, most probably!"

"She's gone—she was taken. Where the hell is she?"

Donald Glass began to sob. He shook his white head, far less than dignified then. "I didn't take Maura. I didn't hurt Angie. I swear, I was in my room. I was in my room. I was in my room—"

"Get every cop you can. We have to search everywhere. Maura is with those other girls, I'm certain, and they're near here," Brock said.

A siren sounded, and then a cacophony of sirens filled the night.

"We'll get him to jail—you can join the hunt," Flannery told Brock.

"I'll get out to the car with him. By God, he's going to talk." Brock said. He set a hand hard on Donald Glass's shoulder, following him and Flannery out to the police cruiser.

A uniformed officer jumped out of the driver's seat and opened the back door for them.

"He's not going to talk, Brock, get on the search—" Flannery began. "Or don't," he said as Brock shoved Glass into the rear of the car and then crawled into the seat next to him.

"I don't have her. I don't have her. I don't have her!" Donald Glass screamed. "Don't kill me. Please, don't kill me!"

"I'm not going to kill you," Brock said. "What I need to know from you is anything I don't. Where around here could someone hide women?"

"But I swear, I didn't—"

"You—or anyone else. Dammit, man, I'm trying to believe you! Talk to me."

"WATER...PLEASE... Don't kill me... Water..."

The flesh Maura had encountered spoke.

"I don't have water. I'm not going to kill you," Maura assured the voice she heard. "I'm Maura Antrim. Who are you?"

"Maura!"

The person struggled in the darkness. Maura felt hands grab for her. "I know you... I know you... I'm Heidi... I'm so scared! I stopped because a car had flashing lights and... I went out to help and there was no one to help, and someone hit me, and... I'm dying, I'm sure. I'm going to die down here. I'm so scared. It's so dark. I don't know... Did they take you, too?"

"Yes, they hit me over the head in my hotel room. You don't have any idea of who did this to you?"

Maura felt the girl shake her head.

"We're not far from the resort—I know that. Not far at all."

"But where...?"

"I think we're in a bit of a sinkhole—covered up years and years ago—but someone used it as something. They shored up the sides with coquina. But they got us in here—there has to be a way out. Can you still move?"

"Barely."

"Okay, so stay still. I'm going to try to find a way to escape."

"No! Don't leave me!" Heidi begged, clinging to her.

"Then you have to come with me," Maura said firmly.

She began to crawl again, and she felt the earth grow wetter.

They were in a drainage culvert. They were probably right off the main highway, and if she could just find the grating…

Her mind was numb, and it was also racing a hundred miles an hour. Angie had called her because she had been meeting someone. That someone had lured Angie out and let her lure Brock out and, of course…

That someone had known Brock. Yes, she'd thought that right away. Known that he would make her go back, that he'd consider himself trained, ready to meet danger.

Brock would want Maura safe.

Whoever it had been walked easily and freely through the resort, knew where to go—how to avoid the eyes of the desk clerk and the cameras that kept watch on the lobby.

Thoughts began to tumble in her mind. One stuck.

It couldn't be. And, of course, it was just one someone…

It wasn't a society or an organization—but rather someone who had known about it.

She suddenly found herself thinking about the long-lost Gyselle, the beautiful woman running from her pursuers, those who would hang her from the History Tree until dead.

Maybe they had been part of a society. Maybe they hadn't. Maybe they had just…

She saw a light! A tiny, tiny piece of light…

THE NIGHT WAS ALIVE. Police were searching everywhere.

Dogs were out, each having been given a whiff of Maura's scent. But while they searched the woods and the house and the gardens and the pool, Brock headed off toward the road.

Donald Glass had spilled everything he knew. No, there had never been a basement; there were foundations, of course, but barely wide enough for one maintenance man. There had been a well, yes, filled in years and years ago.

Outbuildings had been torn down. The wings on the resort were new. There were no hidden houses; the one little nearby cemetery had no mausoleums or vaults…

Where to hide someone?

Warehouses aplenty on the highway. And the drainage tank off the road, ready to absorb excess water when hurricanes came tearing through.

A perfect place for a body to deteriorate quickly.

Donald Glass had been taken off to jail.

That didn't matter to Brock right now. Nothing mattered.

Except that he find Maura.

He reached the road and raced alongside the highway, seeking any entrance to the sunken areas along the pavement.

He ran and ran, and then ran back again, and then noted an area where foliage had been tossed over the drain.

He raced for it.

And as he neared, he heard her. Crying out, thundering against the metal grate.

"Maura!"

He cried her name, surged to the grate and fell to his knees. His pocketknife made easy work of the metal joints. He pulled her out and into his arms, and for a long moment, she clung to him.

And then he heard another cry.

"Heidi—she says there are other women down there… Dead or alive, I don't know."

He pulled Heidi from the drain. She crushed him so hard in a hug that he fell back, and several long seconds passed in which it seemed they were all laughing and crying.

Then, in the distance, he heard the baying of a dog. He shouted, "Over here!" Soon, there were many officers there, many dogs, and he was free to take Maura into his arms and hold her and not let go.

Epilogue

"You know," Maura said, probably confusing everyone gathered in the lobby of the Frampton Ranch and Resort by being the one to speak first. "Sometimes, really, I can still see her—or imagine her—the beautiful Gyselle, running in the moonlight, desperate to live. Legends are hard to shake. And I'm telling you this, and starting the explanation because, in one way, it's my story. And because Gyselle's life has meaning, and legends have meaning, and sometimes we don't see the truth because what we see is the legend."

She saw interest on the faces before her. The employees knew by now that Donald Glass had been taken away. They knew that horrible things had happened the night before, that Angie had been attacked by her host and that Maura had been attacked—but found, and found along with Heidi and the other three missing girls. Heidi was already fine and home with her parents. The other girls were still hospitalized. For Lily Sylvester it would be a long haul. She'd been in the dark, barely fed and given dirty water for months—and it had taken a toll on her internal organs. Lydia

Merkel would most probably be allowed to go home that afternoon, and for Amy Bonham the hospital stay would be about a week.

There was hope for all of them. They'd lived.

The resort guests had all gone. They had been asked to vacate by the police and Marie Glass until the tragedy had been appropriately handled.

The resort was empty except for the staff, Detectives Flannery and Lawrence, and Angie and Maura.

Donald Glass remained gone—biding his time in jail before arraignment. But if things tonight went the way Maura thought they would, that arraignment would never come.

"Thinking about Gyselle brings to mind—to many of us—what happened to Francine Renault. Well, I don't really see her in a long gown running through the forest, but she, too, met her demise on this ranch. And through the years, we suspect, so did many other young women. They didn't all come to the tree. After Francine they were stabbed. Yes, by the same killer. Brutally stabbed to death. As Peter Moore, a cook here back then, was stabbed. It doesn't sound as if it should all relate. One killer, two killers, working independently—or together? All compelled by just one driving motive—revenge."

Blank faces still greeted her. She wasn't a cop or FBI. They were curious, but confused.

"I thought they were random kidnappings," someone murmured.

"Yes and no," Maura said.

Brock stepped forward. "We discovered a longtime

association or society. It was called Sons of Supreme Being. They don't—we believe—really exist anymore. So legend gave way to what might be revamped—and imitated."

"I thought the police were going to explain what really went on here," Nils Hartford said.

"I guess Donald Glass did consider himself a supreme being," his brother added sadly.

"Well, he might have," Maura said. "But…there you go. I'm back to beautiful Gyselle, running through the forest. Her sin being that of a love affair with the owner of the plantation."

"I'm letting Maura do the explaining," Brock said. "She's always been a great storyteller."

Maura turned and looked at Marie Glass. "Donald didn't kill Francine, Marie. You did."

"What?" Marie stared at her indignantly. "I did not kill Francine. My husband killed Francine."

"No, no, he didn't. He didn't kill Francine. Nor did he kill Maureen Rodriguez or the other woman whose remains have been found. Donald loved history—and kept it alive. He loved women. You found your way to take revenge on those who led him astray—and, of course, on Donald himself. Oh, and you killed Peter Moore—that's when you discovered just how much you enjoyed wielding a knife."

"This is insane! How do you think that I—" Marie gestured to herself, demonstrating that she was indeed a tiny woman "—could manage such acts? Oh, you ungrateful little whore!"

"No need to be rude," Brock said. "Marie, you were good—but we have you on camera."

"Really? How did I tie up Angie and get back and…"

"Oh, you didn't tie up Angie."

"Of course not!"

"Angie tied herself up," Brock said calmly.

Angie sprang to her feet. "No! I wasn't even around when Francine Renault was killed. Or the cook. Why on earth do you think that I could be involved?"

"I still don't know why you were involved, Angie," Brock said. "But you were. There was no one else in the woods. We've found sound alibis for everyone else here. Oh, both Mark and Nils Hartford were sleeping with guests that night—a no-no. But you weren't one of those guests. And there's video—the security camera picked it up—of Fred Bentley talking to the night clerk right when it was all going on. What? Did you two think that we were getting close? That we'd figure it out—that Marie's hints about her husband were a little too well planted? Then, of course, there was you—wanting to see where the bones had been discovered. Strange, right? But I'm thinking that the bones washed out in the drainage system somehow—and Marie panicked and wrapped them in hotel sheets, thinking she could dispose of the remains with the laundry. And maybe you were hoping that you hadn't messed up somehow. Maybe you didn't know. But for whatever reason, you and Marie have been kidnapping and killing people. Marie getting her rage out—certain she could frame her husband if it came to it. But you…"

"That's absurd!" Angie cried.

"No, no, it's not. We checked your phone records—you talked to Marie over and over again during the last year. Long conversations. She chose the victims. You helped bring them down."

The hotel staff had all frozen, watching—as if they were caught in a strange tableau.

"You're being ridiculous!" Angie raged. She looked like a chicken, jumping up, arms waving at her sides in fury. "No, it was Marie! I didn't—"

"Oh, shut up!" Marie cried. "I'm not going down alone. I can tell you why—she wanted to hurt Donald as badly as I did. We were willing to wait and watch and eventually find a way to create proof that made the system certain that it was Donald. And those women… Whores! They deserved to suffer. We could have seen that Donald rotted for years before he got the death penalty. There's no record of it—her mother was one of my husband's whores. He paid her off very nicely to have an abortion. The woman took the money—she didn't abort." She looked at Angie. "You should have been an abortion!"

"Oh, Marie, you lie, you horrible bitch!"

Angie tore toward her in a fury.

Rachel stepped up, catching her smoothly and easily, swinging an arm across her shoulders.

She then snapped cuffs on Angie.

And Marie—dignified Marie—was taken by Mike.

She spit at him. She called him every vile name Maura had ever heard.

And then some.

They were taken out. The employees stood in silence, gaping.

Then, suddenly, everyone burst into conversation, some expressing disbelief, some arguing that they were surprised.

"No," Fred Bentley said simply, staring after them. "No."

"Yes. You saw," Brock told him.

"So, what do we do now?" Mark asked.

"Well, Donald Glass is being released. Right now he's sick and horrified at what has happened. He believed that he caused Marie to be cruel. He never knew he had an illegitimate child, and now he's left with the fact that his child…became a killer. He needs time. He's the one who has to make the decisions," Brock said. "For now, he has said to let you know that you don't need to worry while he regroups—everyone will be paid for the next month, no matter what."

There was a murmur of approval, and then slowly the group began to break up.

Fred stared at Brock and Maura for a long time. "Well," he said. "I will be here. I will keep the place in order. Until I know what Donald wants. I'll see that the staff maintain it. I'll be here for—for anything anyone may need." He started to walk away, and then he came back. "I'm… I can't believe it. Imagine, that cute little Angie. Who could figure…? But thank you, Brock. Yeah, thank you so much."

He turned and left, heading behind the restaurant toward the office.

Brock and Maura stood alone in the center of the lobby.

"Shall we go?" he asked her.

"We shall, but..."

"But where, you ask?" Brock teased. "An island. Somewhere with a beautiful beach. Somewhere we can lie on the sand and make up for lost time, hurt for those who died and be grateful for those who lived. You are packed and ready to leave?"

"I am," she told him.

They drove away.

MAURA COULD FEEL the deliciousness of the sea breeze. It swept over her flesh, filtering through the soft gauze curtains that surrounded the bungalow. She could hear the lap of the waves, so close that she could easily run out on the sand and wade into the water.

It was beautiful. Brock had found the perfect place in the Bahamas. It was a private piece of heaven, and no one came near them unless they summoned food or drink with the push of a button. The next bungalow was down the beach, and they were separated by palms and sea grapes and other oceanfront foliage.

It was divine.

Though nothing was more divine than sleeping beside Brock so easily, flesh touching, sometimes just lying together and talking about the years gone by, and sometimes, starting with just the slightest brush against each other, making love.

There would be four days of this particular heaven, but…

"You did talk to your parents, right?" Brock asked Maura.

"Of course! If news about what happened had reached them and they hadn't heard from me…they would have been a bit crazy," Maura assured him. She inched closer to him. "I almost feel bad for my mother—she's so horrified, and she admitted all the messages she'd gotten from you and kept from me… poor thing. And then, I have myself to blame, too. I was hurt that I didn't hear from you—and so I never tried to contact you myself. I thought I was part of your past—a past you wanted closed."

"Never. Never you," he said with a husky voice. Then he smiled again. "But your mom… She is coming to the wedding."

Maura laughed. "Oh, yes. She didn't even try telling me that we were rushing things when I said we were in the Bahamas but coming home to a small wedding in New York at an Irish pub called Finnegan's. And my dad… Well, he thinks that's great. Why wait after all this time? Now or never, in his mind. It's nice, by the way, for your friend to arrange a wedding and reception in one at his place—his place? Her place?"

"Kieran and Craig have been together a long time. Craig is a great coworker and friend. Kieran owns Finnegan's with her brothers—they're thrilled to provide for a small wedding and reception. And you…you don't mind living in New York? For now? Maybe one day, we'll be snowbirds, heading south for the winter. And maybe, when we're old and gray, we'll come home for good. Or, hell, maybe I'll get a transfer. But for now..."

She leaned over and kissed him. "I lost you for twelve years. I'm going to say those vows and move to New York without blinking," she promised. "Besides... Hmm. I'm going to be looking for some new clients—New York seems like a good place to find them."

He smiled, and then he rolled more tightly to her, his face close as he said, "It's amazing. I knew I loved you then. And I never stopped loving you—and I swear, I will love you all the rest of my years, as well. With or without you, I knew I loved you."

"That's beautiful," she whispered. "I love you, too. Always have, always will." She smoothed back his hair.

He caught her hand and kissed it.

Then the kissing continued.

And the ocean breeze continued to caress them both as the sun rose higher in the sky.

Later, much later, Maura knew that the ocean breeze wouldn't be there every morning. They wouldn't be sleeping in an oceanfront bungalow with the sea and sand just beyond them.

And it wouldn't matter in the least.

Because his face would be on the pillow next to hers, every morning, forever after.

* * * * *

FULL FORCE

ELLE JAMES

Thank you to my wonderful family, who understand
when I'm on deadline and allow me the time
during holidays to write.

Thank you to my mother and father, who taught
me the value of hard work and perseverance,
without which I would never have finished one
book, much less one hundred and fifty!

Thank you to my sister, who helps me with
brainstorming when I'm fresh out of ideas.

Thank you to my editors, who keep me
in commas, and commas in the right places!

And thank you to our men and women in
uniform who protect our country and allow
us the freedom to follow our dreams.

Chapter One

The Russian ambassador, Nikolai Kozlov, stormed out of the room, his face a mottled red, his black eyes blazing.

Perched on the edge of her seat, Emily Chastain looped the strap of her purse over her shoulder and glanced across the conference table at Viktor Sokolov, the Russian ambassador's executive assistant. She reminded herself that she'd only been the interpreter. The ambassador wasn't mad at her but at the information she'd translated.

Jay Phillips, the private investigator, shoved his notes into a folder and started to slip them into the briefcase he'd carried into the conference room at the Russian embassy.

Sokolov held up his hand. "*Nyet*," he said in a commanding voice. In Russian he continued. "You will leave your papers and data with me."

Emily translated. "He wants you to leave the documents."

Phillips shrugged and laid the folder on the table. "The papers aren't going to change anything. I signed a nondisclosure, and it pays for me to keep what I know to myself. I don't share the information I compile with anyone other than my client. Otherwise, I would have no business."

Emily gave Sokolov a shorter version of what Phillips had said.

Nevertheless the assistant's heavy black brows veed over his nose and he gathered the stack of papers and photographs into a pile in front of him.

Phillips closed his briefcase and pushed to his feet. "Now that the meeting is over, I have an appointment across town in less than an hour."

"If you no longer require my services, I should be going, too," Emily said in Russian.

Sokolov's intense stare turned on Emily. "You will keep the information you have translated private?"

Emily nodded. "I am very discreet. And I signed a nondisclosure agreement when I took this assignment. If we are done here," she said, "I need to use the ladies' room and then I need to leave before the traffic gets too hard to make it back to my apartment before rush-hour traffic gets bad." She spoke the words in Russian. She started to pick up the notebook in front of her.

A hand came down on the notebook and the ambassador's assistant said, "The notes stay." He, too, spoke in Russian. The hard look on his face brooked no argument.

Phillips stiffened, his eyes widened, but he didn't move from his position by the table.

Her heart beating fast, Emily secured her purse strap on her shoulder and stood. Still shaking from the force of anger the ambassador had displayed, Emily's knees wobbled as she was escorted to the door, alone, without the investigator.

The Russian ambassador had stormed out of the

room yelling so loud and fast, Emily couldn't keep up with his Russian. In his wake, the remaining occupants of the small conference room had sat in stunned silence for moments afterward.

Emily couldn't shake a bad feeling about this particular translation gig. The urge to exit the Russian embassy overwhelmed her. As she crossed the threshold of the room she made a quick glance over her shoulder at the investigator. He attempted to leave but the guard behind him pressed a hand to his shoulder and forced him to sit. The American investigator shot a worried glance at Emily. Again, in Russian, she said, "Perhaps Mr. Phillips would like to share a cab with me?"

The guard behind the investigator shook his head. "*Nyet.*"

Phillips looked at her again and nodded, as if to say she should go while she could. When she didn't move forward, her hovering guard gave her a slight shove that sent her into the hallway. There wasn't much else she could do for the investigator but hope and pray that nobody stood in his way of leaving the embassy.

The guard gripped her elbow and escorted her down the hall. If she hadn't dug her heels into the tile when she passed the restroom he would have marched her all the way to the exit.

Emily pulled free of the hand holding her arm and ducked into the bathroom. For a moment she thought the guard would follow her. When he didn't, she breathed a sigh as the door closed behind her.

What she had translated that day left her shaken.

The investigator had been hired to follow the ambassador's daughter and to find out where she had been going in Washington, DC. Apparently she'd had a number of unescorted clandestine assignations with a young man her father considered dangerous to his position as the Russian ambassador to the US. The investigator had stopped short of naming names but the look he'd exchanged with the ambassador had been clear. The ambassador knew who she was seeing.

The anger Emily had heard in the ambassador's voice led her to believe that he was livid enough to kill the young man and possibly even his daughter, Sachi.

Emily hadn't been altogether sure that she would make it out of the embassy alive. Though she'd never felt threatened before when she'd come to do translations within the Russian embassy, the anger in the ambassador's demeanor left her feeling anything but comfortable.

She quickly splashed water on her face and dried it with a paper towel. Then she straightened her shoulders and pushed through the door to exit the bathroom. As she emerged into the hallway a man wearing a press badge was being escorted into the embassy by two guards, each gripping one of the journalist's arms.

Emily was certain she'd seen the young man before but she couldn't quite place him at the moment.

The guard who had led her from the conference room grabbed her elbow and jerked her toward the exit. Emily was in just as much of a hurry to get out of the embassy as the guard was to get her out. She no longer felt safe.

As she worked her way to the door, a sense of urgency filled her. She had to get out of the building as quickly as possible. At the exit, she was stopped by another guard. The two burly men spoke in Russian, their speech so quick she only caught half of it. It appeared the guard at the door was reluctant to let her leave, whereas the other guard wanted her out as soon as possible. Finally her guard escort got her through the door and gave her a little push toward the gate leading off the embassy compound.

Hugging her purse against her body, and pulling her jacket tightly around her, Emily hurried for the gate. Again, she was stopped and questioned as to why she was at the embassy. She told them she had been there to translate. The guard at the gate waved her through and she was free.

Emily didn't look back. Instead she kept going, walking faster and faster until she was almost running down the street. She didn't stop running until she was several blocks from the embassy. Her heart beating fast, her breathing coming in ragged gasps, she finally stopped long enough to remember where she had parked her car. She had to backtrack to the lot where she had paid to park earlier that day.

As she crossed the street, a vehicle raced toward her without slowing. She quickened her pace but realized she wasn't going to make it across in time. The vehicle barreled forward, increasing speed rather than slowing, as if the driver didn't see her or had made her his target.

Emily dove for the sidewalk and rolled to the side. The vehicle rushing at her bumped up on the curb and nearly ran over her. If she hadn't rolled once more, it would have crushed her. The driver didn't stop to check that she was all right, but sped on, leaving her to pick herself up and dust the dirt off of her clothes.

A man reached down and gripped her elbow. "Are you all right?"

Emily nodded, her heart still pounding so hard she thought it might leap out of her chest. "I'm okay." She tried to get a look at the license plate to report the reckless driver, but the car didn't have a plate on the rear bumper.

Turning to the stranger, she said, "Thank you," and gave him a weak smile. Moving past him, Emily glanced down at the damage done to her trouser leg, which now sported a dirt stain and a tear, wondering what her knee looked like beneath it. It stung and hurt when she flexed it. She couldn't take care of it until she got home. After another glance around, she continued toward the car park. With nothing but a description of a dark sedan having nearly run her over, she gave up hope of turning in the man behind the wheel for reckless driving. Instead she slipped into her car, paid the parking lot attendant and drove out of downtown DC, putting distance between her and the Russian embassy.

Out of the downtown traffic, Emily drove onto a six-lane highway, crowded with people hurrying to get somewhere. A white van behind her sped up, swerved around her to the left and slammed into the side of her vehicle.

Emily held on to the steering wheel with a white-knuckled grip, struggling to keep from hitting the vehicle on her right. The driver on the other side of her honked as she crossed into his lane. Ahead of her, the van dodged in and out of traffic, leaving Emily behind before she could get a look at his license plate.

She slowed, unable to pull to the side of the road. The car behind her honked, the vehicles on either side boxing her in, keeping her moving steadily forward. She had no choice but to continue toward home. Shaken and paranoid, Emily held on tightly to the steering wheel, bracing for the next potential hit-and-run driver. What was wrong with people? Why were the drivers all bent on trying to run her over? After her encounter at the Russian embassy, she could swear they were deliberately attacking her. Or was she imagining it? Traffic was scary enough without aggressive people expressing their road rage with a three-thousand-pound deadly weapon.

By the time she drove into her neighborhood, Emily was tired, stressed and ready to kick her feet up and drink a glass of wine to calm her nerves.

The traffic light ahead turned green as she approached. She pressed the accelerator and entered the intersection.

A dark blue sedan shot out of the side road, completely ignoring the red light.

If Emily hadn't been ultra-aware of her environment, she wouldn't have reacted as quickly as she did. She slammed her foot on the gas pedal, pulling ahead just enough to avoid being T-boned by the other car. It missed hitting her rear bumper by a hair.

"What the heck?" Emily cried. She didn't slow, pushing past the speed limit to the next street. A glance in her rearview mirror showed the vehicle that had almost plowed into her was turning in the middle of the intersection, aiming toward her.

After this third vehicular incident, Emily got a clue. Instead of driving straight to her apartment she drove past her complex, watching closely in her rearview mirror as the dark sedan followed.

She turned at the next corner and the trailing car continued on straight. She breathed a sigh of relief and headed toward her apartment, keeping an eye on the rearview mirror. From all she could tell, no one was following her. She made a circuitous trip around the block before she pulled into the parking lot of her building.

Her heart still pounding, Emily slowed her vehicle and started to turn into her usual parking space.

Although it was still a part of a normal workday, there were several cars in the lot, most of which were empty. When she spotted the dark blue sedan, Emily's heart did a flip-flop.

The windows were too darkly tinted to see inside.

A tightening in the pit of Emily's stomach made her pause before parking. Her heart sped up as she lifted her foot off of the brake and applied it to the accelerator. Instead of turning into her parking space, she whipped through the lot and out the other end of the apartment complex.

As she turned back out onto the road, she glanced into her rearview mirror and saw again the dark sedan pulling out of the parking lot, following her. She raced to the next street and turned.

The blue sedan stayed right on her tail.

Not knowing what to do, she chose a busy thoroughfare and rushed out into the open, hoping and praying the traffic would help put some distance between her and the sedan. Whipping in and out of traffic and dodging vehicles, Emily did manage to put distance between her and her tail. When she thought she'd lost him, she called her friend Grace, using her car's Bluetooth setup.

Grace answered on the first ring. "Hi, Emily, how's it going?"

"I think I'm in trouble," she said, her voice wobbling.

"What kind of trouble?" Grace's voice was sharp, filled with concern.

"I'm not sure," Emily said. "I think I'm being followed, and drivers have tried to run me off the road a couple of times in the past hour. I—I can't go home."

"Try to stay calm. You know you called the right person," Grace said. "Charlie's guys will help. Where are you now?"

Emily glanced around, for the first time aware that she hadn't headed anywhere in particular, just away from trouble. "I'm on 395. I don't know where," she said. "Wait, there's an exit sign." She gave Grace her location and then glanced in her mirror once more. "Crap! There he is again," she said.

"I'm going to text you a map coordinate," Grace said. "It's the address of my new employer. Go straight there, I'll have somebody meet you at the gate."

A beep sounded on her cell phone. Emily took her eyes off the road long enough to select the coordinates for her map on her phone to follow. She'd slowed just enough that the dark sedan behind her was quickly catching up. While her map application calculated the directions, she again weaved in and out of traffic, trying to lose her tail.

"Stay on the phone with me, Emily," Grace said. "I have a team of people here at Charlie's place. They can help you. You just have to get here."

"I'll do the best I can," Emily promised.

She thought she'd been doing well and had lost her tail when she'd finally pulled off the main parkway onto a smaller road. But as soon as the traffic thinned, she looked behind her.

The dark-tinted vehicle was there and speeding up, closing in on her. The road she traveled now was lined with gated driveways. Besides the gates and the driveways, there was nothing else around. No cars. No people. Just her and the sedan that was quickly catching up.

"Are you still with me, Emily?" Grace asked.

"I'm here," she said. This time when she glanced in her rearview mirror the vehicle behind her was racing toward her back bumper. Emily pressed her foot to the accelerator, shooting her little car forward. Her speed increased from fifty to sixty to seventy miles per hour. A caution sign on the side of the road indicated an upcoming curve, with a recommended speed of twenty-five miles per hour.

Afraid the vehicle behind her would rear-end her and send her flying off the road, Emily didn't dare slow down. She gripped the steering wheel and raced into the curve at breakneck speed. As she navigated the radius, the rear end of her vehicle fishtailed and swung around. She almost went into a 360-degree spin, was able to correct her direction, but not soon enough to avoid the vehicle following her.

The car behind her slammed into her left rear fender, sending her back into the spin.

Out of her control, her car slid toward the edge of the road.

Emily squealed and held tight to the steering wheel as her vehicle bumped onto the shoulder, down into a ditch and up an embankment, slamming into a fence post. Upon impact, the airbags deployed, forcing her back against her seat, stunning her for a few precious seconds. Emily rubbed the dust out of her eyes and looked around. The fine powder of the airbag coated her skin and clothes and the dash of the vehicle.

In her rearview mirror, she could see the road behind her and the dark sedan parked at the edge. A man dressed in black, with a black ski mask pulled over his head, got out of the driver's side and stood on the shoulder, staring down at her vehicle.

Emily didn't move, praying her attacker would think she was unconscious and leave.

When he moved toward her, she couldn't sit still, she had to get away.

Emily shifted her vehicle into Reverse and hit the accelerator. The rear tires spun, gaining no traction. She couldn't go forward because of the fence post. She tried turning the steering wheel sharply to the left and hit the accelerator again. The back tire spun, shooting mud up behind her, but the vehicle didn't budge.

"What's happening, Emily?" Grace's voice said over the phone. "What was that noise? Are you okay?"

"No, no, I'm not. I've crashed," Emily managed to croak out as she struggled with what to do. "I have to… I'm getting out…" She couldn't waste time talking. Escape was her only option.

The man on the side of the road scrambled down into the ditch, moving purposefully toward her. Emily tried to open her door to get out, but the door was jammed. She fumbled with the catch on her seat belt and finally got it loose.

Her pulse pounding loudly against her eardrums, Emily crawled across the console to the other side of the vehicle and pulled the door handle. When the door swung open, she fell out onto the ground, rolled onto her side, bunched her feet and knees up beneath her and rose.

When she raised her head above the car, she could see the man in black standing there, his hand rising, a gun held in his grip.

Emily's heart leaped to her throat. She ducked back down behind the car as a shot rang out. Glass shattered, raining down from the window above her as Emily lay flat against the earth. The scent of gasoline, tire rubber and the mud beneath her nose filled her senses. But she couldn't lie there for long. If her pursuer came any closer, he could easily pick her off with his handgun.

Unwilling to die that day, Emily rose onto her hands and knees. Keeping low to the ground, she crawled for the fence, slipped beneath the bottom rail and continued on toward the trees, praying she could find a place to hide until the crazy man following her gave up and went away. Or until Grace's friends arrived to rescue her.

Chapter Two

Frank "Mustang" Ford's cell phone rang through to the Bluetooth in his truck. Declan O'Neill's name appeared on the dash screen.

Mustang thumbed the button on his steering wheel to answer. "What's up, Declan?"

"Are you on your way to the Halverson Estate?"

"Roger," he confirmed. "Five miles away. Why? Need me to stop and pick up some milk or bread?" He chuckled.

"No. I have a mission for you."

"Really?" Mustang sat straighter. "Must be a short deadline if you can't wait until I get to Charlie's place."

"It is," Declan said, his tone clipped. "Be on the lookout for a red Toyota Camry. Grace's friend is en route to Charlie's and has a tail following her. She reported three vehicular attacks since leaving the DC area. She might be in trouble."

"I'll keep an eye out for her. The road out this way appears pretty deserted."

"Then it shouldn't be hard to find her. Let us know when you catch up to her."

"Roger." As he increased his speed, Mustang gripped the steering wheel a little tighter.

A mile or more later a yellow caution sign indicated a sharp curve ahead. Mustang applied his brakes, his gaze scanning the sides of the road and the ditches. If someone was trying to harm Grace's friend, running her off the road in the middle of a curve was the perfect place to do it. Dusk was settling in, causing shadows to merge, making it more difficult for Mustang to distinguish between shadows and objects on the sides of the road.

As soon as he entered the sweeping curve, he spied a dark vehicle parked barely off the shoulder. The driver's-side door hung open and, as far as Mustang could tell, no one was inside or around the vehicle. He slowed, pulled over to the side of the road and off onto the shoulder, giving the vehicle in front of him plenty of space. He shifted into Park, grabbed his flashlight from the center console and pulled his handgun from the shoulder holster beneath his jacket.

Mustang slipped down out of his truck and closed the door quietly. As he rounded the hood and edged toward the dark sedan he spied another vehicle on the other side of the ditch crashed against a fence pole. It, too, seemed abandoned and, from what he could tell, it was red. The front bumper was smashed into the fence post and the driver's-side window was shattered with what looked like a bullet hole at the exact position that would have hit the driver, had the driver been sitting in the seat.

Adrenaline shot through Mustang's veins. Crouching low, he eased toward the abandoned vehicles, dropped down into the ditch and climbed up the embankment to the disabled vehicle where he discovered the passenger door was open. He prayed that whoever had been in the car had escaped. All he could assume at the moment was that whoever had arrived in the dark sedan had been the one to run the other vehicle off the road and to fire the shot that had put the hole in the driver's-side window. That led Mustang to believe the driver of the disabled vehicle was on the run, being chased now by whoever had attacked her.

With his gun held at the ready, he pointed his flashlight with his other hand into the front seat of the disabled vehicle. He was glad to discover there was no blood on the seats or the dash. The airbags had deployed and the vehicle was empty, meaning the driver had escaped. But how long would she last on the run from somebody trying to kill her with a gun? She could be injured. The question was, what direction had she gone in?

He tried to think like a person running from somebody determined to kill her. She would have made for the safety and concealment of the tree line. That meant that she would have slipped beneath the fence into the forest. She might only have seconds before her pursuer caught up to her.

Mustang ran the rest of the way up the embankment, braced his hand on a fence rail and vaulted over the metal railing. As his feet hit the ground, a shot rang out. He raced in the direction he thought the sound had come from, determined to reach the woman before her attacker finished her off. He hoped he wasn't too late.

Mustang raced as fast as he could, leaping over branches, pushing past bushes and trees. His muscles strained and his lungs burned, and still he didn't see anyone ahead of him.

It had been dusk when he'd pulled to the side of the

road. Within the canopy of the trees, darkness had descended. He couldn't see every little branch and tripped over one. He got up and kept moving, arriving finally at the edge of a glen where a little bit of dusk light illuminated a dark figure standing over a lump on the ground. From the man's silhouette, Mustang could tell he was pointing a gun at the figure on the ground. Mustang raised his weapon and fired. The dark figure ducked. When he straightened, he pulled the person up from the ground and held her in front of him.

"Come another step closer and I will shoot her," a voice said in a thick Russian accent.

Mustang took cover behind a tree. "You shoot her and I'll hunt you down and kill you. I will show you no mercy."

Though he spoke with force, Mustang could not help the shaky feeling he felt inside. What he witnessed before him was so similar to the last operation he and his team had conducted in Afghanistan. In that scenario, their bogey had used the bride in a wedding couple as the shield to get him out of a village. That Taliban leader's ploy and Mustang's team decision to spare the bride had cost them all their careers in the marines. And, as had been the case then, he couldn't take the shot now. If he attempted to kill the bad guy, he'd have to go through the body of an innocent victim.

"Okay. I won't shoot," Mustang shouted. "But I reiterate, if you kill the woman, I *will* kill you. And I will make certain that you suffer in the process of dying."

The man holding the hostage inched backward, dragging the woman with him. He made a wide circle, heading back in the direction of the road and the vehicles abandoned there.

Mustang had no recourse but to wait for the man to pass him and continue on his path to the road. At one point Mustang thought he heard the woman sob and, possibly, a softly spoken plea. *Help me.* His heart contracted, squeezing tightly in his chest. He vowed to himself that he'd get her out of her attacker's grasp.

Mustang followed, keeping a safe distance but close enough that he could see what was going on in the shadowy darkness of late dusk. At one point he got too near.

"Do not come closer," the attacker said. He fired a shot.

Mustang ducked low and behind a tree.

Thankfully the woman remained on her feet, still dragged alongside her kidnapper. They closed the distance between them and the vehicles on the side of the road.

Mustang knew he had to stop the kidnapper before he got the woman into the car. If he had been bent on running her off the road and shooting at her inside her vehicle, he would kill her as soon as he got her away. Mustang couldn't let that happen. He had to stop the kidnapper.

Mustang eased through the woods, moving shadow to shadow, inching closer as quietly as he could. When the other two reached the fence, Mustang knew he had to make his move. The kidnapper shoved the woman to the ground and said something to her in Russian. She rolled beneath the fence.

"My finger is on the trigger," the Russian called out. "If you shoot me. I shoot the woman. I might die, but the woman will die, as well."

With the man in his sights, Mustang hesitated.

The woman, who had managed to get beneath the

fence, kicked out a foot, catching her kidnapper in the shin with a hard smack.

Mustang took his chance and pulled the trigger at the same time the Russian yelled and bent over.

The woman on the ground rolled and kept rolling past the fence and down the embankment, out of sight of Mustang. Her attacker climbed over the top of the fence and dropped down on the other side.

Mustang left the concealment of the tree and raced for the fence, vaulting over and landing on the other side. He immediately dropped to his belly on the ground.

A shot rang out.

The woman had managed to roll to the bottom of the ditch, get up and start running from the Russian.

Her attacker rose and pointed his weapon at her.

Mustang aimed and fired, hitting the man's hand, knocking the gun from his grip.

Clutching his injured hand to his chest, the Russian ran for the dark sedan on the roadside.

Mustang glanced from the assailant to the woman. He wanted to stop the Russian from making another attempt on the woman's life. But first he needed to ascertain what injuries the woman might have sustained. Headlights shone in the curve on the road above as the dark sedan sped away with the Russian inside. Meanwhile the woman hadn't stopped. She kept running, tripping over bushes and bramble in the ditch. If she didn't stop soon she'd injure herself even more.

"Mustang," a man shouted. "You out there?"

Mustang breathed a sigh of relief at the sound of Declan's voice.

"Do you need help?" Declan called out.

"Call 9-1-1, get an ambulance out here." Mustang didn't wait for Declan's response. He raced after the woman scrabbling through the ditch. Because of the recent rain the ditch contained pools of standing water and mushy soil.

The woman stumbled and fell into the mud.

Mustang splashed through the water. "Hey!"

His shout seemed to galvanize her and she pushed to her feet and resumed running. Her breathing coming in ragged gasps and sobs.

Mustang increased his speed.

Apparently the woman didn't realize that he was one of the good guys. She had to be so frightened that she was beyond reason. She struggled up the incline toward the road. If Mustang didn't catch up to her soon, she could be hit by an oncoming vehicle as soon as she emerged from the ditch.

The headlights shining on the road above made Mustang kick up his pace and he charged after the woman. Just before she reached the road, he caught her with a flying tackle, sending her sprawling onto the gravel. He pulled her beneath him and rolled her to the side, away from the oncoming car. After the vehicle had passed, he pushed up on his arms and stared down into the shadowy face of the woman. Her features were blurred in the looming darkness, but he could tell she had a scrape on her chin and her eyes were wide and frightened.

She fought, kicking and screaming something in Russian.

Mustang used the weight of his body to hold her against the ground.

When he didn't shift off her, she switched to English. "Let go of me."

Mustang pinned her wrists to the ground to keep her from scratching his eyes out. “Hey, lady. I’m just here to help you.”

Her struggle slowed and finally came to a halt. She stared up at him. “If you’re here to help me, let me go,” she said.

He chuckled. “Sweetheart, I’ll let you go when I’m sure you’re not gonna run out into the traffic.”

She dragged in a long, shaky breath and let it out. “I promise, I won’t run out into the traffic. And I’m not your sweetheart.”

For a long moment Mustang stared down into her face, wishing he could see the color of her eyes in the darkness. Finally he sighed and rolled over, releasing her wrists. “Okay. But I’ll tackle you again if you try to get out onto the highway.”

She sat up, rubbing her wrists where he’d held them so tightly.

“Grace sent us,” Mustang said.

The woman’s head jerked up and she stared into his eyes. “Are you some of Charlie’s men?”

“If you mean do I work for Charlie Halverson, then yes.” Mustang pushed to his feet and extended his hand.

She hesitated a moment before placing her hand in his and letting him pull her to her feet.

“Are you okay?” His gaze raked her body from head to toe, his eyes straining in the darkness. He’d lost the flashlight in his chase to catch her.

She nodded. “I think so. A little banged up and bruised from the car wreck and from being tackled.”

“Sorry about that,” Mustang said.

A smile quirked at the corners of her lips. “I guess

I should thank you for keeping me safe from running out into the middle of the road."

Footsteps sounded on the pavement behind the woman. Declan raced toward them. "Mustang? Emily?" He ground to a halt and shook his head. "An ambulance is on the way. And I called the sheriff's department and the police department and have them looking out for a dark sedan with no license plate."

Mustang shook his head. "The dude will be long gone before anybody gets out here."

Declan stepped up to Emily and held out his hand. "Grace sent us. You must be Emily."

The woman took his hand and nodded. "I'm Emily," she said softly. "Thank you for coming to my rescue."

Declan chuckled and tipped his head at Mustang. "You'll have to thank Mustang. He's the one who came to your rescue."

She raised her eyebrows and shot a glance toward Mustang. "Mustang? Is that your real name or is that a call sign?"

"Call sign," Mustang answered. "Frank Ford." He held out his hand and she took it, giving it a firm shake before releasing it and rubbing her hand on the side of her leg.

The wailing of a siren brought all three heads up at once. Lights blinked around the corner and an ambulance came to a stop beside Mustang's truck. The EMT crew leaped out of their rig and converged on Emily.

She held up her hands and backed away. "I'm okay," she insisted.

Mustang touched her shoulder. "Let them look you over. Even if it doesn't make you feel better, it will make me feel better," he said and stepped back to let the EMT crew get to Emily.

Declan fell in beside Mustang. "Did you get a look at the guy who attacked her?"

Mustang shook his head. "No, it was dark, and the guy wore a ski mask." He stared in the direction the dark sedan had gone. "However, the man had a Russian accent."

Declan's brows rose. "Russian, aye."

Mustang shrugged. "Not that I speak Russian. But it sounded like it to me, and Emily apparently can speak Russian because she said something in Russian when I tackled her."

Declan chuckled. "You tackled her?"

With a frown, Mustang nodded. "I had to, to stop her from running out in the road."

Declan shook his head. "That's no way to make a new friend."

Mustang snorted. "I wasn't trying to make a friend. I was trying to save her from getting run over."

Declan clapped a hand to Mustang's shoulder. "Well, that will make Grace happy. She was worried about Emily."

When the EMTs brought out a stretcher, they were stopped by an emphatic, *No!*

Emily shrugged out of the hands of one of the technicians. "I'm okay, I'm telling you."

"Ma'am, being in a car wreck, and having the airbags deploy, can cause concussion. We'd feel better if you came to the hospital and had one of the doctors look you over."

Emily shook her head. "At no time was I unconscious."

"You don't have to be unconscious to have suffered

a concussion." The EMT gripped her arm. "Please, ma'am, let us take care of you."

She shook off his hand and backed away. "I'm okay and I can take care of myself." She looked around, her gaze catching Mustang's. "If I've suffered any injuries, my friends will make sure that I get to a hospital on time. Won't you?" She directed her challenge at Declan.

Declan chuckled. "We'll get her to the nearest hospital if she starts showing any signs of deteriorating health."

The technician shrugged. "Have it your way." He closed his kit and loaded it into the emergency vehicle. The two other technicians who'd gotten the stretcher out put it into the back of the ambulance and eventually the three of them drove away.

Emily turned and stared at the wreckage of her car. "I don't suppose I'm going to get that out of the ditch anytime soon," she said.

Again Declan chuckled. "No. The only thing that's going to get that vehicle out of the ditch is a tow truck."

Emily sighed and turned to Declan and Mustang. "I take it you're my ride."

Declan nodded. "However, you do have a choice between riding with me—" he tipped his head toward Mustang "—or with Mustang."

Emily's eyes narrowed as she stared from Mustang to Declan and back.

Mustang found himself holding his breath. He didn't know why, and he didn't know the woman, but he wanted her to choose him.

Though she was soaked with the equivalent of swamp water, he had come this far to save her. He didn't want to let it end there.

For several seconds Emily chewed on her bottom lip. Then she drew in a breath, let it go on a sigh and nodded at Mustang. "I'll ride with Mustang," she said softly.

"Well then, let's get you to Charlie's place. It's not too far down the road. That way you can get out of those cold, wet clothes. It's starting to get chilly outside," Declan said.

Emily nodded, a shiver shaking her frame.

Declan grinned. "I'll see you there." He spun on his heels and hurried toward his truck.

When Mustang tried to steer her toward his truck, Emily dug her heels into the pavement. "I can't leave my purse and keys in the car." She started toward the wrecked vehicle.

"I'll get them," Mustang insisted. "Stay here."

He dropped down into the ditch and found his way into the damaged vehicle. After pulling the keys from the ignition, he took longer than he wanted to find the purse. Finally, he had what he needed and returned to Emily's side.

Mustang handed her the purse and keys, gripped her elbow and led her to the passenger side of his pickup. He opened the door to assist her into the seat.

She put her foot on the running board and it slipped, causing her to fall back into Mustang's arms.

He held her until she had her feet firmly on the ground again. "You all right?"

She nodded. Color rose up her neck and into her cheeks. She reached this time for the handle inside the cab of the truck and helped pull herself up into the passenger seat.

Once Emily was settled, Mustang reached around her and clicked the shoulder strap of the seat belt across her lap. As he retracted his elbow, it brushed gently across her breast and he quickly mumbled an apology. A blast of electricity shot through him.

Emily's breath hitched, as if she'd had a similar experience.

Mustang jerked his arm back and stepped away from the side of the truck, slamming the door firmly. He rounded the front of the vehicle and climbed into the driver's seat. Without another word, he started the engine and pulled out onto the road. The shock he'd felt had to have been static electricity. There could be no other explanation. There was no way he'd felt a connection with the cold, wet woman who'd showed a remarkable amount of spirit and courage in her escape from her captor. Mustang barely knew the woman.

Chapter Three

They'd gone maybe a little more than a mile when Mustang pulled off at a large, impressive stone wall and wrought-iron gate. Declan's truck had just pulled through onto the estate and he waved his hand out the window for them to follow.

Mustang drove through and the gate closed slowly behind them.

Emily had heard Grace talk about her new employer, Charlie, or Charlotte Halverson, the widow of a wealthy philanthropist. Grace had gone on and on about the beautiful estate and how kind and caring her employer was to her collection of employees.

Having been the most recent recipient of Charlie's kindness, Emily was anxious to meet the woman. If Charlie had not sent Mustang out to help, Emily was absolutely certain she would not be alive to appreciate the beauty of Charlie's estate at that moment.

She glanced toward the man beside her, studying him in the light from the dash.

He was tall, with broad shoulders and a ruggedly handsome face. Something about his stoic countenance tugged deeply at Emily's insides. Or perhaps she was just grateful he'd arrived when he had and saved her from being shot. Either way, she felt closer to this man than any other stranger she had ever met.

Chills rippled through Emily. She fought to keep her teeth from chattering. Her clothes were damp, and she smelled like swamp water, but she couldn't help that.

"S-s-so you work for Charlie?" she asked.

Mustang gave a curt nod. "Yeah."

"W-w-what do you do for her?" Emily wrapped her hands around her arms and shivered in her seat.

He adjusted the thermostat on the dash to make it blow blessedly warm air. "She hired Declan and then he brought the rest of our team on board. I guess you could say we are kind of a security agency."

"Does the agency have a name?" Emily asked.

Mustang smiled. "Declan's Defenders."

"So, Declan is your leader?" Emily asked.

Mustang nodded. "He was our team lead before. It just seemed natural for him to be lead of Declan's Defenders."

"Before?" Emily stared across the console at the man driving.

Mustang's jaw tightened. "We were in the marines together."

Emily nodded silently. She should have recognized his military bearing. The man didn't have an ounce of flab or fat on him. And when he stood, he held himself straight, shoulders back and head held high, the countenance and bearing of someone who had been in the military, living under strict rules and guidelines.

Mustang shot a glance her way. "So what did you do to piss someone off enough that they want to kill you?"

Emily shook her head. "I have no idea," she said.

"I seriously doubt it was a case of road rage," Mustang noted.

Emily snorted. "Well, if it was road rage, he did a good job of it. He ran me off the road."

"And chased you down with a gun." Mustang's brows dipped. "If I'm not mistaken, that man spoke Russian. And when I tackled you, you spoke in Russian, as well. What's up with that?"

Emily ran a hand through her hair and stared out the window beside her. "I'm a Russian interpreter. No, I'm not Russian, I'm American, but I studied Russian in high school and college. I also studied abroad in Moscow for a semester. Now I teach Russian at Georgetown and I translate for people who speak Russian."

"Was the guy who tried to kill you one of the clients you translated for?"

Emily pressed her lips together. "You know as much as I do. The man wore a ski mask. I couldn't tell you if he was one of my clients." A shiver shook Emily so hard her teeth rattled.

Mustang glanced at her again. "You're cold."

She nodded.

"Sorry, I should have given you this earlier." He reached over the back of the seat, grabbed a blanket and threw it across her lap. "Wrap yourself in that. You need to warm up."

Emily picked at the blanket. "I hate to get it all wet and smelly."

"Don't worry about it. It'll wash."

Mustang followed Declan's taillights as they twisted and turned on the tree-lined road leading to Charlotte Halverson's massive mansion.

Emily wrapped the blanket around her lap, thankful for the warmth. She would be sure to wash and return it when she got back to her apartment. Then she'd begin the hassle of getting her car repaired or replaced. In the meantime she was dependent on Charlotte Halverson and Declan's Defenders to get her around. And she was thankful they'd come through for her when she'd needed them.

As they pulled up in front of the three-story mansion with its many gables and arches, several men descended the marble staircase from the front door. Three women followed, one of whom Emily recognized as Grace. And the other, her friend Riley. The front porch lights shone down on the third woman's gray hair. That had to be Charlotte Halverson. Emily had seen pictures of her in the news and in the papers.

Mustang pulled to a stop and shifted into Park. Before he could get out and around to the other side of the truck, the door opened and Declan held out his hand for her.

Emily pushed the blanket off her lap and accepted the assistance to get down from the truck.

Grace, the first woman to reach her, wrapped her in her arms. "Oh, sweetie, I'm so sorry this happened to you."

"I'm okay. Mustang got there in time." Emily briefly hugged her back and then pulled away. "Sorry. I'm soaked and I'm sure I smell."

Grace's brow furrowed as she held Emily at arm's length and raked her gaze over her from head to toe. "What happened?"

"We'll fill you all in when Emily's had a chance to get out of those damp clothes," Mustang said.

"Right." Grace hooked Emily's arm. "We'll find you

something to wear. I have enough clothes here, I might as well move in permanently."

The gray-haired woman stepped forward. "I've left an open invitation for you and Declan to take the west wing."

Grace smiled at her employer. "Charlie, this is my friend, Emily. Emily, meet Charlotte Halverson, my new boss."

Emily held out her hand. "Nice to m-meet y-you," she said, her teeth rattling. "And th-thank y-you."

"Oh, pish." Charlie took Emily's hand and frowned. "Your hands are like ice. Inside. Now." She grabbed Emily's other elbow and marched her up the steps. The door opened as if automatically.

Once inside, Emily saw a man dressed in a suit, holding the door handle, standing at attention.

"That's Arnold, my butler," Charlie said. "Don't let him intimidate you. I can't get him to wear anything but a suit." She winked at Arnold as she passed him. "But I can't live without him, so he gets his way more often than not. Isn't that right, Arnold?"

"Yes, Mrs. Halverson." Arnold gave her a slight bow.

"Charlie. I've told you to call me Charlie."

Without changing his expression the butler nodded. "Yes, ma'am."

Charlie shook her head and gave a wry grin to Emily. "Please, call me Charlie. Mrs. Halverson was my husband's mother."

Emily forced a smile past her chattering teeth. "Charlie," she repeated softly.

"Mrs. Halverson, would you like me to escort your guest to a bedroom?" Albert asked in his flat, expressionless tone.

Charlie waved a hand. "No need. Grace and I will take her." She charged across a smooth white-marble foyer and started up the stairs.

Feeling like she was being dragged along by a freight train, Emily looked back over her shoulder, her gaze searching for and finding Mustang's.

"I'll be here when you get cleaned up," he said.

She gave him a quick smile and followed Charlie up the stairs, Grace bringing up the rear. Why she should be relieved Mustang was staying, she didn't know. Surrounded by Grace and Charlie, Emily should feel reassured. However she'd never had a man point a gun at her, much less discharge it in an attempt to kill her.

Mustang had been the one to save her. She felt confident that if her attacker tried again to kill her, Mustang would keep him from succeeding. Knowing he was sticking around made her feel much better.

Although Emily had been in a number of posh hotels and opulent embassies, she'd never been inside a multimillionaire's mansion. Everywhere she looked, what appeared to be priceless objects were perched on tables, in alcoves and hung on the walls. She imagined she could pay her rent for a year with even one of the vases or paintings.

Charlie turned right at the top of the staircase. "You can stay in the Banyan Room while you're here."

"Thank you. But as soon as I can, I'd like to return to my apartment."

Grace grabbed Emily's arm. "Sweetie, you can't go back to your apartment as long as that maniac is still out there."

Charlie nodded. "Agreed. And I have plenty of

empty rooms. You'll stay here." Her tone didn't allow for argument.

But Emily couldn't put her life on hold. "I have a job. I work at the university. I have students to teach."

Charlie shook her head. "Honey, you can't teach if you're dead."

A lead weight settled at the pit of Emily's belly.

"And if you show up at the university, who's to say your attacker won't show up, as well?" Grace added. "You would be putting your students at risk of being caught in the crossfire."

The lead weight twisted in Emily's gut. They were right. "But I can't hide here forever. I have bills to pay."

"Then we'll have to figure out who attacked you."

"You can't do it on your own. I'm the only one who knows my life. I won't stand by and let others put themselves at risk for me."

"Then I'll assign one of Declan's Defenders to protect you and help you figure out who has it in for you." Charlie crossed her arms over her chest. "In the meantime, you need a safe place to sleep. Your apartment isn't that place. I have enough security wired into this estate, you won't have to worry about anyone getting in."

Emily smiled and hugged Charlie. "Thank you. If you hadn't sent Mustang to help me, I wouldn't even be here to have this conversation."

"Any one of Declan's Defenders would have done the same. But since Mustang saved your life, he now has a vested interest in keeping you alive." Charlie waved toward the room. "While you get cleaned up, I'll have a word with Declan about assigning Mustang to protect you."

Warmth spread through Emily's body, loosening the knot in her stomach. Despite her desire to get back to work, she didn't want to put herself or her students in danger.

Charlie left Emily and Grace and headed for the staircase.

Grace chuckled. "Charlie is a force to be reckoned with."

"Yes, she is," Emily agreed.

"But she has a heart of gold and would do anything for you." Grace touched Emily's shoulder, guiding her to the other side of the bedroom where a door led to an attached bathroom. "While you get a shower, I'll gather some of my clothes."

Tears filled Emily's eyes. "Thank you, Grace. You saved my life."

Grace laughed. "I didn't save your life. Mustang did."

"Because you had him sent to me." A tear slipped down her cheek. "I don't think I've ever been more afraid in my life."

"Honey, I know what you mean," Grace said, her voice tight, her lips pressing together briefly. "I've been there."

Emily nodded. "Yes, you were. Back when Riley went missing."

"Declan was there when I needed him. He and his men went to bat for me, and for Riley when things got sticky for her, too. They'll help you. And Mustang's a good man. He'll take care of you."

"I want to say I don't need anyone to take care of me but…" A shiver shook her wet frame. "Apparently I do. I've never had a man shoot at me or hold a gun to my head."

"Oh, sweetie." Grace pulled Emily's bedraggled form into her arms. "I'm sorry you had to go through that. Hopefully the team can help figure out who did this to you and why." She turned Emily and gave her a gentle shove in the direction of the bathroom. "For now, get cleaned up and warm. Everything will look better once you are."

"Thank you, Grace." Emily entered the bathroom and closed the door behind her, leaning against it to keep from falling. Another shiver shook her, and another, until her entire body quaked with the tremors. She knew it was shock setting in. If she didn't get into a warm shower soon, she didn't know what would happen. She could pass out or die from hypothermia. After Mustang went to the effort of saving her, that would be a crappy way to repay him.

She pushed away from the door and took stock of the beautiful bathroom. Six of her apartment bathrooms could fit in the space. White quartz counters and sinks shone, sparkling clean. A large bathtub invited the guest to fill it full of warm water, bath salts and oils. Bypassing the tub, Emily walked to the shower, turned on the faucet and waited for the water to warm.

Her hands shook as she stripped out of her wet clothing and dropped the garments to the smooth, tiled floor.

When the water was warmer than her skin, she stepped beneath it and let it run over her head, shoulders and the length of her body. As the heat chased away the chills, she squirted a liberal amount of shampoo into her palm and smoothed it over her hair, digging her fingers in, determined to wash away the smell of stagnant water.

Emily leaned her head back, closed her eyes and

let the water sluice over her. As the soap bubbles slid down over her breasts, a sudden image intruded on her thoughts. An erotic scene, completely at odds with the suspenseful one she'd just lived through. Maybe it was a coping mechanism, but she couldn't get the thought out of her head. One of Mustang rubbing his hands together to create lather and smoothing them all over her body.

Shocked by her own imagination, Emily opened her eyes and took in a deep, steadying breath. She had to be having some kind of post-traumatic lust for the man who'd saved her. She didn't know Mustang from Adam. He could be married, for all she knew. Her heart pounded against her ribs. She could be having lustful thoughts over a married man.

Grabbing the bottle of body wash, she completed her shower in record time, scrubbing every inch of her skin to remove traces of mud and ditch water.

When she emerged from the shower, she found a neat stack of clothing on the counter and a fluffy white towel.

She smiled at Grace's thoughtfulness.

Her lips turned down as she dressed. How could she face Mustang when she'd just been thinking about him naked?

Chapter Four

Mustang paced the floor of one of the spacious living rooms in Charlie's mansion. He'd been inside the home a number of times since going to work for the rich widow. Still, he didn't feel comfortable surrounded by the opulence millions of dollars could afford to buy. He preferred the comfort of his own little house. The one he'd purchased since landing the job with Declan's Defenders.

In all of the years he'd been on active duty, he'd never established roots in any one place. Since signing on with his brothers in arms to a decent job with a steady income and benefits, he'd decided it was time.

His friends had given him a hard time about having a home without a partner. Mustang didn't care. It was his, and he could do anything he wanted with it. If he wanted to paint the walls purple with green polka dots, he could. He didn't have to ask permission of a landlord or the government.

Though he'd prefer to be at his own house, he wasn't about to leave until he knew Emily was safe. Even then, he didn't want to leave without her. After saving her life, he felt responsible for her. Since her attacker had gotten away, she couldn't be one hundred percent safe.

"What do you know about Emily?" Mustang asked Declan.

"Only that she's a friend of Grace's, works at a university teaching Russian and performs as an interpreter when needed." Declan shrugged. "I got all of that today when Grace told me Emily was in trouble."

Mustang made another pass of the living room, feeling like a caged lion ready to bust out and roar. "Grace didn't say anything about her work? Anything or anyone who might have it in for her?"

Declan shook his head. "Nothing."

Stopping in front of a massive fireplace, Mustang ran a hand through his hair. "I should have killed the bastard."

"And if you'd gone after him, you'd have left Emily unprotected." Declan clapped a hand on Mustang's shoulder. "You did the right thing."

"Oh, good." Charlie entered the living room and smiled at Mustang. "I'm glad you stayed."

Declan stepped forward. "How's Emily?"

Mustang hung back, wanting to know the answer and barely willing to wait for Charlie's response.

"She's okay," Charlie said. "Shaken but okay."

Mustang released a silent sigh. He'd worried she might have had injuries not readily apparent.

"She's okay for now, anyway." Charlie directed her gaze at Declan and then Mustang. "However, I'm concerned."

"So are we," Declan responded. "Emily needs someone protecting her at all times, until her attacker can be found and dealt with."

Charlie smiled. "I agree. Who from your team do you suggest?"

Mustang's heart pounded against his ribs as he stepped forward. "I'll do it."

A frown pulled at Charlie's brow. "Are you sure? It will mean being with her 24/7."

"He's young, single and has the skills needed to protect Emily," Declan said.

The corners of Charlie's lips quirked. "Are you sure there's not someone more suited than Mustang?"

"She's mine," Mustang blurted. "I mean, I've already saved her life once. I feel it's my duty to protect her and continue to keep her safe."

Charlie grinned. "I was hoping you'd feel that way. I think she will feel most comfortable with you, for just that reason."

Declan nodded. "I agree. The rest of my men will be backup when not otherwise engaged."

"Good." Charlie raised an eyebrow. "Then, Mustang, you'll be staying here until further notice. You'll be in the room next to Emily's."

"What?" Mustang frowned. "Why here?"

"Unless you or Emily have an airtight security system at your homes, she will not be as safe as she can be here."

"She's right," Declan interjected. "I've gone over all the security devices, cameras and fences. No one will get in without setting off an alarm and having half a dozen guards swarming all over them."

"Can you or Emily top that?" Charlie tilted her head. "If so, by all means. Otherwise, I have plenty of room, as Grace and Declan can attest to."

Mustang pressed his lips together. So much for enjoying his own home. But until Emily's attacker was apprehended and Emily was safe to go about her own life again, Mustang would do what it took to be close enough to protect her. "I'm in."

"Do you need to go back to your home to collect clothing and toiletries?" Charlie asked.

He shook his head. "I keep a go-bag in my truck for emergencies. I can get by on what I have stashed in it."

"Smart man." Charlie clapped her hands together. "Now that we've settled who's protecting Emily, I'll make sure the chef increases the number of plates to serve at dinner." Charlie left the room.

Mustang's head spun.

Declan chuckled. "Charlie doesn't give anyone a chance to say no." His smile faded. "But seriously, man, are you good to go with this?"

Mustang nodded. "I'm good."

"Then get your gear and meet me and some of the others in the basement conference room. I'll have Grace and Emily join us when they're ready."

Mustang headed for the front entrance.

"Pardon me, sir." Arnold, the butler, stood in front of the door. "Are you the owner of the truck that had been parked out front?"

"I'm one of them. Declan's is the other," Mustang replied.

"I hope you don't mind, but I took the liberty of parking both of them in the rear garage."

"Okay." Mustang turned. "Could you point me in the right direction? I need to collect my gear bag."

"I'll show you, sir." Arnold stepped forward, his posture impeccable, his gate measured. He moved swiftly as he led Mustang through the foyer, past a living area, a study and the massive kitchen. They finally reached a back entrance. The butler paused long enough to hold open the door for Mustang to step outside into the light shining down on a porch and sidewalk that weaved through a garden.

Though he'd been to the estate before, Mustang hadn't been there often enough to memorize his way around. Since he'd be staying there indefinitely, he needed to be completely familiar with every building, gate and entry and exit onto the property. He studied what he could in the glow lighting the path.

Once inside the detached garage, Arnold flipped on the light switch.

Mustang blinked. He knew the building was large, but wow. At least twenty cars in a multitude of shapes, models, years and colors formed two rows. "This isn't a garage, it's a warehouse," he muttered.

Arnold nodded. "Mr. Halverson collected cars." He plucked a soft cloth off a shelf and ran it over the hood of a sleek, black Ferrari. "This was one of his favorites."

"Does Charlie drive them?"

"No." Arnold tipped his head toward a long black limousine. "She leaves the drive to the chauffeurs. The traffic in DC is more than she prefers to manage. And many of these wouldn't accommodate her security detail."

"It's a shame no one drives these," Mustang commented. "Why does she keep them?"

"You'll have to ask Mrs. Halverson. I suspect she has a sentimental attachment to them." Arnold folded the soft cloth and replaced it on the shelf. "Your truck is over here." He led the way through a door into another section of the garage where Mustang's black truck was parked next to a four-door sedan Mustang assumed was Grace's. On the other side of the car were three more vehicles he recognized. The black one similar to his belonged to Declan. The charcoal-gray, four-wheel-drive pickup belonged to Mack Balkman, the assistant lead of the team. An olive-drab Hummer was Cole McCastlain's, equipped to transport Dawg, his Belgain Malenoi, his former military war dog. On the far side of the line of vehicles was a Harley-Davidson belonging to Jack Snow. Gus Walsh must have caught a ride with Cole or Mack, otherwise his vehicle would have been in the lineup.

The team had agreed to meet at Charlie's estate before the incident with Emily. Mustang had been on the way when he'd gotten the call. If he hadn't been where he was, Emily would not have survived.

The thought drove him forward to collect his gear. An unexplainable urge to return to the house and lay eyes on his new assignment made him jerk open the truck door and grab the go-bag from behind the rear seat.

"Is that all you need?" Arnold asked.

"That's all." Mustang turned and headed back the way they'd come.

"Pardon me, sir."

Arnold's voice brought Mustang to a halt. He turned, bag in hand, to face the butler.

"Mrs. Halverson asked me to show you an alternate route to return to the main house. She said you never know when it might come in handy. Her words, exactly."

Curious, Mustang returned to Arnold's side. "Lead the way."

The butler spun on his heels and marched toward

what appeared to be a wall of tools. When he reached it, he pulled on a shiny wrench. The wall shook slightly and then a door opened outward. Stairs led downward, in the direction of the house.

"They thought of everything," Mustang said.

"Mr. Halverson felt he should always be prepared for any situation."

"What was he expecting, a war?"

Arnold shrugged. "You never know. Now, if you will follow me." The butler descended the stairs. As he reached the bottom, a light blinked on.

When Mustang stepped through, the door behind him closed. He turned to study the mechanism to re-open it should he need to. A lever on the wall beside the door appeared to be how the lock was triggered. Committing it to memory, he hurried after Arnold.

The tunnel was bright white and well-lit. At one point, the pathway split.

Arnold paused long enough to point to the right. "That way leads to the rose arbor at the end of the garden." He didn't go in that direction. Instead he veered left. Soon they were climbing steps up to another door with a similar lever as the one at the garage.

Arnold pulled the lever. As he did, the light in the tunnel snuffed out.

Mustang stopped two steps below Arnold and waited until the door they'd just reached opened inward. Light from above spilled through the gap and flooded the stairwell as the exit grew wider.

They emerged into the study they'd passed on their way through the house. Once Mustang cleared the door, the wall shifted back into place. Wood paneling and a floor-to-ceiling bookcase completely hid the door.

Arnold pointed to a book on one of the shelves. "If you need to use the tunnel, look for *Moby Dick*."

Mustang leaned forward and read the title on the book binding. *Moby Dick*.

Arnold gave him a slight chin lift. "Go ahead. Give it a try."

Mustang pulled the book, which gave a little resistance. Instead of sliding off the shelf, it tipped and the wall moved, opening to reveal the passage they'd just emerged from.

"I'll take you to your room." Arnold led the way out of the study, up the curving staircase to the second floor of the three-story mansion and turned right. He walked down a long hallway and stopped at a door. "You'll be in this room." The butler nodded at one door farther down the hallway. "Miss Chastain is in the room beside you. There is a connecting door should you need to use it." He pushed open the hall door and stood back for Mustang to enter. "When you've deposited your gear, Mrs. Halverson would like the team to meet in the conference room."

"Roger," Mustang responded automatically. His lips twisted. "You weren't perhaps in the military at some time, were you?"

Arnold gave a slight nod and met Mustang's gaze. "Ten years in the SAS."

Mustang held out his hand. "Always good to meet a brother in arms."

Arnold shook the man's hand. "Always good to have help you can count on." With a nod, he left Mustang and marched down the hallway.

For a long moment Mustang watched the former SAS operative. Only then did he notice a slight limp. Despite

Arnold's limp, Mustang bet the butler could hold his own in a fight. Mrs. Halverson was lucky to have him on staff. Though, to Mustang, being a butler was only a small portion of Arnold's duties. He was her first line of defense in the mansion.

Mustang dropped his gear on the bed and unzipped the bag. It had been several weeks since he'd packed the duffel. He removed the items quickly, throwing clothes in a drawer and his ammo on top of the dresser. When the bag was empty, he zipped it and stored it in the closet. Then he walked to the door connecting to the other room and pressed his ear to the panel. He could hear the sound of a shower and twisted the knob to see if it was locked.

The knob turned easily.

Rather than barge in, he released the knob and left the door closed. He would have liked to see Emily before going downstairs, but he couldn't wait. His team was waiting for him in the conference room. He strode to the French doors, stepped out onto the balcony and leaned over to check the window of the room beside him. No trees grew close enough for someone to climb and gain entry. No ladders had been left nearby and the brick and rock walls were clear of any trellises or climbing vines.

Relatively certain Emily would be all right in the house, Mustang made his way back down the stairs, past a living room and into the study. A door led from inside the study, down a hidden staircase into the basement and a soundproof space Mr. Halverson had used as a conference room before his untimely death. A fourteen-foot mahogany conference table took up much of the room with enough chairs to seat a dozen people. The side walls contained magnetic Dry-Erase whiteboards. Several computer terminals were positioned along the walls with six monitors each, arranged in an array.

Cole McCastlain, the team's radio operator and all-around computer guru, sat at one of the keyboards, alternating between typing furiously and clicking on the mouse.

Gus Walsh and Jack Snow stood behind him, peering over his shoulder at the information on the center screen. While they worked, they ate. A sideboard was set up buffet-style with sandwiches, salads, drinks and something warm and delicious-smelling that Emily guessed was lasagna. When Grace saw her eyeing it, she quickly fixed Emily and Mustang plates and set them on the table.

"For when you're hungry," she said to them both.

"What have you learned about Emily's attacker?" Mustang asked.

"Nothing, yet," Jack said. "We're not even sure where to start."

Declan, Mack, Grace and Charlie stood before another set of monitors set up with several news channel displays, the volume on each turned down low but loud enough they could hear.

Grace stared at one of the television monitors, her brows furrowed. "Emily was at the Russian embassy today. She said she was translating for the ambassador, but couldn't divulge what was said."

Charlie shifted her gaze from one news station to another. "I thought I heard something about an altercation at the Russian embassy earlier today. They had a lockdown. Surely they'll say something about it on the evening news."

"The lockdown must have happened after Emily left," Declan noted.

"I have contacts at a couple of the news stations and local newspapers," Charlie said. "I could call around and get the scoop."

"Wait." Grace pointed to a screen. "Turn that one up."

Mack grabbed the remote and adjusted the volume louder.

A reporter stood in front of large building in downtown DC. Behind him were at least a dozen police cars, SWAT vehicles and fire trucks. He glanced behind him and back at the camera. "Today, at approximately three forty-five in the afternoon, the Russian embassy locked its gates and refused to let anyone in or out. So far, no one inside is talking to explain why they've instituted a lockdown. The State Department has reached out to Russia for answers, but so far no one knows why the Russian embassy has been shut down or who might still be inside."

"What are they saying?" a voice said from behind Mustang. "The Russian embassy is in lockdown?"

Mustang turned to face Emily. Her long blond hair lay in damp strands around her shoulders and her face was scrubbed clean of any makeup. The clothes she wore hung loose on her frame, just some sweatpants and a T-shirt, and she stood barefooted on the Persian rug.

Grace went to her friend, slipped an arm around her shoulders and led her toward the television monitors. "They had a lockdown around three forty-five this afternoon."

"That was right after I left." Emily shook her head. "What happened?"

"No one knows," Charlie said. "No one is getting in or out of the embassy at this time."

"And no one is talking," Declan added. "Did you see or hear anything on your way in or out?"

Emily shook her head. "No."

"Can you share what you translated while inside the embassy?" Mack asked.

Again Emily shook her head, shifting from one foot to the other, her discomfort apparent. "I signed nondisclosure statements. But I can tell you, it was more of a personal nature than political. I wouldn't think it would cause a lockdown."

"Well, something did," Charlie said. "And I wonder who is still inside and why."

Emily looked back at the monitors. "Did they say anything about a Mr. Phillips? He was the man whose report I translated. He was still there when I left the embassy."

Grace responded. "No, nothing."

Mustang stepped up beside Emily and cupped her elbow. He leaned close and whispered, "Are you all right?"

She glanced up into his eyes, a small, grateful smile curling her lips. She gave him a silent nod and leaned into his arm. Together they faced the wall of monitors.

Several of the newscasts displayed various reporters standing in front of the Russian embassy, all reporting on the lockdown. As if on cue, they cut to commercials, all except one station that flashed a still image of a young man on the screen. The man held a microphone, a strand of his dark hair falling over his forehead like an unintentional fashion statement.

Emily gave a small gasp and stiffened against Mustang.

He stared down at her. "What's wrong?"

"I saw that man."

"Where?" Grace asked.

"At the embassy before I left," Emily said. Her brow furrowed. "What are they saying about him?"

"Turn it up," Mustang commanded.

Mack adjusted the volume.

The picture was replaced by a female news anchor. "So far, we have received no word from Tyler Blunt. He was supposed to report in yesterday evening with the station manager, but he hasn't. He hasn't been to his apartment in two days and he isn't answering his phone. If anyone has any information about Tyler Blunt's whereabouts, please notify this station."

"He was in the embassy," Emily said.

"Are you sure?"

Emily nodded. "He was on his way in as I was on my way out."

"Was he going willingly?" Mustang asked.

Emily frowned. "I wasn't sure. They were hustling me out at that time. The young man was flanked by a couple of men."

Grace gripped her arms. "Emily, a reporter is missing. One you saw at the Russian embassy. Then you were attacked after leaving the embassy. Doesn't that sound too coincidental?"

Mustang's jaw tightened. "I don't believe in coincidence."

Emily looked over Grace's shoulder into Mustang's eyes, her own widening. "Neither do I. But what do I have to do with the reporter?"

Chapter Five

Mustang shook his head. “Maybe your attack and Tyler Blunt’s disappearance have nothing to do with each other. But my gut is telling me otherwise.”

A chill rippled down the back of Emily’s neck. “I’ve never even met Tyler Blunt. Sure, I’ve seen him on television news reports, but I’ve never actually had words with him. Why would he and I have anything in common? Other than being in the Russian embassy at the same time, we’ve never been anywhere closer. There has to be another reason for the attack on me.”

Charlie’s eyes narrowed. “Well, we won’t know unless we start asking questions.” She glanced across the room at Declan.

Declan nodded. “We’re on it.” He nodded toward Gus who had been busy clicking away on the mouse and the keyboard of the computer he’d been working for as long as Emily had been in the conference room. “We have Gus searching for anything that might raise red flags.”

Mustang’s eyes narrowed. “Cross-check anything related to the Russian ambassador and Tyler Blunt.”

“Already have,” Cole confirmed. “Nothing is coming up tying Blunt with the ambassador, Nikolai Kozlov. But I’m not finished digging. It could take some time.”

"We might have to get out on the street and ask questions," Mustang said.

"In the meantime, I still have a job to do," Emily said. "I'm supposed to teach a class in Russian literature tomorrow."

"Can't you call in sick?" Charlie asked.

She shook her head. "No. We have a major test coming up. I'm going over everything we've covered for the first half of the semester. Then I'm adminstering the test. I have to be there."

"Once you step foot off Charlie's estate, you could become a target all over again." Mustang said. "Could you pass your notes to someone else and let them perform the review?"

Emily crossed her arms over her chest. "I can't bail on my students."

Mustang frowned heavily. "Their grades mean more to you than your life?"

"They've all worked hard," she said. "If it were any other day in the semester, I might consider skipping. But it's the only class day they have left before midterms. I owe it to them to be there."

"And how will they respond to having a stranger in their classroom?" Mustang stood taller, his shoulders back, his chin held high.

Emily studied the man. Her reaction was probably not a good indication of how the other young men and women would react to the big marine standing or sitting among them. He was far too handsome and built like a tank. Every red-blooded cell in her veins stood up and applauded at the determined man, standing with his shoulders back and head held high.

Her heart pounded and her voice came out as a

squeak. "They'll..." She cleared her throat and started again. "They'll have to deal with it, I suppose." Emily pushed her shoulders back and stood as tall as her five feet, four inches could manage against Mustang's much larger stance. "I have to be there."

Mustang's lips twitched. "So be it. We'll be there." He turned to Declan. "And then we'll come right back here."

Before he finished the last word, she was shaking her head. "I want to go by my apartment and gather some of my clothing and toiletries." She shot a glance at Grace. "No offense, but I like wearing my own things."

Grace smiled. "None taken. I prefer my own stuff, myself."

Mustang nodded. "Okay, but then we're heading right back to this estate."

Again Emily shook her head. "While we're out, I'd like to stop by the office of the organization that hired me as an interpreter. Maybe they will know something about what happened today."

"I know you signed a nondisclosure agreement," Mustang said. "But can you tell us who was involved in the meeting where you translated Russian?"

Emily chewed on her bottom lip. She was not at liberty to tell them what was said, but nowhere in that agreement had it stipulated she couldn't talk about who else was involved. "I was interpreting for an American private investigator. Jay Phillips."

"We'll look him up," Declan said. "And it wouldn't hurt to pay him a visit."

Emily frowned. "My nondisclosure didn't specifically say I couldn't talk about who was in the meeting.

But telling you the investigator's name might be construed as crossing the line."

Declan nodded. "Fair enough. We'll tread lightly when we confront him. Mostly, we want to find out if he's suffering some of the same problems as you are. And if so, we might conclude that whatever was discussed at the meeting could have something to do with whoever is trying to kill you."

Declan's Defenders dug into the buffet, while they went over and over the events leading up to Emily being run off the road. They considered every detail, every angle, as they ate. By the time they finished, Emily was certain she'd have nightmares for the rest of her life.

After everyone had eaten, Emily helped carry plates to the massive kitchen, eager to escape the inquisition. She placed her dishes on the counter beside the sink. When she turned, she almost ran into Mustang.

"Sorry," she said. "I didn't know you were there."

"It's okay," he said. "I was following too close."

Standing so near to Mustang caused a ripple of awareness to shoot across her skin and make her shiver. Emily spun back to the sink, put the stopper in the drain, and started filling it with water and soap.

"My staff will take care of the cleanup," Charlie said.

"If it's all the same to you, Charlie," Emily said, "I need something to keep myself busy. So much has happened that if I don't have anything to do, I'll just dwell on the bad."

Charlie brought her plate to the sink, laid it on the counter and then pressed a hand to Emily's arm. "I understand. I need to keep busy, as well. When my husband died, I went through the entire house cleaning."

"But you have a staff to do all that," Emily pointed out.

Charlie snorted. "Tell me about it. I confused the hell out of them." She chuckled softly. "And you know how big this house is."

Emily glanced her way. "That must have taken you days."

"I called it vacuum therapy. I made a lot of noise with the vacuum, so I could yell when I was mad and nobody would care or hear me. And when I was done, I had a clean house. The added bonus was that I was worn out and finally able to sleep." She waved at the sink. "So have at it."

"Thank you," Emily said.

Charlie smiled and left the kitchen.

Emily slipped her hands into the warm, soapy water as if reaching for some level of normalcy.

Mustang moved up beside her and handed her a plate. "You wash, I'll dry."

"I can do this by myself," she said, not at all certain she wanted the added complication of standing next to a man who made her body hum.

"I know you can do this by yourself," he said. "That was a lot of excitement for one day. I can use the work, as well."

Emily settled into washing each dish carefully before handing it to Mustang to rinse and dry. She felt a sense of safety and comfort with the big marine standing beside her. But every time her hand touched his, a shock of electricity slipped up her arm and spread warmth across her chest. What was it about the man that made her so aware of him? Other than the fact that he stood a head taller than her, and his shoulders were as broad as a door frame. Something about his rugged countenance and his take-charge attitude sent shivers across her skin.

Grace entered the kitchen carrying a stack of plates. "Need help in here?"

Emily almost said yes. Not that she needed help washing dishes. What she needed was help understanding what was going on inside her head and body. Before she could open her mouth to tell Grace yes, she needed help, Mustang answered for her.

"No, thank you, we've got this covered," he said.

"Okay then," Grace said. "If you get a chance, check out the garden. Charlie has the most wonderful roses and a fountain that can be very soothing to sit in front of. And at night everything smells divine."

"I'll do that," Emily promised.

Once all the dishes were deposited in the kitchen, the rest of the team retired to the living area, leaving Mustang and Emily alone to wash.

For a long time they worked in silence, washing and drying one plate, one glass, one fork at a time. Finally, feeling a little out of breath and rattled, Emily handed the last dish to Mustang. While he dried, she wiped her hands on a towel and hung the towel to dry. Despite the mind-numbing work of washing dishes, she still felt nervous and punchy. Perhaps it was from having been shot at, or maybe it was the big marine who had been standing next to her bumping shoulders with her for the last thirty minutes. But Emily had to move, had to leave the room. Needed to get out, needed some fresh air.

"Thank you for helping by drying." She turned and started for the door leading out of the kitchen.

"Hey, wait," Mustang called out.

Emily turned.

Mustang quickly dried the last dish and put it in the cabinet along with the rest. He laid the towel across the oven rail and rubbed his hands along the sides of his jeans. "I'll go with you."

"That's not necessary," Emily said. "I'm just going to wander around the house. I shouldn't run into any problems inside the Halverson estate."

Mustang's brow dipped. "Well, I guess that's okay. But if you decide to go outside for any reason, let me know and I'll go with you."

"Deal." Emily turned and walked away. She wanted to put distance between her and the marine. Following the sound of voices, she entered the living area where the others had congregated.

Grace glanced up from where she was perched on the arm of a sofa next to Declan and smiled. "Thank you for doing dishes."

Emily nodded. "No problem. It helped me work through some of my nerves."

Grace chuckled. "I can think of much better ways to burn off some steam. But whatever works for you, I'm glad it did."

Declan waved toward the other end of the sofa. "Won't you join us?"

Emily shook her head. "Thank you, no. I don't feel much like sitting." She glanced at Charlie. "If you don't mind, I'd like to explore the house."

Charlie smiled. "Go right ahead. Make yourself at home."

"Do you need someone to show you around?" Grace asked.

Emily gave her half a smile. "No, thank you. I'd like to do it on my own. I need some time to think."

Emily left the living room and walked to the next door down the hallway and entered. Inside this room were some more feminine-looking sofas and a white baby grand piano. Drawn to the musical instrument, she entered the room, crossed to the piano and ran her fingers across the keys.

The cool, white ivories against her fingertips brought back memories she thought she'd forgotten. She hadn't touched a piano since she'd left home almost a decade before. Emily couldn't remember a time as a child when she hadn't been taking piano lessons or going to recitals. Her parents had made absolutely sure that she, as their only child, would have some musical skills as well as learning a foreign language.

Teaching Russian at the university seemed so natural. Her musical skills were adequate but not sufficient to take to the stage. Quietly, so as not to draw attention away from the conversations in the other room, she played one of her favorite tunes that she had committed to memory.

Even after ten years her fingers found the keys. The music was a liltingly sad tune that suited her mood. Soon she was lost in time and the sound of the keys hitting against the chords. When the song came to an end she lifted her fingers from the keys and sat for a moment staring at the instrument.

Until she had sat at Charlie's piano, she hadn't realized just how much she missed playing. And how cathartic the music was to her soul.

"That was beautiful."

Jerked back to the present, Emily shot a glance to the door where Mustang leaned against the doorjamb, a gentle smile tugging at the corners of his lips.

"How long have you been standing there?" she asked, heat rising up her neck.

Mustang straightened and walked toward her. "Since you sat down and started playing." He closed the distance and leaned against the grand piano. "I didn't have the heart to interrupt. In fact, I didn't want to interrupt. I didn't want you to know I was there because you looked so at peace and so engrossed in what you were doing. And, call me selfish, but I liked listening. I didn't want you to stop."

Warmth burned up into her cheeks. Emily glanced down at her fingers on the piano keys. "I haven't played in ten years. It must have sounded awful."

Mustang chuckled.

The deep, resonant sound made her shiver all over.

"If that was awful, then I am tone deaf." His smile disappeared. "Don't stop on my account. If you want, I'll leave the room."

Emily shook her head, pushed back from the piano and stood. "No, really, I'm done," she said. "I haven't made it very far in my exploration of the estate."

Mustang's smile returned. "Uh, right. One room over is not very far. Not when you consider the size of this estate. I believe it's over twelve thousand square feet, just the house alone, and the garage is like a warehouse. There must be over twenty thousand square feet just in the garage alone."

Emily walked around him, giving him plenty of space. She didn't want to touch him for fear of having that electrical shock shoot through her again. "Sounds like you've already done your exploring. You must visit here quite a lot."

"It's our base of operations." Mustang fell into step behind her.

She had hoped he wouldn't follow her. But when the sound of his footsteps continued on her heels, she stopped suddenly.

He bumped into her.

"Look." She spun on her heels to find herself standing toe to toe with Mustang. "Could I have a little space? I don't need you following me around inside the house."

Mustang held up his hands. "Sorry, I didn't mean to crowd you."

Emily raised her hands. They fluttered a little, so close to his chest she could touch him. And that was the problem. She sighed. "I just need some time to myself, to think. To breathe. To get a grasp on what happened today."

Mustang captured her flapping hands in his big, warm paws. "I get it. I'll let you be alone."

She should have pulled her hands free, but the warmth of his fingers holding hers made her want to continue just like that until her heartbeat stopped fluttering so fast.

Instead of slowing to a calm, steady beat, her pulse raced even faster. "I have to go." She pulled her hands free, turned and ran. When she reached the hallway, she looked in both directions. Though alone, she wasn't sure where she should go next.

When she saw the study across the hall, she darted into the room lined with bookshelves. Emily loved books. They were her escape, her wells of knowledge, and her friends when she wanted to be alone but not completely alone.

The ornate wood paneling of the study lined the

walls and ceiling. A massive mahogany desk took up one end of the room. To the side was a set of wood-framed French doors.

With her need to escape driving her forward, Emily aimed for the French doors, charging across the room, pulling the handle and stepping out into the night.

Cool night air felt good against her flushed cheeks as she turned to quietly close the French doors behind her. The soft glow of accent lights guided her along a path leading toward a garden. She guessed it was the rose garden Grace had talked about. She could smell them before she even reached the space. The aroma filled her, wrapped around her and soothed her scattered senses.

Neatly trimmed rosebushes lined the walkway with fragrant blooms in a multitude of colors. In the center of the garden stood a fountain. Water bubbled from the top, dropping down to the lower levels. Stone benches surrounded the fountain, inviting Emily to sit.

She dropped onto the smooth, stone surface and rested her face in her hands. So much had happened in the last twelve hours that she could barely wrap her mind around everything.

Her day had started with her Advanced Russian Language class. She'd gone straight from there to the Russian embassy where she had interpreted for the investigator and the ambassador.

Emily snorted. And she'd thought the Russian ambassador had troubles with his daughter having an affair with an American. He only had to deal with a rebellious daughter. Emily had had to deal with somebody shooting at her or trying to run her over or off the road.

Why did someone want her dead?

She glanced up at the fountain as if it could give

her the answers. But the trickling water just continued to dribble, drip and soothe. But not enough. What she needed was answers. The fountain couldn't give them to her, and the roses were no help, other than to smell pretty. She needed to get out and to ask the questions that would lead her to the answers. Hiding away on Charlie's estate would get her nowhere.

Emily squared her shoulders and started to rise. The snap of a twig made her start. She rose and paused, listening. Was that the shuffle of footsteps? Had Mustang followed her out to the garden?

"Mustang?" she called out softly and then listened, straining her ears to hear anything. Her pulse pounded so loudly against her eardrums she could barely discern the sound of the wind rustling in the leaves.

Mustang had asked her to let him know when she went outside. He'd had a reason for that. Even though the estate was equipped with security cameras and guards, someone could possibly get past them.

Someone who wanted to kill her.

Emily started toward the path leading back to the study and the French doors she had come through. She tiptoed softly, listening as she went, creeping along slowly. With the ever-increasing beat of her heart, she moved faster until she was running.

She burst through the French doors and crashed into a wall of muscle.

Chapter Six

"Hey," a deep voice said. Arms wrapped around her and held her close. "I thought I told you to let me know when you went outside."

She buried her face against his chest. "You did. I didn't. I wish I had."

He stiffened, his arms enfolding her tightly. "What's wrong?"

Emily felt foolish. But she didn't want to push away from his warm embrace. "I don't know. I probably was hearing things."

"You want to stay here while I check it out?"

"No," she said and enveloped her arms around his waist, pressing her face closer to his chest.

"You wanna come with me?" he asked.

"No. Can't we just stay here?" she said, her voice muffled against his shirt.

"We can do that, too." He pulled her closer and rested his chin against the top of her head. "We can stay here as long as you like."

"Good," she said. Her lips pushed against his shirt.

"I don't mind holding you like this, but could we at least get away from the windows?" Mustang whispered.

She nodded.

He guided both of them away from the windows and deeper into the study.

Emily didn't know how long she stood there until her heartbeat slowed to a more normal pace, but it didn't seem nearly long enough.

Mustang didn't say another word, just held her.

When at last she raised her head, she gave him a crooked grin. "I'm sorry."

"What's there to be sorry for?" Mustang touched a finger to the side of her cheek. "You had quite the scare today." He pressed his lips to her forehead and then leaned back. "You okay now?"

She nodded, although her pulse had ratcheted up with the feel of his lips against her forehead.

Mustang shifted one of his hands from around her waist to cup the back of her head. "So, what was it you heard outside?"

She gave a broken laugh. "It was probably a stick falling from the tree. The wind was blowing a little. I'm sure it was nothing."

Mustang cupped her cheek. "Still, I'd like to check it out."

Voices sounded in the hallway.

"Oh, there you are." Declan entered the room, followed by Grace.

Emily stepped away from Mustang. Heat rushed into her cheeks.

"We're trying to contact the private investigator that Emily had interpreted for," Declan said, as if continuing a conversation.

"You think he might have had something to do with this?" Mustang asked.

Declan shook his head. "No, but if Emily is having

difficulties, he might also have run into some problems. We tried looking him up and phoning but got no answer. We don't have his cell info, though. Not yet. We'll find his place and head there tomorrow if we still can't raise a response by then."

Grace crossed to get close to Emily and hooked her arm through Emily's. "Are you doing okay?"

"I'm fine."

Grace frowned. "You look a little flushed. Are you sure you're not feverish?"

Emily shook her head. "No, I was just outside for a few minutes."

Grace smiled. "Did you get to visit the rose garden?"

Emily nodded. "It was as you said…beautiful."

"The roses seem to be even more vibrant as the weather cools," Grace said.

Emily nodded again. She'd been too frightened by the sounds of the night to care.

Mustang tipped his head toward the door. "While Emily was out in the garden a few minutes ago, she thought she heard something."

Declan's eyes widened. "You think someone was out there?"

Mustang shrugged. "I don't know. But I'd feel better if someone checked it out."

Declan nodded. "Will do. I'll get Snow to go look with me."

"Good," Mustang said. "I'll stay with Emily."

Declan left the study, calling out in the hallway, "Snow. Got a mission for you."

Grace frowned and stared into Emily's eyes. "What did you hear in the garden?"

"I don't know. Could just be my imagination playing tricks on me."

Grace shook her head. "The guys will make sure. With all the stress, you must be exhausted."

It wasn't until Grace mentioned it that Emily realized she had been tense. Her muscles were tired, and she was starting to feel all the aches and pains of having fallen in the dirt and from being tackled from behind. Her knees still stung and her shoulder felt bruised. "I am tired."

Grace slipped an arm around her waist. "I can give you a tour of the estate tomorrow. Why don't you hit the hay and get some much-needed rest?"

Emily's gaze slid to Mustang's.

He nodded. "Go on. I'll be up in a few minutes. My room is next to yours. If you have any troubles in the night, you just have to call out and I'll be right there."

Though she hated being dependent on anyone, Emily was grateful that Mustang was there and would be on the other side of the door to her bedroom.

She let Grace guide her to the staircase and up to her room. Her friend entered with her and nodded at the French doors on the opposite end of the room. "I love that this room has its own balcony and bathroom."

"It's nice," Emily muttered. Perhaps after a good night's sleep, she might be more enthusiastic, but right now she was too tired to care.

Grace lifted a garment from the end of the queen-size bed. "I found an extra nightgown that you can use until we can get to your apartment and get some of your own things." She laid it back on the comforter and turned to face her. "I wish I had more, but we only just moved a few of our things into our rooms."

"Thank you," Emily said. "I hate to be a bother."

"You're not a bother. What are friends for?" Grace hugged her tightly, then let go and stepped away. "If you need anything tonight, all you have to do is ask."

Tears welled in Emily's eyes. "You've been so good to me."

Grace left her in her room, softly closing the door behind her.

For a long moment Emily stood staring at the nightgown on the bed. Her gaze shifted to the door connecting her room to the one Mustang would be sleeping in that night. A shiver of awareness rippled across her skin. She wasn't quite sure what she was afraid of most. Her attacker…or her lusty attraction to the big marine who had saved her life that day.

MUSTANG MET UP with his team in the hallway as they headed for the door leading out the back of the estate. "What's the plan?" he asked.

Declan nodded at the others. "We're going to check out the garden and do a reconnaissance of the perimeter to make sure everything is in place and the security system is working."

Mustang clapped his hands together, ready to dive into the mission. "Which way do you want me to go?"

"Go with Arnold," Declan said. "He's going to check the front gate."

"Will do." Mustang performed an about-face and headed toward the front of the house where he joined Arnold.

The butler unbuttoned his suit jacket and pulled it to the side, displaying a shoulder holster and handgun tucked inside.

Mustang nodded and pulled his jacket aside to display his own shoulder holster and handgun beneath. No words were necessary for each to know the other was armed.

Arnold opened the front door and they both stepped outside. Rather than walking down the road winding toward the gate, they slipped into the shadows and worked their way quickly, paralleling the road all the way to the front of the estate near the entrance. When they arrived at the gate, Mustang held back in the shadows, providing cover for Arnold as he checked mechanisms to ensure they were working properly. Once his task was complete, he slipped back into the shadows and joined Mustang where he stood.

"Everything seems to be functioning as intended," said the butler.

A soft whistle sounded in the darkness.

Arnold reached for the handgun beneath his jacket.

Mustang touched his arm. "That's one of my guys, indicating he's nearby. That way we don't shoot first and ask questions later."

"Good to know," Arnold acknowledged.

The whistle was one they had used during operations in Afghanistan. A moment later Snow emerged from the shadows and joined them.

"Anything?" Mustang asked.

Snow shook his head. "Not a thing."

Arnold tipped his head toward the stone wall with its wrought-iron gate. "Gate's secure."

"Meet back at the conference room?" Snow asked.

"I'm gonna check the property line on the other side of the gate." Mustang turned and started along the fence line.

"I'll come with you," Snow offered.

They hadn't gone two steps when the sound of an engine revving cut through the night. In the next moment, a loud crash sounded behind them.

Mustang and Snow spun.

A commercial-size dump truck had crashed through the stone wall, leaving it in rubble.

Mustang pulled his handgun from beneath his jacket and aimed it at the truck's driver's-side cab.

Snow did the same.

"Arnold?" Mustang called out.

"I'm okay," he called from the other side of the crashed vehicle.

The truck engine was no longer running, but steam poured out from the radiator beneath the hood.

Clinging to the shadows, Mustang and Snow eased up on the driver's side of the vehicle. From what Mustang could see, there was no one in the driver's seat, or he was lying down.

"I don't see anybody inside," Mustang said.

"That doesn't mean there isn't anyone in there." Snow eased up to the door. "You cover. I'll open."

Mustang took a position where he could fire straight into the cab once the door was open.

Ducking low, Snow reached for the handle on the pickup and threw open the door.

Mustang aimed, his finger barely caressing the trigger and held his fire. As far as he could tell in the darkness, there was no one in the truck. "Clear," he confirmed.

"Clear on this side," Arnold echoed.

Mustang crawled over the rubble to the back of the truck. He didn't find anyone there, either.

"Check this out," Snow said.

Mustang scrambled back over the bits of stone to the cab of the pickup where Snow had leaned in, studying the interior. His teammate backed out and waved for Mustang to lean in.

"He rigged the accelerator by strapping a heavy brick to it." Snow snorted. "But why?"

Mustang's gaze met Snow's and a cold chill ripped across his spine. "Diversionary tactic."

They turned as one toward the house and ran. Declan, Gus, Mack and Cole joined them before they reached the house and fell in beside them as they raced.

"What the hell was that?" Declan asked.

"I'll explain when we get to the house," Mustang yelled. He kept running, his heart thundering against his ribs. He prayed he wasn't too late.

Chapter Seven

Emily had just slipped into the nightgown and robe Grace had provided when she heard the crashing sound. She ran to the French doors, flung them open and stepped out onto the balcony. A cool breeze ruffled the hem of her nightgown and chilled her arms and legs. Behind her, she heard her bedroom door open and close. Still straining to see what had caused the commotion, Emily assumed it was Grace.

"What was that?" she asked without turning.

Footsteps sounded, coming quickly. Before she was aware of the danger, she was shoved from behind.

Emily slammed into the balcony railing and doubled over, pitching over the edge. She flailed, reaching out, trying to find purchase. Her fingers wrapped around the wrought-iron rail and hung on tightly as her body weight jerked her grip loose. Emily screamed. Again the door to her bedroom opened.

"Emily!" Grace yelled.

A man all dressed in black with a black ski mask pulled over his face stood over her.

"Help me!" Emily called out, her arm aching and fingers slipping loose.

A shot rang out.

The man in black vaulted over the railing, grabbing her legs as he came down.

The added weight made her fingers slip free of their grip and she dropped from the second-story balcony, landing with a thud on top of the intruder who'd dragged her down. Not only had he ended up breaking her fall; he'd had the wind knocked out of him and lay still for blessed moments. Now was her chance.

Emily took the opportunity to scramble to her feet and dart away. And she almost made it, but a hand grabbed a hold of her ankle and yanked her back.

"Emily," Grace cried from above. "If you can get away, move to the side so I can get a clean shot."

"Emily! Grace!" cried out male voices in the darkness.

The man holding her ankle released it and scrambled to his feet.

Another shot rang out, the sound reverberating in the darkness.

Her masked attacker stumbled but kept running. As he disappeared into the darkness, the men of Declan's Defenders appeared from the opposite direction.

Emily pointed. "That way!"

Five of the six men took off running after the disappearing attacker.

Mustang stayed behind. Instead of following his counterparts, he hooked an arm around her shoulders and hustled her toward the back door leading into the house.

As soon as they reached the door, Emily turned and braced her hands against Mustang's chest. "Don't worry about me. Go get him," she said.

Mustang shook his head. "I'm not going anywhere."

He edged her in through the door and closed it behind them. Then his gaze raked her from head to toe. "Are you okay?"

As the adrenaline rush receded, Emily could feel every one of the bumps and bruises she had acquired in her fall. "I—think I'm okay."

"What were you doing outside?" he asked. "I thought you'd gone to bed?"

"I heard a crash," she said. "I went out onto my balcony to see what had happened."

"Then how did you end up down here?"

She snorted. "The attacker hit me from inside my bedroom and knocked me over the railing."

Mustang's eyes widened. "You fell from the balcony?" His gaze scanned her once again, slower this time as he seemed to make sure she really was in one piece. "Sweet heaven, you could have broken your neck.

Emily nodded.

Mustang shook his head. "We need to get you to a hospital and check you out for a concussion."

"No need," she said. "I didn't hit my head. In fact, I landed on my attacker."

The next thing she knew, Emily was being scooped up into Mustang's arms and carried into the living room. Nestled against his chest, Emily had to admit she felt safer there. But at the same time, unsettled and very aware of the man.

"I'm quite all right. I can walk on my own," she insisted.

He didn't answer, just kept walking.

"Seriously, I can walk." Emily didn't struggle. She told herself it was because she didn't want to throw him off balance. But the truth was, she really didn't want him to put her down. And he didn't put her down until they reached the living room and he laid her on the couch.

"I'm calling the doctor." He reached for the telephone.

"Don't." Emily shot up from the couch and put her hand over his. That same electric jolt shot through her arm and into her chest that had startled her earlier when they'd first touched. For a moment she forgot what she was going to say. Then it came back to her. "I tell you, I'm okay." She held her arms out to the sides and smiled. "See?"

Mustang frowned mightily. "I'd feel better if you had a doctor at least check to see if you have any concussion."

Emily chuckled softly. "I didn't hit my head. If anybody hit their head, it was my attacker. He's the one who needs to see a doctor about a concussion."

"Hopefully they'll catch him so that they can give him a concussion or send him to the hospital." Mustang ran a hand through his hair.

Emily rubbed her arms with her hands, suddenly aware she was wearing only her night clothes. "I hope they catch him, too."

Mustang stared at her for a moment. Then he reached out and pulled her into his embrace. "Are you cold?"

Emily shrugged. "Not really. I think it's just that the adrenaline has run its course." She shivered, her entire body quaking.

Mustang closed his arms around her, pulled her really close and rested his chin on top of her head. "You scared the crap out of me."

She laughed. "Scared the crap out of *you*? That man

scared the crud out of me. I don't ever want to fall off a balcony again."

"I don't ever want you to fall off a balcony again." For a long moment he held her without saying a word.

Emily didn't move. She enjoyed being up against him with the strength of his muscles beneath her fingertips.

They remained that way until footsteps sounded in the hallway.

"Oh, Emily. Thank God." Grace entered the room and rushed toward her.

Emily stepped back from Mustang to be engulfed in Grace's embrace.

"I nearly had a heart attack. When you went over the balcony rail, I thought for sure you were dead." She hugged Emily so tightly she could barely breathe.

Emily leaned back. "Was it my imagination or were you firing at my attacker?"

Grace grinned. "Don't worry, I've had a lot of practice. I'm a pretty good shot."

"As long as I'm not the one you're shooting at." Emily shook her head, a smile tilting her lips. "When did you learn to fire a gun?"

"Declan's been taking me to the range. He even bought me an HK .40-caliber pistol and a shoulder holster." She patted her jacket and opened it, showing the pistol tucked beneath her arm. "It took some time getting used to wearing it. But I'm glad I did."

Emily laughed. "You and me both." She shivered and rubbed her hands up and down her arms.

Mustang slipped out of his jacket and draped it over Emily's shoulders.

She smiled up at him, grateful for the gesture. The leather jacket still radiated Mustang's body heat and smelled of his cologne. Emily could easily get lost in how good it felt.

Declan, Gus and Jack Snow entered the room.

Mustang's gaze shot to them. "Did you catch him?"

Declan shook his head. "Snow is our fastest runner. He made it out to the fence in time to see the man climb a ladder over the top."

"Why didn't he get him while he was on the ladder?" Mustang asked.

"He was at the top of the fence before Snow could get to him, and then he pushed the ladder to the ground," Declan said.

"He had a car waiting on the other side," Gus said. "By the time Snow got the ladder back up and was at the top of the fence, the guy got away in his car."

"Did you get a license plate?" Mustang asked. He knew the answer before Gus responded.

Gus shook his head. "No license plates."

"I wish we knew why he was targeting Emily." Mustang paced the floor.

Charlie entered the room. "I put a call out for the police. They should be here in the next five minutes."

"I don't know what good they'll be," Emily said. "The guy was wearing gloves. He would not have left any fingerprints."

"Then he wouldn't have left fingerprints in the truck he used to smash the fence," Mustang said.

"And he had to have had some help. He probably had someone waiting in the car to drive him away," Gus said.

"That's right, there have been two men working the operation," Declan said. "One to provide the diversion. The other to get inside the fence."

Mustang stopped pacing, coming to a halt in front of Emily. "All I know is that Emily isn't even safe inside the perimeter of the Halverson estate."

Declan nodded. "Agreed. That's why I've got Mack and Cole guarding the perimeter." Declan tipped his chin toward Mustang. "I need you to stay with Emily through the night. We can't count on her being safe even inside the house. As we've already seen."

Mustang locked gazes with Emily. "She's not getting out of my sight."

Emily's body quivered.

"You two need to get some rest," Declan said. "Tomorrow you're going to the Russian language training class with Emily."

Mustang nodded. "I guess I'd better bone up on my Russian."

Emily tilted her head to the side. "You speak Russian?"

"A little," Mustang said. "It's not like I have a chance to use it much."

Emily grinned. "Then you can help me grade papers."

"Uh, no. My Russian isn't that good."

Declan chuckled. "You haven't heard his Russian."

Mustang's lips twitched. "My Russian is about at the kindergarten level."

"That would be better than most people's," Emily said.

"Tomorrow, Mack and I will chase down the private investigator." He glanced at Emily. "Is there any chance that we can talk to some of the staff at the embassy?"

Emily shrugged. "Some of them live at the embassy.

But for the most part they live on the economy. They have apartments and houses just like the rest of us."

"Then I'll see what Cole can find on the computer. Perhaps we can dig up some addresses and go and question some of the staff to see what might be going on with them."

"Don't forget, I'd like to make a stop at my apartment tomorrow and gather some of my things. I can't continue to borrow from Grace," Emily said.

Mustang nodded. "We can do that."

The police arrived and Arnold ushered them into the living room. They all gave statements on what they'd seen and what had happened to Emily that day. The police made a cursory investigation of Emily's bedroom. As Emily had suspected, they found no fingerprints.

Emily and the others waited in the living room until the police finished their search and left.

By that time, it was getting late and Emily was beyond tired. She glanced down at the robe and nightgown Grace had loaned her and the dirt smeared across them. "I guess I'm going for another shower," she said. She glanced up at Mustang. "I guess you'll have to take your eyes off of me long enough to let me have some privacy in the bathroom."

"Are there any windows in the bathroom?" Mustang asked.

"No," Emily said.

"As long as you let me clear the bathroom first, I'll allow you that privacy."

She raised her eyebrows. "Allow?"

Mustang gave her a twisted grin. "Until we get this attacker situation resolved, you'll have to play by my rules."

Emily frowned. "I'm not used to someone else dictating my life."

"And I'm sure you're not used to being shot at and attacked." Mustang tilted his head to the side, challenging her.

Emily sighed. "Point made." She turned to Grace.

Her friend grimaced. "I'm sorry, but I don't have another nightgown to loan you."

"I have a spare T-shirt," Mustang offered.

Emily nodded. "That'll do. Thank you."

"I guess, then, that we're calling it a night," Charlie said.

She turned to Emily. "I'm sorry this has happened to you on my property. I thought my security was pretty tight, but it seems that I wasn't prepared for a dump truck crashing into my stone wall. Nor did I conceive of someone infiltrating my house. I promise, I'll look through the security footage and determine from where he entered and shore up the locks."

Emily reached for Charlie's hands and squeezed them. "And I'm sorry I brought this trouble into your home."

Charlie waved a hand. "Don't you worry about us. We'll get things under control. That's why I hired Declan's Defenders."

Declan nodded. "Our main job right now is to keep you safe and to figure out who's attacking you."

Mustang frowned. "Not that we're doing such a great job so far."

Emily shook her head. "You are. I would be dead if you hadn't showed up when you did earlier. And you couldn't anticipate a breach in the estate security." Emily sighed. "I appreciate all your help in keeping me safe. Now, if you'll excuse me, I'm beyond tired." She turned and started for the door.

Mustang fell in step beside her and hooked his hand through her elbow. "I'm not trying to push you around. Consider it part of me just trying to do my job."

He climbed the stairs with her. When they reached the top, he walked with her to her bedroom. Once inside, he secured the French doors, locking the dead bolt. Then he checked the closets, beneath the bed and anywhere else someone might potentially hide. He even checked the cupboards and shower in the attached bathroom. When he was satisfied there were no other intruders in her room, he opened the adjoining door between his room and hers. "I'll get you that shirt," he said.

He gripped her arms, marched her across the room and positioned her in the doorway. "Stay right there."

Emily chuckled. "Isn't that taking it a little too far?"

"Not as far as I'm concerned," he said. "Last time I left you alone, you were pushed over a balcony."

Emily shivered. "I have to say, he did take me by surprise."

"And we thought the house was pretty secure." Mustang shook his head. "We can't assume anything." He walked to his go-bag, pulled out a T-shirt and handed it to her. "It's kind of ragged, but it's soft. It'll feel good against your skin."

She took the garment and pressed it against her cheek. "It is soft. I really appreciate it. At least I won't have to sleep in muddy clothes."

She turned and started to pull the adjoining door closed between their rooms.

Mustang caught the handle before she could completely close it. "Leave the door open," he said. "You can close the bathroom, but there are too many other entryways that can allow entry into your room. I would just as soon have my eyes on all of them."

She nodded, entered the bathroom and closed the door behind her.

Mustang waited until he heard the shower turn on. Then he walked into her room again and once more checked the windows, the French doors and the lock on her door to the hallway. He couldn't assume she was safe anywhere. If he didn't have his eyes on her, he had to know that there was no way anyone else could get to her.

While Emily showered, Mustang moved a wing-back chair up against the French doors leading out to the balcony. He pulled another chair from his room into hers and used it to block her bedroom door.

The shower turned off and a moment later Emily emerged, wearing his T-shirt and carrying the borrowed nightclothes. She had pulled her long blond hair into a messy bun on top of her head and there were droplets of water glistening on her shoulders and neck. Wearing his T-shirt, which came down over her thighs, she looked like a young girl in his oversize clothes. However, Mustang wasn't fooled. She was a full-grown woman with all the curves in all the right places. When she touched him, his senses went wild. Staring at her long, slender legs, all he could think about was wrapping those legs around his waist and—

Whoa! He couldn't go there. She was the job, not his next bed partner.

Emily stared at the two chairs. "Are we expecting another attack tonight?"

"No, but I want to be prepared in case one happens."

She nodded at the adjoining door that was closed. "I thought you'd leave the door open between our rooms, so you could keep an eye on me."

Mustang shook his head. "I won't be staying in there."

Emily's brows rose. "Uh, you're not sleeping with me."

He chuckled and nodded toward the chair leaning against the French doors. "I'm sleeping in that chair."

She frowned at the piece of furniture. "That won't be very comfortable."

"If I have any difficulties sleeping, I'll just stretch out on the floor. I've slept in worse places."

"That's right. You're a marine. I imagine you've slept in foxholes or out in the sand of the desert. Or beneath a tank or something like that." She grimaced. "I take it you've been deployed?"

He nodded. "A few times." He didn't bother to inform her that he'd been deployed over eighteen times to twelve different countries across the world. It might sound like bragging and he wasn't into bragging about what he did on active duty. He'd done what was asked of him. Guarding Emily was different. He hoped he didn't screw it up.

Chapter Eight

Emily slipped into the bed, climbed beneath the sheets, pulled the comforter up over her chest and stared at the man standing in front of her. "I mean, I know you are a marine. But what about before that?"

His mouth quirked upward on the corners. "What more do you want to know?"

She tilted her head and touched a finger to her chin. "How about…where did you grow up?"

"In Montana," he replied.

He wasn't going to help her with her interrogation. But Emily was persistent. "What did you do before the marines, in Montana?"

He crossed to the chair by the French doors and dropped down into it. "I was in high school like most kids my age."

Emily gave him a crooked grin. "You aren't going to make this easy, are you?"

His lips twisted into a wry grin. "Okay, so I grew up on a ranch."

Emily leaned forward. "Now we're getting somewhere." She raised her brows. "Go on. What part of Montana are you from? The open plains side or the mountains around Kalispell?"

Mustang tipped his head back against the chair's cushion and closed his eyes. "The nearest town to the ranch I grew up on was Cutbank. It's a town that's as close to Canada as you can get without actually being in Canada. But we didn't live there, we lived out on a ranch just south of that. It's on what they call the Front Range. Mostly plains, but we could see the mountains from my home." He raised his brows and opened his eyes to look across at her. "Does that help?"

Emily nodded. "It gives me an idea of where you're from anyway. So, I suppose, you ride horses?"

Mustang nodded. "I learned to ride before I learned to walk."

Emily's grin broadened. "Wow. Does that mean you're an honest-to-God, real-life cowboy?"

"If by *cowboy* you mean I know the difference between a horse and a cow, then, yes, I guess you could say I'm a cowboy."

"So, did you do all those things that cowboys do out West? You know, like branding and roping and herding the cattle?"

Mustang chuckled. "We did whatever it took to make sure the cattle were healthy and survived the brutal winters that they have out there on the plains in Montana."

"And then you joined the marines straight out of high school?"

Mustang nodded. "It's not like I would inherit the ranch when my parents pass away. My dad is the foreman of the ranch. I either had to sign on as a ranch hand or find another job. And since they had plenty of ranch hands, it was pretty much settled for me. The marines gave me an opportunity to get away from Montana and see the world."

As Emily stared across the room at Mustang, a thought occurred to her. "Do you have someone special in your life? Are you married? I mean, if you are, how are you going to explain sleeping in the same bedroom with another woman?"

Mustang chuckled. "I'm not married."

"Do you have a girlfriend or somebody you left behind in Montana?"

He shook his head. "No, I don't. The nature of the Marine Force Recon missions makes it so that it's hard to maintain a relationship when you could be deployed at any moment."

Emily frowned. "That has to be lonely."

"You don't have time to be lonely. And we have all our team to keep us company."

"I imagine the things you go through in the marines establishes a pretty strong bond between the men of your team," Emily said. "How long have you and your team been together? And are they the same ones you had when you were on active duty?"

"The men of Declan's Defenders are my teammates. Most of us have been together for the past four years. Jack Snow is the slack man—the newest member of the team. But even he's been with us for the past two years. They're my family now, my brothers. I'd take a bullet for any one of them."

"I imagine you would," Emily said.

"What about you?" Mustang asked.

"What about me?" Emily responded. "I don't know too many people I'd take a bullet for." She shrugged. "Although, I suppose I would for Grace."

Mustang shook his head. "No, I want to know more

about you. Like, did you grow up on a ranch or did you grow up in the city?"

"My parents were older when they had me. They did the best they could to make sure I had a well-rounded upbringing. We lived in Virginia, in a suburb of DC." She smiled. "I learned to walk before I learned to ride a bicycle or ride a horse."

"So, you have ridden a horse?" Mustang asked.

"I have." Emily smiled. "Although it was purely through riding lessons. I've never owned my own horse. And we rode English not Western."

"That's more than some people have done. So many kids that grew up in the city have never even seen a horse in person. Yes, they've seen them on television, but they've never stood close to one, so you are fortunate in that respect."

"My parents did try to give me a good understanding of the world and everything in it. And that included a smattering of sports, which I was never very good at, and the riding lessons, which I enjoyed. I had hoped someday to have my own horse."

"And what's stopped you?"

"I live in the city." Emily shrugged. "The traffic and commute are awful. I wouldn't have time to really spend with a horse."

"Why DC? Why did you settle here?" Mustang asked.

Emily slipped down onto the pillow and yawned. "I don't know. I guess I just kind of slid in to the position at the university after completing my undergraduate degree, my masters and my doctorate there."

"You didn't want to explore the world and use your

Russian language training in other parts of the country or the world?" Mustang asked.

Emily smiled. "I did study abroad for a semester in Moscow. And that was great, and I would really like to do some more traveling." She yawned again and stretched. "Just not tonight. The stress must have taken it out of me. I can't..." Emily closed her eyes as she yawned once more, hugely this time. "Sorry... I'm going to sleep now."

"Go ahead. I'll keep you safe while you do." He settled back, stretched his legs out in front of him and crossed his arms behind his head.

"Mmm." She nestled into the pillow, closing her eyes to a slit wide enough to study Mustang. He really was a handsome man. Too bad he was only there to keep her safe. He seemed a bit dangerous to her. At least to her libido. The man had charisma in spades. If she wasn't so darned tired, she might try to seduce him.

Another yawn nearly split her face in two.

Oh, who was she kidding? She didn't know how to seduce a man. So busy making good grades and then helping students make good grades and working as an interpreter, she hadn't taken the time out of her packed schedule to really learn the art of flirting much less dating.

Yeah, she'd gone out with a boy or two in college. She'd even experimented with sex. But she hadn't felt that certain "something" other women had claimed they'd felt. Perhaps her body wasn't built the same way as other women. Maybe she wasn't capable of feeling that special something during sex.

Another yawn made her eyes water. She couldn't

fight it anymore. She had to let go of consciousness and sleep.

She recognized her hesitation and knew it had to do with all that had happened. She didn't want to dream about her attacker. Reliving the horrific experience was what nightmares were made of.

Knowing Mustang was only a few short steps away gave her a sense of relief. Finally she let go and drifted off into a dark abyss.

EMILY RAN, *her breathing ragged, her lungs ready to burst. She didn't know where she was. All around her was a deep, inky blackness. And someone was chasing her.*

Fear clutched at her chest, making it difficult to draw air into her lungs. But she had to keep moving.

Footsteps crunched on leaves and branches behind her.

Her foot caught on a root, pitching her forward. She landed hard in the dirt, the wind knocked from her lungs.

More footsteps sounded behind her.

Move! She had to move!

When she tucked her legs beneath her, they refused to push her to a standing position. With no strength left in her legs, she dragged herself up against a tree and curled into a ball, praying her pursuer couldn't find her. The darkness around her seemed to spin, sucking her downward. One moment she floated through space. The next she was falling...falling...falling.

Emily would have reached out her hands in search of something to hold on to, to break her fall, but she was afraid it would be him...

The sound of a soft cry jerked Mustang awake. He must have dozed off. His gaze shot to the bed and his heart froze in his chest.

Empty.

In a split second he shot to his feet and raced toward the door. The chair stood in the same place he'd positioned it. Reaching over the back of the chair, he gripped the handle, fully expecting the door to open easily, but the lock remained in place.

A keening moan sounded behind Mustang.

He spun and his heart dropped to his knees.

Emily sat on the floor, wedged between the nightstand and the bed, her knees drawn up to her chest, her hands wrapped around her legs, and she was rocking back and forth. Another moan rose from her throat and a tear slipped from the corner of her eye.

"Oh, Emily," Mustang whispered. He hurried to her, switched on the light on the nightstand and dropped down beside her. "You're okay." He captured her hands in his and gently pulled her into his arms. "Hey, sweetheart, wake up."

She struggled, her body rigid, her hands pushing against his chest. "No. Please, no."

"It's okay," he crooned. "I won't let him hurt you."

Emily stopped fighting but her eyes remained closed.

"It's me, Mustang," he said. "Open your eyes. You're safe."

She shook her head, her fingers curling into his shirt.

"You're dreaming. Wake up and look at me." He chuckled, though it caught in his throat. "I'm one of the good guys."

Her eyelids fluttered and then opened. She stared

up at him, blinking, a frown denting her smooth brow. Finally her eyes widened and she melted into his arms.

Mustang wrapped her in his embrace, smoothing his hands down her back. "You're all right. It was just a bad dream. I'm here. I won't let anyone hurt you."

"He was chasing me. I tr-tripped." She dragged in a shaky breath and let it out.

The warmth of her exhalation spread across Mustang's chest. He held her closer and swept his hand over her hair, cupping the back of her head.

She leaned back far enough that she could look up into his eyes. "Thank you."

He shook his head. "For what?"

"For saving me again," Emily said, and laid her cheek against his chest, snuggling closer against him.

"I didn't do anything but wake you up."

"It was enough." She slipped her arms around his waist and held on, as if she might fall if she let go.

Mustang shifted, pulling her into his lap. For a long time he sat there, holding her until her body relaxed against his. She was warm and soft against him, and her hair smelled of flowers and springtime. His T-shirt on her body did little to disguise her curves pressed against his torso and chest.

His groin tightened. Now was not a good time to be turned on by the woman he was there to protect. She didn't need her bodyguard making a pass at her.

But he couldn't control his body's reaction. And if he didn't move soon, she'd become aware of his lack of control.

"We should get you off the floor," he whispered against her ear, fighting the urge to nibble at her lobe.

Her arms tightened around his middle. For a long

moment she didn't say anything. Slowly she loosened her hold around him and nodded. "Okay."

He shifted her off his lap and rose. Instead of reaching a hand down to pull her to a standing position, he bent, scooped her up in his arms and lifted her onto the bed.

She clung to him until he settled her on the comforter. "I could have gotten here on my own," she reminded him. "But thank you." Emily leaned forward and kissed his cheek. Her eyes widened and she dropped back against the pillow. "Sorry. I shouldn't have done that."

Mustang's face tingled where Emily's lips had touched. He pressed his fingers to the spot and gave her a crooked smile. "I didn't mind."

Her cheeks reddened. "Still, I shouldn't have." She snuggled under the sheets then pulled them and the comforter up to her chin and stared at him, her eyes wide.

"You can leave the light on. It won't bother me," Mustang said. He turned toward his chair.

"Mustang?" Emily said, her voice little more than a whisper.

He could hear the desperation and fear lacing the sweet sound of his name on her lips. Without hesitation, he turned back to her. "Yes?"

She chewed on her bottom lip before answering, "Will you stay with me?"

He nodded. "I'm not going anywhere. I'll be in that chair, all night long."

Emily shook her head. "No. Here." She moved over, making room for him on the queen-size bed.

He stared at her and the space beside her and swallowed a groan. "I don't know. That might not be a good idea."

She shrank back against the pillow. "Oh. Okay. I'm sorry. I shouldn't have asked. It's just…when I close my eyes, I'm afraid I'll end up right back in that dream." Her voice faded at the end. With a little more oomph, she added, "It's okay. I'll manage." And she turned over, away from him. "Good night, Mustang," she said.

Mustang stood for a long time, reminding himself he was being paid to watch out for this woman, not to sleep with her. His jeans tightened uncomfortably. Lying in bed with Emily could only be painful and make for a very long, sleepless night. Even more so than sleeping in the chair.

He straightened his shoulders.

No. He should walk away and keep his distance from her. They'd been strangers before that night. They'd be strangers when the threat was neutralized. He didn't need to start anything that would go nowhere. Not that lying in bed with her meant he had her permission to start something.

He started toward the chair, stopped, spun and crossed to the bed. Kicking off his shoes, he stretched out beside Emily on the bed, lying on top of the comforter.

Emily drew in a deep breath and let it out on a sigh. "Thank you."

For a long time Mustang lay staring at the ceiling, his body hard, his fists clenched.

He was just about to slide out of the bed and return

to his chair when Emily rolled over and slid an arm across his chest.

Swallowing hard to keep from groaning, Mustang froze.

Emily pressed her cheek against the side of his chest, her eyes closed, her breathing steady and relaxed.

He couldn't move. What scared him worst was…he didn't want to. He liked having her body next to his. He wanted to hold her all through the night. What scared him even more was he had a feeling one night wouldn't be long enough.

Chapter Nine

Emily woke to sunshine streaming through a window, cutting across the floor and edging beneath the slits of her closed eyes. She blinked them open, winced and closed them again. On her second attempt, she was able to open her eyes fully and welcome the morning with a smile.

She stretched, her arm falling across the opposite side of the bed. It was empty.

Sometime during the night or early morning Mustang had left the bed. The bathroom door stood halfway open and she could hear water running in the sink. Emily rolled onto her side.

Through the gap in the door, she could see him.

Mustang stood shirtless at the sink, smearing shaving cream over his chin.

Emily's breath lodged in her throat and her pulse pounded through her veins.

The man had broad, tanned shoulders. From where she lay, she could see the evidence of scars on his arms and side. They didn't detract at all from his rugged good looks. In fact, they made her heart flutter and warmth spread low in her belly.

He'd held her in his arms when she'd been frightened

by a dream. Then she'd taken advantage of him by asking him to lie beside her in the bed. She had no regrets in that regard. Having his hard body beside hers had chased away all the bad guys of her imagination and made her feel safe and protected.

She'd slept the rest of the night without a recurrence of the horrible nightmare. With sun shining through the window, she met the day with more optimism than she'd had the night before. And more determination to discover who was behind the attacks. She suspected it had something to do with her visit to the Russian embassy. Had the situation with the ambassador's daughter caused such a stir they didn't want the information to leak out? Emily shook her head. Why would they need to keep that such a secret? Who cared besides the ambassador?

Mustang finished shaving and tapped the razor on the side of the sink. Then he turned his head toward her and winked. "Caught ya looking."

Heat flared in Emily's cheeks and she rolled back to her side of the bed. Her bare feet hit the cool wooden floor. She searched the room for her clothes before she remembered they had been covered in mud and too nasty to wear again. The sweatpants and T-shirt Grace had loaned her were gone as well.

"If you're looking for clothes, you'll find the items you arrived in stacked on the dresser. Charlie had them cleaned while you slept."

Relief washed over her as she gathered her pants, shirt, panties and bra. When she started toward the adjoining door, intent on changing out of the revealing T-shirt, she was brought up short by Mustang clearing his throat.

"Ahem. Where are you going?"

She spun to face him, clutching the stack of clothing to her chest. "To change into my clothes."

"If you go into my room and close the door, I won't be able to see you, or protect you against an intruder entering that room." He tipped his head toward the bathroom behind him. "I'm done in here."

She nodded and hurried forward, intent on giving him a wide berth, knowing if she touched him, she'd feel that spark of electricity he managed to generate without trying.

As she walked past him, he reached out a hand and touched her arm.

Emily fought hard not to moan. She came to a halt, gathered her scattered senses and looked up into Mustang's eyes questioningly.

"How do you feel this morning?" he asked, his tone low, intimate and far too sexy for Emily's good.

Those scattered senses scrambled all over again. She struggled to concentrate on what he'd said while staring at his lips, wondering what they would feel like against hers. She shook her head. "Fine," she blurted. "I'm fine." Then she scurried into the bathroom. Once she'd closed the door between them, she leaned against it and let go of the breath she'd been holding.

Why was she so rattled by the man? He was there to protect her, but she was afraid. Not of him, but of her uncontrolled reaction to him. She was nothing more to him than a person he'd been hired to protect. He wasn't there because he was in love with her. The measure of his success on the job was to keep her alive, not to make love to her.

A moan escaped her lips at the idea of making love with the man.

Emily hurried to the sink, turned on the cold water and splashed it into her face.

The shock of the icy water helped bring her back to earth. She scrubbed her face, found a packaged toothbrush under the sink and scrubbed the night's funk off her teeth. She ran a brush through her hair, pulled on her own blouse and pants and felt more in control of her body and mind.

Squaring her shoulders, she braced herself for her next encounter with Mustang. With a deep breath Emily flung open the door, fully expecting to face the man who occupied all of her thoughts.

The room was empty.

A moment of panic flashed through her.

She hurried to the adjoining door into his room.

Mustang stepped in front of her.

"Did you miss me?"

She pressed a hand against his chest and let go of the breath she'd been holding, steadying herself. "No, of course not," she lied.

"Do you always lose your breath walking across the room?"

Emily struggled to come up with some excuse for her reaction to thinking he'd gone.

"I just… I just…" She sighed. "Yes, I missed you."

His lips twisted as he opened his arms. "Come here."

She didn't hesitate. She walked into his arms and rested her cheek against his chest. The steady sound of his heartbeat soothed her immediately. "I thought you'd left."

"Sweetheart, I told you I wasn't leaving you out of my sight."

"But then you were gone," she pointed out.

She stood in the circle of his arms inhaling the scent of his aftershave.

He had put on a polo shirt, tucked it into his jeans and combed his hair.

Even with all those lovely muscles covered, he felt like a solid brick wall.

He flexed his shoulders naturally.

Mustang settled a finger beneath her chin and tipped her head upward. "Hey, I'm not leaving you." He pressed his lips to her forehead. "I'm sticking with you, girl."

"Promise?"

He nodded and lowered his face to brush his lips across hers.

Before he could lift his head, she captured his cheeks between her hands and stood on her toes to press her lips more firmly to his.

His hands slid up her back and cupped her head, bringing her closer to deepen the kiss.

When at last he lifted his head, he stared down into her eyes. "I shouldn't have done that. But I'm not sorry."

Emily shook her head. "I shouldn't have kissed you back."

A knock sounded on the door. "Emily?" Grace's voice rang through the paneling.

Emily stepped back.

Mustang's arms fell to his sides.

"I'm awake," Emily said.

"Breakfast is ready, if you'd like to join us," Grace said.

Emily stared into Mustang's eyes. "I'll be down in a moment."

"Great. See you there," Grace called out. Footsteps sounded, leading away from the door.

Emily took another slight step back. "We'd better go."

Mustang hesitated. "Emily…"

Emily held up a hand. "Let's just leave it here."

He took a step closer. "What if I don't want to leave it here?"

She took a deep breath and let it out slowly. "We should go down."

"I shouldn't have kissed you," Mustang said. "But I couldn't help myself.

"Ditto." Emily shook her head. "It just…complicates things."

He shoved a hand through his hair. "I get it. And your life is pretty complicated right now."

Emily nodded.

He stared at Emily for a long moment. "Then let's uncomplicate this. I'll stay as far away as possible, as long as I can still be effective protecting you." Mustang moved the chair away from the door, unlocked it and opened the door. "After you."

Emily led the way down the stairs and followed the sound of voices coming from the dining room. She wasn't certain how Mustang would stay away from her, if he had to be right beside her to protect her. And she didn't want him to go far. Not with all that had happened. He was her rock in a turbulent sea. She wasn't combat trained and she didn't have any self-defense skills to fight off an attacker.

DECLAN, GRACE, CHARLIE and Arnold the butler were there. Sitting around the dining table. Plates of sausage, eggs, bacon, hash browns and toast lined the middle of the table. Emily's stomach rumbled. She hadn't realized just how hungry she was.

"Glad you could join us," Charlie said. "I trust you slept well?"

Emily didn't bother to tell Charlie about her bad dream or the fact that Mustang had slept with her. Instead she nodded as she took a seat beside Grace. Mustang sat next to Emily.

"Are you still good with the plan we have for today?" Declan asked.

Emily glanced around at the others at the table. "I am. I have a class to teach today. After that I'd like to go with you to talk to the private investigator."

"I had Cole run a background investigation on your private investigator. We didn't find anything unusual. He did do some time in the military in the NCIS." Declan nodded. "What time do you think you will be done with your class?"

"I should be finished by noon."

"I'm not sure it's a good idea for you to be walking around the city. Especially since we don't know who is trying to attack you," Declan said.

"I can't just hide away and wait until my problem goes away," Emily said.

"You put yourself at risk." Declan nodded to Mustang. "I'm not sure one bodyguard will be enough."

"I hate that anybody has to be my bodyguard," Emily admitted.

"I'm sure you didn't ask to be attacked," Mustang said.

"Well, we don't mind providing your protection,"

Charlie said. "The local police are investigating, but it's clear whoever is after you is persistent and resourceful."

"As long as the boss lady says so, we'll provide that protection," Declan told her.

"Correction, I'll be here whether the boss lady says so or not," Mustang said.

Tears welled in Emily's eyes. "Thank you all. I feel so much safer just knowing that you have my back."

"That goes for all of us," Grace said. "We're here for you, Emily."

Emily scooped eggs onto her plate, a piece of bacon and a piece of toast. And then she watched as Mustang loaded his plate with eggs, toast, hash browns, sausage and bacon. And proceeded to consume all.

She picked at her breakfast and drank a small glass of orange juice before she finally pushed her plate away and scooted her chair from the table. "I need to go by my apartment before I go to the university."

Mustang shoved the last bite of his toast into his mouth before pushing back from the table and standing. "I'm ready to go."

"Do you want us to go with you?" Grace said, glancing over at Declan.

"No, I think it will be enough of a disturbance to have one bodyguard in the classroom along with the rest of the students," Emily said, shooting a glance at Mustang.

The former marine would have every student in the classroom wondering why he was there and if he was single. At least the female students. And half of the male students, as well.

"I'll have your car towed to the body shop," Charlie told Emily.

"Thank you." Emily smiled at Charlie. "You've already done so much for me. I'm sure insurance will help with the repairs, if the car is not totaled."

"My guy's a good repairman," Charlie said. "I'll have him give me an estimate."

"Either way," Emily conceded, "I'll be out of a vehicle at least for a couple of weeks. I guess I'd better look into a rental car."

Mustang frowned. "I don't know why you need a rental car as long as you have me. We'll go in my truck."

"You can't be with me all the time," Emily said.

"That's exactly what I will be. With you. All the time." Mustang crossed his arms over his chest. "Until we figure out who your attacker is, and we neutralize him, you're with me 24/7."

"Surely, you have a life of your own?" Emily said.

"Get this," Mustang stressed. "You are my life. Period. Period. Period."

Emily shook her head.

Mustang held up a hand. "Until we get this attacker in hand, you are my only job. We will eat, drink and sleep together as long as we need to."

Heat rushed into Emily's cheeks and she glanced around the room at the others. Grace had a half smile tugging at her lips.

Declan nodded, a serious look on his face. "Mustang's right."

Grace nodded. "He is. We'll all feel better if he's with you 24/7."

"And we'll add additional bodyguards as needed," Charlie offered.

"It seems like so much trouble," Emily said.

Mustang held up his hand again. "End of argument," he said. "Are you ready to go?"

Emily valued her independence, but what they were saying was right. She needed them until they found the attacker and put him away. She nodded. "All right. But no entourage. Just Mustang and me. I'm ready. Let's go."

MUSTANG MADE EMILY wait at the door as he stepped outside. He searched the surrounding area quickly before ushering her out to his truck. He used his body as a shield between her and any potential threat. When he had her settled in the passenger seat, he closed the door and rounded the front of the vehicle to climb into the driver's seat.

With Emily's direction, he maneuvered through the traffic of DC to Arlington, where her apartment was located. When they arrived at her building, he pulled into the parking lot slowly, his gaze scanning the immediate surroundings.

"You can wait in the truck while I go inside and gather a few things," Emily said.

"Nope," Mustang said. "We're both going in." He shifted one hand under his jacket where he kept his Glock in a shoulder holster. Then he dropped down from the truck, rounded to the other side, opened the door and helped Emily to the ground. He kept her in the curve of his other arm, protecting her with his body as they hurried toward the apartment building.

When they stopped in front of her apartment, Emily fumbled with her key until she finally got it into the lock, twisted it and opened the door.

Mustang kept Emily from walking in by placing a

hand on her arm. He drew his weapon and pushed the door wider. After a quick glance around the exterior of her apartment, he entered and tugged her in behind him.

Once inside, Mustang pulled the door closed behind Emily with a soft click. He pressed a finger to his lips, pointed to the corner by the door and then pointed at her. He mouthed the word *Stay.*

Emily frowned but nodded and took up her position in the corner.

Mustang would have preferred to clear her apartment before allowing her to enter, but he couldn't leave her outside for fear somebody might attack her while he was busy searching the apartment. With no other choice, he'd had to bring her in and plant her by the front door while he cleared the rest of the apartment.

He entered the main living area, scanning for any sign of an intruder. The room was sparsely but tastefully furnished with a light gray, modern sofa, a white marble-topped coffee table with matching end tables on either side of the sofa, and a white leather chair and ottoman. Bright red, orange and turquoise pillows provided splashes of color to an otherwise gray-and-white interior. One wall contained an Impressionist painting of a summer wheat field with a bright blue sky. On another wall were black-and-white photographs of bridges, each had been enlarged and printed on canvas.

On an end table was a photograph of a family of three. Emily was front and center between an older man and woman. Mustang assumed they were her parents. He absorbed the decorations in a brief scan as he moved through the living room and into the kitchen. Once he was sure there weren't any bogeys hiding behind the sofa or in the pantry, he entered the bedroom—a room as different from the living room as night was to day. In this room, the bed was covered in a blush pink comforter with a stack of fluffy pillows pushed up against a white-cushioned headboard. The dresser was of a light, whitewashed wood with brushed, stainless-steel pulls.

The painting hanging over the bed was of a young girl wearing an old-fashioned hat and a long white dress. She was carrying a basketful of wildflowers. The entire room was utterly feminine and what he would have expected of Emily. Soft…delicate…and vulnerable. His chest tightened. Mustang didn't like that she was being targeted. He vowed to keep her safe, no matter the cost to himself.

There weren't too many places a person could hide. But he checked them all, looking under the bed, in the closet and behind the shower curtain. When he was convinced there were no other people in the apartment besides him and Emily he called out, "All clear."

Emily entered the bedroom and stared across the floor at him. "Do I have to worry about every place I go?"

Mustang nodded. "Afraid so."

Emily's frown was more sad than angry. She made quick work of finding a small suitcase and stuffing it full of clothes that she might need for the next week. She entered the bathroom and collected toiletries, putting them into a smaller case that fit within her suitcase. When she finished, she zipped the case, lifted it off the bed and set it on the floor. "I just need to gather my book bag and then I'll be ready to go."

Back in the living room she gathered a stack of papers, shoved them into a satchel and looped the strap of the bag over her shoulder.

Mustang carried her suitcase to the door and waited patiently.

Emily's gaze swept the apartment, ending up connecting with Mustang's. "I don't like it."

Mustang nodded. "I understand. Nobody likes it when their personal space is invaded. Or even if their personal space has the risk of being invaded."

Emily shivered. "I feel like I have to be looking over my shoulder every step I take."

"And that's exactly what you have to do. Until we find the attacker," Mustang said.

She squared her shoulders and marched toward the door. "Then let's go. I have a class to teach."

Once again, Mustang was out the door first, checking the parking lot for any vehicles that may have arrived while they were inside or any people that looked suspect. When he felt certain all was clear, he looped his arm around Emily's shoulder, pulled her close to his body and guided her toward the truck.

For the next thirty minutes he contended with DC traffic to get Emily to the university in time for her class to begin. Once they arrived on campus, Mustang parked the truck in a parking garage and went around to let Emily out. They arrived at her classroom with no interference.

Mustang was surprised by the size of the space. It wasn't so much a classroom as it was an auditorium, albeit a small one, with about two dozen students seated among the one hundred or more chairs.

They entered from the back of the auditorium.

Emily paused and touched a hand to his arm. "I'd

prefer if you stayed in the back," she whispered. "Having a stranger in the classroom is enough of a distraction with you being in my face or following me everywhere."

He frowned, studying the room of students. "Do you recognize all of these people?"

She nodded. "All have been in my class from the beginning of the semester." Emily smiled. "They aren't here to hurt me. They're here to learn to speak Russian."

Mustang didn't like that she would be all the way across the room from him. "Is there another door leading into the room near the front?"

Emily shook her head. "Only the ones here at the rear of the classroom." She glanced at the double doors. "I'd feel safer and more comfortable if you guarded the doors rather than guarding me."

"Are these all of the students?" he asked. "Are you expecting more?"

She nodded. "I have exactly twenty-five students. I did a quick count. They're all here." She nodded toward a young man standing near the front of the class. "The student standing is my teacher's assistant. He's enrolled in the masters-level program. He will help me to administer the test."

After one more glance around the room at the students, Mustang nodded. "Okay. But if I say 'hit the ground,' I expect you to drop to your belly." He gave her a fierce glance. "Got that?"

She held up her hand as if swearing an oath, the corners of her lips quirking. "Got it."

"Okay then, go teach." He stood in front of the door, his arms crossed over his chest. He wouldn't allow anyone else to enter the room without going through him.

And if one of the students tried to make a move on Emily, Mustang could be across the room in seconds.

For the next hour Emily conducted a last-minute review, speaking in Russian and in English.

Mustang was entranced by her smooth, sexy voice and the way the Russian language rolled off her lips as if she'd been born to speak it.

If he had only been mildly attracted to her before, he now found himself completely under her spell.

By the look of some of the male students, they were equally captivated. The woman was smart, sexy, and didn't appear to be much older than her students. Some raised their hands and asked questions. She responded with a smile and clearly enunciated words. Emily knew her stuff. No wonder she was in demand as an interpreter.

After the hour was over, she asked her students to put away their books and get out their pencils.

Her teacher's assistant handed out the scanner test forms while Emily distributed the actual tests, facedown.

Once each student had a form and a test, Emily walked to the front of the class, glanced at her watch and then looked up. "You have one hour to complete the test. You may begin."

For the next hour the students worked through their tests at their own paces. By the end of the hour, they trickled up to the front of the room, handed over their completed forms and the test, and left, walking past Mustang as they went. Male and female students only gave him a brief glance as they exited. They appeared to be deep in thought, as if second-guessing their answers.

When the hour ended and there were still students

at their tables, working on their tests, Emily cleared her throat.

"Time's up," she called out. "Put down your pencils and bring your tests and answer sheets to me."

The remaining handful of students submitted their papers and left the room.

Emily and her assistant stacked the tests and the scanner forms. After Emily tucked them into her satchel, she thanked the assistant and told him he could leave.

The assistant brushed past Mustang, eyebrows raised. But the young man didn't comment. Instead he left, letting the door swing closed behind him.

"I need to take my forms to my office and run them through the test-scanning software." Emily looped the satchel's strap over her shoulder and started up the aisle toward Mustang. "The students will want to know their grades as soon as possible. Then we can go see Jay Phillips, the private investigator."

Mustang nodded and held out his hands. "Do you want me to carry anything?"

Emily smiled and shook her head. "No need. I do this all the time." When she started to pass him, he put out his arm.

"Let me go first."

With a sigh, she hung back.

Before Mustang could put his hand out to open the door, it burst outward.

He shoved Emily behind him and dropped into a ready crouch, his hand going to the gun beneath his jacket. He had it pulled and pointed at the intruder before she was completely inside the classroom.

The young woman stood no more than approximately

five feet tall with pitch-black hair, ice-blue eyes and pale skin. She stopped short, the door swinging closed behind her. “Oh!” she said and took a step backward, raising her hands, her eyes wide and frightened. “I’m not here to hurt Miss Chastain,” she said with a heavy Russian accent. “I need her help.”

Mustang refused to move. “Who are you and what do you want with Miss Chastain?”

The woman shot a nervous glance over her shoulder. “Please,” she said softly. “If they find me, I won’t be able to speak freely. I need to talk to Miss Chastain.” She held up her hands higher. “I am not armed.”

Emily touched Mustang’s arm. “Let her talk.”

“She might not have a gun, but she could be carrying a knife.”

“You can…how you say? Frisk me. But please, away from the door. If my bodyguards find me, they will take me back to the embassy.”

Emily stepped around Mustang. “The Russian embassy?”

The woman nodded, shot another glance over her shoulder. “I told my father I wanted to enroll in classes. I ran away from my bodyguards. It is only moments before they find me.” She pressed her hands together. “Please, I must speak with you, Miss Chastain. It is a matter of life and death.”

Chapter Ten

"You must be Sachi," Emily said and moved forward.

Mustang shot out his arm to keep Emily from stepping past him.

"It's okay," Emily said. "Sachi is Russian Ambassador Nikolai Kozlov's daughter." When she tried to lower his arm, it remained firm.

"You can't trust anyone," Mustang said. "Not even another woman."

"Miss Kozlov won't hurt me," Emily said and turned to Sachi. "Will you?"

Sachi stared at Emily wide-eyed. "No, no. Of course not."

"Still, I'd rather make certain she isn't carrying a weapon."

Sachi held out her arms and spread her feet apart. "Please hurry. If my bodyguards find me, I will not have another chance to speak to Miss Chastain."

Mustang ran his hands lightly over her arms, along her sides, down to her shoes and then checked inside her jacket. When he was done, he stepped back and allowed Emily to move forward. "She's clean."

Emily closed the distance between her and Sachi.

Sachi moved away from the door into a corner of the

classroom while Emily flipped one of the light switches near the entrance, plunging that corner into darkness. Then she followed Sachi, with Mustang close behind. "What is it you wanted to discuss?"

Sachi glanced over Emily's shoulder toward the door before she spoke. "My father has made it impossible for me to get out of the embassy alone. He treats me like a child, when I am twenty-six years old."

SACHI COLLAPSED AGAINST Emily, sobbing. Emily wrapped her arms around Sachi and looked over her head into Mustang's eyes.

"Is your love the journalist Tyler Blunt?" Emily asked.

"Yes," Sachi said. "He is. And my father is furious. He thinks Tyler is a risk to his position as the ambassador."

"Why does he think that?" Emily asked.

"He thinks Tyler is only seeing me so he can get bad information about what the Russians are doing in the United States."

"And do you think Tyler is using you?" Emily asked.

"No, of course not." Sachi shook her head. "Tyler loves me."

Emily didn't bother telling the young Russian girl that journalists sometimes could be quite crooked and start relationships with people just to use them for a story. What good would it do when Emily knew nothing of Tyler's true intentions?

Sachi frowned and stared into Emily's eyes. "You don't believe me, do you?"

"I didn't say that," Emily said. "Question is, what do you want me to do about it?"

"My father said he hired a private investigator to follow Tyler," Sachi said. "Who was the private investigator?"

"I'm not at liberty to reveal anything about my conversation with your father," Emily said.

Sachi grabbed her hands and squeezed. "Please, you need to tell me. I think the private investigator might have seen something. Might know something about what Tyler was working on. Maybe he knows something about why Tyler disappeared."

Emily shook her head. "I signed a nondisclosure agreement with your father. If you want to know who the private investigator is, why don't you ask your father?"

"He won't tell me," Sachi said.

Again Emily shook her head. "I'm sorry, I just can't tell you."

More tears welled in Sachi's eyes. "It could be the difference in life and death for Tyler," she said. "What if he's been kidnapped? What if he is being tortured?"

Emily pressed her lips together. "Talk to your dad. I can't say anything."

Sachi dropped Emily's hands, turned and paced a few steps away. Turned and came back. "Tyler said he was working on a project that could have some very serious ramifications. He seemed nervous about it. He thought it was really dangerous."

"Did he say anything about what it was?"

Sachi shook her head. "He didn't want me to know. Not until he had all the details."

"And you think this project that he was working on may have gotten him in trouble?"

Sachi nodded. She ran a hand through her rich black hair and sighed. "I wish he would have told me what the project was. Then at least I would have some kind of place to start looking for him."

Standing in the shadows with the Russian ambassador's daughter, Emily could feel the tension and the fear. If the man she loved had disappeared like Tyler Blunt had disappeared, she, too, would be searching for answers. But she couldn't violate her nondisclosure.

Emily sighed. "Sachi, I can't tell you who the investigator was. That information you will have to get from your father. However, I can check with him and see if he knows anything." She had been going to go talk with the private investigator anyway. It wouldn't hurt, and it wouldn't violate the nondisclosure agreement for her to talk to the investigator. Especially now that she knew who he had been talking about during the interpretation session—Tyler Blunt.

Sachi grasped her hands once again. She stared at Emily. "Please, you will tell me if you learn anything about where Tyler might be?"

Emily nodded. "I'll tell you what I can. But I'll need some way to contact you."

Sachi took a business card from her wallet. She pulled a pen from her purse and wrote a phone number on the back of the card. "Call me if you learn anything."

Emily reciprocated and gave Sachi her number, as well.

Heavy footsteps sounded in the hallway. Sachi heaved a frustrated sigh. "I have to get back to my bodyguards. My father will be angry when he finds that they lost me. I can take his anger. But it isn't fair to the bodyguards when he gets angry."

"Will you be all right?" Emily asked.

Sachi nodded. "As well as can be expected. I will not rest until I find Tyler."

She squeezed Emily's hands one more time before she released them, turned and hurried toward the exit doors. As she reached out to open them, they pushed outward and two burly, heavyset men entered.

Mustang started after Sachi.

Emily's hand shot out and grabbed his arm.

The ambassador's daughter spoke in fluent Russian to the two men. They responded also in Russian. And soon all three left the auditorium. Mustang's gaze followed Sachi out the door. He turned to Emily. "I'd follow her to make sure she's all right, but that would leave you exposed."

Emily shook her head. "She knew the men. She spoke to them as if she had a long-standing relationship with them as her bodyguards."

"Still, she looked scared."

Emily nodded. "She is scared. But not for herself, for her lover, the journalist Tyler Blunt." Emily shook her head.

"Let me guess, you want to go talk to Jay Phillips now?" Mustang said.

Emily's eyes narrowed. "You bet. Your team wanted to follow up with him today anyway. So, we'll do it."

"Okay," Mustang said. "I'll let Declan know we'll handle it."

"And then we can stop by the office that hired me to translate for the embassy." She met Mustang's gaze. "With as much trouble as I've been having lately, do you think Sachi is in trouble, as well?"

Mustang shrugged. "I don't know. But she has two bodyguards. They should keep her safe."

"I'm kind of worried about her," Emily said.

"Do you think her father had something to do with Tyler Blunt's disappearance?"

Emily's lips pressed tightly together. "I don't know, but it's all pretty suspicious. Considering I saw Blunt being led deeper into the embassy instead of out of it."

"Sounds to me like the Russians had something to do with Mr. Blunt's disappearance."

Emily nodded. "You should have seen how mad the ambassador was when he found out that his daughter had been having an affair with the man Jay Phillips had been tasked to follow."

"All the more reason for us to get to this private investigator and ask a few questions of our own."

Emily nodded, slipped her satchel more firmly over her shoulder and started for the door. Mustang beat her to it and stepped outside first. After he had checked both directions of the hallway, he opened the door for her and led her out of the building and back to the lot where he had parked his truck.

He had just settled Emily in her seat when a loud bang sounded, echoing off the walls of the parking garage. Glass shattered the passenger window of his truck just as she was bending over to retrieve a paper that had fallen from her satchel. Instinct took over as he shoved Emily sideways in the front seat and then crouched low behind the metal of the door. Another shot rang out, hitting the front windshield.

Emily shuttered her hand out. "Give me your truck keys," she said.

"Why?" Mustang asked.

"Just do it," she demanded.

He handed her the keys. She scrambled across the console into the driver's seat. "Get in," she ordered.

Another shot pierced the front and back windshields leaving small holes with cracks like spider's legs reaching out. Emily jammed the key into the ignition and turned on the engine.

Mustang scrambled up into the passenger seat and closed the door, still remaining low, out of range of the windshields.

Emily slammed the gearshift into Reverse. She backed out of the parking space, shifted into Drive and hit the accelerator, shooting the truck forward toward the exit. She didn't let the fear of being shot slow her down. She kept her foot on the accelerator, taking turns in the parking garage at a much too fast pace to make her comfortable. But she had to get out of there before someone finally hit their target. Her.

While Emily navigated getting out of the parking garage alive, Mustang was on his cell phone dialing 9-1-1. "I'd like to report an active shooter on campus at the university."

Emily was so angry at herself as she pulled out of the garage and onto the campus street. If she hadn't showed up that day, insisting her students needed to take their tests to get the grade for class, the campus would not have had an active shooter. She was in trouble and had brought that trouble to the campus, putting the students at risk.

As she left campus she vowed not to return until her attacker was captured and put behind bars. She'd get her test results in electronically somehow.

MUSTANG HAD INSISTED Emily keep going until they were miles away from the university campus. He didn't want to stop at all, but he knew they would have to file some kind of report with the police since he had called in the active shooter. He was proud of Emily for keeping a level head and getting them out of the parking garage and off the campus. She was still driving at a fairly fast rate, at the same time not erratic enough to run over pedestrians. He looked back every few minutes to make sure they were not being followed. When he felt certain they were safe, he had her pull over at a gas station, where they arranged for the police to come and question them about the incident.

After Mustang gave his statement to the police, he placed a call to Declan and explained their situation.

"I'm glad you got out of there alive," Declan said.

Mustang glanced over at Emily. "So am I, dude. So am I."

"Do you need me to send another one of the guys out to help protect Emily?" Declan asked. "Or Mack and I can interview Phillips."

Mustang debated taking Declan up on his offer, but they needed to talk with the private investigator, and he might get spooked if there were too many people bombarding him at once. "No, I think we need to do this, just me and Emily."

"Fair enough," Declan said.

"What I need from you and the others is information. Give me the address of this private investigator, Jay Phillips."

"I'm on my way to you," Declan said, "and I'm texting you Phillips's address. Good luck getting information from him. Most investigators don't share private data of the people they investigate. Of course, unless you're the one paying him to do the investigation."

"I don't know why they're targeting me," Emily said as she wrapped her arms around her middle and moved closer to Mustang. "Nothing in that report seems worth all this."

He put his arm around her. "You're safe with me and my team," he said into her hair. "I won't let you down."

Chapter Eleven

Minutes later Declan joined Mustang and Emily at the service station as the police wrapped up their investigation.

"Thought you might need another vehicle," Declan said. He tipped his head at a dark gray sedan pulling into the parking lot. "Charlie sent a backup car. She could have sent a truck, but she said this one blended more easily into the DC traffic."

Mustang shot a glance toward his pickup with the bullet holes in the windshield and side windows. His stomach roiled. Any one of those bullets could have hit Emily. "Tell Charlie thanks." His gaze shifted to Emily. "It might be a good idea to take Emily back to the Halverson estate. She's not safe out here."

Emily shook her head even before he finished speaking. "I'm not going to sit back at Charlie's and wait for the trouble to miraculously disappear. I want to have a word with Jay Phillips. And if that isn't any help, I'm going to request a meeting with the Russian ambassador. I have to get to the bottom of this." As she spoke, her anger became more evident and a bright fire burned in her eyes.

Mustang couldn't help but think how very sexy she

was when riled. He chuckled. "Okay. You're staying with me. But we might need to get you into a bulletproof vest."

"Whatever it takes," she said.

Mack climbed out of the dark gray sedan and handed the keys to Mustang. "She's all yours while your truck in is the shop."

"Good." Mustang cupped the keys in his palm. He filled Declan and Mack in on the rest of the details of their encounter with Sachi Kozlov.

"So, she was having an affair with Tyler Blunt." Declan shook his head. "I can understand her concerns. From what Cole has learned, the man has yet to turn up."

"I know he's the one I saw in the Russian embassy," Emily said. "Surely they wouldn't have done something stupid like kill the man on American soil."

"You would think they wouldn't have done it at the embassy," Mustang said.

"Perhaps that's why they want Emily out of the picture," Mack said. "She saw Blunt there. She could call them out and have the embassy investigated for kidnapping and potentially for murder."

Mustang frowned. "You wouldn't think having an affair with the ambassador's daughter would be enough to make the Russians want to kill the journalist."

"You didn't see how mad the ambassador was," Emily said. "He stormed out of the conference room shouting obscenities. His face was red and there were veins popping out on his forehead. I don't think I've seen anyone quite that mad."

"Well, since we can't find the journalist, we'll have

to settle for the other American in that session with the ambassador," Declan said.

"The address you gave me…is it his home or office?" Mustang asked.

Declan snorted. "His home." He pulled his smartphone from his pocket and clicked some buttons. "I just sent you a text with the office address, too, so you have it. Mack and I will go by his office. You and Emily can swing by his home. We tried calling his work number, but got no response. He might be there, but he's not answering. Same with his home number."

Mustang nodded. "We'll head for his house. Hopefully he can shed some light on what's going on."

"*If* we find him," Emily murmured. "Alive."

Declan climbed into his truck. Mack joined him. They took off in the direction of Phillips's office.

Mustang held the door for Emily and waited while she slipped into the sedan. Then he slid behind the steering wheel, adjusted the seat and mirrors and pulled out into the traffic. He followed the directions given by the map application on his cell phone. Twenty minutes later he pulled into the driveway of a modest town house with a one-car garage.

Just by looking at the building, he couldn't tell if anyone was home. The shades were drawn and the garage door was closed.

He stepped out of the sedan and walked around to hold Emily's door for her.

She joined him and they walked up the driveway to the front door. With every step they took, Mustang scanned the surrounding area, searching for anyone who might take a shot at Emily. He wished she hadn't insisted on coming along for the conversation with Jay

Phillips. She would have been safer staying with Charlie at her estate with the other members of his team guarding her.

But then Mustang wouldn't have been able to keep his sights on her. He'd worry the entire time he was away. He trusted his team to protect her, but he felt more invested in her well-being and wanted to be the one looking out for her.

At the door, Emily pressed the doorbell.

Mustang could hear it echo in the interior of the structure.

After a full minute Emily pressed the button a second time. Again no one answered.

Emily glanced up at Mustang. "I hope the others had more luck at his office." She turned and took a step toward the car.

As Mustang turned with her, he heard a sound. He reached out to capture Emily's elbow, pulling her to a stop beside him. Then he pressed a finger to his lips and tilted his ear at the town house.

Another sound came from behind the door.

Mustang turned and banged on the door with his fist. "Mr. Phillips, we know you're in there. Open the door. We only want to talk to you."

No sounds emanated from inside the home.

Emily leaned closer to the door. "Mr. Phillips, it's me, Emily Chastain, the interpreter from our meeting with Ambassador Kozlov yesterday. I need to talk to you."

Nothing.

"Please, Mr. Phillips." She leaned her forehead against the door panel. "It's important. Someone is trying to kill me. I need your help."

Mustang couldn't let Emily stand out in the open any longer than necessary. He touched her shoulder and turned her toward the vehicle.

They'd just stepped off the porch when the door behind them opened.

Mustang spun and stepped in front of Emily.

A thin man with brown hair and brown eyes poked his head through the gap in the door. "Miss Chastain?"

Emily leaned around Mustang. "Yes. Mr. Phillips, are you okay?"

He shook his head, his gaze darting left then right. "Not really. I'm afraid to step out of my house."

"Has someone tried to attack you, as well?" Emily asked.

He nodded. "If I hadn't had such a good security system installed, I'd likely be a dead man by now." He frowned at Mustang. "Who's he?"

Emily gave the man a weak smile. "He's my bodyguard. I've been having a little trouble myself."

Mustang snorted. "Not just a little."

Phillips shot another glance around and opened the door a little wider. "You can come in."

Mustang followed Emily through the door and closed it.

Phillips reached around him, shot the dead bolt home and armed the security system through a panel on the wall.

"Come into the kitchen. It doesn't have any windows." Phillips led the way down the hall into a modern kitchen with granite countertops and dark cabinets. A small dinette table with four chairs took up a small corner. The private investigator nodded in that direction. "Have a seat and tell me you've had a better past twenty-four hours than I have."

Mustang held a chair for her and Emily sat.

"I can't say that my day's been better." She told him all that had happened in the last twenty-four hours, ending with the attack in the university parking garage.

Phillips ran a hand through his hair, making it stand on end. "Sounds like what I've experienced. I had an appointment across town from the Russian embassy after our meeting with Kozlov. I never made it there. Someone ran me off the road and down into a ditch. Fortunately, I was able to drive back out of it relatively unscathed. At least they let me go from the embassy. For a while, I wasn't sure they would. But I made up a story about my next appointment being with the military for an investigation on a base, and they'd be searching for me if I didn't show up. That seemed to tip them toward releasing me."

"You were luckier than I was. My car is totaled."

Phillips's lips twisted. "Yeah, but I spent the next couple of hours trying to lose the guy who'd run me off the road. I finally ended up hiding the night in a used car lot. I didn't sleep a wink. When I was pretty sure I wasn't going to be followed, I headed back here, only to find the alarm going off and the place surrounded by police." He smiled. "It was nice to know my security service worked. But once the police left, I haven't felt much like going out again. Not when someone is clearly trying to get to me."

"We've tried to call you," Emily interjected. "Mustang and his team."

"I hardly use my landline and let calls go to voice mail."

"Do you have any idea why someone would want to kill you two?" Mustang asked.

"I don't know. I've been trying to figure it out. Now that I know you're involved, it kind of narrows it down to the people and discussion that happened in the Russian embassy." He glanced toward Mustang. "We signed a nondisclosure agreement, but I'm seriously rethinking that at the moment."

"He knows pretty much what was discussed. Sachi Kozlov came to me, worried about her lover, Tyler Blunt, who went missing yesterday."

Phillips's eyes narrowed. "I heard that on the radio. Wow, who would think the ambassador would be angry enough to kill all those involved with his daughter's indiscretions?"

Emily shook her head. "It doesn't make sense."

"No. Something isn't right." Phillips ran his hand through his hair again, his mouth pinched in a tight line and the creases around his eyes deepening, making him appear older than his years. "Someone tried to break into my house."

"Do you have information they might not want shared? Information they might have tried to steal?" Mustang asked.

"Only the files I had on Blunt."

"You gave them the photos you'd taken," Emily said. "What more could they want?"

"I wasn't too worried about the images I left with the ambassador's assistant. Those were only the prints. I have digital copies of those photographs." He frowned.

"Do you suppose they were after the digital copies?"

"They would have to know how to get to them. I have them backed up to the cloud. Even if they got my desktop computer and laptop, they couldn't completely destroy them."

"What was in those pictures?" Mustang asked.

"I followed Blunt, capturing him and Sachi making clandestine assignations. I have photographs of them together outside restaurants and nightclubs."

Emily shrugged. "Again, it's not enough, in my mind, to want to kill us. We signed nondisclosures. We aren't going to the tabloids with the information."

"I'm not even sure they'd care who Sachi is going out with," Mustang said. "It's not like she's the First Daughter or a celebrity."

"True," Phillips said. "I'll go back through those photographs, in case I missed something important."

"Could you forward them to me?" Emily asked. "It might help to have a second set of eyes reviewing them."

Phillips shook his head. "Not yet."

Emily nodded. "I know. The nondisclosure agreement." She empathized, "I wouldn't want you to compromise your integrity."

"But you'd think all bets were off when someone is trying to kill you." Mustang held up his hand. "I understand. It's your word. A person's word is gold."

"And it's my livelihood. If people found out I don't hold true to my promise of complete discretion, I wouldn't have a business."

"You won't have a life if we don't figure this out soon," Mustang said, clearly trying to press the man into disclosing more.

"I get that. I just want to review the photos first and decide what to do. I promise you'll be hearing from me if something turns up. But I'm not handing over every single snapshot. Not yet anyway."

Emily leaned across the table and touched the man's arm. "Will you be all right?"

He shrugged. "I have my security system and enough food in my refrigerator and pantry to last a week." Phillips gave Emily half a smile. "Surely they'll give up after that."

"If you need anything, we can bring it. All you have to do is call." Emily dug in her purse and handed Phillips one of her business cards.

"Got a pen?" Mustang held out his hand.

Emily pulled a pen out of her purse and handed it to him.

Mustang scribbled his and Declan's cell phone numbers on the back of Emily's card. "Call either one of those numbers. We can help."

"Thank you," Phillips said, his shoulders sagging. "I've been in the PI business for twenty years, but I've never been this close to being killed. I pride myself in blending in. But no amount of blending seems to work in this situation. I'll have a look at my images again. I'll let you know if I find anything unusual."

Emily squeezed Phillips's arm. "Thank you. And please, stay safe."

The private investigator narrowed his eyes. "Same goes for you," he said. "I can see someone coming after me, but it doesn't make any sense that they would come after the interpreter."

"I couldn't agree with you more." Mustang stood and touched Emily's arm. "I'd like to get back to the estate before dark."

"Let's make that stop at the organization that hired me to translate. She nodded and pushed to her feet. "Then I'm ready to head back to the estate."

"I'll be in touch, one way or another," Phillips promised. He pulled his own card out of his pocket and handed it over. "This has my private cell on it that I don't give out to everyone."

"Thank you," Emily said.

Mustang held out his hand.

Phillips took it and shook with a surprisingly strong grip. "Prior military?" he asked.

Mustang nodded. "Marines."

Phillips's shoulders squared and his grip tightened on Mustang's hand. "Semper Fi."

"Semper Fi," Mustang echoed. "Stay safe."

Mustang led the way to the door and exited first, performing a swift evaluation of the street, houses and bushes nearby. A car slowed as it approached.

When Emily moved to step out onto the porch, Mustang's arm shot out, stopping her in a clothesline move—straight arm across her chest.

Her eyes widened. "What's wrong?"

The vehicle slid by at a slow pace and Mustang could peer into the interior.

An old man hunched over the wheel, as if struggling to see the road in front of him.

"Nothing. It was just an old man."

She smiled up at him. "Getting punchy?"

He nodded. "After being shot at in the university parking garage, I'm thinking punchy is a good way to be while we're out and about."

Emily shivered. "You're right. She touched his arm, sending a shock of awareness through his body. "You go right on being punchy. I'd rather be safe than sorry."

Her hand slid down his arm to capture his fingers with hers. For a moment he held her hand, enjoying the coolness of her fingertips against his warm palm. Then he released her fingers and wrapped his arm around her shoulders and walked with her to the car.

Once she was safely inside, he got in, shifted into Reverse and pulled out of the driveway onto the street.

They made a quick stop at the office that hired her for the translation. The administrative staff had nothing to add that would help them in their investigation.

It was early afternoon and traffic was just picking up. People from all over the city rushed to get home, causing the roads to clog and vehicles to move at a snail's pace. By the time they reached the Halverson estate, dusk was creeping up on the trees, casting long, dark shadows over the landscape.

Mustang pulled up to the gate and pointed at a section of the stone wall. "They already have the wall back up."

Emily shook her head. "That's amazing."

"I guess when you have as much money as Charlie Halverson, things get done a heck of a lot quicker."

"She seems like such a strong woman, yet she surrounds herself with the best in security systems and personnel."

"For a reason," Mustang said. "Her husband was killed and there was an attempt on her own life. That's how she met Declan. A group of men took her from her limousine in a kidnapping attempt. If Declan had not been there when he was, she could be dead."

"Grace told me about what happened. It's a miracle he got her out alive."

"Right place, right time."

"Right hero." Emily smiled in his direction.

"Declan will be the first to tell you he isn't a hero.

Our team has been operating on the rule of *if you see something that needs doing, you do it.* It's purely reflex."

"Hero reflexes," Emily insisted. "And save your breath. You won't convince me otherwise." She laid a hand on his leg and squeezed lightly.

Before she could remove the hand, Mustang pressed his over hers. "Just promise me you won't tell Declan he's a hero. It would go to his head and he'd be impossible to live with." Mustang gave her a sly grin.

Emily held up her free hand. "I promise."

Mustang maneuvered along the driveway to the big house with one hand on the steering wheel, the other still holding Emily's. He didn't want to let go.

All the way, he kept a watchful eye on the shadows beneath the surrounding trees. Charlie would have beefed up the security, but whoever was after Emily had breached the estate's protection once. He could do it again.

Chapter Twelve

Emily couldn't remember a time when she was more exhausted. The stress of being on guard all day had taken its toll. The only thing holding her up from collapse was Mustang's arm around her as she stood in the foyer, a frown marring her brow, as Charlie greeted her.

"I heard what happened at the university." She gripped Emily's hands in hers. "Are you all right?"

Emily nodded. "I am." She turned to Mustang. "We both are."

Charlie's gaze went to Mustang. "Thank God you were there to get her out alive." She hooked her arm through Emily's. "Come. You must be starving. I want to hear all about your visit to Mr. Phillips. Did you learn anything new?"

Charlie led Emily and Mustang into the kitchen and urged them to sit at the large table while she worked with her chef to deliver a substantial meal for the two of them.

"Aren't you going to eat, too?" Emily asked.

"We finished dinner less than an hour ago. We saved plates for you and Mustang. Will chicken cordon bleu be enough for you?" She placed meals in front of both of them.

"More than enough," Emily said, her stomach rumbling as she sniffed the heavenly scent of roasted chicken wrapped around ham and cheese with a delicate layer of breading. Her mouth watered as she cut off a piece and brought it to her lips.

Heaven. Pure heaven.

She moaned her pleasure.

Beside her, Mustang chuckled. "I don't think I've ever seen anyone eat a bite of chicken with quite that much enthusiasm."

Heat rose in Emily's cheeks. She cut off another slice of the chicken. "We didn't have lunch, did we?"

Mustang shook his head. "We were otherwise occupied staying alive." He took a bite of the chicken, too, and nodded. "This really is good." He nodded to the chef, busy preparing the kitchen for the next day's meals. "My compliments to the chef. Sure beats MREs."

Emily frowned. "MREs?"

"Meals ready to eat," Mustang said. "The prepackaged stuff they feed the troops in the field." He leaned back, his brow rising. "You've never had MREs?"

Emily shook her head. "Never."

"Sweetheart, we have to improve your education. You need to try them so that you'll know just how good this chicken is."

"I know how good it is," Emily said and glanced down at her empty plate. "I don't think I actually took a breath between bites."

Charlie laughed. "Carl, my chef, can make a can of Spam taste like a culinary masterpiece." She gave the chef a chin lift. "Isn't that right, Carl?"

"Yes, ma'am," he answered.

"Carl is prior navy. He was a chef on board the USS

La Salle." Charlie smiled. "My husband knew the ship's captain. When Carl left active duty, the captain asked him if he had a place for him in one of our businesses." Charlie's lips quirked. "John saw his potential, sent him to culinary school and he went to work for us as our personal chef."

"I love it almost as much as I loved cooking for the navy," Carl called out.

Charlie snorted. "I know I'll lose him someday to some fancy restaurant, but I'm enjoying some really good meals in the meantime." She sighed heavily. "So, tell me what happened today."

Emily recounted Sachi's visit, the attack in the parking garage and their visit with Jay Phillips. "I'm sad to report, we're no closer to learning who my attacker is."

"But we do know more than we started out with," Mustang added. "Whoever is after Emily is also after Phillips. Which must have something to do with what was discussed at the meeting with the ambassador."

"And since Sachi spilled the beans about why her father contracted the private investigator in the first place," Emily said, "I can speak freely about the meeting with the PI and the ambassador without violating my nondisclosure agreement."

"Good." Charlie clapped her hands together. "At least there's that. We haven't had much luck here. Cole McCastlain and Jonah Spradlin, my computer guy, have been online all morning, trying to find the dirt on the Russians occupying the embassy. So far, other than being accused of employing an undocumented maid at one of the Russian's town homes, we haven't uncovered anything of significance that would warrant someone wanting you and Mr. Phillips dead."

Emily laid her napkin on the table. "I don't know what else I can do, other than go back to the embassy and ask for a meeting with the ambassador himself." She shrugged. "I'm not sure what good that will do, other than to let him know one of two things. Either I'm on to his attempts on my life or he's got a problem with someone on his staff who feels it necessary to keep his daughter's love affair quiet from the rest of the world."

Mustang shook his head. "I still find it hard to believe a daughter's indiscretions would create enough of a stir to warrant an attack on an interpreter and a PI."

Emily frowned. "Unless it goes back to the fact I saw Tyler Blunt at the embassy the day he disappeared. Do you think that's the crux of the matter? Have the Russians done something nefarious with Tyler?"

"I can have some of Declan's Defenders follow the ambassador," Charlie offered.

"It wouldn't hurt," Mustang said.

"While you're at it, have Viktor Sokolov, the ambassador's assistant, followed," Emily said. "He was at the meeting, as well, along with a couple of their embassy guards. I'm sorry, I didn't get their names."

Charlie tapped her chin with the tip of her finger. "I doubt they would be pulling the strings on your attackers."

Mustang frowned. "If anything, they might be the ones attacking you."

"All I know is I need a shower." She yawned, covering her mouth. "I might call it a night early."

"I'm sure you're exhausted," Charlie said.

Emily gave the older woman a crooked smile. "At least I was able to collect some of my own belongings."

She glanced around, looking for the bag she'd packed. "I must have left my things in the car."

Charlie held up a hand. "I had Arnold take your bag to your room. You go on up. I'll have Carl make you a cup of tea and send it up."

"That's not necessary," Emily said. "I can come down and get it myself."

"Please. I insist." Charlie pressed her lips together. "I like having the company. I just wish the circumstances weren't so dire."

Emily pushed back from the table and stood.

Mustang rose with her and cupped her elbow.

"You don't have to go with me," Emily said. "I can find my way."

With a shake of his head, Mustang didn't slow as he ushered her from the dining room. "I told you, I'm sticking with you. I don't want you out of my sight for more than a couple of seconds."

Emily opened her mouth to argue but ended up saying, "Thank you." Nothing she could say or do would put Mustang at ease. Until her attacker was stopped, she'd have the former marine as her shadow. After all that had happened, she was glad he was there.

As Charlie had indicated, Emily's bag had been brought to her room and deposited on the bed. Thankful for her own clothes, she dug into the garments and selected clean underwear and hesitated over what to sleep in.

She ran her hand over her usual nightgown, though she wondered what Mustang would think of her in it. The gown was a sexy, blush pink babydoll that barely covered her bottom, with matching pink panties. Why she'd tossed it into the bag, she didn't know. Mustang would be sleeping in her bedroom until further notice. The gown was too revealing to wear in the presence of the marine. He might think she was coming on to him.

Her pulse quickened and warmth pooled low in her belly at the thought of standing in front of Mustang in a nightie that didn't conceal much beneath the shear fabric. She shot a glance in his direction.

Mustang had closed and secured the bedroom door before wandering through the room and bathroom. He ended up in front of the French doors leading out onto the balcony. Having pulled the curtain aside, he stared out at the night. The man obviously wasn't interested in seeing her in a nightgown. She'd practically had to beg him to sleep with her the night before, to chase away the lingering shadows of her nightmare. The man was in her room out of necessity not desire.

Emily grabbed a pair of dark leggings and a long-sleeved T-shirt and headed for the shower, closing the bathroom door behind her. She'd stripped out of her clothes and turned on the shower before she realized she'd left her bag of toiletries on the bed.

Wrapping one of the huge, plush towels around her, Emily opened the door and poked her head out.

Mustang stood directly in front of her, only inches away, with one fist raised to knock, the other hand holding her toiletries bag. "Forget this?"

Her eyes widened and heat rushed up her neck into her cheeks. Even more heat raced south to the juncture of her naked thighs beneath the towel. "Uh, yes." When she reached for the bag, her towel slipped. She held it up with one hand and tried again to take the bag.

The corners of Mustang's lips quirked as he handed over the item.

When his fingers touched hers, Emily felt a jolt of something like electricity shoot up her arm and across her chest, making her nipples tighten and her breath catch in her lungs. Her eyes widened as she held the bag he hadn't released yet.

For a long moment she stared into his eyes.

And he stared back.

Finally he let go and backed away, jabbing a thumb over his shoulder. "I'm just going to wait in the adjoining room, but I'll leave the door open." Then he turned and strode into the other room. He paused at the connecting door and glanced back over his shoulder.

Emily stood for a moment longer, unable to draw in a breath. Wow. What had just happened?

He ducked around the corner and the moment was gone.

Clutching the bag to her chest, Emily slipped back into the bathroom and closed the door. Then she turned and leaned against it and tried to remember how to breathe. The man turned her inside out and made her heart flutter. No man had ever done that. Why Mustang? And, for heaven's sake, why now?

MUSTANG PACED THE floor of his bedroom, passing the open connecting door several times before he slowed to a stop and stood staring across Emily's room to the closed bathroom door.

When she'd poked her head out, wearing nothing but a towel, all thoughts of keeping her at arm's length flew out the window. He'd wanted to take her into his arms and hold her naked body against his. Hell, he wanted to do more than that. His gaze drifted to the bed and he groaned. How the heck was he going to keep this mission from becoming too personal? With all that was going on, Emily didn't need a lusty former marine panting after her.

He closed his eyes and willed his body to calm down. But the image that resonated in his mind was one of her creamy shoulders above the terry-cloth towel and her long, sexy legs that would wrap so easily around his waist.

Mustang opened his eyes and forced himself to look at anything but the bed and the bathroom door. He turned into his room and stared at the go-bag he'd carried on more missions than he cared to remember. Perhaps it was time to pack it again and let one of the other team members take on the responsibility of keeping Emily safe and alive.

As soon as the thought entered his head, he pushed it back. No. As much as he trusted his team to support him and to do a good job at any tasking, Mustang couldn't walk away. Emily was his.

He ran a hand through his hair.

Correction… Emily wasn't his. Keeping her alive was his mission. He would not fail. That meant he would not let her out of his sight. He couldn't let someone else provide her protection. He'd just have to manage his baser instincts and do his best not to touch her any more than he had to.

Just as he was coming to that conclusion, the bathroom door opened and Emily stepped out, wearing leggings and a long-sleeved shirt. All the drool-worthy parts of her body were covered and her hair was wet and combed straight back. The sloppy outfit and wet hair didn't make her any less sexy. If anything, the tips of her nipples making little tents against her shirt were more of a tease than exposed flesh.

Another groan rose up his throat and would have escaped if Emily's cell phone hadn't buzzed at that exact moment.

Mustang swallowed hard and hurried forward.

Emily lifted the phone from the bed and frowned down at the display.

Mustang leaned over her shoulder and read the text message.

I might have something. Meet me at Finnegan's Tavern in Arlington in thirty minutes. JP.

"I can be dressed in one minute. Do we have time to make it to Finnegan's in thirty minutes?" Emily grabbed a bra from her suitcase and tucked it beneath her T-shirt, reaching to clasp it in the back. Then she pulled her arms out of the sleeves and into the torso of the shirt. After a few moments of fumbling beneath the fabric, she pushed her arms back through the sleeves and gave him a twisted grin. "You could have turned your back."

"Yeah, sorry. I've always been intrigued at how dexterous a woman can be when dressing."

Emily grabbed a pair of shoes and slipped her feet into them. "I'm ready."

"I'm not sure you should go," Mustang said. "I need to run this by Declan and the team."

"He texted me. He'll be expecting me." Her lips firmed. "I'm going."

"What if it wasn't him who texted? What if it's a setup?"

She grabbed her phone as he stepped closer, calling Phillips.

"Voice mail," she said and hit End.

"See? Might not have been him."

"Or he might be on the road." She stared at him. "I'm going. Like it or not, I'm going."

"Okay. But we do it my way. And we need backup." He led the way down the stairs and into the living area where he found Declan, Grace, Charlie and Charlie's computer guy, Jonah Spradlin. "We just got word from Phillips. He wants to meet in twenty-five minutes. Finnegan's in Arlington. He thinks he has something."

Declan leaned over and kissed Grace. "Snow and I are with you. Mack and Gus are on their way home. We can divert them to the location."

"He texted me," Emily reminded them. "He'll be expecting me, and Mustang. But he might spook if the whole gang of us shows up."

Declan nodded. "Understood. We won't all enter at the same time. In fact, I can position a couple guys outside the tavern to be on the lookout for trouble."

Mustang glanced down at the clock on his cell phone. "We'd better get moving." Whatever Phillips had could be the break they were looking for. They couldn't blow it by being late.

The garage doors were up and the sedan Mustang and Emily had arrived in was pulling out as Mustang, Emily, Declan and Snow emerged from the back door of the big house.

Arnold climbed out, left the driver's door open and then ran around to the other side and opened the door for Emily.

Emily and Mustang slid in and buckled their seat belts.

"I'll have the gate open as you reach it," Arnold promised.

"Thanks," Mustang called out as he shifted into Drive and sped away from the garage.

Declan and Snow climbed into Declan's truck and pulled in behind them.

By the time they reached the gate it was three-quarters of the way open, just enough for him to squeeze the sedan through. Emily had the address of the tavern keyed into the map on her phone. They were on the road to their rendezvous with little time to spare.

With Declan's headlights in the rearview mirror, Mustang felt marginally better about the meeting. He couldn't keep watch in all directions, and the attackers had showed some ability to create a distraction. Having the rest of the team there would make it easier to keep Emily safe.

Pushing the speed limits, Mustang wove through the city, from main roads to those with less traffic, arriving with two minutes to spare.

When Emily reached for the door handle, Mustang shot out a hand to capture her arm. "I'm still not comfortable with you going in. It smells like a setup to me."

Emily let go of the handle as if it burned her hand. "But why would Jay go along with a setup?"

"He might not be in control of his cell phone." He pulled his own phone out of his pocket and punched the key for Declan.

"I'm going in first," Declan answered without preamble.

Mustang chuckled. "You read my mind. We'll wait for your signal."

Declan had parked his truck out of sight of the tavern's front door and approached the building, using the sidewalk, like any other customer intent on a meal or a pint.

Once Declan entered, Mustang gave him a minute or two to get settled and then he gave Emily's arm a gentle squeeze. "Stay low until I get out and come around."

Emily did as he told her, waiting for him to open her door and usher her out of the vehicle. Once again, using his body as a shield, he guided her into the tavern, certain Declan would have made sure it was relatively safe. If it hadn't been, he'd have found a way to notify Mustang before he dared enter with Emily.

Once inside, Mustang scanned the interior. At that moment he wished he had his military rifle and bulletproof body armor on both him and Emily. He didn't know what to expect, but his gut was telling him to count on trouble. For a moment he considered turning around and marching Emily out, high-tailing it back to the Halverson estate.

Then he spotted Declan who gave him an almost imperceptive chin lift. A further study of the interior of the tavern revealed a lack of Jay Phillips.

Emily craned her neck, frowning. "I don't see him."

"He said he'd meet us here in a half hour. We're right on time, he might have gotten tied up in traffic," Mustang reasoned. "Give him a few minutes."

Emily nodded. "You're right. I'm just nervous. I really hope he's come up with something that would give us a clue as to who is targeting us."

Mustang guided her to a table in a corner and took the seat that placed him with his back against the wall.

It also gave him a view of the front entrance and the rear exit.

Rather than sitting across the table from Mustang, Emily chose to sit in the seat beside him, giving her a good view of the entrance.

The waitress came and handed them two dinner menus and a drinks menu. "Can I get you a drink to start with?"

"I'll have coffee," Mustang said, anxious for the woman to move and quit blocking his view of the doors.

"Hot tea for me," Emily said softly.

"I'll be back with your drinks and to take your dinner order."

Mustang didn't bother to tell the waitress they weren't interested in eating. He just wanted her to move on.

Emily lifted her napkin and laid it across her lap, her fingers pulling at the hem, her gaze worried and turned to the entrance.

With a chuckle, Mustang covered her hand with his. "You'd be a terrible secret agent," he said.

She frowned. "Why do you say that?"

"You're wearing your emotions on your face. Anyone looking at you would know you're waiting for someone to enter. Someone you're nervous about meeting or seeing."

Her frown deepened. "How am I wearing my emotions on my face?"

Mustang reached out and brushed his thumb across her brow. "You're frowning fiercely. Why don't you pretend we are here on a date? Not the kind of date where you're about to dump me."

Emily lifted a hand halfway to her face and then let

it drop to her lap. “You’re right. I’m worried, and I’m sure it shows.” She pasted a smile on her face. “There, is that better?”

He winced and gave her a crooked smile. “A little, but a bit scary.” He winked and gave her a natural smile. What wasn’t to smile about? She was a beautiful woman and they were alone at the table together.

She sighed. “You make it look so natural and easy.”

“I think of something besides why we’re here. A more pleasant reason to be sitting here with you. Like if we were on a real date.” He reached out and took her hand in his and wove her fingers through his. Though he gazed into her eyes, he kept a close watch in his peripheral vision on the doors.

Emily’s fingers curled around his. “I wish we were here for that reason. Not because we need information on my attacker. I’d order a glass of wine and stare across the table into your eyes, not frantically watch the door for another man to enter.”

He gently squeezed her hand. “Sounds good to me. Maybe when this is all over, we can do that.” Out of the corner of his eye, he spotted a man fitting Jay Phillips’s build slipping through the front door. He wore a sweatshirt with a hood pulled up over his head.

As soon as he spotted Emily, the man pushed the hood away from his face and hurried toward them.

“Phillips is here,” Mustang announced softly.

Chapter Thirteen

Emily's fingers tightened around Mustang's and she turned toward the investigator.

The man hurried across the bar and sat in the chair opposite Mustang. "I think I was followed," he said and glanced over his shoulder.

Mustang leaned toward Phillips and spoke softly. "We have a couple guys here as backup."

Phillips shook his head. "I should have stayed home. By leaving, I might as well have painted a target on my back."

Emily placed her hand on the man's arm. "Tell us what you came to say. We'll make sure you get out of here safely, won't we?" Her gaze met Mustang's.

He nodded. "We will. But you have to trust me and my team."

"They've been watching me. I had to create a diversion in order for me to get out of my house without being seen. I called the police to my neighbor's house, saying I thought someone was trying to break in. When a couple cruisers arrived, I slipped out the back door of my house and escaped on my motorcycle."

Emily tightened her hold on the private investigator's arm. "Jay, what did you come here to say?"

He pulled a small electronic tablet from a backpack he'd worn over his hoodie. Pressing the on switch, he glanced around and then leaned closer to Emily. "I found something in one of the most recent photographs I took of the ambassador's daughter and the journalist. They were leaving the restaurant at one of the hotels in Alexandria. I snapped the photo as they passed an alley."

As the photo materialized on the screen, Emily leaned in. Though the image was a bit blurry, Emily recognized Sachi Kozlov and Tyler Blunt. They were holding hands as they walked by the alley. "So, we know they were seeing each other. Why is this image so important?"

Phillips touched the screen, enlarging the image. He pointed to the alley behind the couple. "Do you see the people in the background?"

Emily squinted, concentrating on the dimly lit space behind the couple. "A little. There's a man and a woman."

"Look closer." The PI enlarged the image yet again, making it even grainier.

"The man looks familiar, but I can't quite place him."

Phillips pulled the tablet back and thumbed the touch screen until another image popped into view.

Emily's heartbeat kicked up a notch. "The ambassador's assistant, Viktor Sokolov." She glanced up at the PI. "You think the man in the alley is Sokolov?"

Phillips touched the screen and brought up both images side by side.

Emily compared the two, her eyes growing wider. "Looks like him. But who is the woman with him?"

"I don't know, but she looks really young."

Mustang studied the image. "Too young."

"She can't be more than fourteen."

"It's hard to tell by a picture," Phillips admitted. "But she doesn't look happy about being with him. And they're waiting at a door to the back of the hotel."

A chill rippled down the back of Emily's neck. "You think Sokolov is having an affair with a minor? Is that what this is all about?"

Phillips ran a hand through his hair. "I don't know, but what are the chances Blunt and Sokolov happen to be at the same hotel at the same time?"

"Blunt is an investigative reporter. Could he have been probing Sokolov's activities?" Mustang asked.

"We can't know until someone has the opportunity to ask Blunt," Phillips said.

"And you think someone at the embassy has kidnapped Blunt because of what he might know about Sokolov's activities?" Emily asked.

Phillips nodded. "I looked through all of my photos of Blunt and the ambassador's daughter and this is the only one that stood out. Why else would they be after me?"

"And I saw Blunt at the embassy. I know the ambassador was angry about his daughter going out with the journalist, but I can't imagine it being enough to make him want to kidnap or kill the man."

Phillips frowned. "Unless he's in on whatever Sokolov is doing. Either way, this photograph could be what has them spooked and willing to come after me."

"You have the photos backed up in case someone destroys your equipment and computer storage device, right?" Mustang asked.

Phillips nodded. "Yeah, on the cloud. Only I know how to get to them."

"The Russians have been known to be good at hacking," Mustang reminded Phillips.

"That's why I wanted to meet in person. I was afraid if I sent it, with an explanation, it could somehow get diverted into the wrong hands. I've saved them in multiple places. It will take them time to hack into my account. And even more time to hack into multiple accounts."

"Could you send me a copy of that photo now? Our system is secure," Mustang said. "I have people who can do some sleuthing on this Sokolov guy and see what they can come up with."

Mustang gave him the email address to Cole McCastlain.

After a few clicks on the tablet, Phillips looked up. "Sent." He looked again at the front entrance. "Now, I need to go before they catch up with me." Phillips rose from his seat.

Emily rose with him. "Will you be all right?"

Phillips pressed his lips together in a tight line. "Only time will tell."

Mustang held out his hand. "Thanks for bringing this to us at a risk to your own life."

"I wanted someone else to know what I'd found. It wouldn't do anyone any good if I was knocked off before the images could be reviewed even closer."

"Thank you." Mustang held out his hand. "And please, let us help you get somewhere safe. We could put you up for a while, until this blows over."

"Thanks, but I'm going to get out of town." He started toward the entrance.

Before Phillips had taken three steps, Declan launched himself out of his seat and tackled Phillips.

At that moment a loud crash sounded and a vehicle erupted into the tavern, smashing through one of the walls and rolling to a stop mere inches from where Declan lay on top of Phillips.

The crash made Emily rock back on her heels and fall into the seat she'd just vacated.

Declan jumped to his feet, pulled his gun and aimed it at the crashed vehicle.

With the weight lifted from his body, Phillips leaped to his feet and ran for the rear exit.

"Jay!" Emily called out. "It could be a trap!"

But the man was gone, through the back door and out into the night.

"Go after him!" Emily said.

"I won't leave you," Mustang said.

"Fine, then follow me." She ran toward the back door.

Mustang followed close behind. "Don't go out there," he called out.

Just as Emily reached the back door, she heard the sound of an engine starting and then the squeal of tires on the pavement outside the crumbled tavern.

By the time she opened the door and peered out, Phillips was speeding away on his motorcycle.

"Come on." Mustang stepped past her into the night then pulled her into the crook of his arm and ran for the other side of the building where he'd parked the car. "If we hurry, we can catch up to him and maybe make sure he gets away safely."

Emily picked up the pace, running as fast as she could.

They reached the sedan in seconds, climbed in and raced off in the direction Phillips had gone.

Mustang tossed his cell phone to Emily. "Call Declan and let him know where we're going."

Emily fumbled with the device and brought up the contacts list. "Where are we going?"

"After Phillips," Mustang said. He rounded the corner and hit the accelerator, making the sedan leap forward.

Ahead, several blocks away, a bright red taillight glowed on a motorcycle.

"There he is," Mustang murmured, his focus on the vehicle ahead as Emily clicked on the number for Mustang's leader.

Declan answered on the first ring. "Mack and I will catch up to you," he said, without waiting for Emily to fill him in on where they were going. "Just give us a street name and direction."

Emily frantically looked for a street sign and then passed on the information he needed.

"Thanks. We'll be with you as soon as possible," Declan said.

"What happened back there?" Emily asked.

"Another diversion," Declan said. "These people don't believe in being subtle. But don't worry, we'll have your back."

Emily ended the call and concentrated on keeping track of the motorcycle ahead of them. "Are we trying to stop him?" she asked.

"No. I just want to make sure he gets far enough away before someone catches up to him and makes another attempt on his life," Mustang said.

As if conjured by Mustang's words, a van pulled out of a side street ahead and slammed into the motorcycle Phillips was riding.

Phillips flew into the air and landed several yards away, skidding to a stop on the pavement.

"Oh my God," Emily whispered, the horror of the scene making her stomach roil and her hands shake.

Mustang punched his foot harder on the accelerator, speeding toward the downed PI as the vehicle that hit him backed up, dragging the motorcycle beneath its chassis. It bumped up over the mangled wreckage and shifted forward, heading for the man on the ground.

Emily leaned toward the windshield. "Hurry, Mustang! You can't let him run over Jay."

Mustang raced ahead, coming up on the left side of the van. He turned his wheel sharply to the right, making the car hit the van hard on the right rear bumper.

The van spun around, performing a one-hundred-and-eighty-degree turn until it faced the little sedan Mustang and Emily were in.

Emily leaned back in her seat and braced herself. "He's going to hit us—"

The van plowed into them, clipping the front driver's-side bumper, sending them spinning toward the curb and a solid light pole.

At the last moment Mustang swung the steering wheel around. The little sedan crashed into an abandoned warehouse, where part of the old walls came crumbling down around them.

The airbags deployed, slamming Emily back into her seat. No sooner had they exploded in her face than the bags deflated, leaving Emily stunned and powder-coated.

"Get out!" Mustang ordered from beside her. "Get out now!" He pushed his door open, shoving aside rubble to exit.

Emily tried to do the same but couldn't get her door to budge. She unbuckled her seat belt and crawled across the console, escaping out the driver's side.

"What about Jay?" she said, looking back.

A shot rang out nearby.

"The team will help him." Mustang grabbed her hand and took off running through the dark building where their vehicle had landed, with nothing but the dull glow of exterior streetlights shining through windows high up on the walls guiding them.

Emily had no other choice but to follow or have her arm yanked out of its socket. She ran, trying her best to keep up with Mustang's longer stride, dodging abandoned crates and pallets.

In the shadowy expanse, Emily could just make out a row of doors. She had no idea where they led or if they would be locked when they got there. But the sound of several pairs of footsteps pounding behind her kept her moving forward, praying one of the doors opened to the outside where they might have a chance to escape.

Another shot rang out, the sound closer and louder, as if it had been fired from right behind them.

Emily ducked automatically but didn't slow. She pushed harder, running as fast as she could, her lungs burning and her pulse pounding so loudly against her eardrums she could barely hear herself think.

Mustang reached the doors and tried the first one. It opened.

He ran inside, pulling Emily in behind him.

The darkness was complete behind the door.

Emily swept her finger across Mustang's cell phone that she still held in her hand and turned on the flashlight application. The little light illuminated the space enough to let them see they'd ended up in a stairwell where the only way to go was up.

Mustang took the steps two at a time, until he realized Emily couldn't keep up.

She tried, but her legs just weren't as long and strong and she was already struggling for breath, having run the length of what felt like a football field inside the warehouse. But she couldn't stop.

The sound of the door opening at ground level and clanking shut made her climb faster. When they reached the top of the stairs, Mustang shoved open the door and led her into a long hallway with a door leading off to either side.

"Which one?" Emily whispered.

Mustang tried the first. It was locked. The second and third weren't, but he kept moving, trying the doors as he went.

A little over halfway down the hall, he ducked into a door on the right and yanked Emily inside. As he pulled the door closed behind them, the door to the stairwell clanked open at the end of the hallway.

Emily clamped a hand over her mouth to keep from gasping.

Mustang started to twist the lock on the door and stopped.

"Why aren't you locking it?"

"They might think we're in here, if we engage the lock. We need to hide. I'd fight them, but I'm not sure just how many there are. I think I heard three sets of footsteps, but I can't be sure."

Emily shone the cell phone light around the room, locating another door, a modular metal desk, a giant metal cabinet and a large credenza.

Mustang ran for the other door and pushed it open. He shook his head and retreated into the room with Emily. "No good. Only another desk, not big enough for both of us to fit beneath."

Emily pointed to the credenza. "I can fit in that," she offered and started toward it.

Mustang shook his head and pointed to the modular desk. "Get under that," he urged quietly.

Footsteps sounded in the hallway, along with deep, male voices.

Emily dove behind the desk.

Mustang followed, pressing his body against hers, pushing her as far forward as they could both be and still be hidden behind the metal skirting around the front of the office furniture. "Douse the light."

Emily fumbled with the phone and managed to turn off the flashlight.

The sound of doors opening and closing grew closer and faster as more than one man searched the floor for them.

A metal click echoed, as if the doorknob to the room in which they hid had been turned. Footsteps sounded, moving toward the desk.

Emily held her breath.

Behind her Mustang rolled over, placing his back against hers, his body tense, ready to spring should the intruder round the desk and look beneath.

The footsteps seemed to lead away from the desk and toward the other doors. One clicked open and shut pretty quickly. He must have found the broom closet they'd passed and Mustang had rejected as a hiding place. Then the other door clicked open and the steps sounded as if they were going away.

A moment later they were back and stopped in front of the massive desk.

Something thumped softly against the floor.

A voice called out in Russian from the hallway, "Did you find them?"

The man standing in front of the desk responded, "*Nyet*."

"Someone is coming. We must leave."

Emily waited, willing the man on the other side of the desk to go and leave them alone.

Finally he did, his steps leading away from them and out the door to echo in the hallway with the others. Moments later the hallway was silent.

Emily didn't move. Neither did Mustang. After what felt like an eternity, which was probably only a minute, maybe two, Mustang rolled from beneath the desk and held out his hand to Emily.

She grasped it and let him pull her to her feet and into his arms.

He held her for a long time, his arms like steel bands around her middle, reassuring in their strength.

Emily slipped her arms around his neck and looked up into his eyes. "That was…"

She didn't get the chance to finish her sentence.

Mustang's mouth came down on hers, crushing her lips in a kiss that left her knees weak and her heart hammering.

He traced the seam of her lips with his tongue.

When she opened to him, he swept in and claimed her, deepening the kiss until she couldn't think past his mouth on hers.

When he finally lifted his head, he stared down at

her. “I know the timing isn’t great, but I’ve wanted to do that since I first kissed you.”

She smiled at him and then leaned up on her toes and pressed her lips to his. “I wanted you to, ever since you saved me from being shot.”

He took her again, slowly this time, gathering her closer.

Emily could have stayed in his arms forever, but an incessant ringing sounded, pulling her back to reality.

She glanced down at the phone still in her hand. It was dark and silent.

Emily and Mustang glanced around the room and finally located the ringing sound coming from another cell phone lying on the floor.

A second later they heard the sound of footsteps pounding down the hallway toward them.

Mustang grabbed her hand and yanked her into the broom closet inside the office. He managed to pull the door almost all the way closed without clicking the lever, as the outer office door burst open.

Emily stood in the circle of Mustang’s arms, her pulse pounding and her breath lodged in her throat.

Through the gap, she could see the shadow of a man leaning over to grab up the cell phone that was still ringing. He hit the answer key and turned to leave.

Something shifted behind Emily. A broom or a mop, she didn’t know. But it made just enough noise to alert the man in the other room.

He spun toward the door they were hiding behind. Still holding the phone to his ear, he paused.

A shout sounded in the hallway.

The man pocketed his phone, pivoted on his heel and raced out the door.

A distant voice called out, muffled by walls and doors. It sounded like someone yelling, "Mustang! Emily!"

Mustang's hands gripped her arms and his head lowered in the darkness until his lips found hers. "We need to talk. Later. Right now, I need you to stay here. I have to warn Declan in case those thugs are still hanging around. I'll be back when I'm sure the coast is clear." He dropped a kiss on her mouth and then stepped out of the closet.

"Mustang." Emily reached a hand out and grabbed Mustang's arm.

He took her hand in his and raised it to his lips.

If anything happened to him… Emily swallowed hard on the lump in her throat. "Be careful," she whispered.

Chapter Fourteen

Mustang peeked out the door of the office and checked the hallway. It was empty. He held his gun in front of him as he eased out into the hall.

"Mustang! Emily!" Declan's voice called out, this time a little more clearly but muffled by walls.

Mustang thought he'd heard the man who'd been in the office with them run off to the right. Declan's call came from the direction of the stairwell. He glanced in both directions. If he went after the people who'd been looking for him and Emily, he'd leave her exposed. They might return and find her hiding in the broom closet.

Instead of racing after the bad guys, Mustang hunkered low to the floor and held his handgun pointed at the opposite end of the hallway from where Declan would emerge. He'd provide cover for his team as they entered into the hallway and remain close enough to Emily to keep her safe.

As he suspected, Declan emerged from the stairwell a few seconds later. He dove into the hallway, rolled to his feet and came up aiming his weapon at Mustang.

Mustang raised a hand and spoke in a low tone that wouldn't carry any farther than his team leader. "It's me. But there were others here right before you arrived."

Mack and Snow emerged behind Declan and the three of them joined Mustang in front of the office, holding their aim on the other end of the hall.

Declan glanced over Mustang's shoulder. "Where's Emily? Is she all right?"

Mustang nodded. "She's hiding in there. I don't want her to come out until I know for sure someone isn't going to shoot at her."

"Good. Stay here. We'll clear the building." Declan started forward.

"With just the two of you?" Mustang shook his head. "Where's Gus?"

"He stayed behind with the PI and called for the police and an ambulance."

"Is Phillips still alive?" Mustang asked.

"He had a pulse, but he's pretty banged up and he wasn't wearing a helmet. I don't know if he'll make it."

Mustang took in a deep breath and slowly released it. "I didn't lay eyes on all of the men who followed us into the warehouse, but I would guess there were three or four by the sound of their footsteps. You'll be outnumbered."

"Only three?" Declan's teeth flashed in a grin in the shadowed hall. "Remember that time we were outnumbered twenty to six?"

"We're not in Afghanistan," Mustang reminded him.

"Yeah," Declan said. "But I heard gunfire earlier. I'll be dammed if I let those bastards take potshots at my men. Stay with Emily. We've got this." Declan took off running toward the other end of the hallway.

Mack and Snow followed. They disappeared through what appeared to be another stairwell.

Mustang entered the office and locked the door behind him. He'd have to wait until Declan returned before he could leave with Emily.

"Did I hear right?" her voice sounded in the darkness.

"Hear what?"

"Jay Phillips might not pull through?" she said, her voice catching.

"You saw what happened," Mustang reminded her. "He flew through the air. And he wasn't wearing a helmet. The landing itself could have killed him, even if the impact of the car hitting him didn't." He realized how harsh he sounded and added, "Gus is with him. He called an ambulance and the police. He will stay with Phillips to protect him until they arrive."

He crossed the room to stand in front of her shadowy figure, wishing he could see her face and the expression in her eyes.

"It's just… He didn't do anything to warrant being killed," Emily said, her voice so soft and ragged Mustang barely understood her words. "It's not fair."

"And all you did was interpret for him and witness a man being led around the embassy. A man who is now conveniently missing. You don't deserve to die any more than Phillips or Blunt," Mustang reminded her. He pulled her into his arms.

Emily melted against him, her cheek on his chest, her arms going around his waist. "How many people will be hurt by these people?" Her fingers curled into Mustang's shirt.

"I don't know," he said and smoothed his hand over her soft hair.

"When is this going to end?" she whispered.

"Soon, sweetheart," he assured her, though he had

no idea when that might be. He held her for a long time, wishing he could hold her forever and protect her from all the troubles that might come her way. He'd only known her for such a short time, but his attraction to her was so strong he couldn't deny it.

"Mustang?" A soft tap on the door sounded, pulling Mustang back to reality. He stepped away from Emily and went to the door.

Declan, Snow and Mack stood in the hallway. Declan had a flashlight, the beam casting a bright glow in the dark interior of the abandoned warehouse's corridor.

"We didn't see any sign of your attackers anywhere. We checked throughout the warehouse and every one of the offices attached. We even performed a perimeter check of the exterior. The police have arrived."

Emily stepped up beside Mustang.

He slipped his arm around her waist and she leaned into him.

"Has the ambulance arrived?" she asked.

Mack nodded. "It has. They loaded Phillips into it and had him hooked up to oxygen and an IV as they left for the hospital. Gus rode with him in the back of the ambulance."

"Come on," Declan said. "Let's get you back to the Halverson estate before anything else happens."

Mustang couldn't agree with his team leader more.

"I'd rather go to the hospital and check on Jay's status," Emily said.

"Gus will be there with him. He'll keep us informed of Phillips's progress," Declan assured her. "You'll be better off at the estate. You don't want to put anyone else in danger of becoming collateral damage if the attackers follow you to the hospital."

"They could go after Jay," Emily pointed out.

"He's out of it for now. He won't be talking to anyone anytime soon."

"Did anyone collect the backpack he was wearing?" Mustang asked. "He had a tablet inside it with a photo that could help us understand what's going on. He sent it to us, but the tablet might have more."

Mack turned around and jerked his thumb over his shoulder. "You mean this backpack?"

Mustang nodded. "Have you checked the contents? Was the tablet still inside?"

Mack slipped the straps off his shoulders and opened the backpack, from which he pulled the device, its screen shattered. "Let's get it back to Cole and Charlie's computer guy. They should be able to hack into the device and retrieve the data."

They spent an hour with the police, giving a detailed description of what had taken place, describing the van that had hit Jay Phillips and then rammed the car Mustang had been driving into the warehouse.

Mustang made certain Emily was allowed to sit in the back seat of Declan's vehicle throughout the questioning. He wasn't going to leave her exposed anymore than he had to. When the police were done with them, he climbed in next to her and pulled her against his side.

Declan and Mack rode up front, each watching for trouble at intersections and keeping an eye on the rearview mirror.

By the time they passed through the gate at the Halverson estate, Emily had fallen asleep against Mustang's chest.

Declan pulled up to the front of the house and parked just as Arnold appeared, opened the door to the truck and helped Emily down. Still groggy, she stumbled on the first step.

Mustang swept her into his arms and carried her into the house and up the steps to the bedroom he would share with her that night.

"I can walk, you know," she said, though she snuggled into him rather than struggled to be free.

"I know, but it's faster this way. Besides, you have to be exhausted."

"No more so than you."

He shook his head. "I can go several days without sleep and still function."

She yawned into his shirt. "I don't know how you do it."

He deposited her on her feet in the bedroom, closed and locked the door and then pushed the chair against the French doors and another in front of her hallway door, as he had the night before. Just the thought of her standing out on the balcony and being pushed over the edge made his skin crawl. He shuddered at the mental image. He checked under the bed, in the closet and in the bathroom before declaring, "The room is safe."

"Good." Emily smiled. "I'm not sure I have the energy to fight off an intruder at this point. I'm going to get another shower. After running through that abandoned warehouse, I feel like I picked up several pounds of dust." She gathered clothes and ducked into the bathroom.

Mustang entered the adjoining room, leaving the door open between them. He jumped in his shower and rinsed off, straining the entire time to hear even the slightest sound from the other room. Once he finished, he toweled dry and slipped into a pair of shorts he'd sleep in. Normally he slept naked, but he figured sleeping in the nude was pushing the boundaries of the new relationship between himself and Emily. Yes, they shared an amazing kiss, but expecting it to progress to sleeping together naked was presuming too much.

He pulled a T-shirt over his head as he entered Emily's bedroom.

The shower was still going, but soon shut off. A few minutes later the door opened and Emily stepped out, wearing a fluffy, white, terry-cloth robe, her long legs bare below the hem.

Mustang's groin tightened.

She'd combed her damp hair straight back from her forehead and her cheeks were clean and pink from the hot shower. As she stood in front of him, her cheeks grew even pinker. Emily tugged at the terry-cloth belt around her waist and cleared her throat. "I'm tired, but I doubt I'll sleep much." She shifted her gaze from his and looked around the room. "Why don't you take the bed and I'll sleep in the chair?"

He shook his head. "It's your bed. You need the sleep more than I do."

Her lips twisted. "But you didn't sleep much last night. Even marines have to recharge their bodies."

"I catnap. It's enough."

"Bull feathers," she exclaimed. "If you won't take the bed by yourself, then at least sleep in it with me." She lifted her chin. "I'll stay on my side. You won't even know I'm there."

Mustang snorted. "Sweetheart, I'll know you're there. Hell, I'd know you were anywhere in the same room." He shook his head again. "I can't sleep with you."

She frowned. "Why?"

He captured her gaze with a hard one of his own. "Because if I sleep in the same bed as you, I won't be able to keep my hands to myself. It's best if I sleep in the chair."

Her eyes widened and her tongue swept across her lips as if they'd suddenly gone dry. For a long moment she just stared into his eyes. Then she whispered, "What if I don't want you to keep your hands to yourself?"

Mustang closed his eyes tightly to block the image of her standing there in that robe, the valley of her breasts visible in the neckline and her long legs so tantalizingly toned and silky. "I don't think it's a good idea."

Gentle hands touched his chest.

He blinked open his eyes and stared down into Emily's eyes.

"Funny, but I think it's the best idea we've had all day." Her words came out warm and husky, melting into every pore of Mustang's body.

He gripped her arms.

That was his first mistake.

Pulling her close was his downfall.

The terry cloth did little to disguise the curves of her body beneath the robe as she pressed against him.

A groan rose in his throat. "Emily, I'm supposed to protect you, not take advantage of you." He knew he should push her away and take a step back, but his hands refused his brain's logic.

"I think *I'm* the one taking advantage of *you.*" She lifted up on her toes and pressed her lips to his in a gentle kiss.

When her mouth touched his, a firestorm of sensations blasted through his veins. He slid his hands down her arms and onto her hips, pulling her even closer. "I'm barely fit to be around people after being at war for so long," he said, burying his face in her hair.

She chuckled, the sound like silk sliding across his skin. "I've been so busy building my career, I don't even know how to be with a man. You might find me…lacking in experience."

He leaned back and smoothed a strand of her hair out of her face. "Sweetheart, you're pushing all my buttons, so you must be doing something right." Then he kissed her, taking her mouth in a long, sensuous caress.

When she opened to him and returned the kiss, they were closer than they'd ever been and yet he felt as if he couldn't get close enough.

When he finally came up for air, Emily slipped her hands between them and untied the belt on her robe. She stepped back and let the garment fall open, revealing that she wore nothing beneath.

Another groan slipped along Mustang's throat. He cupped her chin and tilted her head up to his. "Are you sure this is what you want?"

She nodded. "I left my nightgown in the bathroom… on purpose." She tilted her head and raised her eyebrows in a challenge he couldn't refuse.

"If at any time you feel uncomfortable, just say the word and I'll back off," he said, already pushing the robe from her shoulders. He paused with his hands on the terry cloth, a frown pulling his brow low. "Wait."

Emily's brow knit in confusion. "For what? I thought it was settled."

He grinned and left her standing in her room to race into his. It took him thirty precious seconds to locate what he needed and return to where they'd left off.

Emily had pulled her robe back up over her shoulders and closed the edges. "Did *you* change your mind? I don't want you to feel any obligation toward me other than protecting me. I hope I didn't push you into a corner. Like you said…if you feel at all uncomfortable, I'll back off."

Mustang laughed and pressed a finger to her lips. "Shh. I haven't changed my mind, but we couldn't go any further without this." He lifted her hand and dropped an accordion of condoms into her palm. "I don't want you to have any regrets."

"My only regret is that we didn't get started sooner." She tossed the condoms on the bed and wrapped her arms around his neck. "Hold me, Mustang. I need to feel your body against mine."

Her words echoed Mustang's own thoughts. He pulled her against him and scooped her up by the backs of her thighs, wrapping those long, sexy legs around his waist. The robe swung around them.

Emily removed her arms from around Mustang's neck and shrugged out of the robe over her shoulders. "I'm not experienced in the art of seduction," she said, "but I learn quickly." The robe dropped to the floor.

He walked her to the bed and set her down on the edge, running his hands from her hips into the curves of her waist and up to cup the swells of her breasts in his palms.

She tightened her legs around his middle and arched her back, pressing against his hands.

Mustang pulled back long enough to yank his shirt over his head.

Emily dropped her legs over the side of the bed and sat up. She pressed her lips to his naked ribs, kissing him there and flicking her tongue against his skin. All the while her hands got busy in the elastic of his shorts. She slipped inside them to cup his backside, pulling him closer. Then she worked his shorts over his hips and down his thighs, easing his erection free in the process.

Impatience won out and Mustang shimmied free of his shorts and stepped out of them to stand naked in front of Emily.

She smiled, her lips forming a seductive curl.

He laid her back and parted her thighs, kissing a path from the bend of her knee to her center.

In less than two days he'd come to care for this woman. Not because she was the job, but because she was smart, sexy and courageous in the face of a deadly threat. She didn't care that he wasn't in the military anymore. It wasn't even a factor as she hadn't known him when he'd been a marine. She wanted him for who he was now.

Mustang parted her folds and thumbed the nubbin he knew would bring her pleasure, really wanting her to like making love to him. He wanted that so much because he couldn't see one time being nearly enough.

WHEN MUSTANG TOUCHED his tongue to that special place, Emily let out a small cry of passion and dug her heels into the mattress, lifting her bottom up. "Please," she said.

"Please what?" Mustang asked, blowing a warm stream of air across that fevered strip of flesh.

"Please, I want more," she moaned, letting her knees drop to the sides, opening herself to him.

He tongued her again, setting off an explosion of nerves that originated at her core and spread outward to the very tips of her extremities.

Emily weaved her hands into his hair and held on until the wave crested and ebbed. Then she pulled on his hair, urging him to give more.

Mustang climbed up the bed and settled between her legs, the tip of his shaft pressing against her entrance. There, he paused and searched the bed for the strip of condoms. When he found it, he leaned up on his knees, tore off one and ripped it open.

Emily took the condom from his hands and rolled it down over his erection, stopped at the base to fondle him. She loved how hard his shaft was in her hand and shivered at the thought of him inside her. And then it couldn't happen soon enough. She tugged on him, guiding him to her. When he touched her there, she shifted her hands to his hips and pulled him into her.

He fit tightly, his girth stretching her deliciously.

Once he'd entered her with his full length, he pulled almost all the way out and drove in again, settling into a smooth, sensuous rhythm.

Emily pressed her feet into the comforter and lifted up, meeting every one of Mustang's thrusts, driving him even deeper.

His body tensed. He dragged in a deep, ragged breath, thrust one last time and held himself there, filling her so completely, she tipped over the edge again and came undone.

His shaft throbbed inside her as her body shook with the force of her release.

When at last she fell back to earth, she lay limp against the mattress, drained and completely satisfied. For the moment.

Mustang dropped down and rolled both of them onto their sides, maintaining their intimate connection.

A chuckle escaped Emily's throat.

Mustang leaned up on his elbow and frowned down at her. "I was expecting a wow, not laughter. Was it that bad?"

She cupped his cheek in her hand. "Not at all. Quite the opposite. I was just realizing how much I've missed all those years of studying and furthering my career. And, wow." Emily shook her head. "Just wow. I really didn't know it could be so good."

Mustang brushed a kiss across her forehead. "Can't tell you how relieved I am to hear that. You had me worried."

"Trust me, sweetheart," Emily said, "you have nothing to worry about. If you treat all your women that way, you'll have no troubles finding one to warm your bed." Her heart squeezed as she spoke the words. Mustang hadn't said he was committing the rest of his life to be with her. Hell, they barely knew each other. At the least, she might have him for a couple more days. After they resolved her attacker issue, Mustang was under no obligation to continue their connection.

The thought of leaving Mustang behind made Emily's chest tighten and a lead weight settle in her gut. He'd become such a part of her life in the past two days, she couldn't imagine a future without him.

But what would keep them together?

Chapter Fifteen

Mustang lay long into the night without falling asleep. His time with Emily had taken an altogether different path than he'd ever imagined. A path he didn't want to see come to an end. Especially such a permanent end as death.

If her attacker managed to slip by him and his team, she could be dead within a week. Heck, within the next twenty-four hours.

His fists clenched. Losing her was not an option. He'd risk his own life to save her. The woman had so much to offer the world in intelligence and kindness.

By the time the sun crept through the gaps in the blinds, Mustang was up and pacing the length of the room, trying to figure out how to capture the attacker without putting Emily up as bait.

"Hey," a soft voice called out.

Mustang stopped halfway across the room and turned to the woman lying in the bed, her hair rumpled and her cheeks flushed with sleep. God, she was beautiful.

He wanted to go to her and make love to her all over again, but the worry eating at his gut kept him at a distance. He knew if he touched her, he wouldn't be able to resist. And he needed a clear mind and a hell of a lot of focus to see this job through. And when it was over…when the attacker was captured and Emily was safe again, then Mustang would start over and woo this beautiful professor the proper way.

She reached out a slender arm and the comforter slipped lower, exposing a tempting breast.

Mustang swallowed a moan and turned away. "I'll leave you to get dressed. We need to come up with a plan today."

"Is it something I said?" she asked.

He turned back to her. "No, it's something we have to do before this can go any further."

She sat up, pulling the comforter over her chest, her cheeks turning a pretty shade of pink. "Having second thoughts?" She trapped her bottom lip between her teeth, a frown furrowing her brow.

"Far from it. Until we find out who is attacking you, I need to keep my focus."

Her frown smoothed and a smile curled the corners of her lips. "And I make you lose focus?" She chuckled. "I suppose that's a compliment."

"Damn right, it's a compliment." He stood in the middle of the room, staring at her, wishing the circumstances were different. "Please," he said. "Just get dressed. I'll be in the other room." He marched out of her bedroom, refusing to look back.

Her soft laughter followed him.

He could hear her moving around, opening the bathroom door, the sound of water running and the tap of a toothbrush against the porcelain sink.

He was so aware of her, he could imagine everything she was doing.

Finally she appeared in the door frame of the adjoining room, buttoning the front of a soft pink blouse she wore with a pair of gray trousers. “Just so you know,” she said, “you make me lose focus, too. But I don’t necessarily consider it a bad thing.”

“It would be bad in my case if my loss of focus left you vulnerable to attack.” He nodded at her bare feet. “I’d wear something comfortable.”

One side of her mouth lifted in a sardonic grin. “In case I have to run?”

He nodded. “Precisely.”

She disappeared into her room and came back wearing a pair of black-leather flats and carrying her cell phone. “Will these do?”

He nodded. “Let’s get downstairs and see if Cole’s made any progress on locating the hotel where Phillips snapped that photo.” He strode to the bedroom door, pulled the chair away and yanked it open. He stood back as Emily passed so close he could smell the scent of her shampoo.

She leaned closer. “Your focus is slipping.” Emily’s grin spread across her face as she walked ahead of him to the top of the staircase.

He hurried past her to take the lead, descending to the main level.

He followed the voices emanating from the dining room.

Declan gave him a chin lift as he entered. “Oh, good, we were just about to come get you.”

“What have you found?” Mustang held a chair for Emily and waited for her to be seated before claiming the chair beside her.

Charlie, Grace, Jonah and Cole sat at the table with half-eaten plates of food in front of them.

"Jonah and Cole were able to hack into Phillips's tablet and retrieve the digital images. We found the one you were talking about that showed Blunt and the ambassador's daughter with Viktor Sokolov in the alley in the background."

Mustang paused in the middle of scooping scrambled eggs onto his plate. "And?"

"We think we know where they were," Cole said.

"The Trinity Hotel." Jonah jabbed his fork at a piece of chicken. "It's located in Alexandria."

Emily pushed back her chair. "Well, let's go check it out."

Mustang grabbed her arm and urged her to take her seat. "Not without a plan. And I'm not so sure you need to go. Declan and the others can check it out. You and I can stay put until they return with whatever they find out."

Emily scowled. "I'm not good at sitting around doing nothing."

"Then you can work with Jonah as he hacks into the embassy database," Charlie said.

Jonah nodded. "I understand you understand Russian. All the information in that database might as well be Greek to me."

Emily seemed to consider the prospect. "You'll let us know what you find, as soon as you find anything?"

Declan held up his hand as if swearing before a judge. "Promise."

"Okay." Emily settled back in her seat. "I'll stay and translate." But she didn't look all that happy about being left behind.

Mustang was more than relieved. He could keep a closer watch on her if she stayed inside the house. But he knew he wouldn't be able to keep her housebound for long. The woman had a life and she'd refuse to be held captive for any length of time.

Grace reached over and covered Emily's hand. "The guys are only trying to keep you safe."

Emily sighed. "I know. I'm not used to being the target of some nut job. If I knew who it was, I'd confront him."

"No, we'd send the police after him," Charlie said. "Whoever these people are, they are playing for keeps. You're not trained in warfare. That's why we have Declan's Defenders. They'll help keep you safe, if you let them."

Mustang wanted to cheer Charlie for her comments, but he kept quiet, letting her words sink in with Emily.

"You're right," she said. "And I'm grateful for all you've done for me. I wouldn't be alive today without their help." She slipped her hand beneath the table and captured Mustang's, giving it a squeeze.

After a quick breakfast, Declan and Cole left the estate, destined for the Trinity Hotel in Alexandria.

Emily and Mustang helped carry dishes into the kitchen where the chef and his staff made quick work of cleaning up.

Jonah led them to the computer room where he had an array of six monitors lined up in front of a single keyboard. He tapped on the keys and brought up a screen filled with files all labeled in Russian.

For the next two hours Emily translated file names and searched through data on the Russian embassy's database. For all the work, they came up with nothing substantial. Names of people, biographies of individuals, schedules of visiting diplomats and records of Russian ships entering American ports all over the US, including some in the DC, Maryland and Virginia area. Nothing jumped out at them as being something that could help them determine who was after her and Jay Phillips or why.

Emily pinched the bridge of her nose and stood. "I need something for a headache."

"Let's take a break." Mustang walked with her to the kitchen where the chef offered them a cup of coffee or hot tea.

"I'd like the tea," Emily said.

"I could use some coffee."

They collected their steaming cups and sat at the solid-oak kitchen table. No sooner had they taken their seats than Emily's cell phone buzzed with an incoming text message.

She glanced down, a frown forming on her brow. "It's from Sachi Kozlov."

Mustang leaned over her shoulder and read the message.

Found Tyler's journal. You need to see this. Meet me at DC's Eastern Flea Market at 2:00 pm. I'll be at the Crepes food truck wearing a gold scarf.

Emily checked the time on her cell phone. "That gives us an hour to get there and find her."

"Us?" Mustang shook his head. "I don't feel good about you being out and about. What if this is a setup? We just did a meeting that didn't end well. Call her back. Ask what's up."

"I'm not calling her back. If she wants to meet, it could be because talking on the phone is difficult. People might be nearby she doesn't want eavesdropping. I won't do anything that might put her at risk."

"I don't like doing anything that puts you at risk," he countered.

"I can go in a disguise," Emily said. "I'm going. You can come with me or not." She responded to Sachi's text.

I will be there.

Mustang already knew he wasn't going to talk Emily out of going. "Fine. But we will have to make your disguise good enough to fool the best. Where's Grace?" He stood and held her chair for her.

She rose and hurried through the house. "Grace? Charlie? I need your help."

Meanwhile, Mustang was on his cell phone clicking on his team lead's number. "Declan, I need your help."

AT PRECISELY 1:58 P.M. Emily, dressed in baggy jeans and a hooded sweatshirt with the hood pulled up over her hair, stood twenty yards from the Crepes food truck at DC's Flea Market at Eastern Market, searching for a woman in a gold scarf. "I don't see her," she said to Mustang, who stood beside her, wearing a similar outfit, his hands in his jacket pocket, resting on his handgun.

"It's not quite two. Give her a minute," he said softly.

From around the other side of the rendezvous truck, a woman emerged, dressed in a gray trench coat and a gold scarf.

Emily's heart beat fast. "There she is." She stepped forward but Mustang's hand held her back.

"Wait a moment in case she was followed." He scanned the area, searching for anyone watching Sachi and her movements.

Emily kept her head down to disguise the fact she wasn't the teenaged boy she was dressed as. She'd scrubbed her face, pulled back her hair and tucked it into the hoodie she'd brought for her disguise. She'd had Grace and Charlie give her thicker eyebrows. Charlie had invested in costume makeup on the off chance Declan's Defenders needed to disguise themselves. She'd been excited that they would actually put the makeup to use for a good cause…keeping Emily safe. Charlie had also found the hooded sweatshirt and helped Emily into it. Then Charlie had hugged her. "Don't lose the hoodie. It will help us find you."

They'd left the estate in the back of a delivery van and caught a taxi once they'd arrived in the DC city limits. They had the taxi drop them off several blocks from the flea market and walked the rest of the way like two guys just hanging out.

"Well?" Emily asked. "Is it safe?"

"I can only hope so. I don't see any suspicious characters."

Sachi had settled into a seat at one of the bistro tables with her back to a shade tree, her face and body cloaked in the shadows.

"We'll order a crepe before we engage with Sachi. Stay close to me," Mustang ordered.

"No argument here," Emily said in her gruffest guy-voice.

They walked over to the crepe truck. Mustang ordered a crepe with strawberries.

Emily stood beside him, watching Sachi out of the corner of her eye.

The woman pulled her scarf over the lower half of her face, but her ice-blue eyes were unforgettable and gave her away.

"I'm going to join her," Emily said.

"Wait for me. It will look more natural if we both sit together. The other tables are filling up."

Emily saw reason and waited for the man in the food truck to finish making the strawberry crepe. Then she and Mustang looked around as if searching for an empty table and not finding it. Sachi's table was the only one with a single occupant.

Mustang carried his plate with the strawberry crepe and stopped in front of Sachi. "Mind if we share your table?"

The Russian ambassador's daughter started to shake her head. "I'm sorry, but I'm waiting for someone."

Emily looked down at Sachi, willing her to recognize her despite the disguise. Finally she whispered. "It's me, Emily."

Sachi's gaze darted to Emily's eyes. Her own narrowed. Then she glanced around nervously and nodded, her gaze lighting on Mustang, whom she seemed to remember from the classroom visit. She relaxed a little. "Please, take a seat." She shifted her chair to make room for them.

"I'll eat, you two talk." Mustang cut off a piece of the crepe and popped it into his mouth.

Sachi glanced down at the purse in her lap. "This was one of the places Tyler and I would meet when I could escape my bodyguards. It's easy to blend into the crowd, as long as I change the color of my scarf. The trick was to wear something unmemorable besides the scarf." Her hand fluttered to the gold cloth. "But that is not the reason I asked you to come." She shifted in her seat and unzipped her oversize purse. "I found these in the safe deposit box Tyler and I share at a local bank. They're the journals he kept when he was doing an investigation."

"Did you find anything about you or the Russian embassy in it?" Emily asked softly, barely moving her lips lest someone see her talking to the stranger.

Sachi nodded, almost imperceptibly. "He was following a story about human trafficking in the DC area. He wrote that he suspected someone in the Russian embassy was responsible for transporting women out of the US." She pulled a small leather-bound journal out of her voluminous bag and pushed it across the table. "I bent the page where Tyler noted that he suspected one of the higher-ranking embassy staff was involved. He'd seen the man outside a hotel with a very young woman who'd appeared to stagger and drag her feet, maybe drugged.

"He'd gone back to that hotel and asked questions of the staff, most of whom knew nothing about any potential human trafficking going on beneath their roof. But some of them were less talkative and more guarded. Tyler had planned a stakeout to capture more evidence on video. He'd even given up a chance to be with me in order to gather the evidence he needed to turn the mastermind behind the human trafficking in to the authorities.

"That had been the night before. Since then, Tyler has disappeared." Sachi's voice faded into a silent sob. "I don't know where he is or who took him."

"Sachi, I was at the embassy two days ago, interpreting for your father. I saw Tyler Blunt there."

The other woman's eyes grew wide. "You saw him? That was the day he disappeared."

"Your father was very angry about your relationship with the journalist," Emily said. "He stormed out of the meeting, shouting."

Sachi shook her head. "He came to me and told me that I had to break up with Tyler. I told him that I would not. I would leave the embassy and him if he banned me from seeing the man I love."

"What did he say?"

"He threatened to pay Tyler to quit seeing me. I told my father I would never speak to him again if he damaged my relationship with Tyler."

"Is your father capable of kidnapping and potentially murdering?" Emily asked quietly.

Sachi shook her head. "I've known my father to get very angry, but he has never hurt another human being. I don't think he would hurt Tyler."

"Have you ever suspected your father of having any dealings with the buying and selling of women to other countries for profit?" Mustang asked between bites of the crepe.

Sachi's eyes opened even wider. "No. Of course not. He was very much in love with my mother, and he's been a good father, so very protective of the women in his family and on his staff. He would never hurt another woman. His anger is legendary, but his kindness is equally revered." She glanced down at her watch. "I've told you all I know. Now I have to get back to my bodyguards before they call my father or send out a search party."

Emily wanted to ask more questions but the woman was clearly packing up her things to leave. "Let us escort you back to your people," Emily offered.

Sachi frowned. "I don't know. It might be better if I show up alone."

"Please," Emily implored. "With so many attempts on my life, what if the information you just passed on to us is what our attackers are after? That could place you in just as much danger as myself and the private investigator who was assigned to follow you and Tyler around."

"No one knows that I know about Tyler's journal and its contents besides you two."

"I'd feel better if we followed you back. You know the investigator is in the hospital?"

"The private investigator who was following us?" Sachi asked. "No, I did not."

"Someone broadsided him on his motorcycle last night and then tried to hit us, as well."

Sachi's hand fluttered over the scarf. "I did not know. Will he live?"

Emily shook her head. "Only time will tell. He was still unconscious, the last word I received."

Sachi shook her head. "I hope he recovers. And, yes, I would like you to follow me, but not so close that it appears obvious to onlookers."

Mustang tossed his crepe into a trash bin as he followed Emily and Sachi from the food truck.

Emily hurried after Sachi, afraid she'd get too far ahead of them to provide any kind of protection should someone try to harm her.

The ambassador's daughter wove her way through the throngs of people milling about the flea market, until she emerged along another street where a homeless man dug in a trash can and a black limousine stood ten yards farther against the curb.

Sachi didn't slow until she reached the limousine.

Emily watched as Sachi came to a stop in front of one of the bodyguards. She frowned heavily at the big, burly man standing at the rear door of the limousine. Then she backed away quickly.

The man caught her arm and yanked her against him. And just like that, the situation went to hell.

Sachi screamed and struggled against the big guy's grip on her.

Emily leaped forward, racing toward Sachi, too far away to be of any real assistance. But she couldn't stand by and do nothing.

Sachi was forced into the back of the limousine.

"Emily," Mustang called out, his footsteps pounding on the ground behind her.

She couldn't stop. Sachi was in trouble and they'd promised to see her safely to her people. The man at the limousine had obviously not been one of her regular bodyguards.

As Emily and Mustang reached the limousine, the burly guy had already slammed the door and was moving toward the front passenger door.

"Hey!" Emily called out.

The man turned and faced her.

Mustang caught up with her before she reached the big man who'd shoved Sachi into the limousine.

Still more footsteps sounded behind Emily and Mustang.

Mustang spun, but not soon enough to block the steel

pipe that crashed down at the base of his skull. He went down and lay as still as death at Emily's feet.

"Mustang?" she cried and dove for the man who'd saved her life on more than one occasion.

A hand caught her hair before she hit the ground and yanked her back.

She screamed and fought, but the man holding her hair clamped strong arms around her middle and lifted her off the ground.

The man who'd wrestled with Sachi pulled open the door to the back seat. Emily was deposited like a sack of potatoes onto the floorboard and the door was slammed shut behind her.

Sachi lay on the floor, sobbing.

"Are these your bodyguards?" Emily demanded.

Sachi shook her head. "I've never seen these men before."

Emily found the door handle and pulled hard, but the door wouldn't open. The locks were obviously controlled by the driver up front. She pounded her fists against the glass windows but they didn't break.

And Mustang lay on the ground, unmoving.

Was he dead?

Oh, dear God, Emily prayed. *Please let him live.*

The limousine pulled away, rounded a corner and left Mustang behind.

Chapter Sixteen

"Hey, mister," a voice said through the fog of Mustang's brain.

Mustang blinked his eyes open and stared sideways at what appeared to be dirt and shoes.

A man squatted beside him and peered into his eyes. "Are you okay? Should I call an ambulance?"

"What happened?"

The man shook his head. "I don't know. I just found you lying here, unconscious. You have a heck of a goose egg on the back of your head and it's bleeding a little. I'm going to call an ambulance." He pulled out his cell phone and looked down at the screen.

"No," Mustang said and pushed to his hands and knees. Pain ripped through the back of his skull and reverberated throughout his head. His thoughts were just starting to gel when he remembered. "Emily." He staggered to his feet and swayed. "Two women. Did you see them?"

The man shook his head, a frown denting his forehead. "No. Just you." He looked around. "No women. I really think you need to see a doctor. You could have a concussion."

Mustang started to shake his head and thought better of it. "No, thank you. I'll be okay. I have to go." He fished in his pocket for his cell phone and punched Declan's number.

Declan answered immediately. "Mustang, where are you? We just arrived at the flea market."

"They're gone," he said, his stomach roiling, his head throbbing with pain and regret.

"What do you mean they're gone?" Declan asked.

"We were escorting Sachi back to her vehicle when someone hit me from behind." He pressed a hand to the back of his head and winced when it came into contact with the goose-egg-size lump at the base of his skull. "I don't know how long I've been out, but they're gone. Nowhere to be seen."

"I'm at the entrance to the market by the kettle corn booth. Do you need me to call an ambulance?"

"I don't need an ambulance," Mustang bit out. "I need to find Emily." He sprinted toward the entrance. "I'm on my way to you."

Minutes later he met up with Declan and Cole.

"I let Charlie know what was happening," Declan said. "We're in luck. The hooded sweatshirt she gave Emily to wear had a GPS tracking chip in the pocket." Declan shook his head. "That woman knows all the tricks. Cole will forward the link to her tracker. Mack, Gus and Snow are on their way. They're bringing firepower, as well."

A huge wave of relief washed over Mustang for all of a split second. Sure, they might find her, but would it be too late?

A few moments later he climbed into Declan's truck and settled back against the passenger seat. Cole got into the back seat.

How had he let this happen? Mustang had seen the limousine and the man who'd shoved Sachi inside. Otherwise, the street had been fairly empty. Where had the man come from who'd hit him in the back of the head? An image flashed in his mind, one of a homeless man digging in the trash near the limousine. Had he been a decoy? Did it matter? The fact was, Emily and Sachi had been taken. He'd bet the men with the limousine weren't her regular bodyguards. She hadn't gone into the vehicle willingly. Mustang was sure Emily wouldn't have gotten in without a fight.

A text came in on Declan's cell phone. He handed it to Mustang. "I'll drive. You communicate."

Mustang read the text out loud. "'Heading to Baltimore on Interstate Highway 295. About one hour ahead of us.'" He frowned. "Why would they go to Baltimore?"

"Guess we're going to find out," Declan said, pressing his foot down hard on the accelerator as he merged onto Highway 295 heading out of DC. Traffic was thick, but not as bad as on a regular workday.

Declan broke all the speed limits, weaving in between cars and eighteen wheelers. They made record time up the highway and probably cut the usual travel time nearly by half.

As they approached Baltimore, another text came through.

Mustang read it. "'Take Interstate 895 to the 695 south bypass.'"

Declan followed the directions. "Mack and the others must be a good fifteen minutes ahead of us."

Mustang nodded, his mind on the road ahead and every potential scenario he could imagine.

"She'll be okay," Declan assured him.

Cole leaned over the back seat and tapped Mustang's shoulder. "We'll get her out of this."

Mustang couldn't respond. He'd let her down. Failed in his duty to protect her. But he couldn't dwell on that. Getting her back alive was his goal. Failure on this mission wasn't an option.

Declan's cell phone rang with Mack's Caller ID on the display screen.

Declan answered via the Bluetooth option on his truck.

Mack's voice sounded over the speaker. "The tracker has slowed considerably and, get this…they're in the Baltimore shipyard. We're not close enough yet to see what terrain we'll have to deal with, but we'll get as close as we can and wait for you to catch up."

"Roger," Declan said. "We should be there in approximately fifteen minutes."

"Where the hell are they taking them?" Mustang muttered.

Declan shook his head and increased their speed. "I don't know, but it can't be good."

THE LIMOUSINE'S WINDOWS had been blackened, not allowing the passengers a view of where they were going. When the vehicle finally stopped, Emily and Sachi were ready to fight for their escape. As soon as the door opened, Emily dove out onto concrete and rolled across the ground. She was up on her feet and ready to run, but she was captured before she could take two steps. Someone with beefy arms caught her around the middle. Dusk had settled in early with an overcast sky, making it difficult to ascertain where she was. All she could see were tall stacks of metal freight containers.

She screamed as loud as she could. It bought her a dirty rag in her mouth and a sack over her head. Then she was flung over her captor's shoulder, her legs clamped tightly by his arm. No matter how much she tried to kick and buck, she couldn't free herself from her stronger captor. She was carried across a long, flat area. Then her abductor was walking across something that wasn't concrete. His footsteps clanged on what sounded like metal, maybe a bridge, and then he stepped down onto another surface.

Emily strained to make out this new sound. Again, it could have been metal, only it wasn't as hollow as the clanging noise. Where had they taken her and Sachi? Muffled sobbing reassured her that Sachi was still with her, even if they were both still kept captive.

She was carried down metal steps and still more steps. Finally the clang of metal against metal indicated a door being opened. With all the sounds of metal, and the shipping containers she'd seen when she'd attempted her escape, Emily had to conclude they had been taken on board a ship. She could smell and hear the lapping of waves.

Her heart constricted and her pulse raced. Escaping from solid walls and doors of a ship would be much more difficult than if she'd been taken to a building. And if the ship went out to sea, there was the matter of where she could escape to.

Emily was dumped on the floor. Someone else landed beside her with an *umph*.

By the time she pulled the sack off her head and the rag from her mouth, the door to her new cell closed and the sound of gears turning on the other side indicated it had been sealed.

Darkness surrounded her. There was no portal and no light leaked around the edges of the door as it was doubtlessly designed to be watertight. That was probably why they'd not bound their hands. Why bother when they were dumping them in this light-deprived cell?

"Sachi?" Emily whispered.

"*Da*," Sachi responded, her voice catching on a sob. "Where are we?"

"I think we're on board a ship." Emily sat on a hard metal floor. This wasn't a cruise ship with carpeting and soft, comfy beds. Since it was located near a shipyard with containers, it was probably a no-frills freighter. She felt her way around the room. Their cell was completely empty, nothing but a box in which to contain them.

"We have to get out of here," Emily said, fighting the feeling that the walls were closing in around her.

"How?" Sachi sniffed.

"There has to be a handle on the door. We just have to find it."

Emily ran her hands along the walls until she located the edges of the door. She found a wheel handle in the middle and tried to turn it. No matter how hard she pulled on it in either direction, it would not budge. "It must be locked from the other side."

She sat next to Sachi, took her hand in hers and tried to think of a way to break the lock. With nothing harder than the clothes they were wearing or the sacks they'd had pulled over their heads, they had no way to break through the door or to apply leverage to the wheel handle. The only way out was if someone let them out.

Emily sighed. “We’ll have to wait until someone opens the door. But we should be ready.”

“Tell me how,” Sachi said. “I’ll help.”

Emily handed her one of the bags their captors had used to subdue them with. “Rip this into long strips.”

“What are we going to do with them?” Sachi asked.

“I have a plan but we need to act fast.” She took the other bag and tore lengths of two-inch-wide strips. Once they had both bags torn up, she tied the strips together into two long ropes.

“We’ll position ourselves on either side of the door, but out of sight as much as possible. When someone comes through the door to look for us, we’ll use one rope to trip him and the other to tie him up.”

“What if there is more than one?” Sachi asked.

“Then we trip the second one through the door. He’ll fall into the first one and we’ll make our escape while they’re picking themselves up off the floor.” The plan was weak at best, and it would only work if someone came through their door.

For the next thirty minutes they sat on either side of the door, waiting in the dark.

“My father thinks my relationship with Tyler is just a passing fling,” Sachi whispered.

“And how do you feel?” Emily asked softly.

“If he asks me to marry him, I will. I love him with all my heart.”

Emily thought of how long she’d known Mustang and how much he was already a part of her life. She didn’t want to think about their eventual parting. She’d never felt that way about any man. And she’d only been with him for two short days. “How long have you known each other?”

Sachi laughed. "Two weeks. Two weeks and I know in my heart he's the one for me."

"Does he feel the same?"

She laughed again, the sound catching on a sob. "He told me that he loves me even before I was sure."

"Do you worry that he might be using you to get closer to what's going on at the embassy?"

"No. He said he'd walk away from any story if it would prove to me that he is truly in love with me." She sighed. "I believe him. He's a good man who only wants to report the truth so that bad things can be fixed and the good can be revealed. Just read his articles and listen to his reports. You would know who he is by his work."

"I've seen some of his investigative reports. He's helped a lot of people." Emily hoped for Sachi's sake that Tyler was really in love with her. How did anyone know for sure?

Muffled footsteps sounded in the hallway outside the door to their cell.

"Once the door opens, don't make a sound," Emily whispered. "They have to think we've disappeared."

Emily moved back, away from the door and out of the path of any light that might spill in.

The screech of the wheel handle turning made her pulse leap. This could be their only chance of escape. They had to make it count.

The door swung outward. A yellowish light poured through, illuminating a rectangle across the middle of the small cell. For someone on the outside looking in, the cell might as well be empty.

Emily pressed up against the wall, making herself as small as possible, while holding on to her end of the makeshift rope.

A man spoke in Russian. "This is the room?"

"*Da*," came the answer.

"They are gone."

"*Nyet*. They are in there." A man stepped through the door.

Emily held her breath and prayed Sachi wouldn't get excited and pull the rope too soon.

The second man entered the doorway.

About the time the first man turned and spotted her, Emily yelled, "Now!"

Both women pulled hard on the rope as the second man stepped through.

His foot caught and he pitched forward, knocking into the man in front of him, hitting him hard enough that both crashed into the opposite wall.

"Go!" Emily cried as she scrambled to her feet.

Sachi dove for the door.

Emily was on her heels.

The ambassador's daughter hesitated in the dim hallway. "Which way?"

Emily slammed the door shut and twisted the wheel handle. Then she shoved a metal locking lever into place before her jailers could recover.

Pounding sounded against the door, making Emily jump back. The men inside shouted, their voices muffled by the thick metal walls.

"Help us!" A feminine cry came from another door farther down the hallway.

"Did you hear that?" Emily asked.

"Someone is crying for help," Sachi said.

Emily ran to the door behind which came the sound of several women crying out for help. She slid the exterior locking lever to the side and spun the wheel handle. Sachi helped her pull the door open. The room was as small as the one they had just escaped. But inside a dozen women were crowded into the cramped space.

A blond-haired, blue-eyed young woman who couldn't have been more than seventeen swayed toward Emily. "Please, help us." Her words were slurred and she seemed barely able to stand.

After a quick glance at the others Emily shook her head. "These women have been drugged."

"Drugs," the blonde said. "They made us take pills."

"We're going to get you out of here," Emily promised.

"Want to go home," the blonde said, tears streaming down her cheeks.

"We'll get you there, but right now you have to think. Are there more of you?"

Three or four of the women closest to Emily nodded.

Emily's heart squeezed hard in her chest. These women were being shipped out of the US, probably to be sold in the sex trade in some foreign country.

Sachi ran to the next door and shoved the locking lever to the side. Emily helped her spin the wheel handle and push open the door. Ten more women sat or lay passed out on the floor.

They went to the next door and opened it. This room appeared empty until a groan sounded from a dark corner.

Emily hurried in.

What appeared to be a pile of dirty clothes was actually a man. As she neared him, she recognized his pale blue shirt and dark hair. "Tyler? Is that you?"

"Tyler?" Sachi called, muttering a string of curses

in Russian as she rushed to his side. "What have they done to you?"

The man lifted his head, exposing a battered face with dried blood from a gash in his cheek and a busted lip.

"Sachi," Emily said, "we have to get out of here and get help."

"I won't leave him." She stroked his cheek and slipped his head onto her lap. "I won't let them hurt him anymore."

"We have to get help, or we won't be able to help any of them. We can't carry Tyler out and the women are too drugged to help themselves."

"Then go," Sachi said. "Get help. I must stay."

Emily would get nowhere with the woman and she couldn't blame her for insisting on staying with the man she loved. But if someone didn't get off the ship and go for help, none of them would be freed.

Emily squared her shoulders. "I'll be back with help," she promised.

She turned and ran down the narrow hallway to the nearest door that might lead to an upper deck and a way off the ship.

The passageways were a maze of twists and turns. Finally she found stairs leading upward. She paused at the bottom, listening for sounds of voices or movement above. When she was fairly certain the deck above was clear, she hurried up the stairs. She swallowed a groan as another hallway greeted her. She ran to the end and through an open door. More steps led upward and she could hear the sounds of motors humming and the clanking of metal on metal.

Emily eased up the stairs until she could see the

upper deck and stacks of shipping containers lined in neat rows, filling the top deck of the ship, bathed in stadium lights. A crane lowered another metal box onto a stack. Men shouted and waved to the man operating the crane.

The boom turned back to the shore and stopped, the engine shutting down.

More men hurried around the deck, securing lines, apparently preparing the ship to leave. Some of the stevedores crossed the gangway to the shore, waving to the men remaining on the ship.

Emily slipped out onto the deck, moving among the shadows. She worked her way to the side of the ship and looked over the edge. The ship rose forty feet out of the water. The dock was at least ten feet away and twenty feet below where she stood. If she made a flying leap, she could miss the dock and fall the forty feet into the water. If she landed wrong in the water, it could be like hitting concrete. She could die before she got help for the others in the hold below.

No, she had to use the gangway if she wanted to get off in one piece. She'd be exposed and possibly caught, but she had to do something or they would all be lost.

Emily waited until the majority of the deckhands were looking the other way and then made her run for it. She made it to the gangway and put one foot onto the metal grate when hands reached out and grabbed her.

"I cannot have my guest leaving so very soon," a man said, his tone deep and threatening.

Emily glanced over her shoulder into the black eyes of Viktor Sokolov, the ambassador's rogue assistant, and he was speaking English.

Chapter Seventeen

"She's on board that one." Mack pointed to the container ship secured at the dock.

Mustang pushed past Mack but was stopped in his tracks when Declan reached out to capture his arm. "We can't just go storming aboard. We need a plan."

"Hell, we need to take a page from our enemy's book and create a diversion," Mack said.

Clenching his fists, Mustang turned to their slack man, Jack Snow. "What have we got?"

Snow grinned and dropped a duffel bag at the team's feet. "I'm glad you asked. You'd be surprised at the variety of munitions Charlie's husband stockpiled in the basement beneath the garage. He has enough weapons to man a small army and enough ammunition to last long enough to survive a zombie apocalypse."

"I'm not interested in a zombie apocalypse. I want to get Emily the hell off that ship in one piece."

"You know, we're not in Afghanistan anymore. Perhaps we should call the police and let them handle this," Cole suggested.

The other five members of the team stared at him as if he'd lost his mind.

"If we involve the police, they might decide to kill

Emily and Sachi and cut their losses." Mustang tipped his head toward the ship.

"Or there will be a big political standoff with the Russian government and the Russian bad guys might commit murder and suicide to keep from being sent to Siberia," Mack said.

Mustang shook his head. "We can't risk it. We have to go in, neutralize the threat and free the hostages. It's what we do. What we're good at." He waved his hand. "Show me what you've got."

Snow pulled out four M4A1 rifles, two submachine guns and magazines filled with bullets for both, half a dozen smoke grenades, a small brick of C4 explosive and the detonators to go with it. He'd also brought six K-Bar knives and their sheaths, and body armor.

"Damn, Snow." Cole laughed. "You don't happen to have a rocket launcher tucked into that, do you?"

"No, but I'm sure Charlie can get you hooked up with one," Snow said with a straight face. "Just say the word."

Declan handed the C4 to Mack. "Make a noise, not enough to sink the ship, but enough to be heard and scare the crew ashore."

Mack took the C4. "How am I supposed to get on board the ship to do that?"

Snow hefted two of the smoke grenades. "I played outfield on my baseball team in high school. Had the best and most accurate distance throwing arm on the team."

"Can you get those smoke grenades on board that ship from the dock?" Declan asked.

"Just point. I'll deliver."

"We need one at the far end of the ship. If that doesn't

make them think they have a shipboard fire, we can toss the other in for good measure," Declan said.

"You've got it."

"Mustang, you're point man," Declan said. "As soon as the crew bails, you're first man in. We'll be right behind you."

Mack showed Mustang the tracking device. "If this is accurate through the metal hull, Emily is somewhere near the bridge."

"I'll cover Mustang's six," Declan said. "Mack, you and Cole set the charges, Gus and Snow cover the gangway and keep anyone from coming back on board once they've disembarked. Our goal is to get in there, retrieve Emily and Sachi, and get the hell out before we're caught in an international incident."

Mack snorted. "What would it hurt? We've already got dishonorable discharges on our records," he said, referring to their refusal to handle a kill that would have involved too much collateral damage during their military days.

Declan claimed a submachine gun and the rounds that went with it. "No matter what the records show, we're honorable men. As long as we keep that in mind, that's all that counts."

"And if the body count mounts?" Gus asked as he buckled his protective vest in place.

"We'll cross that bridge when we get to it. *If* we get to it," Declan said, slipping his body armor over his shoulder.

Once the rest of the men had their bulletproof vests on, Declan asked, "Ready?"

As one, the team replied. "Ready."

Anxious to get started, Mustang checked his handgun in the holster on his hip, grabbed one of the rifles and slipped several magazines into the pouches on his body armor and moved forward through the maze of containers, keeping to the shadows. He wouldn't get ahead of the plan. He'd been with these men long enough to know the value of teamwork and having someone to cover him when he took point.

The bright lights of the shipyard cast deep shadows alongside the large, metal shipping containers, giving Mustang the concealment he needed to get close to the ship.

When he was as near as he could get without being seen, he waited for the signal to board…that signal being the launch of the smoke grenades.

He didn't have long to wait. From his position he could see the arch of the grenade as it flew through the air and landed on the ship's bow, rolling among the stacks of containers. A puff of smoke rose on impact and spread all across that end of the ship.

Shouts echoed in the night and men ran for fire extinguishers. When they couldn't locate the source of the smoke, some made the decision to abandon ship. A dozen men crossed the gangplank.

In the ensuing smoke and confusion, Mustang tucked his rifle against his leg, walked past the men leaving, and boarded the ship, keeping his head down so that anyone he passed wouldn't immediately realize he was a stranger.

Once on board, he waited for Declan to catch up, keeping a close watch for anyone who might be a danger to his teammate.

Declan walked on board, the submachine gun hidden beneath his jacket.

With the tracking device in hand, Mustang headed for the tallest part of the ship and the wheelhouse where the captain commanded the operation of the ship.

Several times before he reached the pilot castle, Mustang had to duck back against the containers to avoid being seen by armed men running around in the smoke.

With Declan covering him, Mustang entered the pilot castle and climbed the steps up to the deck where the bridge was located. At the top, he surprised two guards standing watch at a door Mustang assumed led to the bridge.

Before the men could aim their weapons, Mustang swung the butt of his rifle, hitting the first one in the nose at the same time as he threw a side kick into the other guard's gut. He had them both subdued by the time Declan joined him on the deck.

Wordlessly, Mustang eased open the door to the bridge, holding his rifle at the ready.

Not ten feet from where he was, Mustang spotted Emily standing at the center of the window that stretched from one end of the room to the other.

She was turned to face the door from which Mustang viewed her.

She shook her head imperceptibly and shot a glance to her right.

Mustang's gaze followed Emily's to a man with thick gray hair and piercing black eyes, holding a gun pointed at her chest.

"Come in," the man said. "Please, join my other guest."

Emily shook her head more noticeably. "Don't," she said. "He's got a gun."

"Oh, but I insist. And if you do not come in, I will shoot the interpreter."

Mustang entered, aiming his rifle at the man's chest. "You must be Viktor Sokolov," he guessed.

Sokolov dipped his head in acknowledgment. "I am. And you must be our little interpreter's bodyguard who has made it difficult for us to dispose of her."

Mustang's chest tightened. "Why would you want to kill her? What did she ever do to you?"

Viktor's eyes narrowed. "It is not what she did, but what she witnessed."

"The journalist you detained in the embassy?" Mustang asked. "Where is he now? Or have you disposed of him, as well?"

"All in due time," Viktor said. "It is much easier to dispose of a body at sea than on land."

"And is that what you have planned for Miss Chastain?" Mustang hoped that by keeping the man talking, he'd buy some time to come up with a plan to save Emily.

"Now that she is here, it seems a waste to do away with her, especially when we can get a sizeable sum for a woman with her particular shade of blond hair. And blue eyes are prized."

Mustang muttered a curse beneath his breath. The bastard was trafficking women to foreign markets, and he planned on selling Emily to the highest bidder. Death was too kind for Viktor.

"Don't worry about me," Emily said. "Just shoot the bastard. There are more people at stake here."

Mustang aimed his gun at the man's chest, beyond tempted to pull the trigger.

Viktor snorted. "Shoot me, and you are all dead."

"What do you mean?" Emily asked.

"There are explosives aboard this ship, rigged with a timer. I set it for fifteen minutes…five minutes ago. I am the only one who knows where the explosives are and the only one with the code to disarm the detonator."

Mustang shot a glance at this watch. Ten minutes wasn't enough time to do anything, much less search an entire ship for explosives and disarm said explosives. "You're bluffing."

Viktor's lips curled. "Are you certain? Only time will tell. Now, enough talk. You will clear this ship of all of your personnel in five minutes."

"This ship is worth more than the cargo it carries. Put down your weapon and give up now and you might not get the death penalty."

Viktor shook his head. "Nine minutes and counting. You are meddling in something much bigger than the cost of just one ship. An organization that extends beyond my little portion of the operation. There are people all over the world who will not be happy if they are exposed. People in your own country. In your own government." He chuckled. "I will not give up."

"Let Miss Chastain go and I'll see to it that you are free to go," Mustang lied. "And I'm sure the Russian ambassador would pay dearly to get his daughter back."

The ambassador's assistant shook his head. "You are a fool. Eight minutes."

While Viktor's attention was focused on Mustang, Emily inched toward her captor.

Mustang wanted to tell her to stand fast, to keep from becoming Viktor's next victim. But to say anything would divert Viktor's attention back to her.

He didn't have to ponder that dilemma. In a flash,

Emily dove for the gun in Viktor's hand and shoved it toward the floor.

The sound of a gunshot blasted through the air.

Mustang aimed at Viktor, but couldn't pull the trigger for fear of hitting Emily.

She had hold of the man's wrist, struggling to keep it pointed at the floor, but the man was strong. Slowly he overpowered her, inching the gun toward her chest.

Mustang had to do something. He couldn't stand by and let Viktor kill the woman who'd come to mean more to him than he'd ever imagined a woman could in such a short time. He aimed his gun and pulled the trigger, praying Emily didn't shift at the last moment.

Two gunshots echoed across the bridge.

Viktor slumped over, his body landing on top of Emily's, crushing her beneath him.

Mustang's breath lodged in his throat until Emily's hand moved. "Help," she said, her voice strained and breathy.

Mustang ran to her, shoved Viktor over and bent to Emily. Blood covered her shirt.

"I couldn't get in to help in case Viktor got spooked and pulled the trigger prematurely," Declan said, entering the room behind Mustang. "I texted Mack and told him to hold off on the explosives. We don't know if a small explosion will trigger whatever Viktor has set. Is Emily okay?"

"I don't know." Mustang stared into Emily's gaze. "Were you hit?"

Emily stared at the blood, her eyes widening. She patted her chest and abdomen and let out a sigh. "It's not mine. I'm okay." She struggled to stand. "How many minutes do we have left?" she demanded.

Mustang looked at his watch. “Five.”

“We have to help the others.” Emily ran for the door.

“Wait!” Mustang caught her arm, bringing her to a stop. “We don’t know if there are more guards.”

“I don’t care. There are nearly thirty drugged women that I know of belowdecks, as well as Sachi and Tyler Blunt. We can’t take the risk Viktor was bluffing. We have to get them out now. And some can’t get out on their own.” She shook free of his grasp and ran, heading down stairs into the bowels of the ship.

Mustang raced after her, leaping down the stairs two at a time.

“I’m right behind you,” Declan called out. “I’ll let the others know we’ll need help below.”

A couple decks below the bridge, Emily came to a halt. Women filled the hallway, some staggering, others leaning on those who could help.

Emily entered one of the doors, helped a woman to her feet and half carried, half dragged her out into the hallway. “This way,” Emily said and led the way up the stairs.

Mustang’s heart sank when he saw how many women there were in the small, dark room. He shot a glance at his watch. Four minutes. They could only do the best they could. He lifted a limp form off the floor and tossed it over his shoulder. “Follow me,” he said and looped an arm around a woman staggering in the hallway. He powered up the stairs, out onto the deck, refusing to let the struggling woman slow him down. Once he had them off the ship, he laid the limp woman on the ground. “Take care of her,” he said to the others.

Emily had already returned to the ship.

Three minutes.

Mustang passed Mack, Cole and Gus on their way out, helping two women each. Some of the ladies made it out on their own. When he returned to the lower deck, he found Sachi in the hallway. "Help me, please," she said. "It's Tyler. He's hurt." She led him into a different room where Tyler Blunt attempted to push to his feet.

"Get her out of here," Tyler said as he leaned heavily against the wall.

"Tyler," Sachi said, "I'm not leaving without you." She hooked his arm over her shoulder.

Mustang looped the man's other arm over his shoulder. Between him and Sachi, they got him up the stairs and out onto the deck.

"I can make it from here," Tyler insisted. "Go. Help the others."

With only two minutes remaining, Mustang returned to the lower deck, determined to find Emily and get her out before the ship exploded.

He passed Snow with a woman folded over his shoulder.

"Emily. Have you seen her?"

Snow jerked his head toward the rear. "She was checking the rest of the rooms on this corridor to make sure we didn't leave anyone behind."

"Hurry, get her out of here," Mustang said, nodding at the woman on Snow's shoulder. "We only have seconds to spare."

"Same to you, man." Snow ran down the corridor and up the stairs.

Emily emerged from a room at the end of the hallway. "The rooms are all empty except one." She stood in front of one, her hand on the locking lever.

Deep voices sounded from inside, yelling in Russian.

Emily glanced at Mustang. "They were the men who kidnapped us and brought us to Viktor."

"Go," Mustang said. "Get out of here. We don't have any time left."

"What about them?" she asked, tilting her head at the door. "We can't leave them to die."

"I'll let them out. But I don't want you anywhere near." He turned her toward the stairs. "The longer you take to leave, the more chance of them and me dying in the explosion. If you care at all for me, you'll go."

She shook her head, leaned up on her toes and kissed him full on the lips. "I care," she said. "A lot. I'm going, but I don't want to leave you here." She turned and ran for the stairs.

Mustang grabbed the lock and shoved it to the side. Heaving a sigh, he spun the wheel handle.

As soon as it hit a full stop, the door erupted outward.

Mustang was ready. He jumped back and came out fighting. "Get out of here," he yelled even as he blocked a right jab. "The ship is about to explode," he warned.

The two men weren't listening or couldn't speak English. Either way, Mustang wouldn't make it out in less than a minute. Not if he had to fight his way through the two men. But he wouldn't go down without trying.

He threw a side kick, hitting the bigger guy in the gut. Then he spun and slugged the other man in the chin. Before he could cock his arm to swing again, he was caught from behind by the big guy and his arms were yanked behind him.

The man he'd just clocked in the chin balled his fists and snarled.

A shout in Russian from the other end of the corridor made all three men turn.

Emily stood like an avenging angel with her fists on her hips and her blue eyes blazing. She shouted again in Russian. The two men stared at her, eyes narrowing.

She spoke again, this time in a more urgent tone, and pointed upward.

The big guy said something to the one with his arms cocked, ready to throw a punch.

The man jabbed hard to Mustang's middle, and then he turned and started toward Emily.

Pain made Mustang double over.

The big guy let go and shoved him forward. Then he ran and followed his partner.

Mustang swept out his foot, caught the big man's ankle with his own and sent him sprawling across the narrow hallway and slamming into his partner.

Mustang stepped on top of both men on his way to Emily. He grabbed her hand and ran with her up the steps to the deck above.

They had just made it onto the gangway when the first explosion shook the ship.

The gangway rattled violently.

Mustang grabbed Emily around the waist and leaped for the dock. Behind him the gangway shuddered and buckled, falling into the water.

"Run!" Mustang shouted. Holding Emily's hand, he rushed with her, aiming for the other side of a huge stack of shipping containers.

As he reached the stack, another explosion rumbled inside the ship and then fire and debris shot out of the middle of the stacks of containers, flinging metal shrapnel in every direction.

Mustang pushed Emily behind the containers and dove in after her.

All the women and the rest of his team had taken cover behind the stacks of giant metal boxes.

Mustang didn't relax until he could see every one of Declan's Defenders. Sachi and Tyler were there, too.

He lay on the ground beside Emily, laughter bubbling up his throat.

Emily leaned up on one elbow and frowned down at him. "What's so funny?"

He pulled Emily into his arms and kissed her hard. "Nothing. I'm just so thankful you made it out alive. And, wow, I wish you could have seen yourself shouting at the Russians." A chuckle escaped his chest, relieving the past two days of stress he'd been under. "You were amazing." He kissed her again. "Thank you for saving me."

"Thank you for shooting Viktor and not me," she said and chuckled. "You had me worried for a moment there."

"I had me worried." He smoothed a hand through her hair. "I've never met a woman as courageous as you."

"And I've never met a man who is as determined as you are to keep me safe." She cupped his chin in her palm and brushed her lips across his in a butterfly-soft kiss. "Where do we go from here, now that we know who was behind the attacks on me, Jay and Tyler? I won't need a bodyguard anymore."

"Sweetheart, you're not getting rid of me that easily. Now that I've found you, I won't let you go. I can't. I think I'm falling in love with you."

Epilogue

Emily sat across the dining table from Charlie Halverson. Mustang occupied the seat to her right and Grace the one to her left. "I guess tonight is my last night here at the Halverson estate. Thank you for putting me up for one more night."

"It didn't make any sense for you to go back to your apartment so late when your clothes and toiletries were here," Charlie said. "Besides, I love the company." She smiled around the table at the six men of Declan's Defenders. "While you all were helping the first responders sort through the women and Tyler Blunt, Jonah and I were digging into Viktor Sokolov's personal emails and data files. Since we were able to focus on him, and not all of the embassy staff, we had more success uncovering what he was up to.

"His emails contained information about meeting locations where he collected women. He used a kind of code to describe each to potential buyers. His buyers are all over the world, including contacts in Saudi Arabia, England, Germany, Bangladesh, Japan and Turkey to name only a few." She frowned and pushed a sheet of paper into the center of the table.

On the paper was a design Emily had seen before.

"That's a Celtic knot, a symbol of interconnectedness of all life." She looked from it to Charlie. "What does it have to do with Sokolov and him selling women into the sex trade?"

Mustang tapped the symbol with his finger. "We seem to keep running across it. First Grace found mention of it at Quest Aerospace when she was searching through Riley Lansing's boss's files. He was involved in selling secret blueprints to the Russians."

"And then we saw it again in the ring Riley's sleeper-agent handler had given to her before she died," Mack said, looping his arm over the back of Riley Lansing's chair.

"And Charlie's husband had a similar ring with the same Russian inscription on the inside."

Declan pulled out his smart phone and showed Emily the picture of the inscription.

Emily nodded. "It reads the equivalent of *Always and Forever*." She slipped her hand into Mustang's. "I'm not sure of the significance of the inscription."

Jack Snow ventured a guess. "It could mean that once the person was a part of the Trinity organization, he or she could never escape."

"Whatever it means, it's making me nervous. It seems we're running into it for a reason," Charlie said. "I just wish we knew what that reason was."

Emily sighed. "I'd like to get some fresh air before I call it a night. It's been a long day."

"You should be able to enjoy the rose garden," Charlie said, "now that no one is waiting to attack you." She gave Emily a reassuring smile.

Mustang jumped up from his seat as Emily stood. "I'll go with her, just to make sure she's safe."

Emily's pulse kicked up a notch and her breathing became more labored at the thought of being alone in the dark with Mustang.

They entered the study and exited the house through the French doors.

Immediately, Emily's senses were bombarded with the aroma of blooming roses.

Mustang captured her hand in his and held on as they walked deeper into the rose garden.

When she reached the fountain with the stone benches surrounding it, she paused. "This place is magical. I can see why Charlie loves living here."

Mustang turned her to him. "To me, it's the people who make the place. And right now, you're making it magical just by being you."

"A marine and a poet?" She laid her hands on his chest and could feel his heart beating beneath her fingertips. "Does that mean I'll see you again?"

"I hope so," he said and brushed a strand of her hair away from her cheek. "It's up to you. Would you like to go out with me?"

"Yes," she said, her voice breathy, as if she'd been running hard, when in actuality she'd been holding her breath, praying he'd ask. "I'd love to go out with you."

"Hmm. There's that L-word." Mustang kissed the tip of her nose. "Are you one of those women who believes in love at first sight?"

She shrugged. "How am I supposed to answer that? If I say yes, I might scare you away. If I say no, you might think I'm not a romantic, when I am, very much so."

He touched a finger to her lips. "To set the record

straight, I never thought I believed in love at first sight until I met you."

Emily laughed. "Your first sight of me was one where I had twigs in my hair and a gun pointed at my head. How could you love that?"

"You were so brave." He kissed her forehead and then each of her eyelids.

Emily's knees threatened to buckle under his tenderness.

"So, do you?" he asked.

She couldn't seem to think when he held her and kissed her like that. "Do I what?"

He kissed her long and hard, pushing his tongue past her teeth to caress hers in a sensuous glide.

When he brought his head up, his gaze met hers reflecting in the moonlight the full force of the emotion Emily felt for him.

"Do you believe in love at first sight?" he said as his mouth skimmed across hers so lightly it left her wanting more.

"Yes," she said and wrapped her arms around his neck to bring his lips back to hers.

* * * * *

COMING SOON!

We really hope you enjoyed reading this book. If you're looking for more romance, be sure to head to the shops when new books are available on

Thursday 5th September

To see which titles are coming soon, please visit

millsandboon.co.uk/nextmonth

MILLS & BOON

JOIN US ON SOCIAL MEDIA!

Stay up to date with our latest releases, author news and gossip, special offers and discounts, and all the behind-the-scenes action from Mills & Boon...

millsandboon

millsandboonuk

millsandboon

It might just be true love...